"My Friend. — Welcome to the Carpathians. I am anxiously expecting you. Sleep well to-night. At three to-morrow the diligence will start for Bukovina; a place on it is kept for you. At the Borgo Pass my carriage will await you and will bring you to me. I trust that your journey from London has been a happy one, and that you will enjoy your stay in my beautiful land. — "

Your friend,
"DRACULA."

NIGHTTOUCH

Edited by Gerry Goldberg, Stephen Storoschuk and Fred Corbett.

ST. MARTIN'S PRESS   NEW YORK

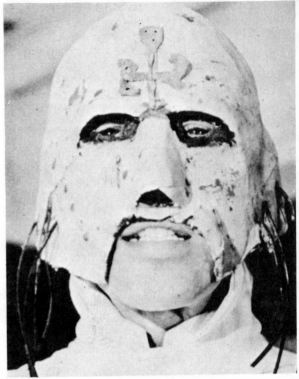

Copyright (c) Gerry Goldberg 1977

Published in the United States by St. Martin's
Press, Inc., New York.
All rights reserved. For information, write:
St. Martin's Press Inc., 175 Fifth Avenue,
New York, N.Y. 10010

ISBN 0-312-57347-2
ISBN 0-312-57348-0 pbk

Published in Canada by General Publishing Co.
Limited, Toronto.
All rights reserved. For information, write:
General Publishing Co. Limited, 30 Lesmill Road,
Don Mills, Ontario M3B 2T6

ISBN 0-7736-1031-6

Library of Congress Cataloging in Publication Data

Main entry under title:

    Nighttouch.
      1. Horror — Literary Collections.
      2. Horror — Quotations, Maxims, Etc.

    1. Goldberg, Gerry.

    PN 6071.H727N5   808.8'016   77-9177

Produced by James-Christen Associates, Toronto, Canada.

PROLOGUE

What is *Nighttouch?* The spectator at a horror movie who covers his eyes. The lover who cannot give himself for fear of losing himself. The whistler in the graveyard. The sleeper tormented, waking up more tired than when he went to sleep.

In the 'nighttouch' of dreams, particularly in those most disturbing messages from the unconscious, nightmares, we meet the hidden, repressed side of our nature which must be experienced if we are to achieve wholeness. The five chapters of this book follow the sequence of stages through which the dreamer of the nightmare passes: "Typically, the dreamer is plunged into an extremely threatening situation, feels overwhelmed by agonizing dread, makes futile attempts to escape, finds every avenue closed, becomes helplessly paralysed, develops a mounting sense of oppression, and awakens in a cold sweat." (Dr. Robert Goldenson, *The Encyclopedia of Human Behavior, 1970*).

Each chapter is framed by quotations from Bram Stoker's *Dracula*. The characters who appear in these quotations represent the range of possible responses to "nighttouch" as embodied by Dracula. At one extreme is Jonathan Harker who seeks to escape from Dracula or to destroy him; at the other, Lucy Westenra, who succumbs to his power and is destroyed. Only one character in the novel comes to terms with him: Mina Harker's powers of perception and self-knowledge are expanded by her experience with Dracula. And, while she is the principal agent of his destruction, she is the only one to appreciate what has been lost through his death.

The chemistry of *Nighttouch* has affected, consciously or unconsciously, the life of everyone. It is a catalyst for our creativity, for our search for self, for glimpses of the beyond. Unable to see, we perceive with more 'primitive' senses messages which elude our waking vision.

Where are you now, Batman? Now that Aunt Heriot has reported Robin missing
And Superman's fallen asleep in the sixpenny childhood seats?
Where are you now that Captain Marvel's *SHAZAM!* echoes round the auditorium,
The magicians don't hear it,
Must all be deaf...or dead...
The Purple Monster who came down from the Purple Planet disguised as a man
Is wandering aimlessly about the streets
With no way of getting back.
...Something in us has faded.
Has the Terrible Fiend, That Ghastly Adversary,
Mr. Old Age, Caught you in his deadly trap,
And come finally to polish you off,
His machinegun dripping with years...?*

g.g., s.s., f.c., august 14, 1976

**Where Are You Now, Batman?* by Brian Patten

CONTENTS

Peter Lorre

Christopher Lee

1. Transylvania

The Dreamer is plunged into a threatening situation.

P.K. Page *Preparation*	11
Bernard Taylor *Forget-Me-Not*	11
John Crowe Ransom *Old Mansion*	20
Louise Bogan *The Cupola*	20
Patricia Highsmith *The Snail Watcher*	22
Miroslav Holub *The Wind in Winter*	25
Gwendolyn MacEwen *The Shadow-Maker*	25
Montague Summers from *The Werewolf;* *The Case of Jean Grenier* (1603)	26
Robert Penn Warren *Eidolon*	27
Dilys Henrik Jones *Road Signs*	28
Peter Fleming *The Kill*	28
Allen Tate *The Wolves*	29
Colin Wilson from *The Occult;* *The Case of Dion Fortune* (1935)	34
George Garrett *The Quest*	34
Ernest Jones from *On the Nightmare*	34

2. The Castle

The Dreamer is overwhelmed by agonizing fear.

Washington Post *'I Can Hear His Screams',* *Says Marine of Beating* (1976)	37
Rod Serling *The Monsters Are Due* *On Maple Street*	37
John Hollander *The Night Mirror*	38
Kenneth Patchen *All The Roary Night*	41
J.C. Nemiah from *Foundations of* *Psychopathology*	47
Akutagawa *The Dragon*	48
Coventry Patmore *The Shadow of Night*	48
Robert Graves *Nobody*	48
C.S. Lewis from *Perelandra*	48
Guy de Maupassant *The Horla*	49
Harry Guest *A Twilight Man*	54
Saint-Denys Garneau *Bird Cage*	55
Emily Bronte *The Horrors of Sleep*	61
Boris Pasternak from *An Essay in* *Autobiography*	61
Patricia Martland *Primitive*	62
Robert Bloch *Mannikins of Horror*	63
David Wagoner *The Man From the* *Top of the Mind*	66
Leonard Wolf from *A Dream of Dracula;* *Altamont, Dec.* 1969	71
William Alexander Percy *Medusa*	71
Edwin Muir *The Bridge of Dread*	72

3. The Prisoner

The Dreamer makes futile attempts to escape but every avenue is closed.

Ivan T. Sanderson from *Investigating* *the Unexplained; The Olitiau* (1932)	75
John Porter *A Day*	75
Siegfried Sassoon *Haunted*	75
Zealia Bishop *The Curse of Yig*	76
Theodore Roethke *Snake*	85
Bruce Elliott *Wolves Don't Cry*	86
Engenio Montale *The Prisoner's Dream*	91
Muriel Rukeyser *The Minotaur*	92
Roger Zelazny *Corrida*	92
Martin I. Ricketts *The Night Fisherman*	94
Howard Nemerov *The Dragonfly*	96

Bela Lugosi

Lon Chaney, Sr.

Vincent Price

Boris Karloff

4. Possession

The Dreamer is paralysed by the attraction to, and his revulsion of, the Nightmare.

John Lame Deer and Richard Erdoes from *Lame Deer, Seeker of Visions*	99
Thomas de Quincey *Solitude*	99
Clifford Dyment *The Snow*	99
Conrad Aiken *Silent Snow, Secret Snow*	100
Joyce Maynard *The Monster Children*	108
Basil Copper from *The Vampire; Haigh and the Brand of Satan* (1948)	110
K.M. O'Donnell *Trial of the Blood*	115
Philip Lamantia *I Am Coming*	120
Montague Summers from *The History of Witchcraft and Demonology; The Case of Hélène-Joséphine Poirier* (1850)	120
Colin Wilson from *The Occult*	124
Edgar Lee Masters *Robert Davidson*	124
Colin Wilson from *The Occult*	125
John Ciardi *Damn Her*	126
Theodore Sturgeon *Bianca's Hands*	126
Thomas Hardy *The Voice*	130

5. Release

The Dreamer temporarily eludes the Nightmare and awakens in a cold sweat, exhausted.

Ted Hughes *Invitation to the Dance*	133
Edgar Allan Poe from *The Premature Burial*	133
H.P. Lovecraft *Cool Air*	135
Mark Strand *Moontan*	135
Alden Nowlan *Siege*	138
Walter de la Mare *Drugged*	140
Robert Louis Stevenson from *The Strange Case of Dr. Jekyll & Mr. Hyde*	141
Dr. Morel from *Etudes Cliniques* (1852)	142
James Dickey *The Ice Skin*	143
Richard Matheson *Blood Son*	144
David Wagoner *Words Above a Narrow Entrance*	145
Alun Lewis *The Sentry*	147
Roy Fuller *The Image*	148
Montague Summers from *The Vampire, His Kith and Kin; The Hanover Vampire* (1925)	149
R.P. Blackmur *Mirage* [*Sea Island Miscellany: IX*]	153
Harlan Ellison from *Blood Thoughts*	153
E.L. Mayo *The Loss*	156
William Dickey *Exploration Over the Rim*	156

Epilogue

158

To the memory of Rod Serling, who shared his dreams with us....

people who gave the book a worth, many thanks to: a friend mel gryfe for his encouragement and suggestions; bernie unger and john p. stoddart, who shared popcorn; *the invaders from mars,* who linger in my mind; jerry title, who spoke so truthfully; forrest j ackerman, who preserves my dreams; robert bloch, who on august 16, 1975 wrote, "if there is a third book — and i sincerely hope there will be..."; tom dunne, who had the faith and the vision; ronnie hoffman and david allen, who are always there; virginia wright and barrie reynolds of james-christen associates, who not only put up with the phone calls and constant revisions but gave their own special touches; *the man from planet x,* who caused many sleepless nights; especially stephen storoschuk and fred corbett, without whose assistance and creative input, my journey into the realms of the nightmare would not of begun again; *the mole people,* who began it at the vaughan road theatre 1957; bram stoker, who gave the world "dracula" in 1897; margaret hamilton as the *wicked witch,* who sent me screaming from the shea's theatre in 1951; my mother, who took me to that show and my father, who placed the first book in my hands; my wife marion, who put up with my nightly *wanderings* and moments of solitude; and finally my daughters sari and shalyn, who remind me of a time forgotten, may *night* bring to them comfort, beauty and wonder....

gerry goldberg *3 a.m.*
july 14, 1977

to robert bloch, ray bradbury, harlan ellison and richard matheson, who *touch* us....

NIGHTTOUCH

TRANSYLVANIA

We wound on our endless way, and the sun sank lower and lower behind us, the shadows of the evening began to creep round us. As the evening fell it began to get very cold, and the growing twilight seemed to merge into one dark mistiness the gloom of the trees, oak, beech, and pine, though in the valleys which ran deep between the spurs of the hills, as we ascended through the Pass, the dark firs stood out here and there against the background of late-lying snow. Sometimes, as the road was cut through the pine woods that seemed in the darkness to be closing down upon us, great masses of greyness, which here and there bestrewed the trees, produced a peculiarly weird and solemn effect, which carried on the thoughts and grim fancies engendered earlier in the evening, when the falling sunset threw into strange relief the ghost-like clouds which amongst the Carpathians seem to wind ceaselessly through the valleys.

I did not know what to do.

Jonathan Harker's Journal, 3, May.

Preparation
P.K. Page

Go out of your mind.
Prepare to go mad.
Prepare to break
split along cracks
inhabit the darks of your eyes
inhabit the whites.

Prepare to be huge.
Be prepared to be small
the least molecule
of an unlimited form.
Be a limited form
and spin in your skin
one point in its whole.

Be prepared to prepare
for what you have dreamed
to burn and be burned
to burst like a pod
to break at your seams.

Be pre-pared. And pre-pare.
But its never like that.
It is where you are not
that the fissure occurs
and the light crashes in.

Forget-Me-Not
Bernard Taylor

"That's the house where Christie lived...."

Sandra followed the direction of the young man's pointing finger and saw, through the window, below them, a shabby cul-de-sac.

"The one at the end," he said. "Right next to that factory wall."

Quickly, Sandra shifted her gaze, but there was only time to catch the briefest glimpse of the drab-looking terrace house before the tube train — travelling overground for this stretch — took them past. The house vanished from sight.

"Who is Christie?" she asked in her New York accent; she was a stranger to England, and curious about everything.

"Who *was* Christie," he corrected her. "Reginald Halliday Christie...Oh, — just a harmless-looking little man who killed — *murdered* — a number of women. He was hanged for it."

"Really?" Sandra thought of the very ordinary house she had just seen. "And he *lived there?*"

"Yes. And committed all the murders there."

She shivered slightly, in spite of the warm September air. The young man went on:

"His victims were all female. Most of them were —" he broke off suddenly, grinning. "Listen to me," he said, " — a fine introduction to London for you!"

She laughed. "No, no, it's fascinating! Anyway, I want to know *everything* —the good *and* the bad." She paused, then added: "It's funny, but somehow I never thought of associating London with any kind of violence...."

"Oh, we have our share," he said, then, changing the subject, asked: "Have you got a place to stay?"

"Yes, I've booked into a hotel for a while. Just till I can find a room or an apartment...."

"That might not be so easy."

She smiled, undeterred. "I'll find something. I'll start looking tomorrow. I've got a whole week before I start school."

Sandra, pretty, blonde, twenty-six years old, had come to London from the U.S.A. to teach in the London Education system — just for a year, on an exchange basis. For months she had looked forward to it, and now the actual day of her arrival was here; it was one of the most exciting days of her life.

"The next stop is yours," the young man said. He had been scribbling on a piece of paper and now, as she stood up, he handed it to her. "My name and phone number," he explained. "Perhaps when you've settled you might give me a ring...."

"Thanks. I'll do that." She stuffed the note into her pocket and picked up her two suitcases. "You've been a great help. Honestly, I don't know how I'd have managed."

He was eager to be even more helpful. "Can you find your way to the hotel?" he asked.

She nodded. "I got me a street map. An *A to Z.*" (She pronounced it *Zee*.) "I'll get there okay." The tube was slowing. She moved towards the doors. "Bye. And thanks again."

He turned to wave a hand. "Goodbye. Nice to meet you. Don't forget — 'phone me...."

Outside the station she looked at the slip of paper he had given her. *David Hampshire,* she read. Below the name was his telephone number. "Yeh, maybe I will give him a call," she said to herself.

With the help of her *A to Z* it was relatively easy to locate the hotel, and the room to which she was then shown looked cozy and inviting. Left alone, she kicked off her shoes, lit a cigarette and lay back on the bed. She was relaxed. There was no one to drag her into conversation; no one to tell her that she shouldn't smoke: she was wonderfully comfortable and alone. "But don't get *too* comfortable· girl·'" she told herself. "Don't get *too* settled. You've got to go out and find something a little more *permanent*. And if David was *right*, that is *not* going to be *easy*." She was not worried, though, the hunting might be fun. And anyway, one thing was certain: she was going to *adore* her stay in London — absolutely *adore* it.

David proved to be right. Finding something a little more permanent proved to be *very difficult*. My God! she

thought, it's as bad as New York! It seemed that no matter how swift she was to answer the ads in the papers, or those in the shop windows, she was always just one bit too late; the room or the flat was always gone. But she'd get *something*, she told herself: she wasn't easily daunted. In the meantime, the hotel made a comfortable haven.

It was during her flat-searching that she found, in a small corner-bookshop, the volume on Christie. As soon as she saw the title: *Reginald Christie, Mass Murderer,* she remembered her conversation on the tube with David. The book was secondhand and at a ridiculously low price. Sorting out the still strange coins from her purse she handed them, along with the book, to the assistant. "I'll take it," she said.

She began to read the book that same afternoon, continuing with it in the evening. And even when she went down to the little café, she took it with her to study over her steak pie and chips.

The story was absolutely *fascinating*. Reginald Halliday Christie was known to have killed at least seven women — by strangulation — and then to have secreted their bodies either in the house or the adjoining garden. His wife had been one of the victims, and a young tenant of the house another. Equally horrifying to Sandra, with her sheltered upbringing, was the fact that after killing each of the women he had undressed them and — and....She closed her eyes tight. The image in her mind was too terrible to bear.

Later, when she took up the book again, she came upon a photograph of the house. The sight of it caused her to catch at her breath. *Ten, Rillington Place,* she read....But was that the name she had seen on the street sign...? No, surely not. Quickly she flicked through the pages to the appendix. Yes, there it was: *Ruston Close. That* was the name *she* had seen. After Christie's trial and execution the local authorities had — for obvious reasons — renamed the ugly little dead-end street. She remembered suddenly that David had pointed out the house just before she got off the tube. With a strange little thrill she realised that *Ruston Close* was very, very near....

That night she found herself thinking more about the house where Christie had lived. And the things that had happened there. Stop it! she admonished herself; she was getting morbid!

What she needed was to start work — to meet people, make a few nice friends....She thought of David. He had said he'd be glad to hear from her — maybe she'd give him a ring. Yes, that was a good idea. For some minutes she made a concerted effort to find the scrap of paper on which he had written his telephone number. Then, meeting with no success, she gave up the attempt. She'd find it later; there was plenty of time. She went back to her reading.

All at once, there was Christie, staring at her from the page. He had a thin, rather gaunt aspect. The hair on his domed head was thinning, and the cold, pale eyes that peered out through the steel-rimmed spectacles were merciless. He had been photographed standing in the tiny, untidy garden of his home, standing with his plump smiling wife ... Sandra found herself addressing the unfortunate, unattractive victim:

"You poor, poor thing," she whispered, "you wouldn't be smiling if you *knew*...."

Her first day at school the following Monday was very tiring. But that was to be expected, — teaching was never an easy job, no matter *what* the age of your pupils. Sandra was given a class of eleven-year-olds, — a vital, noisy group that left her, at four o'clock, feeling drained and exhausted. She departed through the school gates with aching feet, a throat sore from constant shouting, and a mouth that was dry and dusty from the chalk-laden air. Reaching Edgware Road tube station, she got on the train and settled back with a sigh of relief: her first day was *over*. The feeling was only temporary, though — she'd have to face another day tomorrow, *and* the day after, *and* the day after that. The days stretched before her into infinity. "Don't worry," she told herself, "it's just because you're not used to it. It'll be all right in time...." And there was another problem, also: the need for a flat of her own. The worry nagged like a toothache. She'd try again this weekend, she decided — *really* make an all—out effort. There *had* to be something *somewhere*. She lit a cigarette and, gazing from the window, idly noted the stations as they passed by; after Edgware Road came Paddington, then Royal Oak, then Westbourne Park, then Ladbroke Grove, then — And suddenly *the house* was there — Christie's house — standing forlorn and dirty at the end of the cul-de-sac, shadowed by the tall, grey, ugly chimney. She turned as the train sped past, craning her neck to catch the last little glimpse.

Every day that week she saw the house. Sitting on the tube, she found herself counting the stations — almost impatient — just waiting for the street to come in sight. And always, at the end of the street was the house. But it looked so — innocuous, she thought. It was hard to believe that *that* was the scene of so many hideous crimes.

And yet...there *was something* about the place, that last tired—looking three-story dwelling. Something about the whole street. And then she realised what it was that gave it all that air of — difference: the street was uninhabited. No people walked there, no children played. The windows were dark and empty — some of them boarded up.

In the mornings, on the way to school, she couldn't see the house — the train, running on the left tracks, was too far over, affording her no possible view. But on the way back — well — that was a different matter. Her days at school could be bearable when there was something to look forward to. And Sandra *did* look forward to the house. Each teaching day, with thumping heart and damp palms, she watched, waited for the house to come into view. Soon — she could *see* — the *house* was waiting for *her*.

Once the imaginative pattern has been set, and has stirred the creative obsessions, the rest follows.

Colin Wilson, *The Occult* (1971)

She *needed* something to look forward to at this time. Somehow, her life was becoming increasingly lonesome. It just wasn't *that easy* to make friends. For some people it was, but not for Sandra. The warm, satisfying relationships she had envisaged somehow seemed never to materialize. Why was it? she wondered. She *had* tried, too. Though there was, at school, no one with whom she thought she'd really *like* to be friends, she had, even so, made two or three half-hearted attempts to strike up more than the passing acquaintanceship. But her attempts where not very successful, and she was forced to continue with the amusements of her own designing.

Having no television set and no radio, she spent a great deal of her time reading, getting the books from the local library. Many of the books she read were about Christie. Reginald...Halliday...Christie....What a name! she thought. The syllables just rolled off the tongue...*Reginald...Halliday...Christie...Beautiful*. She felt she was beginning to know him *so* well — she almost thought of him as — Reginald....But that was silly.

One afternoon, returning from school, she looked down at the street and saw workmen moving about. And there was a bulldozer and other machines of demolition! "My God!" she whispered; then louder: *"They're knocking it down!"* A woman on the opposite seat looked up from her knitting and gave her an odd, uncomprehending glance.

And they *were* knocking it down. The next day on her return, Christie's house was just a pile of rubble, and the workmen were starting on the house next door.

At school in the staff-room, one of the young teachers came to her holding out a newspaper. "Here," he said, "you're the one who's always reading about Christie...." He pointed to a short column on the back page. Concealing her eagerness, she took the paper from him, read the words. It only told her what she already knew. But *why* tear it down? she asked herself. The reason given here: *space needed for redevelopment* — was just not good enough. It was *Christie's* house. They shouldn't have done it. It just wasn't fair.

Smiling, shrugging, as if not really interested, she handed the paper back to its owner.

It was that same evening that she found the flat.

She had stopped at a small shop to buy cigarettes (— she was smoking far too much these days —) when she saw the card in the window. *Flat to Let*, it said. *Suit young working person. 6 lb. per week.* Yes, she could afford that much, she reckoned. Quickly she made a note of the address, then set off at once to find it.

And now it was hers. She had paid Mr. Malaczynski, the Polish landlord, a month's rent in advance, and told him that she'd be moving in the very next day. She'd take the school day off, she decided. (She didn't feel like going anyway; there was nothing to look forward to anymore.)

There were three flats available, the landlord had told her, so she could have her choice. She chose the one on the first floor. At the moment the ground-floor flat was occupied by the landlord himself. "But only for a short time," he had explained. "I'll be moving to another house this coming weekend." Then, continuing in his accented English: "Will you mind being here on your own for a while? It won't be long before the other flats are let."

"Oh, no," she had assured him. "It won't bother me in the least." Nor would it. She had her *own place* — at *last*. Nothing would bother her now.

The next day she paid her hotel bill and moved into the flat. Now at last, she had finally arrived. She stood in her bed-sitting room and looked around her. She had just the two rooms — this one which was fairly large — and a smaller kitchen next door. The bathroom was on the floor above, and she'd have to share it with the incoming tenant — whoever that might turn out to be. But it didn't matter. The flat was hers. It was small, but it was *hers.*

All the walls were a sort of greyish white. Not attractive. But she'd repaint them in time, she thought. For the present they'd look alright with a bit of colour added: — a few pictures, ornaments. It was going to be fun shopping for things. She could make the place — she was sure — really attractive. Though it was by no means perfect — particularly to a sophisticated New Yorker — it had endless possibilities.

After she had unpacked, she spent a long time arranging her few things, trying — futilely — to add a touch of her own personality. It couldn't be done, she discovered — not in a day. It could only come with *living* there.

In the course of her sorting-out, she came across David Hampshire's name and 'phone number. She put the scrap of paper carefully between the leaves of her address book. She would invite him round for supper, she decided — but not just yet; not till she was well and truly settled.

She stayed up late that night, cleaning and scrubbing. There was so much to be done when moving into a new place. Eventually, totally exhausted, she got into bed and lay there, smoking a cigarette. She gazed about her. The room didn't look *quite* so bare, anyway. On the wall nearest the foot of the bed she had pinned a postcard-size reproduction of Murillo's *Peasant Boy Leaning on a Sill.* She had bought the small print at the National Gallery during her first days in London. She loved the soft, muted tones of the picture and the boy's wide, happy smile. Next to it, making something of a contrast, she had displayed the photograph of Christie and his wife. She had torn the picture from her book.

Lying there, very comfortable, she made vague plans about what she would do with the flat. She'd have to make a list of all the things that were needed — and there were so many things — still, it would come, gradually. Sighing, she put out her cigarette. She felt tired, but happy. Switching off the small lamp, she turned over to go to sleep.

Four hours later, she was still wide-awake. In spite of her great exhaustion from the hectic day, sleep just would not come. Shifting restlessly, she was aware of the dawn lightening the pale curtains at the window. She gave a groan of exasperation — she *had* to get some rest. At last, some time after, she drifted off.

The real difficulty begins when dreams...do not point to anything tangible—especially when they show a kind of foreknowledge....

C.G. Jung, *Aims of Psychotherapy* (1931)

She awoke hours later, having slept right through the strident ringing of her alarm clock. She saw with a shock that the time was after eleven! — it was no good going in to school now. She'd 'phone in and explain. Anyway, she remembered, next week was half-term holiday; it hardly seemed worth going in — not just for those few remaining hours.

She made good use of the rest of the day. After her 'phone call to the headmistress, Sandra went out shopping. She bought china, saucepans, cutlery — those items necessary for the furnishing of a home. And that evening she cooked supper for herself — no more eating out at cafés. The meal was a pleasant — (though somewhat lonely) — affair, and she experienced a real sense of achievement. After that, she washed the dishes, then read for a few hours.

She wasn't sure when the idea came to her — or whether it had been there all the time, just waiting to be acknowledged. But it was the picture of Christie that actually *set* it. It had to be. For one thing, his eyes followed her all the time. And everytime she looked up from her book, he was looking at her. She had to go there. She had to go to the place where Reginald Christie had lived and breathed — and killed.

It was very late when she left the house. The last tubes had gone, and only the occasional car disturbed the silence of the dingy street. Her footsteps echoing on the pavements, she walked in the general direction of Ruston Close. She had consulted her *A to Z*, and knew exactly which way to go.

And suddenly it was there.

She came upon it at once, and the shock of the expected discovery almost took her breath away. Her heart beating wildly, she stood at the entrance to the close, gazing before her at the familiar shape of the chimney, only slightly darker than the dark night sky.

Everything was so quiet. On her right a cinema poster flapped against a wall — it was the only sound in the stillness. Nothing else moved. Completely deserted, the cul-de-sac stretched dark and forbidding before her, the windows of the remaining houses like dead, blind eyes.

Sandra found that she was holding her breath. She exhaled, slowly. The atmosphere — there *was* an atmosphere — poured over her. The place had its own feeling; and it reached out to her as she stood there on the street corner, clutching at her with soft, grasping fingers, drawing her in.

She tried to walk softly, but the cold wind that swirled around the corner followd her, buffeting, so that her raincoat flapped noisily against her legs. No moon or stars were visible; the old street was all a dark greyness, almost at one with the sky.

And then she had reached the end. Standing beneath the chimney, she peered into the gloom of the place where Christie's house had stood.

As she gazed, shivering, the moon appeared from behind a cloud. All at once the scene was lit up before her, and she saw in the sudden light that the house-wall on the right — the one adjoining the factory wall — had not, like all the others, been torn down. It stood there still. And there, yawning in the wall — like grotesque mouths — were the fireplaces — *Christie's* fireplaces. Scraps of torn, discoloured wallpaper still adhered to some of the surfaces around.

Crossing over the rubble, she touched the wall with the tips of her fingers. Then, gaining courage, she laid her whole hand, flat, against it. Underneath her palm the wallpaper was brittle and flaking. After a moment, she took hold of a piece of the paper...and pulled....There was a loud tearing noise, and a strip — about nine inches long and four inches wide — came away in her grasp. She had taken the piece from an area just above her own head. It might well, she thought, be an area that Reginald (— *Christie!* she corrected herself —) had actually touched; have actually leaned his own domed, balding head against. Carefully she eased the strip — it was made from

several thicknesses — into a roll, then tucked it away inside her coat.

Arriving back at the downstairs entrance to her own flat, she let herself in and climbed the stairs. The silence was as complete as that which she had just left. It would be even *more* silent when the landlord left tomorrow....

In her room, she unrolled the paper and laid it flat on the table. She was pleased. It made a nice souvenir. Then, later, she pasted it on the greying wall — just to the right of the gas fire, slightly above the level of her head. She studied the result judiciously for some moments, then, with a smile of satisfaction, she climbed into bed. But once again, rest did not come easily. It was only after tossing and turning for a very long time that she eventually dropped off into a fitful, uneasy sleep — a sleep disturbed by dreams that kept her peace at bay.

Next day she awoke very late. Still, it being Saturday, this time it didn't matter. She lay in bed looking at Reginald's wallpaper. It really stood out against the dull background of the painted wall. The paper had been so affected by dirt and age that it was difficult to determine what its original colour had been. Probably blue, she decided at last; blue with some kind of small design on it. Flowers? Yes, perhaps, but she couldn't possibly identify what species. She gazed at the paper for a long, long time. Yes, definitely flowers, she decided, and the background most certainly blue. It had probably been quite pretty when newly bought. She felt rather smug; for one thing, she hadn't remembered tearing off such a large piece. With a last look, she turned over and went back to sleep.

She stayed up very late again on Saturday night, then slept well into the afternoon of the following day. She awoke about two o'clock, feeling sluggish and heavy-headed — not feeling like getting up at all. Anyway, there was nothing she had planned to do, no shopping could be done, and there was no one she had planned to see, so the day — or what was left of it — was her own. She could do exactly as she pleased. Later on, she thought, she'd get up and make herself a snack — something light — maybe a boiled egg. But she wasn't really hungry. Propping up the pillows behind her head, she sat up, lit a cigarette, and reached for her book. It was a new one from the library, all about famous trials. There was a particularly interesting chapter on Reginald.

She forgot about eating until it was quite late. Hardly worth it now, she thought. She'd just have a cup of coffee and a biscuit.

As she waited for the water to boil, her thoughts went back to her own home in New York City — the home she had shared with her parents and her four sisters. My God! Sandra thought, if my mother could see me now she'd have a fit! There had always been so much emphasis placed on regular habits — regular meals and regular sleeping times. But Sandra had wanted this independence, this solitude. They were all part of her reasons for coming to this strange city.

All around her, the house was as silent as a tomb. There was no longer even the soft, considerate movements of the landlord to disturb the stillness. He had left the day before and, until the new tenants moved in she would be completely alone.

Having no intention of going out, there seemed little purpose in getting dressed, so when the coffee was made she carried it back to bed. Over the rim of the cup she gave a casual glance at the strip of wallpaper. Then she looked harder, studying intently the size, the shape and the colour of the piece. It seemed different somehow. But *how?* And *how could* it? No. It was silly, such a thing just wasn't possible. She stared at it, unblinking. But it was *true*. It *was* different. The piece of paper had grown bigger.

She hardly stirred from the house all that week, except to go to the shop for cigarettes and the odd items of food; not so much for the latter, as she had found that her appetite had decreased considerably.

And there was the silence in the house. It was complete. She began to wish that she owned a television set, a radio or a record-player. It was as if the silence, unchecked, seemed to gain in potency and, with Reginald's wallpaper, grew with each passing day.

Friday came, then Saturday, then Sunday, and then Monday loomed up over her head, threatening, and suddenly she knew that she just could not face the prospect of school that day. She couldn't face those children in the classrooms, the idle talk with the other teachers during the breaks between sessions. She'd just have to telephone in again, tell them she was sick. They'd understand. She got to the telephone on the floor and started to dial the school's number. Half-way through she stopped, replaced the receiver, then turned and went back up the stairs to her room. There was no need to call them, anyway, she rationalized later; *they* would call *her* as soon as they discovered her absence. But then, in a moment the thought came to her: How could they? No one at the school was aware of her new address or telephone number. She had not even told her parents, she realised — in fact, she had not even *written* to her parents since before leaving the hotel. Only Mr. Malaczynski, the landlord, knew of her whereabouts, and he didn't really count.

Monday went by in silence. Tuesday morning came. She forced herself to get up, and began to get ready for school. There was a pounding in her head, and a constricted feeling at her temples as if a metal band had been placed there and was being slowly tightened. The pain was throbbing. She sat down on the chair and pulled on her boots. The wallpaper had spread inches during the night.

She was fully dressed. It was time to go. But the thought of facing those people — the teachers, the children — All those questions that would have been asked: "Has anyone seen or heard from Miss Timms?" "Does anyone know Miss Timms' address?..." And the questions and the comments when she *did* get there: "Where *were* you?...What happened?''...''You should have let us know''...''Are you ill?...Why didn't you telephone?...'' All those looks, all those words....

It was the thought of the looks, the faces, the words that settled the matter. She took off all her clothes, threw them over the back of the chair and got back into bed.

She was awakened some hours later by someone tapping at her door. She got out of bed and slipped on her dressing-gown. ''Who is it?'' she called.

The landlord's voice came to her, the Polish accent strong: ''It's Mr. Malaczynski....''

Sandra opened the door a few inches. ''Yes, what it is?''

He smiled broadly at her. ''It's just that —'' He broke off, gazing at her with concern. ''Are you all right?''

''Yeh, I'm fine. Why?''

''You....You don't look well....Are you ill?''

She felt a growing impatience under the well-meaning questions. ''Of course I'm not ill. What did you want?'' Her tone was slightly sharp.

''I'm very sorry,'' he said, wilting a little under the edge on her voice. ''I just wanted to tell you that if you hear footsteps above, there is no need to be frightened. Mr. Robertson, the new tenant, is moving in today. He is an old man. He will not cause you worry with rock-and-roll music.'' He smiled again, trying to break through the impatient, cold exterior she presented. He added lamely: ''He will be here soon.''

There seemed to be nothing more to say. They looked at each other for a few seconds, and Sandra, trying to ease the warmth into her voice, said: ''Thank you, very much....'' He smiled back at her, grateful. ''Thank *you*,'' he answered, and moved towards the stairs.

When he had gone from sight, she closed the door and walked over to the mirror. She stood there, gazing at her reflection.

She certainly didn't look one hundred percent, she had to admit. Her face was drawn and pale, and the lines around her eyes made her look older than her twenty-six years. And her hair needed washing, she observed. It hung limp, lifeless and uncombed to her shoulders. She'd do it tomorrow, she decided.

About seven o'clock she heard the arrival of the new tenant; she could hear the soft movements of his feet as he moved around on the floor above. What was his name? Robertson? Yes, that's what Malaczynski had said. Perhaps they could be friends. It might be nice to talk to someone. Just a little talk. Just something to relieve the silence....

The days went by. And each day was like the one before. The only way of actually seeing that time had progressed was by watching the wallpaper. It looked different each time she awoke. Always it grew during the night — some nights more than others. The silence grew with it.

The arrival of Mr. Robertson upstairs had made no difference to the house at all. It was just as quiet. Other people were plagued with neighbours who played their radios and their records too loudly — not so Sandra. Mr. Robertson had none of these and lived as silently as

herself. The only evidence of his presence was the soft sound of his feet as he occasionally moved about the room. These faint noises did nothing to alleviate the stillness. They just seemed to emphasise it. The stillness grew louder all the time, and the paper seemed to feed upon the stillness. Yes! *That* was what was *happening*. She suddenly realised. Although normally silent — the house — throughout the day — it was at night when the silence became absolute, so strong, so complete that it was almost tangible. And it was during the night that the wallpaper seemed to grow at such an alarming rate....

All the plans for transforming the ugly little flat into something that was truly her own were now forgotten. They had ceased to be important. Sandra sat on the bed, a cup of cold, untouched coffee in her hand, looking about her. What was happening to her? She didn't understand it. How long had she been here in this room — three weeks? — four? She shivered violently. The room was cold, and she had run out of shillings for the meter. She'd have to go down to the shop to get some more. Sighing, she put down her cup and began to get dressed.

As she moved quietly about, the idea came into her mind that she should buy herself a radio. She had seen some inexpensive transistors not too far away. And she could just about afford it from the little she had left of her savings. The idea added impetus to her movements and she finished dressing quickly, anxious to be out. As she turned towards the door she caught sight of her reflection. Hurriedly she crossed to the sink and splashed cold water on her face. (The soap she had bought on her first day lay unused, still in its wrapper.) Then she raked a hand through her tangled hair.

First of all she got the supply of shillings. She got them from the bank — two pounds' worth. Now, she thought, she'd get that radio.

It was while she stood outside the entrance to the bank, wondering which way to go, that the weakness came over her. Suddenly she felt that her legs were about to give way. Her knees wobbled, she thought she was about to fall and she clutched at the wall for support.

''Are you feeling all right, love?...''

She turned at the soft voice and tried to focus on the man who stood there, leaning towards her. For a moment she stared at herself, mirrored in the lenses of his steel-rimmed glasses, and then she turned, swinging away on her unsteady feet.

Back in her room, she collapsed, gasping, on the bed. It was a long time before she gathered the strength to undress and get in between the sheets. On the wall, Reginald's paper was enormous.

Later, feeling calm again, she lay back and studied the paper. It had now spread in all directions, reaching out to the right as far as the mirror, and on the left almost as far as the shabby wardrobe. But she was no longer shocked by it. It had long since ceased to amaze her in any way. She looked at it now with acceptance, interest. After all, there was nothing she could *do* about it.

With the change in its size, the wallpaper had also changed in quality — or rather than that — it appeared to be *newer*. In fact it looked brand-new, now. She wondered how she could ever have had to *decide* on its colour; it was quite obviously blue, a rather pretty pale blue. Likewise, the flowers that dotted its surface were now easily identifiable. They were the prettiest forget-me-nots, always among her favourite flowers. She thought: So goddamn *English,* too, and found herself smiling. The wallpaper was like a fungus — a creeping, thriving, rapacious, beautiful, beautiful fungus.

She had pinned it up on the wall far away from the paper, and even though the mass of paper had not yet reached it, she could see that the lovely little picture had become infected. It started with just a tiny dot of blue down in one corner. She had noticed it one morning — her eyes seemed to be drawn to it — a little spot that had surely not been in the original. She knew what was happening. The little peasant boy *did not,* though, and — like Mrs. Christie in the photograph — he smiled his smile, unaware of the nearness of the evil. Unconcerned, he continued to lean on the sill, his tanned, peasant-boy's face beaming, while the

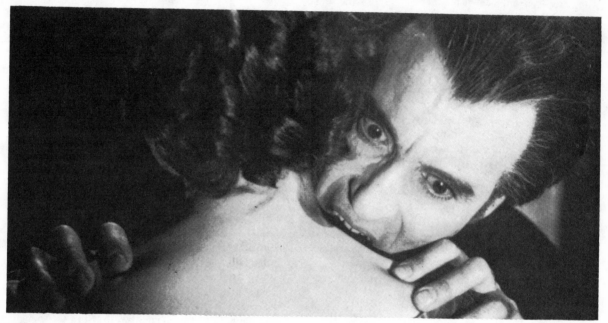

After a while, she got out of bed, lit the gas fire and put on some water for coffee. Nervously she stretched out a hand and touched the paper. It felt slightly damp, yet the other walls — the grey ones — were quite dry under her fingers. Gently she tried to insert a fingernail under the edge of the paper, but she couldn't do it — the paper was too firmly fixed. With the second try — in a different spot — she only succeeded in breaking her nail. Without any sense of disappointment, she picked up her coffee and moved back to the bed.

School, her job as a teacher, her home in New York — all seemed to be disconnected somehow. None of it was real. Not any more. These were the only things that were real: this room, this silence, and Reginald's forget-me-not wallpaper.

The paper had spread *so far* now. It had reached the far end of the wall and was beginning to turn the corner. There seemed to be no pattern to its actual movement — it just seemed to move, creeping, spreading — rather like liquid spilt on a polished surface. Some areas of the wall would be left bare, she noticed. Then, later, she would see that they had been filled in. The paper was relentless and very, very thorough.

Even the little postcard of the peasant boy was not safe.

forget-me-nots grew up around him. Sandra thought the picture was prettier. It's a pity, she thought, that Murillo can't be here to see it. Looking towards the photograph of Reginald and his wife, she was not surprised to see that it remained exactly as before. No forget-me-nots grew on *that* one. Looking closer, she saw that the paper was spreading *underneath* it.

Nothing was staying the same. Nothing. Even the quality of the silence was changing. Looking towards the window she saw the reason why. Snow was falling, thick and fast, the great soft shapes tumbling against the pane, settling. They fell without sound, insulating her more completely against the outside world.

And suddenly, she began to grow afraid. It had to stop. Everything had to stop. She had to do *something*. She didn't know what she was afraid of, but the fear grew, unexplainable, threatening, at any moment it would engulf her. She knew at once that she had to see someone, *talk* to someone. But who? There was no one she knew. Not Mr. Robertson; she had only glimpsed him on the stairs on two or three occasions. He had nodded to her, smiling, a slow-moving, sad old man of seventy-odd. He couldn't help. *Who* then?

David. David Hampshire. She saw his face before she

thought of his name; that nice young man who had been so helpful on the tube that day of her arrival.

She took the piece of paper bearing his 'phone number and snatched a handful of coins from the shelf. Then, throwing on a coat and slippers, she went downstairs. Carefully, her hands trembling, she dialled his number.

"Hello?..." And there was his voice.

"Hello? ... David?"

"Yes. Who's that?"

She paused, then said quickly: "Sandra Timms."

"Who?"

Oh God, oh Jesus, he'd forgotten. "I'm the girl you met on the tube. The American girl...." She could hear herself almost whimpering. "Don't you remember?... You helped me...."

And then she heard the smile in his voice as recollection returned.

"Oh, yes!" he said. "Yes, of course, I remember. How are you? Have you been okay?"

She began to blurt out her need for help. She had not meant to do this; she had meant to ask him to come round to see her — to tell him then — to do it more — casually. But somehow the desperation inside her had taken over, and she was pleading with him.

"Help me. You've got to help me!"

"But what's wrong?" he asked, his voice loaded with concern.

"I don't know — I don't know — I don't know!..."

"Right, listen," he said, forcing the calmness into the situation. "Tell me where you are. I'll drive round straight-away." He took up a pencil. "Give me your address."

She was almost incoherent, but he managed to write down the address she gabbled out.

"I'll be there in fifteen minutes."

"Yes, yes! Please hurry....*Please hurry!*" And she was gone.

David heard the click of the receiver and put the phone down. As he reached for his coat he looked at the address he had scribbled on the notepad. He stopped, gazing at it. Perhaps she was having some kind of joke with him — *some joke* on a night like *this!* He screwed the paper into a ball and tossed it into the wastebasket. It doesn't make sense, he thought, there was no longer any such address as 10, *Rillington Place.*

Reaching her own room, Sandra ran in and closed the door behind her. In her absence the wallpaper had spread even further. Almost three walls were covered now, and the peasant boy had been completely wiped out. Reginald continued to smile.

Fifteen minutes, he had said. Fifteen minutes. She could hold out that long. It wasn't very long. Not too long. She could try counting them off — that might help. Count the seconds: One, two, three, four, five, six, seven....She closed her eyes, shutting out the forget-me-nots that grew all around her. Eight...nine...ten....Now

the silence was getting in the way. Where was she? Eight...nine...ten...eleven....She tried to shut her ears to the silence, but it was no good. It got through. Whatever you did it got through. Make some coffee, smoke a cigarette, do *something*. Act naturally. The paper had crept onto the fourth wall now. It was moving faster than ever. She hurried to the kitchen, lit the gas under the kettle. That's it — be steady — be calm. Get the jar of coffee — don't spill any. One spoonful...sugar...milk ready...the wallpaper had gotten into the kitchen too. There were forget-me-nots everywhere. Take no notice. David will be here soon. Everything will be all right then. You can wait till then. Not long now. The water's boiling. The sound of the steam and the gas are the only sounds. Turn off the gas, pour on the water. Silence. The coffee's made. Add the milk. Sip it slowly. Concentrate...concentrate....She looked at the clock. Half an hour had gone by since she had called David! What had happened to him? Why wasn't he here? Fifteen minutes, he had told her. It was over half an hour....She sipped at the coffee. It was stone-cold, and she put it down in disgust. She moved from the kitchen, back into the larger room, walking slowly, forcing her way through the silence. The silence was like the sea, and it was rising, moment by moment. Reginald liked the silence. He smiled into it from his forget-me-not heaven. Would David *never* come?

Yes! He was *here!* At *last!* The gentle tap at her door had taken her completely by surprise. She pressed herself against the silence, pushing a way through. She got to the door, opened it. She saw the thin face, the smile and the blue eyes behind the glasses. She spun, and the sweet, sweet forget-me-not fungus lurched, reaching out. The whole room was blue, quivering in silence. Then the man spoke. After a second, the silence itself was shattered.

"I wonder if I could borrow a little milk?" the man on the landing had said, holding out an empty cup. "I've just moved in downstairs...." The girl — dirty, emaciated, her tangled hair hanging about her face — just stood there in the open doorway, staring at him dumbly from wide, frightened eyes. He smiled at her, adding: "My name is Reg," and suddenly she screamed. Her voice echoed in the quiet house — the sound of something in pain. The screams continued, the loudness cutting into the snowbound silence. When the screaming stopped, her mouth went on moving, opening and closing like the mouth of a ventriloquist's dummy.

Being a man of "ordinary' constitution" I have done my best to make my soul monstrous. A blind swimmer, I have made myself clairvoyant. I have seen, I have become the amazed lover of what I have seen, wanting to identify myself with it.

Max Ernst, *Inspiration to Order* (1924)

Old Mansion

John Crowe Ransom

As an intruder I trudged with careful innocence
To mask in decency a meddlesome stare,
Passing the old house often on its eminence,
Exhaling my foreign weed on its weighted air.

Here age seemed newly imaged for the historian
After his monstrous châteaux on the Loire,
A beauty not for depicting by old vulgarian
Reiterations which gentle readers abhor.

Each time of seeing I absorbed some other feature
Of a house whose annals in no wise could be brief
Nor ignoble; for it expired as sweetly as Nature,
With her tinge of oxidation on autumn leaf.

It was a Southern manor. One need hardly imagine
Towers, white monoliths, or even ivied walls;
But sufficient state if its peacock *was* a pigeon;
Where no courts kept, but grave rites and funerals.

Indeed, not distant, possibly not external
To the property, were tombstones, where the catafalque
Had carried their dead; and projected a note too charnel
But for the honeysuckle on its intricate stalk.

Stability was the character of its rectangle
Whose line was seen in part and guessed in part
Through trees. Decay was the tone of old brick and
shingle.
Green blinds dragging frightened the watchful heart

To assert, "Your mansion, long and richly inhabited,
Its exits and entrances suiting the children of men,
Will not forever be thus, O man, exhibited,
And one had best hurry to enter it if one can."

And at last, with my happier angel's own temerity,
Did I clang their brazen knocker against the door,
To beg their dole of a look, in simple charity,
Or crumbs of legend dropping from their great store.

But it came to nothing — and may so gross denial
Which has been deplored with a beating of the breast
Never shorten the tired historian, loyal
To acknowledge defeat and discover a new quest —

The old mistress was ill, and sent my dismissal
By one even more wrappered and lean and dark
Than that wrapped concierge and imperturbable vassal
Who bids you begone from her master's Gothic park.

Emphatically, the old house crumbled; the ruins
Would litter, as already the leaves, this petted sward;
And no annalist went in to the lords or the peons;
The antiquary would finger the bits of shard.

But on retreating I saw myself in the token,
How loving from my foreign weed the feather curled
On the languid air; and I went with courage shaken
To dip, alas, into some unseemlier world.

The Cupola

Louise Bogan

A mirror hangs on the wall of the draughty cupola.
Within the depths of glass mix the oak and the beech
leaf,
Once held to the boughs' shape, but now to the shape of
the wind.

Someone has hung the mirror here for no reason,
In the shuttered room, an eye for the drifted leaves,
For the oak leaf, the beech, a handsbreadth of darkest
reflection.

Someone has thought alike of the bough and the wind
And struck their shape to the wall. Each in its season
Spills negligent death throughout the abandoned
chamber.

...man has...a shadow side to his nature which is not just made up of small weaknesses and blemishes, but possesses a positively demoniacal impetus...a delirious monster...the blood-lust of the beast....

C.G. Jung, *The Psychology of the Unconscious* (1953)

Long, crooked shadows fell over the river and muffled sounds crept along the murky banks. In the creaking of the thick beech branches, in the rustling of the willows trailing their leaves in the water, I heard the utterances of the mysterious beings of whom Olga had spoken. They took on peculiar shapes, serpentine and peaked of face, having a bat's head and a snake's body. And they coiled themselves around a man's legs, drawing his will to live out of him until he sat down on the ground, in search of a slumber from which there was no awakening.

Jerzy Kosinski: *The Painted Bird* (1965)

The Snail Watcher

Patricia Highsmith

When Mr. Peter Knoppert began to make a hobby of snail-watching, he had no idea that his handful of specimens would become hundreds in no time. Only two months after the original snails were carried up to the Knoppert study, some thirty glass tanks and bowls, all teeming with snails, lined the walls, rested on the desk and windowsills, and were beginning even to cover the floor. Mrs. Knoppert disapproved strongly, and would no longer enter the room. It smelled, she said, and besides she had once stepped on a snail by accident, a horrible sensation she would never forget. But the more his wife and friends deplored his unusual and vaguely repellent pastime, the more pleasure Mr. Knoppert seemed to find in it.

"I never cared for nature before in my life," Mr. Knoppert often remarked — he was a partner in a brokerage firm, a man who had devoted all his life to the science of finance — "but snails have opened my eyes to the beauty of the animal world."

If his friends commented that snails were not really animals, and their slimy habitats hardly the best example of the beauty of nature, Mr. Knoppert would tell them with a superior smile that they simply didn't know all that *he* knew about snails.

And it was true. Mr. Knoppert had witnessed an exhibition that was not described, certainly not adequately described, in any encyclopaedia or zoology book that he had been able to find. Mr. Knoppert had wandered into the kitchen one evening for a bite of something before dinner, and had happened to notice that a couple of snails in the china bowl on the drainboard were behaving very oddly. Standing more or less on their tails, they were weaving before each other for all the world like a pair of snakes hypnotized by a flute player. A moment later, their faces came together in a kiss of voluptuous intensity. Mr. Knoppert bent closer and studied them from all angles. Something else was happening: a protuberance like an ear was appearing on the right side of the head of either snail. His instinct told him that he was watching a sexual activity of some sort.

The cook came in and said something to him, but Mr. Knoppert silenced her with an impatient wave of his hand. He couldn't take his eyes from the enchanted little creatures in the bowl.

When the earlike excrescences were precisely together rim to rim, a whitish rod like another small tentacle shot out from one ear and arched over toward the ear of the other snail. Mr. Knoppert's first surmise was dashed when a tentacle sallied from the other snail, too. Most peculiar, he thought. The two tentacles withdrew, then shot forth again, one after the other, and then as if they had found some invisible mark, remained fixed in the other snail. Mr. Knoppert peered intently closer. So did the cook.

"Did you ever see anything like this?" Mr. Knoppert asked.

"No. They must be fighting," the cook said indifferently and went away.

That was a sample of the ignorance on the subject of snails that he was later to discover everywhere.

Mr. Knoppert continued to observe the pair of snails for nearly an hour, until first the ears, then the rods withdrew, and the snails themselves relaxed their attitudes and paid no further attention to each other. But by that time, a different pair of snails had begun a flirtation, and were slowly rearing themselves to get into a position for kissing. Mr. Knoppert told the cook that the snails were not to be served that evening. He took the whole bowl of them up to his study. And snails were never again served in the Knoppert household.

That night, he searched his encyclopaedias and a few general science books he happened to possess, but there was absolutely nothing on snails' breeding habits, though the oyster's dull reproductive cycle was described in detail. Perhaps it hadn't been a mating he had seen after all, Mr. Knoppert decided after a day or two. His wife Edna told him either to eat the snails or get rid of them — it was at this time she stepped on a snail that had crawled out onto the floor — and Mr. Knoppert might have, if he hadn't come across a certain sentence in Darwin's *Origin of Species* on a page given to gastropoda. The sentence was in French, a language Mr. Knoppert did not know, but the word *sensualité* made him tense like a bloodhound that has suddenly found the scent. He was in the public library at the time, and laboriously he translated the sentence with the aid of a French-English dictionary. It was a statement of less than a hundred words, saying that snails manifested a sensuality in their mating that was not found anywhere in the animal kingdom. That was all. It was from the notebook of Henri Fabre. Obviously, Darwin had decided not to translate it for the average reader, but to leave it in its original language for the scholarly few who really cared. Mr. Knoppert considered himself one of the scholarly few now, and his round, pink face beamed with self-esteem.

He had learned that his snails were the fresh water type that laid their eggs in sand or earth, so he put moist earth and a little saucer of water into a big wash-pan and transferred his snails into it. Then he waited for something to happen. Not even another mating happened. He picked up the snails one by one and looked at them, without seeing anything suggestive of pregnancy. But one snail he couldn't pick up. The shell might have been glued to the earth. Mr. Knoppert suspected the snail had buried its head in the ground to die. Two more days went by, and on the morning of the third, Mr. Knoppert found a spot of crumbly earth where the snail had rested. Curious, he investigated the crumbles with a match stem, and to his delight discovered a pit full of shiny new eggs. Snail eggs!

He hadn't been wrong. Mr. Knoppert called his wife and the cook to look at them. The eggs looked very much like big caviar, only they were white instead of black or red.

"Well, naturally they have to breed some way," was his wife's comment.

Mr. Knoppert couldn't understand her lack of interest. He had to go look at the eggs every hour that he was at home. He looked at them every morning to see if any change had taken place, and the eggs were his last thought every night before he went to bed. Moreover, another snail was now digging a pit. And another pair of snails was mating! The first batch of eggs turned a grayish color, and minuscule spirals of future shells became discernible on their surfaces. Mr. Knoppert's anticipation rose to higher pitch.

At last a morning arrived when he looked down into the egg pit and saw the first tiny moving head, the first stubby little antennae uncertainly exploring its nest. Mr. Knoppert was as happy as the father of a new child. Every one of the thirty or more eggs in the pit came miraculously to life. He had seen the entire reproductive cycle evolve to a successful conclusion. And the fact that no one, at least no one that he knew of, was acquainted with a fraction of what he knew, lent his knowledge a thrill of discovery, the piquancy of the esoteric. Mr. Knoppert made notes on successive matings and egg hatchings. He narrated snail biology to sometimes fascinated, more often shocked friends and guests, until his wife squirmed with embarrassment.

The world's largest snail, captured in West Africa, has died of dehydration, its owner Christopher Hudson said....The previous largest snail also belonged to Mr. Hudson whose obsession with snails caused his 20-year-old wife to leave him earlier this year.

Reuter, *London, June* (1977)

"But where is it going to stop, Peter? If they keep on reproducing at this rate, they'll take over the house!" his wife told him after fifteen or twenty pits had hatched.

"There's no stopping nature," he replied good-humoredly. "They've only taken over the study. There's plenty of room there."

So more and more glass tanks and bowls were moved in. Mr. Knoppert went to the market and chose several of the more lively looking snails, and also a pair he found mating, unobserved by the rest of the world. More and more egg pits appeared in the dirt floors of the tanks, and out of each pit crept finally from thirty to forty baby snails, transparent as dewdrops, gliding up rather than down the strips of fresh lettuce that Mr. Knoppert was quick to give all the pits as edible ladders for them. Matings went on so often that he no longer bothered to watch them. But the thrill of seeing the white caviar become shells and start to move — that never diminished however often he witnessed it.

His colleagues in the brokerage office noticed a new zest for life in Peter Knoppert. He became more daring in his moves, more brilliant in his calculations, became in fact a little vicious in his outlook, but he brought money in for his company. By unanimous vote, his basic salary was raised from forty to sixty thousand per year. When anyone congratulated him on first achievements, Mr. Knoppert was quick to give all the credit to his snails and the beneficial relaxation he derived from watching them.

He spent all his evenings with his snails in the room that was no longer a study but a kind of aquarium. He loved to strew the tanks with fresh lettuce and pieces of boiled potatoes and beets, then turn on the sprinkler system that he had installed in the tanks to simulate natural rainfall. Then all the snails would liven up and begin eating, mating, or merely gliding with obvious pleasure through the shallow water. Mr. Knoppert often let a snail climb onto his forefinger — he fancied his snails enjoyed this human contact — and he would feed it a piece of lettuce by hand, would observe the snail from all sides, finding as much aesthetic satisfaction as another man might have from contemplating a Japanese print.

By now, Mr. Knoppert did not allow anyone to set foot in his study. Too many snails had the habit of crawling around on the floor, of going to sleep glued to chair bottoms and to the backs of books on the shelves. Snails spent most of their time sleeping, especially the older snails. But there were enough less indolent snails who preferred love-making. Mr. Knoppert estimated that about a dozen pairs of snails must be kissing all the time. And certainly there was a multitude of baby and adolescent snails.

They were impossible to count. But Mr. Knoppert did count the snails sleeping and creeping on the ceiling alone, and arrived at something between eleven and twelve hundred. The tanks, the bowls, the underside of his desk and the bookshelves must surely have held fifty times that number. Some of them had been up there for weeks, and he was afraid they were not taking in enough nourishment. But of late he had been a little too busy, and too much in need of the tranquility that he got simply from sitting in the study in his favorite chair.

During the month of June, he was so busy, he often worked late in the evening at his office over the reports that were piling in at the end of the fiscal year. He made calculations, spotted a half dozen possibilities of gain, and reserved the most daring, the least obvious moves for his private operations. By this time next year, he thought, he should be three or four times as well off as now. He saw his bank account multiplying as easily and rapidly as his snails. He told his wife this, and she was overjoyed. She even forgave him the appropriation of the study, and the stale, fishy smell that was spreading throughout the whole upstairs.

"Still, I do wish you'd take a look just to see if anything's happening, Peter," she said to him rather anxiously one morning. "A tank might have overturned or something, and I wouldn't want the rug to be ruined. You haven't been in the study for nearly a week, have you?"

Mr. Knoppert hadn't been in for nearly two weeks. He didn't tell his wife that the rug was pretty much ruined already. "I'll go up tonight," he said.

But it was three more days before he found time. He went in one evening just before bedtime and was surprised to find the floor absolutely covered with snails, with three or four layers of snails. He had difficulty closing the door without mashing any. The dense clusters of snails in the corners made the room look positively round, as if he stood inside some huge, conglomerate stone. Mr. Knoppert gazed around him with his mouth open in astonishment. They had not only covered every surface, but thousands of snails hung down into the room from the chandelier in a grotesque coagulation.

Mr. Knoppert felt for the back of a chair to steady himself. He felt only a lot of shells under his hand. He had to smile a little: there were snails in the chair seat; piled up on one another like a lumpy cushion. He really must do something about the ceiling, and immediately. He took an umbrella from the corner, brushed some of the snails off it, and cleared a place on his desk to stand on. The umbrella tore the wallpaper, and then the weight of the snails pulled down a long strip that hung almost to the floor. Mr. Knoppert felt suddenly frustrated and angry. The sprinklers would make them move. He pulled the lever.

The sprinklers came on in all the tanks, and the seething activity of the entire room increased at once. Mr. Knoppert slid his feet along the floor, through the tumbling snails that made a sound like pebbles on a beach, and directed a couple of the sprinklers at the ceiling. That was a mistake, he saw at once. The softened paper began to tear, and he dodged one slowly falling mass only to be hit by a swinging festoon of snails, really hit quite a stunning blow on the side of the head. He went down on one knee, dazed. He should open a window, he thought, the air was stifling. And there were snails crawling over his shoes and up his trousers legs .

He shook his feet irritably. He was just going to the door, intending to call for one of the servants to help him, when the chandelier fell on him. Mr. Knoppert sat down heavily on the floor. He saw now that he couldn't possibly get the window open, because the snails were fastened thick and deep over the windowsill. For a moment, he felt he couldn't get up, felt as if he were suffocating. It was not only the smell of the room, but everywhere he looked long wall-paper strips covered with snails blocked his vision as if he were in a prison.

"Edna!" he called, and was amazed at the muffled, ineffective sound of his voice. The room might have been soundproof.

He crawled to the door, heedless of the sea of snails he

crushed under hands and knees. He could not get the door open. There were so many snails on it, crossing and recrossing the crack of the door on all four sides, they actually resisted his strength.

"Edna!" A snail crawled into his mouth. He spat it out in disgust. Mr. Knoppert tried to brush the snails off his arms. But for every hundred he dislodged, four hundred seemed to slide upon him and fasten to him again, as if they deliberately sought him out as the only comparatively snail-free surface in the room. There were snails crawling over his eyes. Then just as he staggered to his feet, something else hit him — Mr. Knoppert couldn't even see. He was fainting! At any rate, he was on the floor. His arms felt like leaden weights as he tried to reach his nostrils, his eyes, to free them from the sealing, murderous snail bodies.

"Help!" He swallowed a snail. Choking, he widened his mouth for air and felt a snail crawl over his lips onto his tongue. He was in hell! He could feel them gliding over his legs like a glutinous river, pinning his legs to the floor. "Ugh—!" Mr. Knoppert's breath came in feeble gasps. His vision grew black, a horrible, undulating black. He could not breathe at all, because he could not reach his nostrils, could not move his hands. Then through the slit of one eye, he saw directly in front of him, only inches away, what had been, he knew, the rubber plant that stood in its pot near the door. A pair of snails were quietly making love on it. And right besides them, tiny snails as pure as dewdrops were emerging from a pit like an infinite army into their widening world.

The Wind in Winter
Miroslav Holub

For too long have we stretched the bowstring of air.

All night we heard the menacing
grumble of engines,
we brought in the wind.

Then it happened. The heap toppled
and layer after layer
pack after pack
the snow dogs tumble,
their howls flogging the fields,

the wind returns, the rubber wind
brings back
the night and darkness
the sky and memory.

Thus we are alone, stripped of the landscape,
the last remnant of air in our lungs
and an evil laugh on our lips.

Such an evil laugh.

Borne helplessly towards some hideous fate the terrified dreamer struggles to escape, but finds himself paralysed, his body seemingly divorced from his conscious efforts. As he struggles, intermittent twitches and strangled cries interrupt the bursts of rapid eye movement and the paradoxical EEG record, till, after half a minute, he finally wakes. Our new knowledge enables us to understand that he really was paralysed.

Ian Oswald, *Sleep* (1968)

The Shadow-Maker
Gwendolyn MacEwen

I have come to possess your darkness, only this.

My legs surround your black, wrestle it
As the flames of day wrestle night
And everywhere you paint the necessary shadows
On my flesh and darken the fibres of my nerve;
Without these shadows I would be
In air one wave of ruinous light
And night with many mouths would close
Around my infinite and sterile curve.

Shadow-maker create me everywhere
Dark spaces (your face is my chosen abyss),
For I said I have come to possess your darkness,
Only this.

from **The Werewolf**
The Case of Jean Grenier (1603)
Montague Summers

During the early spring of the year 1603 there spread through the St. Sever districts of Gascony in the extreme south-west of France, the department Landes, a veritable reign of terror. From a number of little hamlets and smaller villages young children had begun mysteriously to disappear off the fields and roads, and of these no trace could be discovered. In one instance even a babe was stolen from its cradle in a cottage whilst the mother had left it for a short space safe asleep, as she thought. People talked of wolves; others shook their heads and whispered of something worse than wolves. The consternation was at its height when the local magistrate advised the puisné Judge of the Barony de la Roche Chalais and de la Châtellenie that information had been laid before him by three witnesses, of whom one, a young girl named Marguerite Poirier, aged thirteen, of the outlying hamlet of Saint-Paul, in the Parish of Espérons, swore that in full moon she had been attacked by a savage beast, much resembling a wolf....The girl stated that one midday whilst she was watching cattle, a wild beast with rufulous fur, not unlike a huge dog, rushed from the thicket and tore her kirtle with its sharp teeth. She only managed to save herself from being bitten owing to the fact she was armed with a stout iron-pointed staff with which she hardly warded herself. Moreover, a lad of some thirteen or fourteen years old, Jean Grenier, was boasting that it was he who attacked Marguerite as a wolf, and that but for her stick he would have torn her limb from limb as he had already eaten three or four children.

Jeanne Gaboriaut, aged eighteen, deposed that one day when she was tending cattle with Jean Grenier in her company (both being servants of a well-to-do farmer of Saint-Paul, Pierre Combaut), he coarsely complimented her as a bonny lass and vowed he would marry her. When she asked who his father was, he said: ''I am a priest's bastard.'' She remarked that he was sallow and dirty, to which he replied: ''Ah, that is because of the wolf's-skin I wear.'' He added that a man named Pierre Labourat had given him this pelt, and that when he donned it he coursed the woods and fields as a wolf. There were nine werewolves of his coven who went to the chase at the waning of the moon on Mondays, Fridays, and Saturdays, and who were wont to hunt during the twilight and just before the dawn. He lusted for the flesh of small children, which was tender, plump, and rare. When hungry, in wolf's shape he had often killed dogs and lapped their hot blood, which was not so delicious to his taste as that of young boys, from whose thighs he would bite great collops of fat luscious brawn.

These informations were lodged on 29th May, 1603. Jean Grenier was arrested and brought before the Higher Court on the following 2nd June, when he freely made a confession of the most abominable and hideous

werewolfery, crimes which were in every particular proved to be only too true. He acknowledged that when he had called himself the by-blow of a priest he had lied. His father was Pierre Grenier, nicknamed ''le Croquant'', a day-labourer of the hamlet Saint-Antoine de Pizon, which is situate toward Coutras. He had run away from his father, who beat him and whom he hated, and he got his living as best he could by mendicity and cowherding. A youth named Pierre de la Tilhaire, who lived at Saint-Antoine, one evening took him into the depths of a wood and brought him into the presence of the Lord of the Forest. This Lord was a tall dark man, dressed all in black, riding a black charger. He saluted the two lads, and dismounting he kissed Jean, but his mouth was colder than ice. Presently he rode away down a distant glade. This was about three years ago, and on a second meeting he had given himself to the Lord of the Forest as his bond-slave. The Lord had marked both boys on each thigh with a kind of misericorde, or small stiletto. He had treated them well, and all swigged off a bumper of rich wine. The Lord had presented them each with a wolf-skin, which when they donned, they seemed to have been transformed into wolves, and in this shape they scoured the countryside. The Lord accompanied them, but in a much larger shape, (as he thought) as an ounce or leopard. Before donning the skin they anointed themselves with an unguent. The Lord of the Forest retained the unguent and the wolf's pelt, but gave them to Jean whenever he asked for their use. He was bidden never to pare the nail of his left thumb, and it had grown thick and crooked like a claw. On more than one occasion he had seen several men, of whom he recognized some four or five, with the Lord of the Forest, adoring him. Jean Grenier then related with great exactitude his tale of infanticide. On the first Friday of March, 1603, he had killed and eaten a little girl, aged about three, named Guyonne. He had attacked the child of Jean Roullier, but there came to the rescue the boy's elder brother, who was armed and beat him away. Young Roullier was called as a witness and remembered the exact place, hour, and day when a wolf had flown out from a thicket at his little brother, and he had driven the animal off, being well weaponed. It would be superfluous and even wearisome to chronicle the cases, one after another, in which the parents of children who had been attacked by the wolf, boys and girls wounded and in many cases killed, came forward and exactly corroborated the confession of Jean Grenier.

The Court ordered Pierre Grenier, the father, who Jean accused of sorcery and werewolfism, to be laid by the heels, and hue and cry was made for Pierre de la Tilhaire. The latter fled, and could not be caught, but Pierre Grenier on being closely interrogated proved to be a simple rustic, one who clearly knew nothing of his son's crimes. He was released.

...on 6th September, 1603, President Dassis pronounced sentence upon the loup-garou. The utmost clemency was shown. Taking into consideration his youth and extreme ignorance Jean Grenier was ordered to be straitly enclosed in the Franciscan friary of S. Michael the Archangel, a house of the stricter Observance, at Bordeaux, being warned that any attempt to escape would be punished by the gallows without hope of remission or stay.

Pierre de Lancre, who has left us a very ample account of the whole case, visited the loup-garou at St. Michael's in the year 1610, and found that he was a lean and gaunt lad, with small deep-set black eyes that glared fiercely. He had long sharp teeth, some of which were white like fangs, others black and broken, whilst his hands were almost like claws with horrid crooked nails. He loved to hear and talk of wolves, often fell upon all fours, moving with extraordinary agility and seemingly with greater ease than when he walked upright as a man. The Fathers remarked that at first, at least, he rejected simple plain food for foulest offal. De Lancre calls attention to the fact that Grenier or Garnier seems for some reason to be a name not infrequently borne by werewolves.

Jean Grenier told de Lancre that the Lord of the Forest, who was certes none the other than the demon, had twice entered his room at the Friary, tempting him, but that he had warded off the evil one by the Sign of the Cross. The hapless youth, tended to the last by the good religious, died in November, 1611.

Eidolon
Robert Penn Warren

All night, in May, dogs barked in the hollow woods;
Hoarse, from secret huddles of no light,
By moonlit bole, hoarse, the dogs gave tongue.
In May, by moon, no moon, thus: I remember
Of their far clamor the throaty, infatuate timbre.

The boy, all night, lay in the black room,
Tick-straw, all night, harsh to the bare side.
Staring, he heard; the clotted dark swam slow.
Far off, by wind, no wind, unappeasable riot
Provoked, resurgent, the bosom's nocturnal disquiet.

What hungers kept the house? under the rooftree
The boy; the man, clod-heavy, hard hand uncurled;
The old man, eyes wide, spittle on his beard.
In dark was crushed the may-apple: plunging, the rangers
Of dark remotelier belled their unhouseled angers.

Dogs quartered the black woods: blood black on
May-apple at dawn, old beech-husk. And trails are lost
By rock, in ferns lost, by pools unlit.
I heard the hunt. Who saw, in darkness, how fled
The white eidolon from the fanged commotion rude?

Lycanthropy was a form of insanity...men are most attacked with this madness in February...they skulk in cemeteries and live alone like ravening wolves. Clinically they would be classified as cases of sadism, frequently combined with cannibalism and necrophilia.

J. Grimm, *Deutsche Mythologie* (1876)

Those who are changed into the demon werewolf suddenly fall to the ground as if seized with epilepsy, and there they lie without life or motion. Their actual bodies do not move from the spot where they have fallen, nor do their limbs turn to the hairy limbs of a wolf but the soul or spirit by some fascination quits the inert body and enters the spectrum or paoua of a wolf, and when they have glutted their foul lupine lusts and cravings by the Devil's power, the soul re-enters the former human body.

Gaspar Peucer, *De Themonantria* (1553)

The dammed-up instinct-forces in civilized man are immensely more destructive...than the instincts of the primitive, who in a modest degree is constantly living with his negative instincts.

C.G. Jung, *Psychological Types* (1953)

Road Signs
Dilys Henrik Jones

For miles now the road ran through
The forest edge,
And always we saw signs,
Clear in any language —
The atavistic image from the nursery tales,
The long, lean shape.

Not that we met anyone who'd seen,
Himself, a wolf;
One man's father, long ago, had done so,
And there was always a boy,
But he had lived in the next village —
Or so they said.

Nevertheless they kept the signs new painted,
After all one never knew
In some dark, frozen winter they might come,
Once more, the wolves.

The Kill
Peter Fleming

In the cold waiting room of a small railway station in the west of England two men were sitting. They had sat there for an hour, and were likely to sit there longer. There was a thick fog outside. Their train was indefinitely delayed.

The waiting room was a barren and unfriendly place. A naked electric bulb lit it with wan, disdainful efficiency. A notice, NO SMOKING, stood on mantelpiece; when you turned it around, it said NO SMOKING on the other side, too. Printed regulations relating to an outbreak of swine fever in 1924 were pinned neatly to one wall, almost, but maddeningly not quite, in the center of it. The stove gave out a hot, thick smell, powerful already but increasing. A pale leprous flush on the black and beaded window showed that a light was burning on the platform outside, in the fog. Somewhere water dripped with infinite reluctance onto corrugated iron. ·

The two men sat facing each other over the stove on chairs of an unswerving woodenness. Their acquaintance was no older than their vigil. From such talk as they had had, it seemed likely that they were to remain strangers.

The younger of the two resented the lack of contact in their relationship more than the lack of comfort in their surroundings. His attitude towards his fellow beings had but recently undergone a transition from the subjective to the objective. As with many of his class and age, the routine, unrecognized as such, of an expensive education, with the triennial alternative of those delights normal to wealth and gentility, had atrophied many of his curiosities. For the first twenty-odd years of his life he had read humanity in terms of relevance rather than reality, looking on people who held no ordained place in his own existence much as a buck in a park watches visitors walking up the drive: mildly, rather resentfully inquiring — not inquisitive. Now, hot in reaction from this unconscious provincialism, he treated mankind as a museum, gaping conscientiously at each fresh exhibit, hunting for the noncumulative evidence of man's complexity with indiscriminate zeal. To each magic circle of individuality he saw himself as a kind of free-lance tangent. He aspired to be a connoisseur of men.

There was undoubtedly something arresting about the specimen before him. Of less than medium height, the stranger had yet that sort of ranging leanness that lends vicarious inches. He wore a long black overcoat, very shabby, and his shoes were covered with mud. His face had no color in it, though the impression it produced was not one of pallor; the skin was of a dark sallow, tinged with gray. The nose was pointed, the jaw sharp and narrow. Deep vertical wrinkles, running down towards it from the high cheekbones, sketched the permanent groundwork of a broader smile than the deep-set honey-colored eyes seemed likely to authorize. The most striking thing about the face was the incongruity of its frame. On the back of his head the stranger wore a bowler hat with a very narrow brim. No word of such casual implications as a tilt did justice to its angle. It was clamped, by something at least as holy as custom, to the back of his skull, and that thin, questing face confronted the world fiercely from under a black halo of nonchalance. The man's whole appearance suggested *difference* rather than aloofness. The unnatural way he wore his hat had the significance of indirect comment, like the antics of a performing animal. It was as if he was part of some older thing, of which *Homo sapiens* in a bowler hat was an expurgated edition. He sat with his

The Wolves
Allen Tate

There are wolves in the next room waiting
With heads bent low, thrust out, breathing
At nothing in the dark; between them and me
A white door patched with light from the hall
Where it seems never (so still is the house)
A man has walked from the front door to the stair.
It has all been forever. Beasts claw the floor.
I have brooded on angels and archfiends
But no man has ever sat where the next room's
Crowded with wolves, and for the honour of man
I affirm that never have I before. Now while
I have looked for the evening star at a cold window
And whistled when Arcturus split his light,
I've heard the wolves scuffle, and said: So this
Is man; so — what better conclusion is there —
The day will not follow night, and the heart
Of man has a little dignity, but less patience
Than a wolf's, and a duller sense that cannot
Smell its own mortality. (This and other
Meditations will be suited to other times
After dog silence howls his epitaph.)
Now remember courage, go to the door,
Open it and see whether coiled on the bed
Or cringing by the wall, a savage beast
Maybe with golden hair, with deep eyes
Like a bearded spider on a sunlit floor
Will snarl — and man can never be alone.

shoulders hunched and his hands thrust into his overcoat pockets. The hint of discomfort in his attitude seemed due not so much to the fact his chair was hard as to the fact that it was a chair.

The young man had found him uncommunicative. The most mobile sympathy, launching consecutive attacks on different fronts, had failed to draw him out. The reserved adequacy of his replies conveyed a rebuff more effectively than sheer surliness. Except to answer him, he did not look at the young man. When he did, his eyes were full of an abstracted amusement. Sometimes he smiled, but for no immediate cause.

Looking back down their hour together, the young man saw a field of endeavor on which frustated banalities lay thick, like the discards of a routed army. But resolution, curiosity, and the need to kill time all clamored against an admission of defeat.

"If he will not talk," thought the young man, "then I will. The sound of my own voice is infinitely preferable to the sound of none. I will tell him what has just happened to me. It is really a most extraordinary story. I will tell it as well as I can, and I shall be very much surprised if its impact on his mind does not shock this man into some form of self-revelation. He is unaccountable without being *outré*, and I am inordinately curious about him."

Aloud he said, in a brisk and engaging manner: "I think you said you were a hunting man?"

The other raised his quick, honey-colored eyes. They gleamed with inaccessible amusement. Without answering, he lowered them again to contemplate the little beads of light thrown through the ironwork of the stove onto the skirts of his overcoat. Then he spoke, He had a husky voice.

"I came here to hunt," he agreed.

"In that case," said the young man, "you will have heard of Lord Fleer's private pack. Their kennels are not far from here."

"I know them," replied the other.

"I have just been staying there," the young man continued. "Lord Fleer is my uncle."

The other looked up, smiled, and nodded, with the bland inconsequence of a foreigner who does not understand what is being said to him. The young man swallowed his impatience.

"Would you," he continued, using a slightly more peremptory tone than heretofore, "would you care to hear a new and rather remarkable story about my uncle? Its dénouement is not two days old. It is quite short."

From the vastness of some hidden joke, those light eyes mocked the necessity of a definite answer. At length: "Yes," said the stranger, "I would." The impersonality in his voice might have passed for a parade of sophistication, a reluctance to betray interest. But the eyes hinted that interest was alive elsewhere.

"Very well," said the young man.

Drawing his chair a little closer to the stove, he began:

As perhaps you know, my uncle, Lord Fleer, leads a retired, though by no means an inactive life. For the last two or three hundred years, the currents of contemporary thought have passed mainly through the hands of men whose gregarious instincts have been constantly awakened and almost invariably indulged. By the standards of the eighteenth century, when Englishmen first became self-conscious about solitude, my uncle would have been considered unsociable. In the early nineteenth century, those not personally acquainted with him would have thought him romantic. Today, his attitude towards the sound and fury of modern life is too negative to excite comment as an oddity; yet even now, were he to be involved in any occurrence which could be called disastrous or interpreted as discreditable, the press would pillory him as a "Titled Recluse."

The truth of the matter is, my uncle has discovered the elixer, or, if you prefer it, the opiate, of self-sufficiency. A man of extremely simple tastes, not cursed with overmuch imagination, he sees no reason to cross frontiers of habit which the years have hallowed into rigidity. He lives in his castle (it may be described as commodious rather than comfortable), runs his estate at a slight profit, shoots a little, rides a great deal, and hunts as often as he can. He never sees his neighbors except by accident, thereby leading them to suppose, with sublime but unconscious arrogance, that he must be slightly mad. If he is, he can at least claim to have padded his own cell.

My uncle has never married. As the only son of his only brother, I was brought up in the expectation of being his heir. During the war, however, an unforeseen development occurred.

In this national crisis my uncle, who was of course too old for active service, showed a lack of public spirit which earned him locally a good deal of unpopularity. Briefly, he declined to recognize the war, or, if he did recognize it, gave no sign of having done so. He continued to lead his own vigorous but (in the circumstances) rather irrelevant life. Though he found himself at last obliged to recruit his hunt servants from men of advanced age and uncertain mettle in any crisis of the chase, he contrived to mount them well, and twice a week during the season himself rode two horses to a standstill after the hill foxes which, as no doubt you know, provide the best sport the Fleer country has to offer.

When the local gentry came and made representations to him, saying that it was time he did something for his country besides destroying its vermin by the most unreliable and expensive method ever devised, my uncle was very sensible. He now saw, he said, that he had been standing too aloof from a struggle of whose progress (since he never read the paper) he had been only indirectly aware. The next day he wrote to London and ordered *The Times* and a Belgian refugee. It was the least he could do, he said. I think he was right.

The Belgian refugee turned out to be a female, and dumb. Whether one or both of these characteristics had been stipulated for by my uncle, nobody knew. At any rate, she took up her quarters at Fleer: a heavy; unat-tractive girl of twenty-five, with a shiny face and small black hairs on the backs of her hands. Her life appeared to be modeled on that of the larger ruminants, except, of course, that the greater part of it took place indoors. She ate a great deal, slept with a will, and had a bath every Sunday, remitting this salubrious custom only when the housekeeper, who enforced it, was away on her holiday. Much of her time she spent sitting on a sofa, on the landing outside her bedroom, with Prescott's *Conquest of Mexico* open on her lap. She read either exceptionally slowly or not at all, for to my knowledge she carried the first volume about with her for eleven years. Hers, I think, was the contemplative type of mind.

The curious, and from my point of view the unfortunate, aspect of my uncle's patriotic gesture was the gradually increasing affection with which he came to regard this unlovable creature. Although, or more probably because, he saw her only at meals, when her features were rather more animated than at other times, his attitude towards her passed from the detached to the courteous, and from the courteous to the paternal. At the end of the war there was no question of her return to Belgium, and one day in 1919 I heard with pardonable mortification that my uncle had legally adopted her, and was altering his will in her favor.

Time, however, reconciled me to being disinherited by a being who, between meals, could scarcely be described as sentient. I continued to pay an annual visit to Fleer, and to ride with my uncle after his big-boned Welsh hounds over the sullen, dark-gray hill country in which — since its possession was no longer assured to me — I now began to see a powerful, though elusive, beauty.

I came down here three days ago, intending to stay for a week. I found my uncle, who is a tall, fine-looking man with a beard, in his usual unassailable good health. The Belgian, as always, gave me the impression of being impervious to disease, to emotion, or indeed to anything short of an act of God. She had been putting on weight since she came to live with my uncle, and was now a very considerable figure of a woman, though not, as yet, unwieldy.

It was at dinner, on the evening of my arrival, that I first noticed a certain *malaise* behind my uncle's brusque, laconic manner. There was evidently something on his mind. After dinner he asked me to come into his study. I detected, in the delivery of the invitation, the first hint of embarrassment I had known him to betray.

The walls of the study were hung with maps and the extremities of foxes. The room was littered with bills, catalogues, old gloves, fossils, rat-traps, cartridges, and feathers which had been used to clean his pipe — a stale diversity of jetsam which somehow managed to produce an impression of relevance and continuity, like the debris in an animal's lair. I had never been in the study before.

"Paul," said my uncle as soon as I had shut the door, "I am very much disturbed."

I assumed an air of sympathetic inquiry.

"Yesterday," my uncle went on, "one of my tenants came to see me. He is a decent man, who farms a strip of land outside the park wall to the northward. He said that he had lost two sheep in a manner for which he was wholly unable to account. He said he thought they had been killed by some wild animal."

My Uncle paused. The gravity of his manner was really portentous.

"Dogs?" I suggested, with the slightly patronizing diffidence of one who has probability on his side.

My uncle shook his head judiciously. "This man had often seen sheep which had been killed by dogs. He said that they were always badly torn — nipped about the legs, driven into a corner, worried to death; it was never a clean piece of work. These two sheep had not been killed like that. I went down to see them for myself. Their throats had been torn out. They were not bitten or nuzzled. They had both died in the open, not in a corner. Whatever did it was an animal more powerful and more cunning than a dog."

I said, "It couldn't have been something that had escaped from a traveling menagerie, I suppose?"

"They don't come into this part of the country," replied my uncle; "there are no fairs."

We were both silent for a moment. It was hard not to show more curiosity than sympathy as I waited on some further revelation to stake out my uncle's claim on the latter emotion. I could put no interpretation on those two dead sheep wild enough to account for his evident distress.

He spoke again, but with obvious reluctance.

"Another was killed early this morning," he said in a low voice, "on the Home Farm. In the same way."

For lack of any better comment, I suggested beating the nearby coverts. There might be some —

"We've scoured the woods," interrupted my uncle brusquely.

"And found nothing?"

"Nothing....Except some tracks."

"What sort of tracks?"

My uncle's eyes were suddenly evasive. He turned his head away.

"They were a man's tracks," he said slowly. A log fell over in the fireplace.

Again a silence. The interview appeared to be causing him pain rather than relief. I decided that the situation could lose nothing through the frank expression of my curiosity. Plucking up courage, I asked him roundly what cause he had to be upset? Three sheep, the property of his tenants, had died deaths which, though certainly unusual, were unlikely to remain for long mysterious. Their destroyer, whatever it was, would inevitably be caught, killed, or driven away in the course of the next few days. The loss of another sheep or two was the worst he had to fear.

When I had finished, my uncle gave me an anxious, almost a guilty look. I was suddenly aware that he had a confession to make.

"Sit down," he said. "I wish to tell you something."

This is what he told me:

A quarter of a century ago, my uncle had had occasion to engage a new housekeeper. With the blend of fatalism and sloth which is the foundation of the bachelor's attitude to the servant problem, he took on the first applicant. She was a tall, black, slant-eyed woman from the Welsh border, aged about thirty. My uncle said nothing about her character, but described her as having "powers." When she had been at Fleer some months, my uncle began to notice her, instead of taking her for granted. She was not averse to being noticed.

One day she came and told my uncle that she was with child by him. He took it calmly enough till he found that she expected him to marry her, or pretended to expect it. Then he flew into a rage, called her a whore, and told her she must leave the house as soon as the child was born. Instead of breaking down or continuing the scene, she began to croon to herself in Welsh, looking at him sideways with a certain amusement. This frightened him.

He forbade her to come near him again, had her things moved into an unused wing of the castle, and engaged another housekeeper.

A child was born, and they came and told my uncle that the woman was going to die; she asked for him continually, they said. As much frightened as distressed, he went through passages long unfamiliar to her room. When the woman saw him, she began to gabble in a preoccupied kind of way, looking at him all the time, as if she were repeating a lesson. Then she stopped, and asked that he should be shown the child.

It was a boy. The midwife, my uncle noticed, handled it with a reluctance almost amounting to disgust.

"That is your heir," said the dying woman in a harsh, unstable voice. "I have told him what he is to do. He will be a good son to me, and jealous of his birthright." And she went off, my uncle said, into a wild yet cogent rigmarole about a curse, embodied in the child, which would fall on any whom he made his heir over the bastard's head. At last her voice trailed away, and she fell back, exhausted and staring.

As my uncle turned to go, the midwife whispered to him to look at at the child's hands. Gently unclasping the podgy, futile little fists, she showed him that on each hand the third finger was longer than the second....

Here I interrupted. The story had a certain queer force behind it, perhaps from its obvious effect on the teller. My uncle feared and hated the things he was saying.

"What did that mean," I asked; "the third finger longer than the second?"

"It took me a long time to discover," replied my uncle. "My own servants, when they saw I did not know, would not tell me. But at last I found out through the doctor who had it from an old woman in the village. People born with their third finger longer than their second become werewolves. At least" — he made a perfunctory effort at amused indulgence — "that is what the common people here think."

"And what does that — what is that supposed to mean?" I, too, found myself throwing rather hastly sops to skepticism. I was growing strangely credulous.

"A werewolf," said my uncle, dabbling in improbability without self-consciousness, "is a human being who becomes, at intervals, to all intents and purposes a wolf. The transformation — or the supposed transformation — takes place at night. The werewolf kills men and animals, and is supposed to drink their blood. Its preference is for men. All through the Middle Ages, down to the seventeenth century, there were innumerable cases (especially in France) of men and women being legally tried for offenses which they had committed as animals. Like the witches, they were rarely acquitted, but, unlike the witches, they seem seldom to have been unjustly condemned." My uncle paused. "I have been reading the old books," he explained. "I wrote to a man in London who is interested in these things when I heard what was believed about the child."

"What became of the child?" I asked.

"The wife of one of my keepers took it in," said my uncle. "She was a stolid woman from the North who, I think, welcomed the opportunity to show what little store she set by the local superstitions. The boy lived with them till he was ten. Then he ran away. I had not heard of him since then till" — my uncle glanced at me almost apologetically — "till yesterday."

We sat for a moment in silence, looking at the fire. My imagination had betrayed my reason in its full surrender to the story. I had not got it in me to dispel his fears with a parade of sanity. I was a little frightened myself.

"You think it is your son, the werewolf, who is killing the sheep?" I said at length.

"Yes. For a boast: or for a warning: or perhaps out of spite, at a night's hunting wasted."

"Wasted?"

My uncle looked at me with troubled eyes.

"His business is not with sheep," he said uneasily.

For the first time I realized the implications of the Welshwoman's curse. The hunt was up. The quarry was the heir to Fleer. I was glad to have been disinherited.

"I have told Germaine not to go out after dusk," said my uncle, coming in pat on my train of thought.

The Belgian was called Germaine; her other name was Vom.

I confess I spent no very tranquil night. My uncle's story had not wholly worked in me that "suspension of disbelief" which someone speaks of as being the prime requisite of good drama. But I have a powerful

imagination. Neither fatigue nor common sense could quite banish the vision of that metamorphosed malignancy ranging, with design, the black and silver silences outside my window. I found myself listening for the sound of loping footfalls on a frost-baked crust of beech leaves....

Whether it was in my dream that I heard, once, the sound of howling, I do not know. But the next morning I saw, as I dressed, a man walking quickly up the drive. He looked like a shepherd. There was a dog at his heels, trotting with a noticeable lack of assurance. At breakfast my uncle told me that another sheep had been killed, almost under the noses of the watchers. His voice shook a little. Solicitude sat oddly on his features as he looked at Germaine. She was eating porridge, as if for a wager.

After breakfast we decided on a campaign. I will not weary you with the details of its launching and its failure. All day we quartered the woods with thirty men, mounted and on foot. Near the scene of the kill our dogs picked up a scent which they followed for two miles and more, only to lose it on the railway line. But the ground was too hard for tracks, and the men said it could only have been a fox or a polecat, so surely and readily did the dogs follow it.

The exercise and the occupation were good for our nerves. But late in the afternoon my uncle grew anxious; twilight was closing in swiftly under a sky heavy with clouds, and we were some distance from Fleer. He gave final instructions for the penning of the sheep by night, and we turned our horses' heads for home.

We approached the castle by the back drive, which was little used: a dank, unholy alley, running the gauntlet of a belt of firs and laurels. Beneath our horses' hooves flints chinked remotely under a thick carpet of moss. Each consecutive cloud from their nostrils hung with an air of permanency, as if bequeathed to the unmoving air.

We were perhaps three hundred yards from the tall gates leading to the stableyard when both horses stopped dead, simultaneously. Their heads were turned towards the trees on our right, beyond which, I knew, the sweep of the main drive converged on ours.

My uncle gave a short, inarticulate cry in which premonition stood aghast at the foreseen. At the same moment something howled on the other side of the trees. There was relish, and a kind of sobbing laughter, in that hateful sound. It rose and fell luxuriously, and rose and fell again, fouling the night. Then it died away, fawning on society in a throaty whimper.

The forces of silence fell unavailingly on its rear; its filthy echoes still went reeling through our heads. We were aware that feet went loping lightly down the iron-hard drive...two feet.

My uncle flung himself off his horse and dashed through the trees. I followed. We scrambled down a bank and out into the open. The only figure in sight was motionless.

Germaine Vom lay doubled up in the drive, a solid, black mark against the shifting values of the dusk. We ran forward....

To me she had always been an improbable cipher rather than a real person. I could not help reflecting that she died, as she had lived, in the livestock tradition. Her throat had been torn out.

The young man leant back in his chair, a little dizzy from talking and from the heat of the stove. The inconvenient realities of the waiting room, forgotten in his narrative, closed in on him again. He sighed, and smiled rather apologetically at the stranger.

"It is a wild and improbable story," he said. "I do not expect you to believe the whole of it. For me, perhaps, the reality of its implications has obscured its almost ludicrous lack of verisimilitude. You see, by the death of the Belgian I am heir to Fleer."

The stranger smiled: a slow, but no longer an abstracted smile. His honey-colored eyes were bright. Under his long black overcoat his body seemed to be stretching itself in sensual anticipation. He rose silently to his feet.

The other found a sharp, cold fear drilling into his vitals. Something behind those shining eyes threatened him with appalling immediacy, like a sword at his heart. He was sweating. He dared not move.

The stranger's smile was now a grin, a ravening convulsion of the face. His eyes blazed with a hard and purposeful delight. A threat of saliva dangled from the corner of his mouth.

Very slowly he lifted one hand and removed his bowler hat. Of the fingers crooked about its brim, the young man saw that the third was longer than the second.

from **The Occult**
The Case of Dion Fortune (1935)
Colin Wilson

...She was lying on a bed thinking highly unpleasant and negative thoughts about a friend who had done her an injury. In a semi-dozing state, 'there came to my mind the thought of casting off all restraint and going berserk. The ancient Nordic myths rose before me, and I thought of Fenris, the Wolf-horror of the North. Immediately I felt a curious drawing-out sensation from my solar plexus, and there materialised beside me on the bed a large wolf....I could distinctly feel its back pressing against me as it lay beside me....I knew nothing of the art of making elementals at that time, but had accidentally stumbled upon the right method — the brooding highly charged with emotion, the invocation of the appropriate natural force, and the condition between sleeping and waking in which the etheric double readily extrudes.'

Although scared stiff, she managed not to panic, and ordered the creature off of the bed. It seemed to change into a dog, and went out through the corner of the room. That night, someone else in the house reported dreams of wolves, and of seeing the eyes of a wild animal shining in the darkness. She decided to seek the advice of her teacher — almost certainly Crowley — who told her that she had to 'absorb' the creature she had made. But since it had been created out of the desire to settle accounts with a particular person, she had to begin by forgetting her longing for revenge. And, as if by coincidence, the ideal opportunity for revenge presented itself at that exact time. 'I had enough sense to see that I was at the dividing of the ways, and if I were not careful would take the first step on the Left-hand path; she decided to forgive the offender, and to re-absorb the wolf, which she describes:

It came in through the northern corner of the room again (subsequently I learnt that the north was considered among the ancients as the evil quarter), and presented itself on the hearthrug in quite a mild and domesticated mood. I obtained an excellent materialisation in the half-light, and could have sworn that a big Alsatian was standing there looking at me. It was tangible, even to the dog-like odour.

From it to me stretched a shadowy line of ectoplasm; one end was attached to my solar plexus, and the other disappeared in the shaggy fur of its belly....I began by an effort of the will and imagination to draw the life out of it along this silver cord, as if sucking lemonade up a straw. The wolf-form began to fade, the cord thickened and grew more substantial. A violent emotional upheaval started in myself; I felt the most furious impulses to go berserk and rend and tear anything and anybody that came to hand, like the Malay running amok....The wolf-form now faded into a shapeless grey mist. This too absorbed along the silver cord. The tension relaxed, and I found myself bathed in perspiration.

The Quest
George Garrett

The road was menaced by a dwarf,
sharp-tongued with a mind like a trap
for tigers. Later a dragon loomed,
snorted fire and made his wings flap

like starchy washing in brisk wind.
Farther still, the obsolete castle and
the improbable giant overlooked
nothing living in the land.

One is a long time coming to the point
where the enchanted may be free,
all charms be neutralized and everything
be what it, shining, seems to be.

from **On the Nightmare**
Ernest Jones

...the soul is 'a thin, unsubstantial human image, in its nature a sort of vapour, film or shadow, the cause of life and thought in the individual in animates independently possessing the personal consciousness and vilition of its corporeal owner, past or present capable of leaving the body far behind, to flash swiftly from place to place mostly impalpable and invisible, yet also manifesting physical power, and especially appearing to men waking or asleep, as a phantasm separate from the body of which it bears the likeness; continuing to exist and appear to men after the death of that body; able to enter into, possess, and act in the bodies of other men, of animals, and even of things.

It was believed that the real body of the Werewolf lay asleep in bed while his spirit roved the woods in the form of a wolf; further, when the wolf was wounded, corresponding wounds were to be found on the human body that remained at home...these travelling dreams can symbolize a considerable number of repressed wishes: the wish for freedom from compulsion, one which the idea of a wolf very well represents....

M.D. Conway, *Demonology and Devil-Lore: Vol. i.* (1879)

"The oldest and strongest emotion of mankind is fear, and the oldest and strongest kind of fear is fear of the unknown." *H.P. Lovecraft*

L. Sprague DeCamp, *Lovecraft*, a Biography (1975)

I felt a little strangely, and not a little frightened. It seemed to me that we were simply going over and over the same ground again; and so I took note of some salient point, and found that this was so. I would have liked to have asked the driver what this all meant, but I really feared to do so, for I thought that, placed as I was, any protest would have had no effect in case there had been an intention to delay. By-and-by, however, as I was curious to know how time was passing, I struck a match, and by its flame looked at my watch; it was within a few minutes of midnight. This gave me a sort of shock, for I suppose the general superstition about midnight was increased by my recent experiences. I waited with a sick feeling of suspense.

Jonathan Harker's Journal, 5, May.

THE CASTLE

"I myself am of an old family, and to live in a new house would kill me. A house cannot be made habitable in a day; and, after all, how few days go to make up a century. I rejoice also that there is a chapel of old times. We Transylvanian nobles love not to think that our bones may lie amongst the common dead. I seek not gaiety nor mirth, not the bright voluptuousness of much sunshine and sparkling waters which please the young and gay. I am no longer young; and my heart, through weary years of mourning over the dead, is not attuned to mirth. Moreover, the walls of my castle are broken; the shadows are many, and the wind breathes cold through the broken battlements and casements. I love the shade and the shadow, and would be alone with my thoughts when I may." *Count Dracula*

Jonathan Harker's Journal, 7, May.

'I Can Hear His Screams', Says Marine of Beating

Washington Post, May 5, 1976

WASHINGTON — "All I can hear is his screaming for us to stop and asking for the mercy of God....I need help to forget it...we were like animals."

The voice in the tape-recorded interview broke repeatedly as a member of the U.S. Marines described how he and other marines — goaded on by a drill instructor who shouted "Kill! Kill! Kill!" — clubbed a 20-year-old mentally handicapped recruit into unconsciousness.

The recruit, Pte. Lynn McClure, died 13 weeks after the beating at the San Diego, Calif., base without regaining consciousness.

"He was screaming 'God no, Please! What did I do?' It was cruel. The drill instructor didn't have to let us fight that long...he could have stopped it," said the marine as he described to a private investigator why he has not slept peacefully since the incident occurred.

The marine, who said on the tape that he wants to tell the corps what actually happened to McClure and will do so any way he can, believes he delivered the fatal blow to the recruit's head during pugil stick (padded staffs) training on Dec. 6, 1975.

"It's all I can see at night when I go to bed...there's no going to sleep....It turns my world upside down."

John Gyorkos, an Oceanside, Calif., lawyer the McClure family has retained in a $3.5 million suit against the Marine Corps, released the tapes but would not divulge the names of two marines interviewed.

According to the marines and the law firm's chief investigator Irving Richards, an exhausted and reluctant McClure — who was 5 feet 6 inches and 115 pounds — was ordered to fight one marine after another until he dropped unconscious in the dirt.

The marine who described himself as McClure's best friend gave this account:

"...At first he (McClure) wouldn't fight....The DI made him....He was yelling at the colored guy and telling him to hit McClure....He kept on doing it and pretty soon McClure started crying and laying on the ground. Then he tried to take off running.

"They would catch him and bring him back in there. Pretty soon it just seemed they were doing it for pleasure." McClure was told to pick out somebody to fight and pointed to his best friend — the Marine who made the statement to McClure family investigators.

"I said, 'I don't want to fight you.' The DI said 'if you two guys do not put forth effort, I am going to have these other two guys come out and just beat the hell out of you.' These other guys were pretty good size.

"So we go out there, and I was trying to take it easy with him. And all of a sudden he took off again. They caught him and brought him back and the DI fought McClure to show him the moves."

Then another Marine fought McClure, continued his best friend, "and was really beating the hell out of him....The DI was telling him: 'Kill him.' He was saying, 'Kill! Kill! Kill!' "...

The Monsters Are Due On Maple Street

Rod Serling

It was Saturday afternoon on Maple Street and the late sun retained some of the warmth of a persistent Indian summer. People along the street marveled at winter's delay and took advantage of it. Lawns were being mowed, cars polished, kids played hopscotch on the sidewalks. Old Mr. Van Horn, the patriarch of the street, who lived alone, had moved his power saw out on his lawn and was fashioning new pickets for his fence. A Good Humor man bicycled in around the corner and was inundated by children and by shouts of "Wait a minute!" from small boys hurrying to con nickels from their parents. It was 4:40 p.m. A football game blared from a portable radio on a front porch, blending with the other sounds of a Saturday afternoon in October. Maple Street. 4.40 p.m. Maple Street in its last calm and reflective moments — before the monsters came.

Steve Brand, fortyish, a big man in an old ex-Marine set of dungarees, was washing his car when the lights flashed across the sky. Everyone on the street looked up at the sound of the whoosh and the brilliant flash that dwarfed the sun.

"What was that?" Steve called across at his neighbor, Don Martin, who was fixing a bent spoke on his son's bicycle.

Martin, like everyone else, was cupping his hands over his eyes, to stare up at the sky. He called back to Steve, "Looked like a meteor, didn't it? I didn't hear any crash though, did you?"

Steve shook his head. "Nope. Nothing except that roar."

Steve's wife came out on the front porch. "Steve?" she called. "What was that?"

Steve shut off the water hose. "Guess it was a meteor, honey. Came awful close, didn't it?"

"Much too close for my money," his wife answered. "Much too close."

She went back into the house, and became suddenly conscious of something. All along Maple Street people

38

paused and looked at one another as a gradual awareness took hold. All the sounds had stopped. All of them. There was a silence now. No portable radio. No lawn mowers. No clickety-click of sprinklers that went round and round on front lawns. There was a silence.

Mrs. Sharp, fifty-five years of age, was talking on the telephone, giving a cake recipe to her cousin at the other end of town. Her cousin was asking Mrs. Sharp to repeat the number of eggs when her voice clicked off in the middle of the sentence. Mrs. Sharp, who was not the most patient of women, banged furiously on the telephone hook, screaming for an operator.

Pete Van Horn was right in the middle of sawing a 1x4 piece of pine when the power saw went off. He checked the plug, the outlet on the side of the house and then the fuse box in his basement. There was just no power coming in.

Steve Brand's wife, Agnes, came back out on the porch to announce that the oven had stopped working. There was no current or something. Would Steve look at it? Steve couldn't look at it at that moment because he was pre-occupied with a hose that suddenly refused to give any more water.

Across the street Charlie Farnsworth, fat and dumpy, in a loud Hawaiian sport short that featured hula girls with pineapple baskets on their heads, barged angrily out toward the road, damning any radio outfit that manu-factured a portable with the discourtesy to shut off in the middle of a third-quarter forward pass.

Voices built on top of voices until suddenly there was no more silence. There was a conglomeration of questions and protests; of plaintive references to half-cooked dinners, half-watered lawns, half-washed cars, half-finished phone conversations. Did it have anything to do with the meteor? That was the main question — the one most asked. Pete Van Horn disgustedly threw aside the electric cord of his power mower and announced to the group of people who were collected around Steve Brand's station wagon that he was going on over to Bennett Avenue to check and see if the power had gone off there, too. He disappeared into his back yard and was last seen heading into the back yard of the house behind his.

Steve Brand, his face wrinkled with perplexity, leaned against his car door and looked around at the neighbors who had collected. "It just doesn't make sense," he said. "Why should the power go off all of a sudden *and* the phone line?"

Don Martin wiped bicycle grease off his fingers. "Maybe some kind of an electrical storm or something."

Dumpy Charlie's voice was always unpleasantly high. "That just don't seem likely," he squealed. "Sky's just as

Is it not always when we seek merely to control, rather than transmute our demons, that they inevitably erupt in more virulent form to mock, beset, and tempt us anew?

Dorothy Norman, *The Hero* (1949)

The Night Mirror
John Hollander

What it showed was always the same—
A vertical panel with him in it
Being a horrible bit of movement
At the edge of knowledge, overhanging
The canyons of nightmare. And when the last
Glimpse was enough—his grandmother,
Say, with a blood-red face, rising
From her Windsor chair in the warm lamplight
To tell him something—he would scramble up,
Waiting to hear himself shrieking, and gain
The ledge of the world, his bed, lit by
The pale rectangle of window, eclipsed
By a dark shape, but a shape that moved
And saw and knew and mistook its reflection
In the tall panel on the closet door
For itself. The silver corona of moonlight
That gloried his glimpsed head was enough
To send him back into silences (choosing
Fear in those chasms below), to reject
Freedom of wakeful seeing, believing,
And feeling, for peace and the bondage to horrors
Welling up only from deep within
That dark planet head, spinning beyond
The rim of the night mirror's range, huge
And cold, on the pillow's dark side.

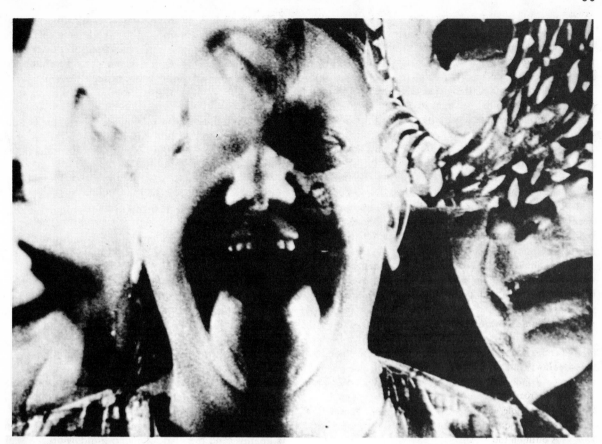

blue as anything. Not a cloud. No lightning. No thunder. No nothin'. How could it be a storm?''

Mrs. Sharp's face was lined with years, but more deeply by the frustrations of early widowhood. ''Well, it's a terrible thing when a phone company can't keep its line open,'' she complained. ''Just a terrible thing.''

''What about my portable radio,'' Charlie demanded. ''Ohio State's got the ball on Southern Methodist's eighteen-yard line. They throw a pass and the damn thing goes off just then.''

There was a murmur in the group as people looked at one another and heads were shaken.

Charlie picked his teeth with a dirty thumb nail. ''Steve,'' he said in his high, little voice, ''why don't you go downtown and check with the police?''

''They'll probably think we're crazy or something,'' Don Martin said. ''A little power failure and right away we get all flustered and everything.''

''It isn't just the power failure,'' Steve answered. ''If it was, we'd still be able to get a broadcast on the portable.''

There was a murmur of reaction to this and heads nodded.

Steve opened the door to his station wagon. ''I'll run downtown. We'll get this all straightened out.''

He inched his big frame onto the front seat behind the wheel, turned on the ignition and pushed the starter button. There was no sound. The engine didn't even turn over. He tried it a couple of times more, and still there was no response. The others stared silently at him. He scratched his jaw.

''Doesn't that beat all? It was working fine before.''

''Out of gas?'' Don offered.

Steve shook his head. ''I just had it filled up.''

''What's it mean?'' Mrs. Sharp asked.

Charlie Farnsworth's piggish little eyes flapped open and shut. ''It's just as if — just as if everything had stopped. You better *walk* downtown, Steve.''

''I'll go with you,'' Don said.

Steve got out of the car, shut the door and turned to Don. ''Couldn't be a meteor,'' he said. ''A meteor couldn't do *this*.'' He looked off in thought for a moment, then nodded. ''Come on, let's go.''

They started to walk away from the group, when they heard the boy's voice. Tommy Bishop, aged twelve, had stepped out in front of the others and was calling out to them.

''Mr. Brand! Mr. Martin. You better not leave!''

Steve took a step back toward him.

''Why not?'' he asked.

''They don't want you to,'' Tommy said.

Steve and Don exchanged a look.

''*Who* doesn't want us to?'' Steve asked him.

Tommy looked up toward the sky. ''Them,'' he said.

''Them?'' Steve asked.

''Who are 'them'?'' Charlie squealed.

''Whoever was in that thing that came by overhead,'' Tommy said intently.

Steve walked slowly back toward the boy and stopped close to him. ''What, Tommy?'' he asked.

''Whoever was in that thing that came over,'' Tommy repeated. ''I don't think they want us to leave here.''

Steve knelt down in front of the boy ''What do you mean, Tommy? What are you talking about?

''They don't want us to leave, that's why they shut everything off.''

''What makes you say that?'' Irritation crept into Steve's voice. ''Whatever gave you *that* idea?''

Mrs. Sharp pushed her way through to the front of the crowd. ''That's the craziest thing I ever heard,'' she announced in a public-address-system voice. ''Just about the craziest thing I ever did hear!''

Tommy could feel the unwillingness to believe him. ''It's always that way,'' he said defensively, ''in every story I've ever read about a space ship landing from outer space!''

Charlie Farnsworth whinnied out his derision.

Mrs. Sharp waggled a bony finger in front of Tommy's mother. ''If you ask me, Sally Bishop,'' she said, ''you'd better get that boy of yours up to bed. He's been reading too many comic books or seeing too many movies or something.''

Sally Bishop's face reddened. She gripped Tommy's shoulders tightly. ''Tommy,'' she said softly. ''Stop that kind of talk, honey.''

Steve's eyes never left the boy's face. ''That's all right, Tom. We'll be right back. You'll see. That wasn't a ship or anything like it. That was just a — a meteor or something, likely as not — '' He turned to the group, trying to weight his words with an optimism he didn't quite feel. ''No doubt it did have something to do with all this power failure and the rest of it. Meteors can do crazy things. Like sun spots.''

''That's right,'' Don said, as if picking up a cue. ''Like sun spots. That kind of thing. They can raise cain with radio reception all over the world. And this thing being so close — why there's no telling what sort of stuff it can do.'' He wet his lips nervously. ''Come on, Steve. We'll go into town and see if that isn't what's causing it all.''

Once again the two men started away.

''Mr. Brand!'' Tommy's voice was defiant and frightened at the same time. He pulled away from his mother and ran after them. ''Please, Mr. Brand, please don't leave here.''

There was a stir, a rustle, a movement among the people. There was something about the boy. Something about the intense little face. Something about the words that carried such emphasis, such belief, such fear. They listened to these words and rejected them because intellect and logic had no room for spaceships and greenheaded things. But the irritation that showed in the eyes, the murmuring and the compressed lips had nothing to do with intellect. A little boy was bringing up fears that shouldn't be brought up; and the people on Maple Street this Saturday afternoon were no different from any other set of human beings. Order, reason, logic were slipping, pushed by the wild conjectures of a twelve-year-old boy.

''Somebody ought to spank that kid,'' an angry voice muttered.

Tommy Bishop's voice continued defiant. It pierced the murmurings and rose above them. ''You might not even be able to get to town,'' he said. ''It was that way in the story. *Nobody* could leave. Nobody except — ''

''Except who?'' Steve asked.

''Except the people they'd sent down ahead of them. They looked just like humans. It wasn't until the ship landed that — ''

His mother grabbed him by the arm and pulled him back. ''Tommy,'' she said in a low voice. ''Please, honey...don't talk that way.''

''Damn right he shouldn't talk that way,'' came the voice of the man in the rear again. ''And we shouldn't stand here listening to him. Why this is the craziest thing I ever heard. The kid tells us a comic-book plot and here we stand listening — ''

The individual is forced to turn inward; he becomes obsessed with the new form of the problem of identity, namely, Even-if-I-know-who-I-am, I-have-no-significance. I am unable to influence others. The next step is apathy. And the step following that is violence. For no human being can stand the perpetually numbing experience of his own powerlessness.

Rollo May, *Love and Will* (1969)

His voice died away as Steve stood up and faced the crowd. Fear can throw people into a panic, but it can also make them receptive to a leader and Steve Brand at this moment was such a leader. The big man in the ex-Marine dungarees had an authority about him.

''Go ahead, Tommy,'' he said to the boy. ''What kind of story was this? What about the people that they sent out ahead?''

''That was the way they prepared things for the landing, Mr. Brand,'' Tommy said. ''They sent four people. A mother and a father and two kids who looked just like humans. But they weren't.''

There was a murmur — a stir of uneasy laughter. People looked at one another again and a couple of them smiled.

''Well,'' Steve said, lightly but carefully, ''I guess we'd better run a check on the neighbourhood, and see which ones of us are really human.''

His words were a release. Laughter broke out openly. But soon it died away. Only Charlie Farnsworth's horse whinny persisted over the growing silence and then he too lapsed into a grim quietness, until all fifteen people were looking at one another through changed eyes. A twelve-year-old boy had planted a seed. And something was growing out of the street with invisible branches that began to wrap themselves around the men and women and pull them apart. Distrust lay heavy in the air.

Suddenly there was the sound of a car engine and all heads turned as one. Across the street Ned Rosen was sitting in his convertible trying to start it, and nothing was happening beyond the labored sound of a sick engine getting deeper and hoarser and finally giving up altogether. Ned Rosen, a thin, serious-faced man in his thirties, got out of his car and closed the door. He stood there staring at it for a moment, shook his head, looked across the street at his neighbors and started toward them.

"Can't get her started, Ned?" Don Martin called out to him.

"No dice," Ned answered. "Funny, she was working fine this morning."

Without warning, all by itself, the car started up and idled smoothly, smoke briefly coming out of the exhaust.

Ned Rosen whirled around to stare at it, his eyes wide. Then, just as suddenly as it started, the engine sputtered and stopped.

All The Roary Night
Kenneth Patchen

It's dark out, Jack
The stations out there don't identify themselves
We're in it raw-blind, like burned rats
It's running out
All around us
The footprints of the beast,
    one nobody has any notion of
The white and vacant eyes
Of something above there
Something that doesn't know we exist
I smell heartbreak up there, Jack
A heartbreak at the center of things—
And in which we don't figure at all

"Started all by itself!" Charlie Farnsworth squealed excitedly.

"How did it do that?" Mrs. Sharp asked. "How could it just start all by itself?"

Sally Bishop let loose her son's arm and just stood there, shaking her head. "How in the world — " she began.

Then there were no more questions. They stood silently staring at Ned Rosen who looked from them to his car and then back again. He went to the car and looked at it. Then he scratched his head again.

"Somebody explain it to me," he said. "I sure never saw anything like that happen before!"

"He never did come out to look at that thing that flew overhead. He wasn't even interested." Don Martin said heavily.

"What do you say we ask him some questions," Charlie Farnsworth proposed importantly. "I'd like to know what's going on here!"

There was a chorus of assent and the fifteen people started across the street toward Ned Rosen's driveway. Unity was restored, they had a purpose, a feeling of activity and direction. They were *doing* something. They weren't sure what, but Ned Rosen was flesh and blood — askable, reachable and seeable. He watched with growing apprehension as his neighbors marched toward him. They stopped on the sidewalk close to the driveway and surveyed him.

Ned Rosen pointed to his car. "I just don't understand it, any more than you do! I tried to start it and it *wouldn't* start. You saw me. All of you saw me."

His neighbors seemed massed against him, solidly, alarmingly.

"I don't understand it!" he cried. "I swear — I don't understand. What's happening?"

Charlie Farnsworth stood out in front of the others. "Maybe you better tell us," he demanded. "Nothing's working on this street. Nothing. No lights, no power, no radio. Nothing except one car — *yours!*"

There were mutterings from the crowd. Steve Brand stood back by himself and said nothing. He didn't like what was going on. Something was building up that threatened to grow beyond control.

"Come on, Rosen," Charlie Farnsworth commanded shrilly, "let's hear what goes on! Let's hear how you explain your car startin' like that!"

Ned Rosen wasn't a coward. He was a quiet man who didn't like violence and had never been a physical fighter. But he didn't like being bullied. Ned Rosen got mad.

"Hold it!" he shouted. "Just hold it. You keep your distance. All of you. All right, I've got a car that starts by itself. Well, that's a freak thing — I admit it! But does that make me some sort of a criminal or something? I don't know why the car works — it just does!"

The crowd were neither sobered nor reassured by Rosen's words, but they were not too frightened to listen. They huddled together, mumbling, and Ned Rosen's eyes went from face to face till they stopped on Steve Brand's. Ned knew Steve Brand. Of all the men on the street, this seemed the guy with the most substance. The most intelligent. The most essentially decent.

"What's it all about, Steve?" he asked.

"We're all on a monster kick, Ned," he answered quietly. "Seems that the general impression holds that maybe one family isn't what we think they are. Monsters from outer space or something. Different from us. Fifth columnists from the vast beyond." He couldn't keep the sarcasm out of his voice. "Do you know anybody around here who might fit that description?"

Rosen's eyes narrowed. "What is this, a gag?" He looked around the group again. "This a practical joke or something?'' And without apparent reason, without logic, without explanation, his car started again, idled for a moment, sending smoke out of the exhaust, and stopped.

A woman began to cry, and the bank of eyes facing Ned Rosen looked cold and accusing. He walked to his porch steps and stood on them, facing his neighbors.

''Is that supposed to incriminate me?'' he asked. ''The car engine goes on and off and that really does it, huh?''

He looked down into their faces. ''I don't understand it. Not any more than you do.''

He could tell that they were unmoved. This couldn't really be happening, Ned thought to himself.

''Look,'' he said in a different tone. ''You all know me. We've lived here four years. Right in this house. We're no different from any of the rest of you!'' He held out his hands toward them. The people he was looking at hardly resembled the people he'd lived alongside of for the past four years. They looked as if someone had taken a brush and altered every character with a few strokes. ''Really,'' he continued, ''this whole thing is just...just weird — ''

...The attractiveness of giving one's self over to the mob lies in the excitement without individual consciousness—no more alienation, no sense of isolation, and none of that fatiguing burden of personal responsibility;...This is what constitutes the attraction—indeed, at times the horrendous joy—of war and mass riots. They assume from us our individual personal responsibility for the daimonics.

Rollo May, *Love and Will* (1969)

''Well, if that's the case, Ned Rosen,'' Mrs. Sharp's voice suddenly erupted from the crowd — ''maybe you'd better explain why — '' She stopped abruptly and clamped her mouth shut, but looked wise and pleased with herself.

''Explain what?'' Rosen asked her softly.

Steve Brand sensed a special danger now. ''Look,'' he said, ''let's forget this right now — ''

Charlie Farnsworth cut him off. ''Go ahead. Let her talk. What about it? Explain what?''

Mrs. Sharp, with an air of great reluctance, said, ''Well, sometimes I go to bed late at night. A couple of times — a couple of times I've come out on the porch, and I've seen Ned Rosen here, in the wee hours of the morning, standing out in front of his house looking up at the sky.'' She looked around the circle of faces. ''That's right, looking up at the sky as if — as if he was waiting for something.'' She paused for emphasis, for dramatic effect. ''As if he was looking for something!'' she repeated.

The nail on the coffin, Steve Brand thought. One, dumb, ordinary, simple idiosyncrasy of a human being — and that probably was all it would take. He heard the murmuring of the crowd rise and saw Ned Rosen's face

turn white. Rosen's wife, Ann, came out on the porch. She took a look at the crowd and then at her husband's face.

''What's going on, Ned?'' she asked.

''I don't know what's going on,'' Ned answered. ''I just don't know, Ann. But I'll tell you this. I don't like these people. I don't like what they're doing. I don't like them standing in my yard like this. And if any one of them takes another step and gets close to my porch — I'll break his jaw. I swear to God, that's just what I'll do. I'll break his jaw. Now go on, get out of here, all of you!'' he shouted at them. ''Get the hell out of here.''

''Ned,'' Ann's voice was shocked.

''You heard me,'' Ned repeated. ''All of you get out of here.''

None of them eager to start an action, the people began to back away. But they had an obscure sense of gratification. At least there was an opponent now. Someone who wasn't one of them. And this gave them a kind of secure feeling. The enemy was no longer formless and vague. The enemy had a front porch and a front yard and a car. And he had shouted threats at them.

They started slowly back across the street forgetting for the moment what had started it all. Forgetting that there was no power, and no telephones. Forgetting even that there had been a meteor overhead not twenty minutes earlier. It wasn't until much later, as a matter of fact, that anyone posed a certain question.

Old man Van Horn had walked through his back yard over to Bennet Avenue. He'd never come back. Where was he? It was not one of the questions that passed through the minds of any of the thirty or forty people on Maple Street who sat on their front porches and watched the night come and felt the now menacing darkness close in on them.

There were lanterns lit all along Maple Street by ten o'clock. Candles shone through living-room windows and cast flickering, unsteady shadows all along the street. Groups of people huddled on front lawns around their lanterns and a soft murmur of voices was carried over the Indian-summer night air. All eyes eventually were drawn to Ned Rosen's front porch.

He sat there on the railing, observing the little points of light spotted around in the darkness. He knew he was surrounded. He was the animal at bay.

His wife came out on the porch and brought him a glass of lemonade. Her face was white and strained. Like her husband, Ann Rosen was a gentle person, unarmored by temper or any proclivity for outrage. She stood close to her husband now on the darkened porch feeling the suspicion that flowed from the people around lanterns, thinking to herself that these were people she had entertained in her house. These were women she talked to over clotheslines in the back yard; people who had been friends and neighbors only that morning. Oh dear God, could all this have happened in those few hours? It must be a nightmare, she thought. It had to be a nightmare that she could wake up from. It couldn't be anything else.

Across the street Mabel Farnsworth, Charlie's wife,

shook her head and clucked at her husband who was drinking a can of beer. "It just doesn't seem right though, Charlie, keeping watch on them. Why he was right when he said he was one of our neighbors. I've known Ann Rosen ever since they moved in. We've been good friends."

Charlie Farnsworth turned to her disgustedly. "That don't prove a thing," he said. "Any guy who'd spend his time lookin' up at the sky early in the morning — well there's something wrong with that kind of person. There's something that ain't legitimate. Maybe under normal circumstances we could let it go by. But these aren't normal circumstances." He turned and pointed toward the street. "Look at that," he said. "Nothin' but candles and lanterns. Why it's like goin' back into the Dark Ages or something!"

He was right. Maple Street had changed with the night. The flickering lights had done something to its character. It looked odd and menacing and very different. Up and down the street, people noticed it. The change in Maple Street. It was the feeling one got after being away from home for many, many years and then returning. There was a vague familiarity about it, but it wasn't the same. It was different.

Ned Rosen and his wife heard footsteps coming toward their house. Ned got up from the railing and shouted out into the darkness.

"Whoever it is, just stay right where you are. I don't want any trouble, but if anybody sets foot on my porch, that's what they're going to get — trouble!" He saw that it was Steve Brand and his features relaxed.

"Ned," Steve began.

Ned Rosen cut him off. "I've already explained to you people, I don't sleep very well at night sometimes. I get up and I take a walk and I look up at the sky. I look at the stars."

Ann Rosen's voice shook as she stood alongside of him. "That's exactly what he does. Why this whole thing, it's — it's some kind of a madness or something."

Steve Brand stood on the sidewalk and nodded grimly. "That's exactly what it is — some kind of madness."

Charlie Farnsworth's voice from the adjoining yard was spiteful. "You'd best watch who you're seen with, Steve. Until we get this all straightened out, you ain't exactly above suspicion yourself."

Steve whirled around to the outline of the fat figure that stood behind the lantern in the other yard. "Or you either, Charlie," he shouted. "Or any of the rest of us!".

Mrs. Sharp's voice came from the darkness across the street. "What I'd like to know is — what are we going to do? Just stand around here all night?"

"There's nothing' else we can do," Charlie Farnsworth said. He looked wisely over toward Ned Rosen's house. "One of 'em'll tip their hand. They got to."

It was Charlie's voice that did it for Steve Brand at this moment. The shrieking, pig squeal that came from the layers of fat and the idiotic sport shirt and the dull, dumb,

blind prejudice of the man. "There's something *you* can do, Charlie," Steve called out to him. "You can go inside your house and keep your mouth shut!"

"You sound real anxious to have that happen, Steve," Charlie's voice answered him back from the little spot of light in the next yard. "I think we'd better keep our eye on you, too!"

Don Martin came up to Steve Brand, carrying a lantern. There was something hesitant in his manner, as if he were about to take a bit in his teeth, but wondered whether it would hurt. "I think everything might as well come out now," Don said. "I really do. I think everything should come out."

People came off porches, from front yards, to stand around in a group near Don who now turned directly toward Steve.

"Your wife's done plenty of talking, Steve, about how odd you are," he said.

Charlie Farnsworth trotted over. "Go ahead. Tell us what she said," he demanded excitedly.

Silence, solitude and darkness are actually elements in the production of the infantile anxiety from which the majority of human beings have never become free.

Sigmund Freud, *The Uncanny The Complete Psychological Works of Sigmund Freud: Vol. XVII* (1919)

Steve Brand knew this was the way it would happen. He was not really surprised but he still felt a hot anger rise up inside of him. "Go ahead," he said. "What's my wife said? Let's get it *all* out." He peered around at the shadowy figures of the neighbors. "Let's pick out every goddamned peculiarity of every single man, woman and child on this street! Don't stop with me and Ned. How about a firing squad at dawn, so we can get rid of all the suspects! Make it easier for you!"

Don Martin's voice retreated fretfully. "There's no need getting so upset, Steve — "

"Go to hell, Don," Steve said to him in a cold and dispassionate fury.

Needled, Don went on the offensive again but his tone held something plaintive and petulant. "It just so happens that, well, Agnes has talked about how there's plenty of nights you've spent hours in your basement working on some kind of radio or something. Well none of us have ever *seen* that radio — "

"Go ahead, Steve," Charlie Farnsworth yelled at him. "What kind of a 'radio set' you workin' on? I never seen it. Neither has anyone else. Who do you talk to on that radio set? And who talks to you?"

Steve's eyes slowly traveled in an arc over the hidden faces and the shrouded forms of neighbors who were now accusers. "I'm surprised at you, Charlie," he said quietly. "I really am. How come you're so goddamned dense all of a sudden? Who do I talk to? I talk to monsters from outer space. I talk to three-headed green men who fly over here in what look like meteors!''

Agnes Brand walked across the street to stand at her husband's elbow. She pulled at his arm with frightened intensity. ''Steve! Steve, please,'' she said. ''It's just a ham radio set,'' she tried to explain. ''That's all. I bought him a book on it myself. It's just a ham radio set. A lot of people have them. I can show it to you. It's right down in the basement.''

Steve pulled her hand off his arm. ''You show them nothing,'' he said to her. ''If they want to look inside our house, let them get a search warrant!''

Charlie's voice whined at him. ''Look, buddy, you can't afford to — ''

''Charlie,'' Steve shouted at him. ''Don't tell me what I can afford. And stop telling me who's dangerous and who isn't. And who's safe and who's a menace!'' He walked over to the edge of the road and saw that people backed away from him. ''And you're with him — all of you,'' Steve bellowed at them. ''You're standing there all set to crucify — to find a scapegoat — desperate to point some kind of a finger at a neighbor!'' There was intensity in his tone and on his face, accentuated by the flickering light of the lanterns and the candles. ''Well look, friends, the only thing that's going to happen is that we'll eat each other up alive. Understand? *We are going to eat each other up alive!*''

Charlie Farnsworth suddenly ran over to him and grabbed his arm. ''That's not the *only* thing that can happen to us,'' he said in a frightened, hushed voice. ''Look!''

''Oh, my God,'' Don Martin said.

Mrs. Sharp screamed. All eyes turned to look down the street where a figure had suddenly materialized in the darkness and the sound of measured footsteps on concrete grew louder and louder as it walked toward them. Sally Bishop let out a stifled cry and grabbed Tommy's shoulder.

The child's voice screamed out, ''It's the monster! It's the monster!''

There was a frightened wail from another woman, and the residents of Maple Street stood transfixed with terror as something unknown came slowly down the street. Don Martin disappeared and came back out of his house a moment later carrying a shotgun. He pointed it toward the approaching form. Steve pulled it out of his hands.

''For God's sake, will somebody think a thought around here? Will you people wise up? What good would a shotgun do against — ''

A quaking, frightened Charlie Farnsworth grabbed the gun from Steve's hand. "No more talk, Steve," he said. "You're going to talk us into a grave! You'd let whoever's out there walk right over us, wouldn't yuh? Well, some of us won't!"

He swung the gun up and pulled the trigger. The noise was a shocking, shattering intrusion and it echoed and re-echoed through the night. A hundred yards away the figure collapsed like a piece of clothing blown off a line by the wind. From front porches and lawns people raced toward it.

Steve was the first to reach him. He knelt down, turned him over and looked at his face. Then he looked up toward the semi-circle of silent faces surveying him.

"All right, friends," he said quietly. "It happened. We got our first victim — Pete Van Horn!"

"Oh, my God," Don Martin said in a hushed voice. "He was just going over to the next block to see if the power was on — "

Mrs. Sharp's voice was that of injured justice. "You killed him, Charlie! You shot him dead!"

Charlie Farnsworth's face looked like a piece of uncooked dough, quivering and shaking in the light of the lantern he held.

"I didn't know who he was," he said. "I certainly didn't know who he was." Tears rolled down his fat cheeks. "He comes walking out of the dark — how am I supposed to know who he was?" He looked wildly around and then grabbed Steve's arm. Steve could explain things to people. "Steve," he screamed, "you know why I shot. How was I supposed to know he wasn't a monster or something?"

Steve looked at him and didn't say anything. Charlie grabbed Don.

"We're all scared of the same thing," he blubbered. "The very same thing. I was just tryin' to protect my home, that's all. Look, all of you, that's all I was tryin' to do!" He tried to shut the sight of Pete Van Horn who stared up at him with dead eyes and a shattered chest. "Please, please, please," Charlie Farnsworth sobbed, "I didn't know it was somebody we knew. I swear to God I didn't know — "

The lights went on in Charlie Farnsworth's house and shone brightly on the people of Maple Street. They looked suddenly naked. They blinked foolishly at the lights and their mouths gaped like fishes'.

"Charlie," Mrs. Sharp said, like a judge pronouncing sentence, "how come you're the only one with lights on now?"

Ned Rosen nodded in agreement. "That's what I'd like to know," he said. Something inside tried to check him, but his anger made him go on. "How come, Charlie? You're quiet all of a sudden. You've got nothing to say out of that big, fat mouth of yours. Well, let's hear it, Charlie? Let's hear why you've got lights!"

Again the chorus of voices that punctuated the request and gave it legitimacy and a vote of support. "Why, Charlie?" the voices asked him. "How come you're the only one with lights?" The questions came out of the night to land against his fat wet cheeks. "You were so quick to kill," Ned Rosen continued, "and you were so quick to tell us who we had to be careful of. Well maybe you *had* to kill, Charlie. Maybe Pete Van Horn, God rest his soul, was trying to tell us something. Maybe he'd found out something and had come back to tell us who there was among us we should watch out for."

We live on a placid island of ignorance in the midst of black seas of infinity, and it was not meant that we should voyage far. The sciences, each straining in its own direction, have hitherto harmed us little; but some day the piecing together of dissociated knowledge will open up such terrifying vistas of reality, and of our frightful position therein, that we shall either go mad from the revelation or flee from the deadly light into the peace and safety of a new dark age.

H.P. Lovecraft

Charlie's eyes were little pits of growing fear as he backed away from the people and found himself up against a bush in front of his house. "No," he said. "No, please." His chubby hands tried to speak for him. They waved around, pleading. The palms outstretched, begging for forgiveness and understanding. "Please — please, I swear to you — it isn't me! It really isn't me."

A stone hit him on the side of the face and drew blood. He screamed and clutched at his face as the people began to converge on him.

"No," he screamed. "No."

Like a hippopotamus in a circus, he scrambled over the bush, tearing his clothes and scratching his face and arms. His wife tried to run toward him, somebody stuck a foot out and she tripped, sprawling head first on the sidewalk. Another stone whistled through the air and hit Charlie on the back of the head as he raced across his front yard toward his porch. A rock smashed at the porch light and sent glass cascading down on his head.

"It isn't me," he screamed back at them as they came toward him across the front lawn. "It isn't me, but I know who it is," he said suddenly, without thought. Even as he said it, he realized it was the only possible thing to say.

People stopped, motionless as statues, and a voice called out from the darkness. "All right, Charlie, who is it?"

He was a grotesque, fat figure of a man who smiled now through the tears and the blood that cascaded down his face. "Well, I'm going to tell you," he said. "I am now going to tell you, because I know who it is. I really know who it is. It's..."

"Go ahead, Charlie," a voice commanded him. "Who's the monster?"

Don Martin pushed his way to the front of the crowd.

"All right, Charlie, now! Let's hear it!"

Charlie tried to think. He tried to come up with a name. A nightmare engulfed him. Fear whipped at the back of his brain. "It's the kid," he screamed. "That's who it is. It's the kid!"

Sally Bishop screamed and grabbed at Tommy, burying his face against her. "That's crazy," she said to the people who now stared at her. "That's crazy. He's a little boy."

"But he knew," said Mrs. Sharp. "He was the only one who knew. He told us all about it. Well how did he know? How *could* he have known?"

Voices supported her. "How could he know?" "Who told him?" "Make the kid answer." A fever had taken hold now, a hot, burning virus that twisted faces and forced out words and solidified the terror inside of each person on Maple Street.

Tommy broke away from his mother and started to run. A man dove at him in a flying tackle and missed. Another man threw a stone wildly toward the darkness. They began to run after him down the street. Voices shouted through the night, women screamed. A small child's voice protested — a playmate of Tommy's, one tiny voice of sanity in the middle of a madness as men and women ran down the street, the sidewalks, the curbs, looking blindly for a twelve-year-old boy.

And then suddenly the lights went on in another house — a two-story, gray stucco house that belonged to Bob Weaver. A man screamed, "It isn't the kid. It's Bob Weaver's house!"

A porch light went on at Mrs. Sharp's house and Sally Bishop screamed, "It isn't Bob Weaver's house. It's Mrs. Sharp's place."

"I tell you it's the kid," Charlie screamed.

The lights went on and off, on and off down the street. A power mower suddenly began to move all by itself lurching crazily across a front yard, cutting an irregular path of grass until it smashed against the side of the house.

"It's Charlie," Don Martin screamed. "He's the one." And then he saw his own lights go on and off.

They ran this way and that way, over to one house and then back across the street to another. A rock flew through the air and then another. A pane of glass smashed and there was the cry of a woman in pain. Lights on and off, on and off. Charlie Farnsworth went down on his knees as a piece of brick plowed a two-inch hole in the back of his skull. Mrs. Sharp lay on her back screaming, and felt the tearing jab of a woman's high heel in her mouth as someone stepped on her, racing across the street.

From a quarter of a mile away, on a hilltop, Maple Street looked like this, a long tree-lined avenue full of lights going on and off and screaming people racing back and forth. Maple Street was a bedlam. It was an outdoor asylum for the insane. Windows were broken, street lights sent clusters of broken glass down on the heads of women and children. Power mowers started up and car engines and radios. Blaring music mixed with the screams and shouts and the anger.

Up on top of the hill two men, screened by the darkness, stood near the entrance to a space ship and looked down on Maple Street.

"Understand the procedure now?" the first figure said. "Just stop a few of their machines and radios and telephones and lawn mowers. Throw them into darkness for a few hours and then watch the pattern unfold."

"And this pattern is always the same?" the second figure asked.

"With few variations," came the answer. "They pick the most dangerous enemy they can find and it's themselves. All we need do is sit back — and watch."

"Then I take it," figure two said, "this place, this Maple Street is not unique?"

Figure one shook his head and laughed. "By no means. Their world is full of Maple Streets and we'll go from one to the other and let them destroy themselves." He started up the incline toward the entrance of the space ship. "One to the other," he said as the other figure followed him. "One to the other." There was just the echo of his voice as the two figures disappeared and a panel slid softly across the entrance. "One to the other," the echo said.

When the sun came up on the following morning Maple Street was silent. Most of the houses had been burned. There were a few bodies lying on sidewalks and draped over porch railings. But the silence was total. There simply was no more life. At four o'clock that afternoon there was no more world, or at least not the kind of world that had greeted the morning. And by Wednesday afternoon of the following week, a new set of residents had moved into Maple Street. They were a handsome race of people. Their faces showed great character. Great character indeed. Great character and excellently shaped heads. Excellently shaped heads — two to each new resident!

Now the CAMERA PANS UP for a shot of the starry sky and over this we hear the Narrator's Voice.

NARRATOR'S VOICE
The tools of conquest do not necessarily come with bombs and explosions and fall-out. There are weapons that are simply thoughts, attitudes, prejudices — to be found only in the minds of men. For the record, prejudices can kill suspicion can destroy and a thoughtless, frightened search for a scapegoat has a fall-out all of its own for the children...and the children yet unborn.
(a pause)
And the pity of it is, that these things cannot be confined to....The Twilight Zone!

FADE TO BLACK
From Rod Serling's closing narration. "The Monsters Are Due on Maple Street," The Twilight Zone, January 1, 1960, CBS Television Network.

from Foundations of Psychopathology
J.C. Nemiah

Illustrative Case: *Anxiety Reaction*

I had been feeling sort of tense all day — nothing out of the ordinary. My hands had been perspiring, and my head felt a little full and tight, and I didn't feel so comfortable and relaxed and in contact with people as I often do now.

I wasn't really prepared for what happened during the evening. I was sitting around with a small group of friends talking casually about this and that, when somebody mentioned something about homosexuality. Suddenly I began to sweat hard and my heart began to race; I could feel it pounding uncomfortably. I lost contact with everyone there and could pay attention only to myself and what I was feeling. I knew it was that homosexual business that had triggered it off, and I tried to get my mind off it, to tell myself not to be silly — there was nothing to be scared about.

By sheer will power I seemed to get control of myself, but I realized that I was more nervous now, even though I was talking with the group and trying to appear relaxed and at ease. I'm sure I looked relaxed enough and that no one knew what I was feeling inside. Somehow, I was afraid now of being afraid again; I was getting more and more anxious that someone was going to mention homosexuality again and set me off once more. To make a long story short, someone did and it really got me going. My heart began to race and pound; I began to sweat and felt as if I couldn't get enough air into my lungs. I can't quite describe that to you; it was as if something were expanding inside my chest and crowding everything else there out of the way; it made me want to take deep, rapid breaths — or to get to the window for fresh air. It was a feeling partly physical and partly of panic.

I don't know what I was afraid was going to happen. It was partly a fear that the other people there knew what was going on inside of me and that I'd make a fool of myself. But somehow during all of it I knew that people couldn't really know what I was feeling, and they really wouldn't care if they did. But that didn't help; this unnamable terror just seemed to take hold of me and I had the feeling I just *had* to get out of that room. I had to move; I had to do something; I just couldn't sit there any longer. I really can't tell you what I was scared of; not knowing was one of the worst parts of the whole thing. Well — I didn't move. I just sat there sweating it out, and pretty soon things began to quiet down. For the rest of the evening I was sort of tense, but I did not have any more of those terrible, panicky feelings.

The more awake we are, the greater is the violence of the paroxysm. I have experienced the affection stealing upon me while in perfect possession of my faculties, and have undergone the greatest tortures, being haunted by specters, hags, and every sort of phantom — having, at the same time, a full consciousness that I was labouring under incubus, and that all the terrifying objects around me were the creation of my own brain.

R. Macnish, *The Philosophy of Sleep* (1834)

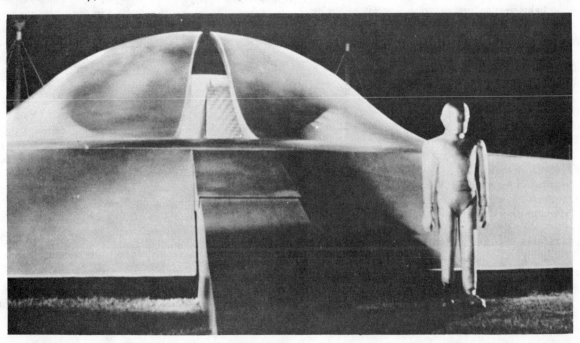

The Dragon
Akutagawa

A priest wants to take revenge on a certain monastery; the monks are always making fun of his red nose. So by a pond near the monastery he sets up a board with the sign: 'On March the third, a dragon shall ascend from this pond.' It has the expected effect. The news spreads, and on the third of March, there are vast crowds waiting at the side of the pond. The monks are deeply embarrassed; they are aware that when the dragon fails to materialise, they will somehow get the blame. As the day drags on, the crowds stretch for miles around, and the priest begins to regret his joke. Gradually he becomes affected by the atmosphere of intense expectancy, and finds himself staring eagerly at the calm surface of the pond. Then, quite suddenly, clouds appear in the sky; there is a tremendous storm; and in the midst of the thunder and lightning, the smoky shape of a dragon flashes out of the pond, and ascends to the sky. Everyone sees it.

Later, when the priest confesses that it was he who set up the notice board, no one believes him.

The most important statement in this story concerns the eager, tense expectancy of the crowd, which affects even the priest who painted the notice board. He knows there is no dragon; yet the telepathic pressure of thousands of believers finally compels his own instincts into tune with it. There is no self-division. And the psychic pressure is like the rhythmic tramp of feet that cracked the walls of Jericho. First, the clouds form out of the clear sky. Then the storm, the visible symbol of the release of tension; something is about to happen. To call the dragon a mass hallucination would be to miss the whole point. It is a mass *projection,* a spontaneous manifestation of the forces of the subconscious. Like all magic.

The Shadow of Night
Coventry Patmore

How strange it is to wake
    And watch while others sleep,
Till sight and hearing ache
    For objects that may keep
The awful inner sense
    Unroused, lest it should mark
The life that haunts the emptiness
    And horror of the dark.

How strange the distant bay
    Of dogs; how wild the note
Of cocks that scream for day,
    In homesteads far remote;
How strange and wild to hear
    The old and crumbling tower,
Amidst the darkness, suddenly
    Take life and speak the hour....

Nobody
Robert Graves

Nobody, ancient mischief, nobody,
Harasses always with an absent body.

Nobody coming up the road, nobody,
Like a tall man in a dark cloak, nobody.

Nobody about the house, nobody,
Like children creeping up the stairs, nobody.

Nobody anywhere in the garden, nobody,
Like a young girl quiet with needlework, nobody.

Nobody coming, nobody, not yet here,
Incessantly welcomed by the wakeful ear.

Until this nobody shall consent to die
Under his curse must everyone lie—

The curse of his envy, of his grief and fright,
Of sudden rape and murder screamed in the night.

from Perelandra
C.S. Lewis

Slowly, shakily, with unnatural and inhuman movements a human form, scarlet in the firelight, crawled out on to the floor of the cave. It was the Un-man, of course: dragging its broken leg and with its lower jaw sagging open like that of a corpse, it raised itself to a standing position. And then, close behind it, something else came up out of the hole. First came what looked like branches of trees, and then seven or eight spots of light, irregularly grouped like a constellation. Then a tubular mass which reflected the red glow as if it were polished. His heart gave a great leap as the branches suddenly resolved themselves into long wiry feelers and the dotted lights became the many eyes of a shell-helmeted head and the mass that followed it was revealed as a large roughly cylindrical body. Horrible things followed — angular, many jointed legs, and presently, when he was in three parts, united only by a kind of wasp's waist structure — three parts that did not seem to be truly aligned and made it look as if it had been trodden on — a huge, many legged, quivering deformity, standing just behind the Un-man so that the horrible shadows of both danced in enormous and united menace on the wall of rock behind them.

The Dream is a meaningful expression of the psyche, a symbolically disguised expression of repressed unconscious wishes.

Sigmund Freud, *The Interpretation of Dreams* (1938)

The Horla
Guy de Maupassant

Mar. 8. What a lovely day! I have spent all the morning lying on the grass in front of my house, under the enormous plantain tree which covers and shades and shelters the whole of it. I like this part of the country; I am fond of living here because I am attached to it by deep roots, the profound and delicate roots which attach a man to the soil on which his ancestors were born and died, to their traditions, their usages, their food, the local expressions, the peculiar language of the peasants, the smell of the soil, the hamlets, and to the atmosphere itself.

I love the house in which I grew up. From my windows I can see the Seine, which flows by the side of my garden, on the other side of the road, almost through my grounds, the great and wide Seine, which goes to Rouen and Havre, and which is covered with boats passing to and fro.

On the left, down yonder, lies Rouen, populous Rouen with its blue roofs massing under pointed Gothic towers. Innumerable are they, delicate or broad, dominated by the spire of the cathedral, full of bells, which sound through the blue air on fine mornings, sending their sweet and distant iron clang to me, their metallic sounds, now stronger and now weaker, according as the wind is strong or light.

What a delicious morning it was! About eleven o'clock, a long line of boats drawn by a steam-tug, as big as a fly, and which scarcely puffed while emitting its thick smoke, passed my gate.

After two English schooners, whose red flags fluttered toward the sky, there came a magnificent Brazilian three-master; it was perfectly white and wonderfully clean and shining. I saluted it, I hardly know why, except that the sight of the vessel gave me great pleasure.

May 12. I have had a slight feverish attack for the last few days, and I feel ill, or rather I feel low-spirited.

Whence come those mysterious influences which change our happiness into discouragement, and our self-confidence into diffidence? One might almost say that the air, the invisible air, is full of unknowable Forces, whose mysterious presence we have to endure. I wake up in the best of spirits, with an inclination to sing in my heart. Why? I go down by the side of the water, and suddenly, after walking a short distance, I return home wretched, as if some misfortune were awaiting me there. Why? Is it a cold shiver which, passing over my skin, has upset my nerves and given me a fit of low spirits? Is it the form of the clouds, or the tints of the sky, or the colors of the surrounding objects which are so changeable, which have troubled my thoughts as they passed before my eyes? Who can tell? Everything that surrounds us, everything that we see without looking at it, everything that we touch without knowing it, everything that we handle without feeling it, everything that we meet without clearly distinguishing it, has a rapid, surprising, and inexplicable effect upon us and upon our organs, and through them on our ideas and on our being itself.

How profound that mystery of the Invisible is! We cannot fathom it with our miserable senses: our eyes are unable to perceive what is either too small or too great, too near to or too far from us; we can see neither the inhabitants of a star nor of a drop of water; our ears deceive us, for they transmit to us the vibrations of the air in sonorous notes. Our senses are fairies who work the miracle of changing that movement into noise, and by that metamorphosis give birth to music, which makes the mute agitation of nature a harmony. So with our sense of smell, which is weaker than that of a dog, and so with our sense of taste, which can scarcely distinguish the age of a wine!

Oh! If we only had other organs which could work other miracles in our favor, what a number of fresh things we might discover around us!

May 16. I am ill, decidedly! I was so well last month! I am feverish, horribly feverish, or rather I am in a state of feverish enervation, which makes my mind suffer as much as my body. I have without ceasing the horrible sensation of some danger threatening me, the apprehension of some coming misfortune or of approaching death, a presentiment which is, no doubt, an attack of some illness still unnamed, which germinates in the flesh and in the blood.

May 18. I have just come from consulting my medical man, for I can no longer get my sleep. He found that my pulse was high, my eyes dilated, my nerves highly strung, but no alarming symptoms. I must have a course of shower baths and of bromide of potassium.

May 25. No change! My state is really very peculiar. As the evening comes on, an incomprehensible feeling of disquietude seizes me, just as if night concealed some terrible menace toward me. I dine quickly, and then try to read, but I do not understand the words, and can scarcely distinguish the letters. Then I walk up and down my drawing-room, oppressed by a feeling of confused and irresistible fear, a fear of sleep and a fear of my bed.

About ten o'clock I go up to my room. As soon as I have entered I lock and bolt the door. I am frightened — of what? Up till the present time I have been frightened of nothing. I open my cupboards, and look under my bed; I listen — I listen — to what? How strange it is that a simple feeling of discomfort, of impeded or heightened circulation, perhaps the irritation of a nervous center, a slight congestion, a small disturbance in the imperfect and delicate functions of our living machinery, can turn the most light-hearted of men into a melancholy one, and make a coward of the bravest? Then, I go to bed, and I wait for sleep as a man might wait for the executioner. I wait for its coming with dread, and my heart beats and my legs tremble, while my whole body shivers beneath the warmth of the bedclothes, until the moment when I suddenly fall asleep, as a man throws himself into a pool of stagnant water in order to drown. I do not feel this perfidious sleep coming over me as I used to, but a sleep which is close to me and watching me, which is going to seize me by the head, to close my eyes and annihilate me.

I sleep — a long time — two or three hours perhaps — then a dream — no — a nightmare lays hold of me. I feel that I am in bed and asleep — I feel it and I know it — and I feel also that somebody is coming close to me, is looking at me, touching me, is getting onto my bed, is kneeling on my chest, is taking my neck between his hands and squeezing it — squeezing it with all his might in order to strangle me.

I struggle, bound by that terrible powerlessness which paralyzes us in our dreams; I try to cry out — but I cannot; I want to move — I cannot; I try, with the most violent efforts and out of breath, to turn over and throw off this being which is crushing and suffocating me — I cannot!

And then suddenly I wake up, shaken and bathed in perspiration; I light a candle and find that I am alone, and after that crisis, which occurs every night, I at length fall asleep and slumber tranquilly till morning.

June 2. My state has grown worse. What is the matter with me? The bromide does me no good, and the shower-baths have no effect whatever. Sometimes, in order to tire myself out, though I am fatigued enough already, I go for a walk in the forest of Roumare. I used to think at first that the fresh light and soft air, impregnated with the odor of herbs and leaves, would instill new life into my veins and impart fresh energy to my heart. One day I turned into a broad ride in the wood, and then I diverged toward La Bouille, through a narrow path, between two rows of exceedingly tall trees, which placed a thick, green, almost black roof between the sky and me.

A sudden shiver ran through me, not a cold shiver, but a shiver of agony, and so I hastened my steps, uneasy at being alone in the wood, frightened stupidly and without reason, at the profound solitude. Suddenly it seemed as if I were being followed, that somebody was walking at my heels, close, quite close to me, near enough to touch me.

I turned round suddenly, but I was alone. I saw nothing behind me except the straight, broad ride, empty and bordered by high trees, horribly empty; on the other side also it extended until it was lost in the distance, and looked just the same — terrible.

I closed my eyes. Why? And then I began to turn round on one heel very quickly, just like a top. I nearly fell down, and opened my eyes; the trees were dancing round me and the earth heaved; I was obliged to sit down. Then, ah! I no longer remembered how I had come! What a strange idea! What a strange, strange idea! I did not the least know. I started off to the right, and got back into the avenue which had led me into the middle of the forest.

June 3. I have had a terrible night. I shall go away for a few weeks, for no doubt a journey will set me up again.

July 2. I have come back, quite cured, and have had a most delightful trip into the bargain. I have been to Mont Saint-Michel, which I had not seen before.

Within each of us there is another whom we do not know. He speaks to us in dreams and tells us how differently *he* sees us from how *we* see ourselves. When we find ourselves in an insolubly difficult situation, this stranger in us can sometimes show us a light which is more suited than anything else to change our attitude fundamentally.

C.G. Jung, *The Meaning of Psychology for Modern Man* (1934)

What a sight, when one arrives as I did, at Avranches toward the end of the day! The town stands on a hill, and I was taken into the public garden at the extremity of the town. I uttered a cry of astonishment. An extraordinarily large bay lay extended before me, as far as my eyes could reach, between two hills which were lost to sight in the mist; and in the middle of this immense yellow bay, under a clear, golden sky, a peculiar hill rose up, somber and pointed in the midst of the sand. The sun had just disappeared, and under the still flaming sky stood out the outline of that fantastic rock, which bears on its summit a picturesque monument.

At daybreak I went to it. The tide was low, as it had been the night before, and I saw that wonderful abbey rise up before me as I approached it. After several hours' walking, I reached the enormous mass of rock which supports the little town, dominated by the great church. Having climbed the steep and narrow street, I entered the most wonderful Gothic building that has ever been erected to God on earth, large as a town, and full of low rooms which seem buried beneath vaulted roofs, and of lofty galleries supported by delicate columns.

I entered this gigantic granite jewel, which is as light in its effect as a bit of lace and is covered with towers, with slender belfries to which spiral staircases ascend. The flying buttresses raise strange heads that bristle with chimeras, with devils, with fantastic animals, with monstrous flowers, are joined together by finely carved arches, to the blue sky by day, and to the black sky by night.

When I had reached the summit, I said to the monk who accompanied me: ''Father, how happy you must be here!'' And he replied: ''It is very windy, Monsieur''; and so we began to talk while watching the rising tide, which ran over the sand and covered it with a steel cuirass.

And then the monk told me stories, all the old stories belonging to the place — legends, nothing but legends.

One of them struck me forcibly. The country people, those belonging to the Mornet, declare that at night one can hear talking going on in the sand, and also that two goats bleat, one with a strong, the other with a weak voice. Incredulous people declare that it is nothing but the screaming of the sea birds, which occasionally resembles bleatings, and occasionally human lamentations; but belated fishermen swear that they have met an old shepherd, whose cloak-covered head they can never see, wandering on the sand, between two tides, round the little town placed so far out of the world. They declare he is guiding and walking before a he-goat with a man's face and a she-goat with a woman's face, both with white hair, who talk incessantly, quarreling in a strange language, and then suddenly cease talking in order to bleat with all their might.

''Do you believe it?'' I asked the monk. ''I scarcely know,'' he replied; and I continued: ''If there are other beings besides ourselves on this earth, how comes it that we have not known it for so long a time, or why have you not seen them? How is it that I have not seen them?''

He replied: ''Do we see the hundred-thousandth part of what exists? Look here; there is the wind, which is the strongest force in nature. It knocks down men, and blows down buildings, uproots trees, raises the sea into mountains of water, destroys cliffs and casts great ships onto the breakers; it kills, it whistles, it sighs, it roars. But have you ever seen it, and can you see it? Yet it exists for all that.''

I was silent before this simple reasoning. That man was a philosopher, or perhaps a fool; I could not say which exactly, so I held my tongue. What he had said had often been in my own thoughts.

July 3. I have slept badly; certainly there is some feverish influence here, for my coachman is suffering in the same way as I am. When I went back home yesterday, I noticed his singular paleness, and I asked him: ''What is the matter with you, Jean?''

''The matter is that I never get any rest, and my nights devour my days. Since your departure, Monsieur, there has been a spell over me.''

However, the other servants are all well, but I am very

frightened of having another attack, myself.

July 4. I am decidedly taken again; for my old nightmares have returned. Last night I felt somebody leaning on me who was sucking my life from between my lips with his mouth. Yes, he was sucking it out of my neck as a leech would have done. Then he got up, satiated, and I woke up, so beaten, crushed, and annihilated that I could not move. If this continues for a few days, I shall certainly go away again.

July 5. Have I lost my reason? What has happened? What I saw last night is so strange that my head wanders when I think of it!

As I do now every evening, I had locked my door; then, being thirsty, I drank half a glass of water, and I accidently noticed that the water-bottle was full up to the cut-glass stopper.

Then I went to bed and fell into one of my terrible sleeps, from which I was aroused in about two hours by a still more terrible shock.

Picture to yourself a sleeping man who is being murdered, who wakes up with a knife in his chest, a gurgling in his throat, is covered with blood, can no longer breathe, is going to die and does not understand anything at all about it — there you have it.

Persons suffering an attack experience incapability of motion, a torpid sensation in their sleep, a sense of suffocation and oppression, as if from one pressing them down, with inability to cry out, or they utter inarticulate sounds. Some imagine often that they even hear the person who is going to press them down, that he offers lustful violence to them but flies when they attempt to grasp him with their fingers.

Paulus Aeginata, *Sydenham Transactions* (1839)

Having recovered my senses, I was thirsty again, so I lighted a candle and went to the table on which my water-bottle was. I lifted it up and tilted it over my glass, but nothing came out. It was empty! It was completely empty! At first I could not understand it at all; then suddenly I was seized by such a terrible feeling that I had to sit down, or rather fall into a chair! Then I sprang up with a bound to look about me; then I sat down again, overcome by astonishment and fear, in front of the transparent crystal bottle! I looked at it with fixed eyes, trying to solve the puzzle, and my hands trembled! Somebody had drunk the water, but who? I? I without any doubt. It could surely only be I? In that case I was a somnambulist — was living, without knowing it, that double, mysterious life which makes us doubt whether there are not two beings in us — whether a strange, unknowable, and invisible being does not, during our moments of mental and physical torpor, animate the inert body, forcing it to a more willing obedience than it yields to ourselves.

Oh! Who will understand my horrible agony? Who will understand the emotion of a man sound in mind, wide-awake, full of sense, who looks in horror at the disappearance of a little water while he was asleep, through the glass of a water-bottle! And I remained sitting until it was daylight, without venturing to go to bed again.

July 6. I am going mad. Again all the contents of my water-bottle have been drunk during the night; or rather I have drunk it!

But is it I? Is it I? Who could it be? Who? Oh! God! Am I going mad? Who will save me?

July 10. I have just been through some surprising ordeals. Undoubtedly I must be mad! And yet!

On July 6, before going to bed, I put some wine, milk, water, bread, and strawberries on my table. Somebody drank — I drank — all the water and a little of the milk, but neither the wine, nor the bread, nor the strawberries were touched.

On the seventh of July I renewed the same experiment, with the same results, and on July 8 I left out the water and the milk and nothing was touched.

Lastly, on July 9 I put only water and milk on my table, taking care to wrap up the bottles in white muslin and to tie down the stoppers. Then I rubbed my lips, my beard, and my hands with pencil lead, and went to bed.

Deep slumber seized me, soon followed by a terrible awakening. I had not moved, and my sheets were not marked. I rushed to the table. The muslin round the bottles remained intact; I undid the string, trembling with fear. All the water had been drunk, and so had the milk! Ah! Great God! I must start for Paris immediately.

July 12. Paris. I must have lost my head during the last few days! I must be the plaything of my enervated imagination, unless I am really a somnambulist, or I have been brought under the power of one of those influences — hypnotic suggestion, for example — which are known to exist, but have hitherto been inexplicable. In any case, my mental state bordered on madness, and twenty-four hours of Paris sufficed to restore me to my equilibrium.

Yesterday after doing some business and paying some visits, which instilled fresh and invigorating mental air into me, I wound up my evening at the Théâtre Français. A drama by Alexander Dumas the Younger was being acted, and his brilliant and powerful play completed my cure. Certainly solitude is dangerous for active minds. We need men around us who can think and can talk. When we are alone for a long time, we people space with phantoms.

I returned along the boulevards to my hotel in excellent spirits. Amid the jostling of the crowd I thought, not without irony, of my terrors and surmises of the previous week, because I believed, yes, I believed, that an invisible being lived beneath my roof. How weak our mind is; how quickly it is terrified and unbalanced as soon as we are confronted with a small, incomprehensible fact. Instead of dismissing the problem with: "We do not understand because we cannot find the cause," we immediately imagine terrible mysteries and supernatural powers.

July 14. *Fête* of the Republic. I walked through the streets, and the crackers and flags amused me like a child. Still, it is very foolish to make merry on a set date, by Government decree. People are like a flock of sheep, now steadily patient, now in ferocious revolt. Say to it: "Amuse yourself," and it amuses itself. Say to it: "Go and fight with your neighbor," and it goes and fights. Say to it: "Vote for the Emperor," and it votes for the Emperor; then say to it: "Vote for the Republic," and it votes for the Republic.

Those who direct it are stupid, too; but instead of obeying men they obey principles, a course which can only be foolish, ineffective, and false, for the very reason that principles are ideas which are considered as certain and unchangeable, whereas in this world one is certain of nothing, since light is an illusion and noise is deception.

July 16. I saw some things yesterday that troubled me very much.

I was dining at my cousin's, Madame Sablé, whose husband is colonel of the Seventy-sixth Chasseurs at Limoges. There were two young women there, one of whom had married a medical man, Dr. Parent, who devotes himself a great deal to nervous diseases and to the extraordinary manifestations which just now experiments in hypnotism and suggestion are producing.

He related to us at some length the enormous results obtained by English scientists and the doctors of the medical school at Nancy, and the facts which he adduced appeared to me so strange that I declared that I was altogether incredulous.

"We are," he declared, "on the point of discovering one of the most important secrets of nature, I mean to say, one of its most important secrets on this earth, for assuredly there are some up in the stars, yonder, of a different kind of importance. Ever since man has thought, since he has been able to express and write down his thoughts, he has felt himself close to a mystery which is impenetrable to his coarse and imperfect senses, and he endeavors to supplement the feeble penetration of his organs by the efforts of his intellect. As long as that intellect remained in its elementary stage, this intercourse with invisible spirits assumed forms which were commonplace though terrifying. Thence sprang the popular belief in the supernatural, the legends of wandering spirits, of fairies, of gnomes, of ghosts, I might even say the conception of God, for our ideas of the Workman-

Some kind of Being, most often a shaggy animal, or else a hideous human form presses on the sleeper's breast, or pinions his throat and tries to strangle him. The terror increases with the suffocation, every effort at defence is impossible, since all his limbs are paralysed as though by magical power....The danger, the terror, becomes ever greater, and then at last a final frightful effort overcomes the adverse Being, a vigorous movement wakens the dreamer from his sleep, and all is over—only the cold sweat over the whole body and a loudly audible beating of the heart serve to remind the waking person...of the horrible and deathly terror he has just had to endure.

D. Cubasch, *Der Alp* (1877)

A Twilight Man
Harry Guest

The black flakes on the quiet wind
    drift through the rib-cage:
Charred reductions of evidence—
    letters, dossiers,
Photographs. The bonfire
    crackles to silence.
Smell of dew supersedes
    the acridity
In back of the heat.
    A wry peace now. Embers
Creep, write enigmatically, twist,
    fade. No messages.
Scraps float, soon lost in the
    thicker air contours abandon.
A skeletal hand disturbs
    the site, prods, stains the
Bone. Faces, afternoons on
    sofas, decisions, success, now
Ash. The head tilts towards the
    stars of slower change
Whose light prickles the empty eye-
    sockets and, dropping into the black
Skull, vanishes, unretained.
    Water beads coldly on
Spine, jaw, poised knuckle,
    and the darkness settles
Substantiate since the last red
    point has gone leaving only
Meaningless wafers for the night to
    obliterate, disperse.

Creator, from whatever religion they may have come down to us, are certainly the most mediocre, the stupidest, and the most unacceptable inventions that ever sprang from the frightened brain of any human creature. Nothing is truer than what Voltaire says: 'If God made man in His own image, man has certainly paid Him back again.'

But for rather more than a century, men seem to have had a presentiment of something new. Mesmer and some others have put us on an unexpected track, and within the last two or three years especially, we have arrived at results really surprising.''

My cousin, who is also very incredulous, smiled, and Dr. Parent said to her: ''Would you like me to try and send you to sleep, Madame?''

''Yes, certainly.''

She sat down in an easy-chair, and he began to look at her fixedly, as if to fascinate her. I suddenly felt myself somewhat discomposed; my heart beat rapidly and I had a choking feeling in my throat. I saw that Madame Sablé's eyes were growing heavy, her mouth twitched, and her bosom heaved, and at the end of ten minutes she was asleep.

''Go behind her,'' the doctor said to me; so I took a seat behind her. He put a visiting-card into her hands, and said to her: ''This is a looking-glass; what do you see in it?''

She replied: ''I see my cousin.''

''What is he doing?''

''He is twisting his mustache.''

''And now?''

''He is taking a photograph out of his pocket.''

''Whose photograph is it?''

''His own.''

That was true, for the photograph had been given me that same evening at the hotel.

''What is his attitude in this portrait?''

''He is standing up with his hat in his hand.''

She saw these things in that card, in that piece of white pasteboard, as if she had seen them in a looking-glass.

The young women were frightened, and exclaimed: ''That is quite enough! Quite, quite enough!''

But the doctor said to her authoritatively: ''You will get up at eight o'clock tomorrow morning; then you will go and call on your cousin at his hotel and ask him to lend you the five thousand francs which your husband asks of you, and which he will ask for when he sets out on his coming journey.''

Then he woke her up.

On returning to my hotel, I thought over this curious *séance* and I was assailed by doubts, not as to my cousin's absolute and undoubted good faith, for I had known her as well as if she had been my own sister ever since she was a child, but as to a possible trick on the doctor's part. Had not he, perhaps, kept a glass hidden in his hand, which he showed to the young woman in her sleep at the same time as he did the card? Professional conjurers do things which are just as singular.

However, I went to bed, and this morning, at about half past eight, I was awakened by my footman, who said to me: "Madame Sablé has asked to see you immediately, Monsieur." I dressed hastily and went to her.

She sat down in some agitation, with her eyes on the floor, and without raising her veil said to me: "My dear cousin, I am going to ask a great favor of you."

"What is it, cousin?"

"I do not like to tell you, and yet I must. I am in absolute want of five thousand francs."

"What, you?"

"Yes, I, or rather my husband, who has asked me to procure them for him."

I was so stupefied that I hesitated to answer. I asked myself whether she had not really been making fun of me with Dr. Parent, if it were not merely a very well-acted farce which had been got up beforehand. On looking at her attentively, however, my doubts disappeared. She was trembling with grief, so painful was this step to her, and I was sure that her throat was full of sobs.

I knew that she was very rich and so I continued: "What! Has not your husband five thousand francs at his disposal? Come, think. Are you sure that he commissioned you to ask me for them? Are you absolutely sure?"

She hesitated for a few seconds, as if she were making a great effort to search her memory, and then she replied: "Yes — yes, I am quite sure of it."

"He has written to you?"

She hesitated again and reflected, and I guessed the torture of her thoughts. She did not know. She only knew that she was to borrow five thousand francs of me for her husband. So she told a lie.

"Yes, he has written to me."

"When, pray? You did not mention it to me yesterday."

"I received his letter this morning."

"Can you show it to me?"

"No; no — no — it contained private matters, things too personal to ourselves. I burned it.

"So your husband runs into debt?"

She hesitated again, and then murmured: "I do not know."

Thereupon I said bluntly: "I have not five thousand francs at my disposal at this moment, my dear cousin."

She uttered a cry, as if she were in pain and said: "Oh! oh! I beseech you, I beseech you to get them for me."

She got excited and clasped her hands as if she were praying to me! I heard her voice change its tone; she wept and sobbed, harassed and dominated by the irresistible order that she had received.

"Oh! oh! I beg you to — if you knew what I am suffering — I want them today."

I had pity on her: "You shall have them by and by, I swear to you."

"Oh! thank you! thank you! How kind you are."

I continued: "Do you remember what took place at your house last night?"

Bird Cage
Saint-Denys Garneau

Tr. F.R. Scott

I am a bird cage
A cage of bone
With a bird

The bird in the cage of bone
Is death building his nest

When nothing is happening
One can hear him ruffle his wings

And when one has laughed a lot
If one suddenly stops
One hears him cooing
Far down
Like a small bell

It is a bird held captive
It is a death in my cage of bone

Would he not like to fly away
Is it you who will hold him back
Is it I
What is it

He cannot fly away
Until he has eaten all
My heart
The source of blood
With my life inside

He will have my soul in his beak.

I knew a bus driver who once, through no fault of his own, ran over and killed a little girl. For nights his sleep was disturbed by dreams in which again he cried out and slammed his foot upon the brake, doing so with such force that he broke the wooden bed-end.

Ian Oswald, *Sleep* (1968)

If we labor under the illusion that we shall automatically arrive safely, or arrive at all, and then be free placidly to play the role of the hero, we are mistaken. If we imagine we can bask in the glory of success in the wake of any achievement whatever, we have already become the dragon.

Dorothy Norman, *The Hero* (1949)

"Yes."

"Do you remember that Dr. Parent sent you to sleep?"

"Yes."

"Oh! Very well then; he ordered you to come to me this morning to borrow five thousand francs, and at this moment you are obeying that suggestion."

She considered for a few moments, and then replied: "But as it is my husband who wants them — "

For a whole hour I tried to convince her, but could not succeed, and when she had gone I went to the doctor. He was just going out, and he listened to me with a smile, and said: "Do you believe now?"

"Yes, I cannot help it."

"Let us go to your cousin's."

She was already resting on a couch, overcome with fatigue. The doctor felt her pulse, looked at her for some time with one hand raised toward her eyes, which she closed by degrees under the irresistible power of this magnetic influence. When she was asleep, he said:

"Your husband does not require the five thousand francs any longer! You must, therefore, forget that you asked your cousin to lend them to you, and, if he speaks to you about it, you will not understand him."

Then he woke her up, and I took out a pocketbook and said: "Here is what you asked me for this morning, my dear cousin." But she was so surprised, that I did not venture to persist; nevertheless, I tried to recall the circumstance to her, but she denied it vigorously, thought that I was making fun of her, and in the end, very nearly lost her temper.

There! I have just come back, and I have not been able to eat any lunch, for this experiment has altogether upset me.

July 19. Many people to whom I have told the adventure have laughed at me. I no longer know what to think. The wise man says: Perhaps?

July 21. I dined at Bougival, and then I spent the evening at a boatmen's ball. Decidedly everything depends on place and surroundings. It would be the height of folly to believe in the supernatural on the *Ile de la Grenouillière* (Frog-Island). But on the top of Mont Saint-Michel or in India, we are terribly under the influence of our surroundings. I shall return home next week.

July 30. I came back to my own house yesterday. Everything is going on well.

August 2. Nothing fresh; it is splendid weather, and I spend my days in watching the Seine flow past.

August 4. Quarrels among my servants. They declare that the glasses are broken in the cupboards at night. The footman accuses the cook, she accuses the needlewoman, and the latter accuses the other two. Who is the culprit? It would take a clever person to tell.

August 6. This time, I am not mad. I have seen — I have seen — I have seen! — I can doubt no longer — *I have seen it!*

I was walking at two o'clock among my rose-trees, in the full sunlight — in the walk bordered by autumn roses which are beginning to fall. As I stopped to look at a Géant de Bataille, which had three splendid blooms, I distinctly saw the stalk of one of the roses bend close to me, as if an invisible hand had bent it, and then break, as if that hand had picked it! Then the flower raised itself, following the curve which a hand would have described in carrying it toward a mouth, and remained suspended in the transparent air, alone and motionless, a terrible red spot, three yards from my eyes. In desperation I rushed at it to take it! I found nothing; it had disappeared. Then I was seized with furious rage against myself, for it is not wholesome for a reasonable and serious man to have such hallucinations.

But was it a hallucination? I turned to look for the stalk, and I found it immediately under the bush, freshly broken, between the two other roses which remained on the branch. I returned home, then, with a much disturbed mind; for I am certain now, certain as I am of the alternation of day and night, that there exists close to me an invisible being who lives on milk and on water, who can touch objects, take them and change their places; who is, consequently, endowed with a material nature, although imperceptible to sense, and who lives as I do, under my roof —

August 7. I slept tranquilly. He drank the water out of my decanter, but did not disturb my sleep.

I ask myself whether I am mad. As I was walking just now in the sun by the riverside, doubts as to my own sanity arose in me; not vague doubts such as I have had hitherto, but precise and absolute doubts. I have seen mad people, and I have known some who were quite intelligent, lucid, even clear-sighted in every concern of life, except on one point. They could speak clearly, readily, profoundly on everything; till their thoughts were caught in the breakers of their delusions and went to pieces there, were dispersed and swamped in that furious and terrible sea of fogs and squalls which is called *madness.*

I certainly should think that I was mad, absolutely mad, if I were not conscious that I knew my state, if I could not fathom it and analyze it with the most complete lucidity. I should, in fact, be a reasonable man laboring under a hallucination. Some unknown disturbance must have been excited in my brain, one of those disturbances which physiologists of the present day try to note and to fix precisely, and that disturbance must have caused a profound gulf in my mind and in the order and logic of my ideas. Similar phenomena occur in dreams, and lead us through the most unlikely phantasmagoria, without causing us any surprise, because our verifying apparatus and our sense of control have gone to sleep, while our imaginative faculty wakes and works. Was it not possible that one of the imperceptible keys of the cerebral finger-board had been paralyzed in me? Some men lose the recollection of proper names, or of verbs, or of numbers, or merely of dates, in consequence of an accident. The localization of all the avenues of thought has been accomplished nowadays; what, then would there be surprising in the fact that my faculty of controlling the unreality of certain hallucinations should be destroyed for the time being?

I thought of all this as I walked by the side of the water. The sun was shining brightly on the river and made earth delightful, while it filled me with love for life, for the swallows, whose swift agility is always delightful in my eyes, for the plants by the riverside, whose rustling is a pleasure to my ears.

By degrees, however, an inexplicable feeling of discomfort seized me. It seemed to me as if some unknown force were numbing and stopping me, were preventing me from going further and were calling me back. I felt that painful wish to return which comes on you when you have left a beloved invalid at home, and are seized by a presentiment that he is worse.

I, therefore, returned despite myself, feeling certain that I should find some bad news awaiting me, a letter or a telegram. There was nothing, however, and I was surprised and uneasy, more so than if I had had another fantastic vision.

August 8. I spent a terrible evening, yesterday. He does not show himself any more, but I feel that He is near me, watching me, looking at me, penetrating me, dominating me, and more terrible to me when He hides himself thus than if He were to manifest his constant and invisible presence by supernatural phenomena. However, I slept.

August 9. Nothing, but I am afraid.

August 10. Nothing; but what will happen tomorrow?

August 11. Still nothing. I cannot stop at home with this fear hanging over me and these thoughts in my mind; I shall go away.

August 12. Ten o'clock at night. All day long I have been trying to get away, and have not been able. I contemplated a simple and easy act of liberty, a carriage ride to Rouen — and I have not been able to do it. What is the reason?

August 13. When one is attacked by certain maladies, the springs of our physical being seem broken, our energies destroyed, our muscles relaxed, our bones to be as soft as our flesh, and our blood as liquid as water. I am experiencing the same in my moral being, in a strange and

distressing manner. I have no longer any strength, any courage, any self-control, nor even any power to set my own will in motion. I have no power left to *will* anything, but some one does it for me and I obey.

August 14. I am lost! Somebody possesses my soul and governs it! Somebody orders all my acts, all my movements, all my thoughts. I am no longer master of myself, nothing except an enslaved and terrified spectator of the things which I do. I wish to go out; I cannot. *He* does not wish to; and so I remain, trembling and distracted in the armchair in which he keeps me sitting. I merely wish to get up and to rouse myself, so as to think that I am still master of myself: I cannot! I am riveted to my chair, and my chair adheres to the floor in such a manner that no force of mine can move us.

Then suddenly, I must, I *must* go to the foot of my garden to pick some strawberries and eat them — and I go there. I pick the strawberries and I eat them! Oh! my God! my God! Is there a God? If there be one, deliver me! save me! succor me! Pardon! Pity! Mercy! Save me! Oh! what sufferings! what torture! what horror!

August 15. Certainly this is the way in which my poor cousin was possessed and swayed, when she came to borrow five thousand francs of me. She was under the power of a strange will which had entered into her, like another soul, a parasitic and ruling soul. Is the world coming to an end?

But who is He, this invisible being that rules me, this unknowable being, this rover of a supernatural race?

Invisible beings exist, then! How is it, then, that since the beginning of the world they have never manifested themselves in such a manner as they do to me? I have never read anything that resembles what goes on in my house. Oh! If I could only leave it, if I could only go away and flee, and never return, I should be saved; but I cannot.

August 16. I managed to escape today for two hours, like a prisoner who finds the doors of his dungeon accidentally open. I suddenly felt that I was free and that He was far away, and so I gave orders to put the horses in as quickly as possible, and I drove to Rouen. Oh! how delightful to be able to say to my coachman: "Go to Rouen!"

I made him pull up before the library, and I begged them to lend me Dr. Herrmann Herestauss's treatise on the unknown inhabitants of the ancient and modern world.

Then, as I was getting into my carriage, I intended to say: "To the railway station!" but instead of this I shouted — I did not speak, but I shouted — in such a loud voice that all the passers-by turned round: "Home!" and I fell back onto the cushion of my carriage, overcome by mental agony. He had found me out and regained possession of me.

August 17. Oh! What a night! what a night! And yet it seems to me that I ought to rejoice. I read until one o'clock in the morning! Herestauss, Doctor of Philosophy and Theogony, wrote the history and the manifestation of all those invisible beings which hover around man, or of whom he dreams. He describes their origin, their domains, their power; but none of them resembles the one which haunts me. One might say that man, ever since he has thought, has had a foreboding and a fear of a new being, stronger than himself, his successor in this world, and that, feeling him near, and not being able to foretell the nature of the unseen one, he has, in his terror, created the whole race of hidden beings, vague phantoms born of fear.

Having, therefore, read until one o'clock in the morning, I went and sat down at the open window, in order to cool my forehead and my thoughts in the calm night air. It was very pleasant and warm! How I should have enjoyed such a night formerly!

There was no moon, but the stars darted out their rays in the dark heavens. Who inhabits those worlds? What forms, what living beings, what animals are there yonder? Do those who are thinkers in those distant worlds know more than we do? What can they do more than we? What do they see which we do not? Will not one of them, some day or other, traversing space, appear on our earth to conquer it, just as formerly the Norsemen crossed the sea in order to subjugate nations feebler than themselves?

We are so weak, so powerless, so ignorant, so small — we who live on this particle of mud which revolves in liquid air.

I fell asleep, dreaming thus in the cool night air, and then, having slept for about three quarters of an hour, I opened my eyes without moving, awakened by an indescribably confused and strange sensation. At first I saw nothing, and then suddenly it appeared to me as if a page of the book, which had remained open on my table, turned over of its own accord. Not a breath of air had come in at my window, and I was surprised and waited. In about four minutes, I saw, I saw — yes I saw with my own eyes — another page lift itself up and fall down on the others, as if a finger had turned it over. My armchair was empty, appeared empty, but I knew that He was there, He, and sitting in my place, and that He was reading. With a furious bound, the bound of an enraged wild beast that wishes to disembowel its tamer, I crossed my room to seize Him, to strangle Him, to kill Him! But before I could reach it, my chair fell over as if somebody had run away from me. My table rocked, my lamp fell and went out, and my window closed as if some thief had been surprised and had fled out into the night, shutting it behind him.

So He had run away; He had been afraid; He, afraid of me!

So tomorrow, or later — some day or other, I should be able to hold him in my clutches and crush him against the ground! Do not dogs occasionally bite and strangle their masters?

August 18. I have been thinking the whole day long. Oh! yes, I will obey Him, follow His impulses, fulfill all His wishes, show myself humble, submissive, a coward. He is the stronger; but an hour will come.

August 19. I know, I know, I know all! I have just read

the following the *Revue du Monde Scientifique:* "A curious piece of news comes to us from Rio de Janeiro. Madness, an epidemic of madness, which may be compared to that contagious madness which attacked the people of Europe in the Middle Ages, is at this moment raging in the Province of San-Paulo. The frightened inhabitants are leaving their houses, deserting their villages, abandoning their land, saying that they are pursued, possessed, governed like human cattle by invisible, though tangible beings, by a species of vampire, which feeds on their life while they are asleep, and which, besides, drinks water and milk without appearing to touch any other nourishment.

"Professor Don Pedro Henriques, accompanied by several medical savants, has gone to the Province of San-Paulo, in order to study the origin and the manifestations of this surprising madness on the spot, and to propose such measures to the Emperor as may appear to him to be most fitted to restore the mad population to reason."

Ah! Ah! I remember now that fine Brazilian three-master which passed in front of my windows as it was going up the Seine, on the eighth of last May! I thought it looked so pretty, so white and bright! That Being was on board of her, coming from there, where its race sprang from. And it saw me! It saw my house, which was also white, and He sprang from the ship on to the land. Oh! Good heavens!

Now I know, I can divine. The reign of man is over, and He has come. He whom disquieted priests exorcised, whom sorcerers evoked on dark nights, without seeing him appear. He to whom the imaginations of the transient masters of the world lent all the monstrous or graceful forms of gnomes, spirits, genii, fairies, and familiar spirits. After the coarse conceptions of primitive fear, men more enlightened gave him a truer form. Mesmer divined him, and ten years ago physicians accurately discovered the nature of his power, even before He exercised it himself. They played with that weapon of their new Lord, the sway of a mysterious will over the human soul, which had become enslaved. They called it mesmerism, hypnotism, suggestion, I know not what. I have seen them diverting themselves like rash children with this horrible power! Woe to us! Woe to man! He has come, the — the — what does He call Himself — the — I fancy that He is shouting out His name to me and I do not hear Him — the — yes — He is shouting it out — I am listening — I cannot — repeat — it — Horla — I have heard — the Horla — it is He — the Horla — He has come! —

Ah! the vulture has eaten the pigeon, the wolf has eaten the lamb; the lion has devoured the sharp-horned buffalo; man has killed the lion with an arrow, with a spear, with gunpowder; but the Horla will make of man what man has made of the horse and of the ox: His chattel, His slave, and His food, by the mere power of His will. Woe to us!

But, nevertheless, sometimes the animal rebels and kills the man who has subjugated it. I should also like — I shall be able to — but I must know Him, touch Him, see Him! Learned men say that eyes of animals, as they differ from ours, do not distinguish as ours do. And my eye cannot distinguish this newcomer who is oppressing me.

Why? Oh! Now I remember the words of the monk at Mont Saint-Michel: "Can we see the hundred-thousandth part of what exists? Listen; there is the wind which is the strongest force in nature; it knocks men down, blows down buildings, uproots trees, raises the sea into mountains of water, destroys cliffs, and casts great ships onto the breakers; it kills, it whistles, it sighs, it roars — have you ever seen it, and can you see it? It exists for all that, however!"

And I went on thinking: my eyes are so weak, so imperfect, that they do not even distinguish hard bodies, if they are as transparent as glass! If a glass without quicksilver behind it were to bar my way, I should run into it, just like a bird which has flown into a room breaks its head against the windowpanes. A thousand things, moreover, deceive a man and lead him astray. How then is it surprising that he cannot perceive a new body which is penetrated and pervaded by the light?

A new being! Why not? It was assuredly bound to come! Why should we be the last? We do not distinguish it, like all the others created before us? The reason is, that its nature is more delicate, its body finer and more finished than ours. Our make-up is so weak, so awkwardly conceived; our body is encumbered with organs that are always tired, always being strained like locks that are too complicated; it lives like a plant and like an animal nourishing itself with difficulty on air, herbs, and flesh; it is a brute machine which is a prey to maladies, to malformations, to decay; it is broken-winded, badly regulated, simple and eccentric, ingeniously yet badly made, a coarse and yet a delicate mechanism, in brief, the outline of a being which might become intelligent and great.

There are only a few — so few — stages of development in this world, from the oyster up to man. Why should there not be one more, when once that period is accomplished which separates the successive products one from the other?

Why not one more? Why not, also, other trees with immense, splendid flowers, perfuming whole regions? Why not other elements besides fire, air, earth, and water? There are four, only four, nursing fathers of various beings! What a pity! Why should not there be forty, four hundred, four thousand! How poor everything is, how mean and wretched — grudgingly given, poorly invented, clumsily made! Ah! the elephant and the hippopotamus, what power! And the camel, what suppleness!

But the butterfly, you will say, a flying flower! I dream of one that should be as large as a hundred worlds, with wings whose shape, beauty, colors, and motion I cannot even express. But I see it — it flutters from star to star, refreshing them and perfuming them with the light and harmonious breath of its flight! And the people up there gaze at it as it passes in an ecstasy of delight!

What is the matter with me? It is He, the Horla who haunts me, and who makes me think of these foolish things! He is within me, He is becoming my soul; I shall kill Him!

August 20. I shall kill Him. I have seen Him! Yesterday I sat down at my table and pretended to write very assiduously. I knew quite well that He would come prowling round me, quite close to me, so close that I might perhaps be able to touch Him, to seize Him. And then — then I should have the strength of desperation; I should have my hands, my knees, my chest, my forehead, my teeth to strangle Him, to crush Him, to bite Him, to tear Him to pieces. And I watched for Him with all my over-excited nerves.

I had lighted my two lamps and the eight wax candles on my mantelpiece, as if, by this light I should discover Him.

My bed, my old oak bed with its columns, was opposite to me; on my right was the fireplace; on my left the door, which was carefully closed, after I had left it open for some time, in order to attract Him; behind me was a very high wardrobe with a looking-glass in it, which served me to dress by every day, and in which I was in the habit of inspecting myself from head to foot every time I passed it.

So I pretended to be writing in order to deceive Him, for He also was watching me, and suddenly I felt, I was certain, that He was reading over my shoulder, that He was there, almost touching my ear.

I got up so quickly, with my hands extended, that I almost fell. Horror! It was as bright as at midday, but I did not see myself in the glass! It was empty, clear, profound, full of light! But my figure was not reflected in it — and I, I was opposite to it! I saw the large, clear glass from top to bottom, and I looked at it with unsteady eyes. I did not dare advance; I did not venture to make a movement; feeling certain, nevertheless, that He was there, but that He would escape me again, He whose imperceptible body had absorbed my reflection.

How frightened I was! And then suddenly I began to see myself through a mist in the depths of the looking-glass, in a mist as it were, or through a veil of water; and it seemed to me as if this water were flowing slowly from left to right, and making my figure clearer every moment. It was like the end of an eclipse. Whatever hid me did not appear to possess any clearly defined outlines, but was a sort of opaque transparency, which gradually grew clearer.

At last I was able to distinguish myself completely, as I do every day when I look at myself.

I had seen Him! And the horror of it remained with me, and makes me shudder even now.

August 21. How could I kill Him, since I could not get hold of Him? Poison? But He would see me mix it with the water; and then, would our poisons have any any effect on His impalpable body? No — no — no doubt about the matter. Then? — then?

August 22. I sent for a blacksmith from Rouen and ordered iron shutters of him for my room, such as some private hotels in Paris have on the ground floor, for fear of thieves, and he is going to make me a similar door as well. I have made myself out a coward, but I do not care about that!

September 10. Rouen, Hotel Continental. It is done; it is done — but is He dead? My mind is thoroughly upset by what I have seen.

Well then, yesterday, the locksmith having put on the iron shutters and door, I left everything open until midnight, although it was getting cold.

Suddenly I felt that He was there, and joy, mad joy took possession of me. I got up softly, and I walked to the right and left for some time, so that He might not guess anything; then I took off my boots and put on my slippers carelessly; then I fastened the iron shutters and going back to the door quickly I double-locked it with a padlock, putting the key into my pocket.

Suddenly I noticed that He was moving restlessly round me, that in His turn He was frightened and was ordering me to let Him out. I nearly yielded, though I did not quite, but putting my back to the door, I half opened it, just enough to allow me to go out backward, and as I am very tall, my head touched the lintel. I was sure that He had not been able to escape, and I shut Him up quite alone, quite alone. What happiness! I had Him fast. Then I ran downstairs into the drawing-room which was under my bedroom. I took the two lamps and poured all the oil onto the carpet, the furniture, everywhere; then I set fire to it and made my escape, after having carefully double-locked the door.

I went and hid myself at the bottom of the garden, in a clump of laurel bushes. How long it was! how long it was! Everything was dark, silent, motionless, not a breath of air and not a star, but heavy banks of clouds which one could not see, but which weighed, oh! so heavily on my soul.

I looked at my house and waited. How long it was! I already began to think that the fire had gone out of its own accord, or that He had extinguished it, when one of the lower windows gave way under the violence of the flames, and a long, soft, caressing sheet of red flame mounted up the white wall, and kissed it as high as the roof. The light fell on to the trees, the branches, and the leaves, and a shiver of fear pervaded them also! The birds awoke; a dog began to howl, and it seemed to me as if the day were breaking! Almost immediately two other windows flew into fragments, and I saw that the whole of the lower part of my house was nothing but a terrible furnace. But a cry, a horrible, shrill, heart-rendering cry, a woman's cry, sounded through the night, and two garret windows were opened! I had forgotten the servants! I saw the terror-struck faces, and the frantic waving of their arms!

Then, overwhelmed with horror, I ran off to the village, shouting: "Help! help! fire! fire!" Meeting some people who were already coming on to the scene, I went back with them to see!

By this time the house was nothing but a horrible and magnificent funeral pile, a monstrous pyre which lit up the whole country, a pyre where men were burning, and where He was burning also, He, He, my prisoner, that new Being, the new Master, the Horla!

Suddenly the whole roof fell in between the walls, and a volcano of flames darted up to the sky. Through all the windows which opened on to that furnace, I saw the flames darting, and I reflected that He was there, in that kiln, dead.

Dead? Perhaps? His body? Was not his body, which was transparent, indestructible by such means as would kill ours?

If He were not dead? Perhaps time alone has power over that Invisible and Redoubtable Being. Why this transparent, unrecognizable body, this body belonging to a spirit, if it also had to fear ills, infirmities, and premature destruction?

Premature destruction? All human terror springs from that! After man the Horla. After him who can die every day, at any hour, at any moment, by any accident, He came, He who was only to die at his own proper hour and minute, because He had touched the limits of his existence!

No — no — there is no doubt about it — He is not dead. Then — then — I suppose I must kill *myself!*

The Horrors of Sleep
Emily Bronte

Sleep brings no joy to me,
  Remembrance never dies,
My soul is given to mystery,
  And lives in sighs.

Sleep brings no rest to me;
  The shadows of the dead
My wakening eyes may never see
  Surround my bed.

Sleep brings no hope to me,
  In soundest sleep they come,
And with their doleful imag'ry
  Deepen the gloom.

Sleep brings no strength to me,
  No power renewed to brave;
I only sail a wilder sea,
  A darker wave.

Sleep brings no friend to me
  To soothe and aid to bear;
They all gaze on, how scornfully,
  And I despair.

Sleep brings no wish to fret
  My harassed heart beneath;
My only wish is to forget
  In endless sleep of death.

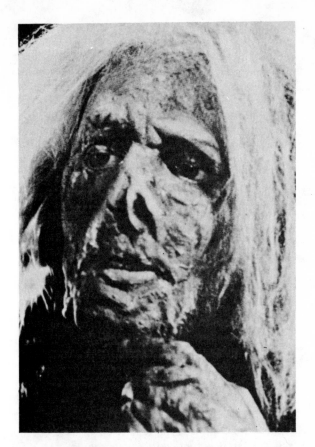

from An Essay in Autobiography
Boris Pasternak

...we have no conception of the inner torture which precedes suicide. People who are physically tortured on the rack keep losing consciousness, their suffering is so great that its unendurable intensity shortens the end. But a man who is thus at the mercy of the executioner is not annihilated when he faints from pain, for he is present at his own end, his past belongs to him, his memories are his and, if he chooses, he can make use of them, they can help him before his death.

But a man who decides to commit suicide puts a full stop to his being, he turns his back on his past, he declares himself a bankrupt and his memories to be unreal. They can no longer help or save him, he has put himself beyond their reach. The continuity of his inner life is broken, his personality is at an end. And perhaps what finally makes him kill himself is not the firmness of his resolve but the unbearable quality of this anguish which belongs to no one, of this suffering in the absence of the sufferer, of this waiting which is empty because life has stopped and can no longer fill it.

What is certain is that they all suffered beyond description, to the point where suffering has become a mental sickness. And, as we bow in homage to their gifts and to their bright memory, we should bow compassionately before their suffering.

Primitive
Patricia Martland

I am alone with fear
   in a world that is afraid
I hold my own too dear
and danger is prowling near
   my tribal bird-winged glade
   I wait the horrible raid.

Golem (go lim), n. Heb., orig., embryo; later, monster (hence Yid. sense "dolt"); in Jewish legend, a man artificially created by cabalistic rites; robot; automaton.

It is said that the origin of the story goes back to the seventeenth century. According to the lost formulas of the Kabbalah, a rabbi (Judah Loew ben Bezabel) made an artificial man — the foresaid Golem — so that he would ring the bells and take over all the menial tasks of the synagogue.

He was not a man exactly, and had only a sort of dim, half-conscious vegetative existence. By the power of a magic tablet which was placed under his tongue and which attracted the free sidereal energies of the universe, this existence lasted during the daylight hours.

One night before evening prayer, the rabbi forgot to take the tablet out of the Golem's mouth, and the creature fell into a frenzy, running out into the dark alleys of the ghetto and knocking down those who got in his way, until the rabbi caught up with him and removed the tablet.

At once the creature fell lifeless....

Gustav Meyrink, *Der Golem* (1915)

"All my stories, unconnected as they may be, are based on the fundamental lore or legend that this world was inhabited at one time by another race who, In practicing black magic, lost their foothold and were expelled, yet live on outside, ever ready to take possession of this earth again." *H.P. Lovecraft*

L. Sprague DeCamp, *Lovecraft, A Biography* (1975)

"Freedom and power, but above all, power! Power over all trembling creatures, over the whole ant-heap!" — *Raskolnikov*

Dostoevsky, *Crime and Punishment* (1866)

Mannikins of Horror
Robert Bloch

Colin had been making the little clay figures for a long time before he noticed that they moved. He had been making them for years there in his room, using hundreds of pounds of clay, a little at a time.

The doctors thought he was crazy; Doctor Starr in particular, but then Doctor Starr was a quack and a fool. He couldn't understand why Colin didn't go into the workshop with the other men and weave baskets, or make rattan chairs. That was useful "occupational therapy," not foolishness like sitting around and modelling little clay figures year in and year out. Doctor Starr always talked like that, and sometimes Colin longed to smash his smug, fat face "Doctor" indeed!

Colin knew what he was doing. He had been a doctor once: Doctor Edgar Colin, surgeon — and brain-surgeon at that. He had been a renowned specialist, an authority, in the days when young Starr was a bungling, nervous interne. What irony! Now Colin was shut up in a madhouse, and Doctor Starr was his keeper. It was a grim joke. But mad though he was, Colin knew more about psychopathology than Starr would ever learn.

Colin had gone up with the Red Cross base at Ypres; he had come down miraculously unmangled, but his nerves were shot. For months after that final blinding flash of shells Colin had lain in a coma at the hospital, and when he had recovered they said he had *dementia praecox*. So they sent him here, to Starr.

Colin asked for clay the moment he was up and around. He wanted to work. The long, lean hands, skilled in delicate cranial surgery, had not lost their cunning — their cunning that was like a hunger for still more difficult tasks. Colin knew he would never operate again; he wasn't Doctor Colin any more, but a psychotic patient. Still he had to work. Knowing what he did about mental disorders, his mind was tortured by introspection unless he kept busy. Modelling was the way out.

As surgeon he had often made casts, busts, anatomical figures copied from life to aid his work. It had been an engrossing hobby, and he knew the organs, even the complicated structure of the nervous system, quite perfectly. Now he worked in clay. He started out making ordinary little figures in his room. Tiny mannikins, five or six inches high, were moulded accurately from memory. He discovered an immediate knack for sculpture, a natural talent to which his delicate fingers responded.

Starr had encouraged him at first. His comma ended, his stupor over, he had been revivified by this new-found interest. His early clay figures gained a great deal of attention and praise. His family sent him funds; he bought instruments for modelling. On the table in his room he soon placed all the tools of a sculptor. It was good to handle instruments again; not knives and scalpels, but things equally wonderful: things that cut and carved and reformed bodies. Bodies of clay, bodies of flesh — what did it matter?

It hadn't mattered at first, but then it did. Colin, after months of painstaking effort, grew dissatisfied. He toiled eight, ten, twelve hours a day, but he was not pleased — he threw away his finished figures, crumpled them into brown balls which he hurled to the floor with disgust.

His work wasn't good enough.

The men and women looked like men and women in miniature. They had muscles, tendons, features, even epidermal layers and tiny hairs Colin placed on their small bodies. But what good was it? A fraud, a sham. Inside they were solid clay, nothing more — and that was wrong. Colin wanted to make complete miniature mortals, and for that he must study.

It was then that he had his first clash with Doctor Starr, when he asked for anatomy books. Starr laughed at him, but he managed to get permission.

So Colin learned to duplicate the bony structure of man, the organs, the quite intricate mass of arteries and veins. Finally, the terrific triumph of learning glands, nerve-structure, nerve-endings. It took years, during which Colin made and destroyed a thousand clay figures. He made clay skeletons, placed clay organs in tiny bodies. Delicate, precise work. Mad work, but it kept him from thinking. He got so he could duplicate the forms with his eyes closed. At last he assembled his knowledge, made clay skeletons and put the organs in them, then allowed for pin-pricked nervous system, blood vessels, glandular organization, dermic structure, muscular tissue — everything.

And at last he started making brains. He learned every convolution of the cerebrum and cerebellum; every nerve-ending, every wrinkle in the grey matter of the cortex. Study, study, disregard the laughter, disregard the thoughts, disregard the monotony of long years imprisoned; study, study, make the perfect figures, be the greatest sculptor in the world, be the greatest surgeon in the world, be a creator.

Doctor Starr dropped in every so often and subtly tried to discourage such fanatical absorption. Colin wanted to laugh in his face. Starr was afraid this work was driving Colin madder than ever. Colin knew it was the one thing that kept him sane.

Because lately when he wasn't working, Colin felt things happen to him. The shells seemed to explode in his head again, and they were doing things to his brain — making it come apart, unravel like a ball of twine. He was disorganized. At time he seemed no longer a person but a thousand persons, and not one body, but a thousand distinct and separate structures, as in the clay men. He was not a unified human being, but a heart, a lung, a liver, a bloodstream, a hand, a leg, a head — all distinct, all growing more and more disassociated as time went on. His brain and body were no longer an entity. Everything within him was falling apart, leading a life of its own.

Nerves no longer co-ordinated with blood. Arm didn't always follow leg. He recalled his medical training, the hints that each bodily organ lived an individual life.

Each cell was a unit for that matter. When death came, you didn't die all at once. Some organs died before others, some cells went first. But it shouldn't happen in life. Yet it did. That shellshock, whatever it was, had resulted in a slow unravelling. And at night Colin would lie and toss, wondering how soon his body would fall apart — actually fall apart twitching hands and throbbing heart and wheezing lungs; separated like the fragments torn from a spoiled clay doll.

He had to work to keep sane. Once or twice he tried to explain to Doctor Starr what was happening, to ask for special observation — not for his sake, but because perhaps science might learn something from data on his case. Starr had laughed, as usual. As long as Colin was healthy, exhibited no morbid or homicidal traits, he wouldn't interfere. Fool!

Colin worked. Now he was building bodies — real bodies. It took days to make one; days to finish a form complete with chiselled lips, delicate aural and optical structures correct, tiny fingers and toe-nails perfectly fitted. But it kept him going. It was fascinating to see a table full of little miniature men and women!

Doctor Starr didn't think so. One afternoon he came in and saw Colin bending over three little lumps of clay with his tiny knives, a book open before him.

"What are you doing there?" he asked.

"Making the brains for my men," Colin answered.

"Brains? Good God!"

Starr stopped, Yes, they *were* brains! Tiny, perfect reproductions of the human brain, perfect in every detail, built up layer on layer with unconnected nerve-endings, blood vessels to attach them in craniums of clay!

"What —" Starr exclaimed.

"Don't interrupt. I'm putting in the thoughts," Colin said.

Thoughts? That was sheer madness, beyond madness. Starr stared aghast. Thoughts in brains for clay men?

Starr wanted to say something then. But Colin looked up and the afternoon sun streamed into his face so that Starr could see his eyes. And Starr crept out quietly under that stare; that stare which was almost — *godlike.*

The next day Colin noticed that the claymen moved.

"Frankenstein," Colin mumbled. "I am Frankenstein." His voice sank to a whisper. "I'm not like Frankenstein. I'm like God. Yes, like God."

He sank to his knees before the table-top. The two little men and women nodded gravely at him. He could see thumb-prints in their flesh, his thumb-prints, where he'd smoothed out the skulls after inserting the brains. And yet they lived!

"Why not? Who knows anything about creation, about life? The human body, physiologically, is merely a mechanism adapted to react. Duplicate that mechanism *perfectly* and why won't it live? Life is electricity, perhaps.

I opened mine in terror. The idea so possessed my mind, that a thrill of fear ran through me, and I wished to exchange the ghastly image of my fancy for the realities around....I could not so easily get rid of my hideous phantom; still it haunted me....I recurred to my ghost story....O! if I could only contrive one which would frighten my reader as I myself had been frightened that night!...

Mary Shelley's Introduction to *Frankenstein or The Modern Prometheus* (1831)

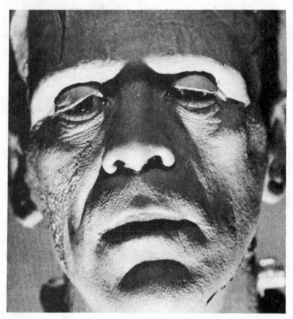

Well, so is thought. Put thought into perfect simulacra of humanity and they will live."

Colin whispered to himself, and the figures of clay looked up and nodded in eerie agreement.

"Besides, I'm running down. I'm losing my identity. Perhaps a part of my vital substance has been transferred, incorporated in these new bodies. My — my disease — that might account for it. But I can find out."

Yes, he could find out. If these figures were animated by Colin's life, then he could control their actions, just as he controlled the actions of his own body. He created them, gave them a part of his life. They *were* him.

He crouched there in the barred room, thinking, concentrating. And the figures moved. The two men moved up to the two women, grasped their arms, and danced a sedate minuet to a mentally-hummed tune; a grotesque dance of little clay dolls, a horrid mockery of life.

Colin closed his eyes, sank back trembling. It was true!

The effort of concentration had covered him with perspiration. He panted, exhausted. His own body felt weakened, drained, And why not? He had directed four minds at once, performed actions with four bodies. It was too much. But it was real.

"I'm God," he muttered. "God."

But what to do about it? He was a lunatic, shut away in an asylum. How to use his power?

"Must experiment, first," he said aloud.

"What?"

Doctor Starr had entered, unobserved. Colin cast a hasty glance at the table, found to his relief that the mannikins were motionless.

"I was just observing that I must experiment with my clay figures," he said, hastily.

The doctor arched his eyebrows. "Really? Well you know, Colin, I've been thinking. Perhaps this work here isn't so good for you. You look peaked, tired. I'm inclined to think you're hurting yourself with all this; afraid hereafter I'll have to forbid your modelling work."

"Forbid it?"

Doctor Starr nodded.

"But you can't — just when I've — I mean, you can't! It's all I've got, all that keeps me going, alive. Without it I'll —"

"Sorry."

"You can't."

"I'm the doctor, Colin. Tomorrow we'll take away the clay. I'm giving you a chance to find yourself, man, to live again —"

Colin had never been violent until now. The doctor was surprised to find lunatic fingers clawing at his throat, digging for the jugular vein with surgically skilled fingers. He went over backwards with a bang, and fought the madman until the aroused guards came and dragged Colin off. They tossed him on his bunk and the doctor left.

It was dark when Colin emerged from a world of hate. He lay alone. They had gone, the day had gone. Tomorrow they and the day would return, taking away his figures — his beloved figures. His *living* figures! Would they crumple them up and destroy them, destroy actual *life?* It was murder!

Colin sobbed bitterly, as he thought of his dreams. What he had meant to do with his power — why, there were no limits! He could have built dozens, hundreds of figures, learned to concentrate mentally until he could operate a horde of them at will. He would have created a little world of his own; a world of creatures subservient to him. Creatures for companionship, for his slaves. Fashioning different type of bodies, yes, and different types of brains. He might have reared a private little civilization.

And more. He might have created a race. A new race. A race that bred. A race that was developed to aid him. A hundred tiny figures, hands trained, teeth filed, could saw through his bars. A hundred tiny figures to attack the guards, to free him. Then out into the world with an

army of clay; a tiny army, but one that could burrow deeply in the earth, travel hidden and unseen into high places. Perhaps, some day, a world of little clay men, trained by him. Men that didn't fight stupid wars to drive their fellows mad. Men without the brutal emotions of savages, the hungers and lusts of beasts. Wipe out flesh! Substitute godly clay!

But it was over. Perhaps he was mad, dreaming of these things. It was over. And one thing he knew: without the clay he would be madder still. Tonight he could feel it, feel his body slipping. His eyes, staring at the moonlight, didn't seem to be a part of his own form any longer. They were watching from the floor, or from over in the corner. His lips moved, but he didn't feel his face. His voice spoke, and it seemed to come from the ceiling rather than from his throat. He was crumpling himself, like a mangled clay figure.

The afternoon's excitement had done it. The great discovery, and then Starr's stupid decision. Starr! He'd caused all this. He was responsible. He'd drive him to madness, to a horrid, unnamed mentally-diseased state he was too blind to comprehend. Starr had sentenced him to death. If only he could sentence Starr!

Perhaps he could.

What was that? The thought came from far away — inside his head, outside his head. He couldn't place his head. He couldn't place his thoughts any more — body going to pieces like this. What was it now?

Perhaps he could kill Starr.

How?

Find out Starr's plans, his ideas.

How?

Send a clay man.

What?

Send a clay man. This afternoon you concentrated on bringing them to life. They live. Animate one. He'll creep under the door, walk down the hall, listen to Starr. If you animate the body, *you'll* hear Starr.

Thoughts buzzing so....

But how can I do that? Clay is clay. Feet would wear out long before they got down the hall and back. Clay ears — perfect though they may be — would shatter under the conveyance of actual sounds.

Think. Make the thoughts stop buzzing. There is a way....

Yes, there was a way! Colin gasped. His insanity, his doom, were his salvation! If his faculties were being disorganized, and he had the power of projecting himself into clay, why not project special faculties into the images? Project his hearing into the clay ears, by concentration? Remodel clay feet until they were identical replicas of his own, then concentrate on walking? His body, his senses, were falling apart. Put them into clay!

He laughed as he lit the lamp, seized a tiny figure and began to recarve the feet. He kicked off his shoes, studied carefully, looked at the charts, worked, laughed, worked

The Man From the Top of the Mind
David Wagoner

From immaculate construction to half death,
See him: the light bulb screwed into his head,
The vacuum tube of his sex, the electric eye.
What lifts his foot? What does he do for breath?

His nickel steel, oily from neck to wrist,
Glistens as though by sunlight where he stands.
Nerves bought by the inch and muscles on a wheel
Spring in the triple-jointed hooks of his hands.

As plug to socket, or flange upon a beam,
Two become one; yet what is he to us?
We cry, "Come, marry the bottom of our minds.
Grant us the strength of your impervium."

But clad in a seamless skin, he turns aside
To do the tricks ordained by his transistors—
His face impassive, his arms raised from the dead,
His switch thrown one way into animus.

Reach for him now, and he will flicker with light,
Divide preposterous numbers by unknowns,
Bump through our mazes like a genius rat,
Or trace his concentric echoes to the moon.

Then, though we beg him, "Love us, hold us fast,"
He will stalk out of focus in the air,
Make gestures in an elemental mist,
And falter there—as we will falter here

And turns in rage upon our horrible shapes—
When the automaton pretends to dream
Those nightmares, trailing shreds of his netherworld,
Who must be slaughtered backward into time.

— and it was done. Then he lay back on the bed in darkness, thinking.

The clay figure was climbing down from the table. It was sliding down the leg, reaching the floor. Colin felt his feet tingle with shock as they hit the floor. Yes! *His* feet.

The floor trembled, thundered. Of course. Tiny vibrations, unnoticed by humans, audible to clay ears. *His* ears.

Another part of him — Colin's actual eyes — saw the little creeping figure scuttle across the floor, saw it squeeze under the door. Then darkness, and Colin sweated on the bed, concentrating.

Clay Colin could not see. He had no eyes. But instinct, memory guided.

Colin walked in the giant world. The foot came out, the foot of Colossus. Colin edged closer to the woodwork as the trampling monster came down, crashing again at the floor with monstrous vibrations.

Then Colin walked. He found the right door by instinct — the fourth door down. He crept under, stepped up a foot onto the carpet. At least, the grassy sward seemed a

foot high. His feet ached as the cutting rug bit sword-blades into his soles. From above, the thunder of voices. Great titans roared and bellowed a league in the air.

Doctor Starr and Professor Jerris. Jerris was all right; he had vision. But Starr....

Colin crouched under the mighty barrier of the arm-chair, crept up the mountainside to the great peaks of Starr's bony knees. He strained to distinguish words in the bellowing.

"This man Colin is done for, I tell you. Incipient break-down. Tried to attack me this afternoon when I told him I was removing his clay dolls. You'd think they were live pets of his. Perhaps he thinks so."

Colin clung to the trousers below the knees. Blind, he could not know if he would be spied; but he must cling close, high, to catch words in the tumult.

Jerris was speaking.

"Perhaps he thinks so. Perhaps they are. At any rate — what are you doing with a doll on your leg?"

Doll on your leg? Colin!

Colin on the bed in his room tried desperately to with-draw life; tried to withdraw hearing and sensation from the limbs of his clay self, but too late. There was an in-credulous roar; something reared out and grasped him, and then there was an agonizing squeeze....

"When I found so astonishing a power placed within my hands, I hesitated a long time concerning the manner in which I should employ it. Although I possessed the capacity of bestowing animation, yet to prepare a frame for the reception of it, with all its intricacies of fibres, muscles, and veins, still remained a work of inconceivable difficulty and labour. I doubted at first whether I should attempt the creation of a being like myself, or one of simpler organization; but my imagination was too much exalted by my first success to permit me to doubt of my ability to give life to an animal as complex and wonderful as man." *Dr. Frankenstein*

Mary Shelley, *Frankenstein or The Modern Promotheus* (1831)

In 1392 Pierre Recordi, a Carmelite friar, was sentenced to imprisonment for life for invoking demons and making wax images to win the love of women. He moulded the wax with his own blood and spittle (magically mingling his own body with the woman's body represented by the image). Then he buried the image under the woman's threshold. He said he had seduced three women in this way and had given thanks to Satan with sacrifices afterwards.

J. Trachtenburg, *Jewish Magic and Superstition* (1939)

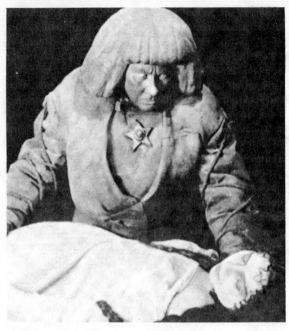

Colin sank back in bed, sank back into a world of red, swimming light.

Sun shone in Colin's face. He sat up. Had he dreamed?

"Dreamed?" he whispered.

He whispered again. "Dreamed?"

He couldn't hear. He was deaf.

His ears, his hearing faculty, had been focused on the clay figure, and it was destroyed last night when Starr crushed it. Now he was deaf!

The thought was insanity. Colin swung himself out of bed in panic, then toppled to the floor.

He couldn't walk!

The feet were on the clay figure, he'd willed it, and now it was crushed. He couldn't walk!

Disassociation of his faculties, his members. It was real, then! His ears, his legs, had in some mysterious way been lent vitally to that crushed clay man. Now he had lost them. Thank heaven he hadn't sent his eyes!

But it was horror to stare at the stumps where his legs had been; horror to feel in his ears for bony ridges no longer there. It was horror and it was hate. Starr had done this. Killed a man, crippled him.

Right then and there. Colin planned it all. He had the power. He could animate his clay figures, and then give them a *special* life as well. By concentrating, utilizing his peculiar physical disintegration, he could put part of himself into clay. Very well, then. Starr would pay.

Colin stayed in bed. When Starr came in the afternoon he did not rise. Starr mustn't see his legs, or realize that he could no longer hear. Starr was talking, perhaps about the clay figure he'd found last night, clinging to his leg; the clay figure he'd destroyed. Perhaps he spoke of destroying these clay figures that he now gathered up, together with the rest of the clay. Perhaps he asked after Colin's health; why he was in bed.

Colin feigned lethargy, the introspection of the schizoid. And Starr gathered up the rest of the clay and went away.

Then Colin smiled. He pulled out the tiny clay form from under the sheets; the one he'd hidden there. It was a perfect man, unusually muscled arms, and very long fingernails. The teeth, too, were very good. But the figure was incomplete. It had no face.

Colin began to work, very fast there as the twilight gathered. He brought a mirror and as he worked on the figure he smiled at himself as though sharing a secret jest with someone — or something. Darkness fell, and still Colin worked from memory alone; worked delicately, skillfully, like an artist, like a creator, breathing life into clay. Life into clay....

"I tell you the damned thing *was* alive! Jerris shouted. He'd lost his temper at last, forgot his superior in office. "I saw it!"

Starr smiled.

"It was clay, and I crushed it," he answered. "Let's not argue any longer."

Jerris shrugged. Two hours of speculation. Tomorrow he'd see Colin himself, find out what the man was doing. He was a genius, even though mad. Starr was a fool. He'd evidently aggravated Colin to the point of physical illness, taking away his clay.

Jerris shrugged again. The clay — and last night, the memory of that tiny, perfectly formed figure clinging to Starr's pants-leg where nothing could have *stuck* for long. It had *clung*. And when Starr crushed it, there had been a framework of clay bones protruding, a viscera hung out, and it had writhed — or seemed to writhe in the light.

"Stop shrugging and go to bed," Starr chuckled. It was matter-of-fact chuckle, and Jerris heeded it. "Quit worrying about a nut. Colin's crazy, and from now on I'll treat him as such. Been patient long enough. Have to use force. And — I wouldn't talk about clay figures any longer if I were you."

The tone was a command. Jerris gave a final shrug of acquiescence and left the room.

Starr switched off the light and prepared to doze there at the night-desk. Jerris knew his habits.

Jerris walked down the hall. Strange, how this business upset him! Seeing the clay figure this afternoon had really made him quite sick. The work was so perfect, so wonderfully accurate in miniature! And yet the forms were clay, just clay. They hadn't moved as Starr kneaded them in his fists. Clay ribs smashed in, and clay eyes popped from actual sockets and rolled over the tabletop — nauseous! And the little clay hairs, the shreds of clay skin so skilfully overlaid! A tiny dissection, this destruction. Colin, mad or sane, was a genius.

Jerris shrugged, this time to himself. What the devil! He blinked awake.

And then he saw — it.

Like a rat. A little rat scurring down the hall, upright, on two legs instead of four. A little rat without fur,

without a tail. A little rat that cast the perfect tiny shadow of — *a man!*

It had a face, and it looked up. Jerris almost fancied he saw its eyes *flash* at him. It was a little brown rat made of clay — no, it was a little clay man like those Colin made. A little clay man, running swiftly towards Starr's door, crawling under it. A perfect little clay man, alive!

Jerris gasped. He was crazy, like the rest, like Colin. And yet it had run into Starr's office, it was moving, it had eyes and a face and it was clay.

Jerris acted. He ran — not towards Starr's door, but down the hall to Colin's room. He felt for keys; he had them. It was a long moment before he fumbled at the lock and opened the door, another before he found the lights, and switched them on.

And it was a terribly long moment he spent staring at the thing on the bed — the thing with stumpy legs, lying sprawled back in a welter of sculpturing-tools, with a mirror flat across its chest, staring up at a sleeping face that was not a face.

The moment *was* long. Screaming must have come from Starr's office for perhaps thirty seconds before Jerris heard it. Screaming turned into moans and still Jerris stared into the face that was not a face; the face that changed before his eyes, melting away, scratched away by invisible hands into a pulp.

It happened like that. Something wiped out the face of the man on the bed, tore the head from the neck. And the moaning rose from down the hall.

Jerris ran. He was the first to reach the office, by a good minute. He saw what he expected to see.

Starr lay back in his chair, his head on one side. The little clay man had done its job and Doctor Starr was quite dead. The tiny brown figure had dug perfectly-formed talons into the sleeping throat, and with surgical skill applied talons, and perhaps teeth, to the jugular at precisely the most fatal spot in the vein. Starr died before he could dislodge the diabolically clever image of a man, but his last wild clawing had torn away the face and head.

Jerris ripped the monstrous mannikin off and crushed it; crushed it to a brown pulp between his fingers before others arrived in the room.

Then he stooped down to the floor and picked up the torn head with the mangled face, the miniature, carefully-modelled face that grinned in triumph, grinning in death.

Jerris shrugged himself into a shiver as he crushed into bits the little clay face of Colin, the creator.

I saw the pale student of unhallowed arts kneeling beside the thing he had put together. I saw the hideous phantasm of a man stretched out....

Mary Shelley's Introduction to *Frankenstein or The Modern Prometheus* (1831)

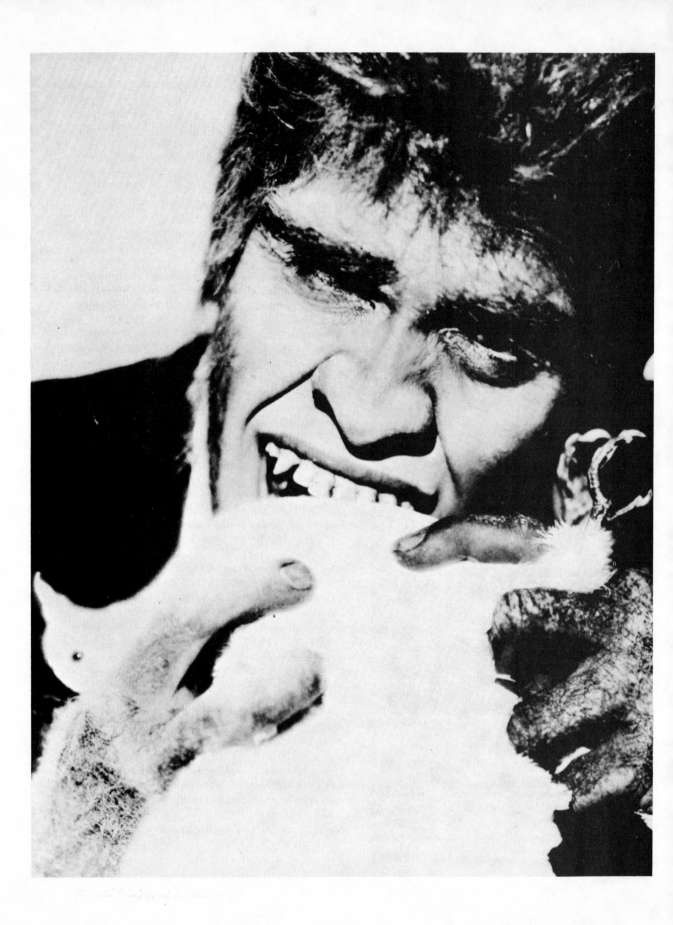

from A Dream of Dracula
Energy Without Grace, The Atavistic Revolution
Altamont, Dec. 6, 1969
Leonard Wolf

Mick Jagger. Red-lipped and twitching, the young, smirking, brilliant vampire of the air waves, flinging incoherent, brightly colored fantasies to his beseeching fans.

He's arriving at Altamont: that great, free festival of love. Jiggling. Mick Jagger. Jiggling. Hurrying to get right in there. Into the holes opened in the upturned faces. Thousands of them. Hundreds of thousands of faces in the sprawling meadows waiting for the one, the only, the true performance, the one that achieves madness. Waiting for the music to reassure them: Altamont, a funky, electronic, neomedieval extravaganza with expensive textures, sophisticated raunchiness. Sensuality at once sly and berserk. The pale, dry figure with the carmine lips faking a trembling ecstasy to a music that is hard, compelled, hysteric. But also brilliant, to a point of genius. A musical understanding of the ugly, the drug-driven, the squalid, scrabbling at the transcendental. A music whose energy is so vast that one almost does not notice that when it stops, there is no peace.

He mounts the bandstand as the sun goes down. The three hundred thousand have been there for hours, entertained by half a dozen other rock groups, but now Belial himself is here and the energy of expectation sweeps across the meadow like wind through a field of grain.

The demonic clown reaches for the green velvet (or is it rubber?)-clad microphone. Jagger, full-lipped, sharp-faced as a starved rat, jiggles; his enormously intelligent blue eyes sweep the crowd, calculating what there is to work with. The pulsations of the music seem to be hurrying the blood. Jagger vibrates. The evening breeze and an impatient gesture of his hand send his scarf and cloak out behind him in a nervous flutter. The microphone is the hypnotic center of the encounter that is about to take place. It is green and rigid, with a bulbous tip, and Jagger crowds the tip, opening his mouth wide, gaping over it, gaping like an insatiable fish as he dares the crowd to guess what he's doing. His lower jaw trembles. Belial, Asmodeus, Baal, whoever Jagger is, taunts the three hundred thousand. He crouches, croons, shouts, leaps, carrying the microphone with him. His hair falls over one eye; with a practiced gesture of impatience he flings it away. His mouth gapes and gapes and the music tears at the dusk.

The faces around the stage are baked in a rich red light. Hieronymous Bosch in the service of the festival's promoters has arranged them: there are the Hell's Angels, trivial demons, earning their beer as they guard the floodlights or hustle impassioned maenads from the stage.

In the vampire's embrace, any number of sexual dilemmas are out-witted. His kiss permits all unions: men and women; men and men; women and women; fathers and daughters; mothers and sons. Moreover, his is an easy love that evades the usual failures of the flesh. It is the triumph of passivity, unembarrassing, sensuous, throbbing, violent and cruel.

And it stands for death. Or Life-in-Death. Death in motion. A style of monstrosity congenial to our age. It is, says Hanns Heinz Ewer's Lotte, "a wild insanity...a new, searing creed is emerging...the insanity of blood."

Leonard Wolf, *A Dream of Dracula* (1972)

There he stood, enfolded in darkness. Dracula. Our *Eidolon,* the willing representative of the temptations, and the crimes, of the Age of Energy. He is huge, and we admire size; strong, and we admire strength. He moves with the confidence of a creature that has energy, power, and will. Granted that he has energy without grace, power without responsibility, and that his will is an exercise in death. We need only to look a little to one side to see how tempting is the choice he makes: available immortality. He has collected on the devil's bargain: the infinitely stopped moment. What does it matter that his flesh is dead? He can move, he can kiss and kill. With only a moderate intake of blood, he can stay young.

Leonard Wolf, *A Dream of Dracula* (1972)

Medusa
William Alexander Percy

There is a tale of brow and clotted hair
Thrust in the window of a banquet room
Which froze eternally the revellers there,
The lights full on them in their postured doom:
The queen still held the carmine to her lips,
The king's mouth stood wide open for its laugh,
The jester's rigid leer launched silent quips;
Only a blind man moved and tapped his staff.
I cannot guess that physiognomy
The sight of which could curdle into stone
The gazer, though pities, horrors, terrors I
Have made encounter of and sometimes known.
But I knew one who turned to stone with terror
Of facing quietly a flawless mirror.

And the stoned freaks swaying by now to a music that they can no longer hear.

The many-headed beast opens its mouth. Jagger seems ready to swallow the microphone in his. A spotlight catches his eyes and they shine like stars on a frosty night.

A fat girl can no longer stand it. Her clothes are off. Too naked to be ashamed, responding to lust or an even more private frenzy, she sways toward the stage. So much white flesh offering itself to an indifferent god who leaps in epileptic joy while his face takes on the look of a prim Bryn Mawr virgin in the arms of a coal-black lover.

"I need a good woman," he groans, "to keep me satisfied."

And the wallowing, white flesh offers herself, in the interests of music, love, the movie industry, or an over-whelming selfpity, but the offer is spurned. Belial's mouth is busy, and she is lead away, weeping, all that soft generosity wasted.

Meanwhile, somewhere in that field of desire and Coca-Colas, hashish, LSD and old-fashioned, ordinary picnic pleasure, a child is born.

And then, the trouble that has been slowly building up around the stage quickens its pace. The Angels, using pool cues, break up or intensify a fight.

Grace Slick, whose homely beauty in the place breathes a loveliness bizarrely out of keeping with the aura surrounding Jagger, repeats softly, "Easy. Easy." If he heard it, her voice could pacify the Nemean lion. But despite the loudspeakers (which, anyhow, kept breaking down) her gentleness seems not to reach where it is needed.

"You got to keep your bodies off each other," she says, "unless you intend love."

It does no good. Something is doomed to happen down there. The greedy cameras want it. It may be that the crowd — touched by the various frenzies that have come its way that day — also wants it. But suddenly there is a tall, green-suited young black man in a splatter of con-fusing movement to the left of the stage. Someone is holding — or not holding him; someone is crying out; someone has a knife; someone has a gun. Someone is pushing, shoving, screaming. The man in the green suit is dead.

Mick Jagger is at his lascivious green microphone, and Altamont, the free festival of joy, goes on. From one of the towers built to hold the spotlights, a single watcher who has escaped the attention of the Angels of Hell looks down. Behind him in the sable night, the stars shine. And shine.

The Black Rider flung back his hood, and behold! he had a kingly crown; and yet upon no head visible was it set. The red fires shone between it and the mantled shoulders vast and dark. From a mouth unseen there came a deadly laughter.

J.R.R. Tolkien, *The Lord of the Rings* (1965)

The Bridge of Dread
Edwin Muir

But when you reach the Bridge of Dread
Your flesh will huddle into its nest
For refuge and your naked head
Creep in the casement of your breast,

And your great bulk grow thin and small
And cower within its cage of bone,
While dazed you watch your footsteps crawl
Toadlike across the leagues of stone.

If they come, you will not feel
About your feet the adders slide,
For still your head's demented wheel
Whirls on your neck from side to side

Searching for danger. Nothing there.
And yet your breath will whistle and beat
As on you push the stagnant air
That breaks in rings about your feet

Like dirty suds. If there should come
Some bodily terror to that place,
Great knotted serpents dread and dumb,
You would accept it as a grace.

Until you see a burning wire
Shoot from the ground. As in a dream
You'll wonder at that flower of fire,
That weed caught in a burning beam.

And you are past. Remember then,
Fix deep within your dreaming head
Year, hour or endless moment when
You reached and crossed the Bridge of Dread.

I looked out over the beautiful expanse, bathed in soft yellow moonlight till it was almost as light as day. In the soft light the distant hills became melted, and the shadows in the valleys and gorges of velvety blackness. The mere beauty seemed to cheer me; there was peace and comfort in every breath I drew. There was some sense of freedom in the vast expanse, inaccessible though it was to me, as compared with the narrow darkness of the courtyard.

But I am not in heart to describe beauty, for when I had seen the view I explored further; doors, doors, doors everywhere, and all locked and bolted. In no place save from the windows in the castle walls is there an available exit.

The castle is a veritable prison, and I am a prisoner! I seemed to want a breath of fresh air, though it were of the night. I am beginning to feel this nocturnal existence tell on me. It is destroying my nerve. I start at my own shadow, and am full of all sorts of horrible imaginings.

Jonathan Harker's Journal, 8, May.

THE PRISONER

As I leaned from the window my eye was caught by something moving. I was at first interested and somewhat amused, for it is wonderful how small a matter will interest and amuse a man when he is a prisoner. But my very feelings changed to repulsion and terror. At first I could not believe my eyes. I thought it was some trick of the moonlight, some weird effect of shadow; but I kept looking, and it could be no delusion. I saw the whole man emerge from the window and begin to crawl down the castle wall over the dreadful abyss, *FACE DOWN* with his cloak spreading out around him like great wings.

What manner of man is this, or what manner of creature is it in the semblance of man? I feel the dread of this horrible place overpowering me; I am in fear — awful fear — and there is no escape for me; I am encompassed about with terrors that I dare not think of....

Jonathan Harker's Journal, Evening, 12, May.

from Investigating The Unexplained
The Olitiau (1932)
Ivan T. Sanderson

...I regained shallow water and was floundering about among the slippery boulders, Gerald suddenly yelled "Look out!" Whipping around toward him, I was confronted by an apparition, such as I had never imagined existed, about fifteen feet away and just above the level of my eyes. It was coming straight at me awfully fast, so I ducked down into the water....We had measured the river at that point, and it was forty feet wide, plus or minus a couple of feet. The wings of this creature spread across at least a third of this span and, as seen by Gerald looking downstream and I looking upstream, and judging by the fact that it was dead center, there appeared to both of us to be the same width of sky between its wing-tips and the trees that lined the banks of the river to either side. Our diaries say "at least a twelve-foot wingspan." The size of this creature really shook me, because there are no birds with such a wingspan in Africa. In fact, the only bird with a comparable one is the great condor of the Andes. Worse was the fact that I got a very good and close look at its face and, to put it facetiously, "That weren't no boid." Its lower jaw hung down and, as the last light of the sun was directly shining onto its face, I could have counted the huge white teeth if I had had the time. They were a good two inches long, all about the same length, and all equally separated by spaces of the same width.

Now this is the one feature of this "apparition" that I will admit would seem to be more reptilian than mammalian. However, some bats have rather small canines, so that their jaws as seen from the front, do seem to present a strangely regular semicircle of about equally-sized teeth. This animal that flew at me had a muzzle more like that of a monkey than of a dog or of any kind of reptile, in that it was not drawn out to a point. The whole animal was coal black in color, including the wings, which were quite opaque. It did not appear to be hairy, but then neither do most bats until you examine them in your hand. The few strokes of its flight that I saw before I "went to ground," as it were, were very leisurely for the speed that it was going, and they were of the "flapping" motion of a fruit bat rather than the clawing of the lesser bats, which actually "swim" through the air.

A Day
John Porter

There is a day of the dragon
when men's eyes flash
and their minds coil behind
like wreaths of smoke;
Days when the trees are statues
crystallised from the atmosphere
in fragile linking cracks.

Haunted
Siegfried Sassoon

Evening was in the wood, louring with storm.
A time of drought had sucked the weedy pool
And baked the channels; birds had done with song.
Thirst was a dream of fountains in the moon,
Or willow-music blown across the water
Leisurely sliding on by weir and mill.

Uneasy was the man who wandered, brooding,
His face a little whiter than the dusk.
A drone of sultry wings flicker'd in his head.
The end of sunset burning thro' the boughs
Died in a smear of red; exhausted hours
Cumber'd, and ugly sorrows hemmed him in.

He thought: 'Somewhere there's thunder,' as he strove
To shake off dread; he dared not look behind him,
But stood, the sweat of horror on his face.

He blunder'd down a path, trampling on thistles,
In sudden race to leave the ghostly trees.
And: 'Soon I'll be in open fields,' he thought,
And half remembered starlight on the meadows,
Scent of mown grass and voices of tired men,
Fading along the field-paths; home and sleep
And cool-swept upland spaces, whispering leaves,
And far off the long churring night-jar's note.

But something in the wood, trying to daunt him,
Led him confused in circles through the thicket.
He was forgetting his old wretched folly,
And freedom was his need; his throat was choking.
Barbed brambles gripped and clawed him round his
  legs,
And he floundered over snags and hidden stumps.
Mumbling: 'I will get out! I must get out!'
Butting and thrusting up the baffling gloom,
Pausing to listen in a space 'twixt thorns,
He peers around with peering, frantic eyes.

An evil creature in the twilight looping,
Flapped blindly in his face. Beating it off,
He screeched in terror, and straightway something
  clambered
Heavily from an oak, and dropped, bent double,
To shamble at him zigzag, squat and bestial.

Headlong he charges down the wood, and falls
With roaring brain—agony—the snap't spark—
And blots of green and purple in his eyes.
Then the slow fingers groping on his neck,
And at his heart the strangling clasp of death.

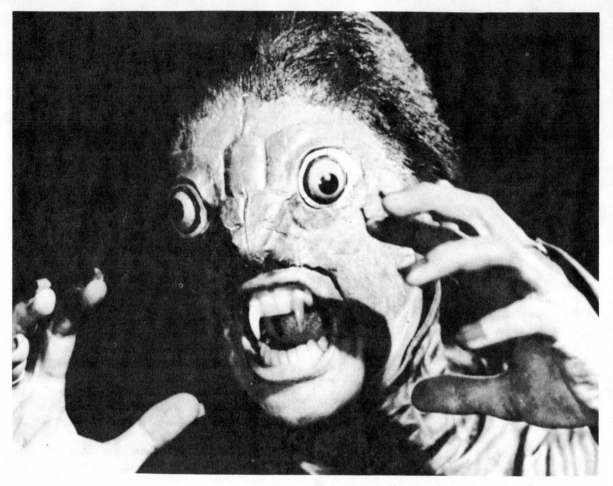

The Curse of Yig
Zealia Bishop

In 1925 I went into Oklahoma looking for snake lore, and I came out with a fear of snakes that will last me the rest of my life. I admit it is foolish, since there are natural explanations for everything I saw and heard, but it masters me none the less. If the old story had been all there was to it, I would not have been so badly shaken. My work as an American Indian ethnologist has hardened me to all kinds of extravagant legendry, and I know that simple white people can beat the redskins at their own game when it comes to fanciful inventions. But I can't forget what I saw with my own eyes at the insane asylum in Guthrie.

I called at that asylum because a few of the oldest settlers told me I would find something important there. Neither Indians nor white men would discuss the snake-god legends I had come to trace. The oil-boom newcomers, of course, knew nothing of such matters, and the red men and old pioneers were plainly frightened when I spoke of them. Not more than six or seven people mentioned the asylum, and those who did were careful to talk in whispers. But the whisperers said that Dr. McNeill could show me a very terrible relic and tell me all I wanted to know. He

could explain why Yig, the half-human father of serpents, is a shunned and feared object in central Oklahoma, and why old settlers shiver at the secret Indian orgies which make the autumn days and nights hideous with the ceaseless beating of tom-toms in lonely places.

It was with the scent of a hound on the trail that I went to Guthrie, for I had spent many years collecting data on the evolution of serpent-worship among the Indians. I had always felt, from well-defined undertones of legend and archeology, that great Quetzalcoatl — benign snake-God of the Mexicans — had had an older and darker prototype; and during recent months I had well-nigh proved it in a series of researches stretching from Guatemala to the Oklahoma plains. But everything was tantalizing and incomplete, for above the border the cult of the snake was hedged about by fear and furtiveness.

Now it appeared that a new and copious source of data was about to dawn, and I sought the head of the asylum with an eagerness I did not try to cloak. Doctor McNeill was a small clean-shaven man of somewhat advanced years, and I saw at once from his speech and manner that he was a scholar of no mean attainments in many branches outside his profession. Grave and doubtful when I first made known my errand, his face grew thoughtful as he carefully scanned my credentials and the letter of introduction which a kindly old ex-Indian agent had given me.

"So you've been studying the Yig-legend, eh?" he reflected sententiously. "I know that many of our Oklahoma ethnologists have tried to connect it with Quetzalcoatl, but I don't think any of them have traced the intermediate steps so well. You've done remarkable work for a man as young as you seem to be, and you certainly deserve all the data we can give.

"I don't suppose old Major Moore or any of the others told you what it is I have here. They don't like to talk about it, and neither do I. It is very tragic and very horrible, but that is all. I refuse to consider it anything supernatural. There's a story about it that I'll tell you after you see it — a devilish sad story, but one that I won't call magic. It merely shows the potency that belief has over some people. I'll admit there are times when I feel a shiver that's more than physical, but in daylight I set all that down to nerves. I'm not a young fellow any more, alas!

"To come to the point, the thing I have is what you might call a victim of Yig's curse — a physically living victim. We don't let the bulk of the nurses see it, although most of them know it's here. There are just two steady old chaps whom I let feed it and clean out its quarters — used to be three, but good old Stevens passed on a few years ago. I suppose I'll have to break in a new group pretty soon; or change much, and we old boys can't last forever. Maybe the ethics of the near future will let us give it a merciless release, but it's hard to tell.

"Did you see that single ground-glass basement window over in the east wing when you came up the drive? That's where it is. I'll take you there myself now. You needn't make any comment. Just look through the movable panel in the door and thank God the light isn't any stronger. Then I'll tell you the story — or as much as I've been able to piece together."

We walked downstairs very quietly, and did not talk as we threaded the corridors of seemingly deserted basement. Doctor McNeill unlocked a gray-painted steel door, but it was only a bulkhead leading to a further stretch of hallway. At length he paused before a door marked B 116, opened a small observation panel which he could use only by standing on tiptoe, and pounded several times upon the painted metal, as if to arouse the occupant, whatever it might be.

A faint stench came from the aperture as the doctor unclosed it, and I fancied his pounding elicited a kind of low, hissing response. Finally he motioned me to replace him at the peep-hole, and I did so with a causeless and increasing tremor. The barred, ground-glass window, close to the earth outside, admitted only a feeble and uncertain pallor; and I had to look into the malodorous den for several seconds before I could see what was crawling and wriggling about on the straw-covered floor, emitting every now and then a weak and vacuous hiss. Then the shadowed outlines began to take shape, and I perceived that the squirming entity bore some remote resemblance to a human form laid flat on its belly. I clutched at the door-handle for support as I tried to keep from fainting.

The moving object was almost of human size, and entirely devoid of clothing. It was absolutely hairless, and its tawny-looking back seemed subtly squamous in the dim ghoulish light.

Around the shoulders it was rather speckled and brownish, and the head was very curiously flat. As it looked up to hiss at me I saw that the beady little black eyes were damnably anthropoid, but I could not bear to study them long. They fastened themselves on me with a horrible persistence, so that I closed the panel graspingly and left the creature to wriggle about unseen in its matted straw and spectral twilight. I must have reeled a bit, for I saw that the doctor was gently holding my arm as he guided me away. I was stuttering over and over again:

"B-but for God's sake, what is it?"

Doctor McNeill told me the story in his private office as I sprawled opposite him in an easy-chair. The gold and crimson of late afternoon changed to the violet of early dusk, but still I sat awed and motionless. I resented every ring of the telephone and every whir of the buzzer, and I could have cursed the nurses and interns whose knocks now and then summoned the doctor briefly to the outer office. Night came, and I was glad my host switched on all the lights. Scientist though I was, my zeal for research was half forgotten amid such breathless ecstasies of fright as a small boy might feel when whispered witch-tales go the rounds of the chimney-corner.

It seems that Yig, the snake-god of the central plains tribes — presumably the primal source of the more southerly Quetzalcoatl or Kukulcan — was an odd, half-anthropomorphic devil of highly arbitrary and capricious nature. He was not wholly evil, and was usually quite well disposed toward those who gave proper respect to him and his children, the serpents; but in the autumn he became abnormally ravenous and had to be driven away by means of suitable rites. That was why the tom-toms in the Pawnee, Wichita, and Caddo country pounded ceaselessly week in and week out in August, September, and October; and why the medicine-men made strange noises with rattles and whistles curiously like those of the Aztecs and Mayas.

Yig's chief trait was a relentless devotion to his children — a devotion so great that the redskins almost feared to protect themselves from the venomous rattlesnakes which thronged the region. Frightful clandestine tales hinted of his vengeance upon mortals who flouted him or wreaked harm upon his wriggling progeny; his chosen method being to turn his victim, after suitable tortures, to a spotted snake.

In the old days of the Indian Territory, the doctor went on, there was not quite so much secrecy about Yig. The plains tribes, less cautious than the desert nomads and Pueblos, talked quite freely of their legends and autumn ceremonies with the first Indian agents, and let considerable of the lore spread out through the neighboring regions of white settlement. The great fear came in the land-rush days of eighty-nine, when some extraordinary incidents had been rumored, and the rumors sustained, by what seemed to be hideously tangible proofs.

Indians said that the new white men did not know how to get on with Yig, and afterward the settlers came to take that theory at face value. Now no old-timer in middle Oklahoma, white or red, could be induced to breathe a word about the snake-god except in vague hints. Yet after all, the doctor added with almost needless emphasis, the only truly authenticated horror had been a thing of pitiful tragedy rather than of bewitchment. It was all very material and cruel — even that last phase which had caused so much dispute.

Doctor McNeill paused and cleared his throat before getting down to his special story, and I felt a tingling sensation as when a theatre curtain rises. The thing had begun when Walker Davis and his wife Audrey left Arkansas to settle in the newly opened public lands in the spring of 1889, and the end had come in the country of the Wichitas — north of the Wichita River, in what is at present Caddo Country. There is a small village called Binger there now, and the railway goes through; but otherwise the place is less changed than other parts of Oklahoma. It is still a section of farms and ranches — quite productive in these days — since the great oil-fields do not come very close.

We — or our primitive forefathers — once believed that the return of the dead, unseen forces, and secret injurious powers were realities, and were convinced that they actually happened. Nowadays we no longer believe in them, we have _surmounted_ those modes of thought; but we do not feel quite sure of our new beliefs, and the old ones still exist within us ready to seize upon any confirmation.

Sigmund Freud, *The Uncanny The Complete Psychological Works of Sigmund Freud: Vol. XVII* (1919)

Walker and Audrey had come from Franklin County in the Ozarks with a canvas-topped wagon, two mules, an ancient and useless dog called Wolf, and all their household goods. They were typical hill-folk, youngish and perhaps a little more ambitious than most, and looked forward to a life of better returns for their hard work than they had had in Arkansas. Both were lean, raw-boned specimens; the man sandy, and gray-eyed, and the woman short and rather dark, with a black straightness of hair suggesting a slight Indian admixture.

In general, there was very little of distinction about them, and but for one thing their annals might not have differed from those of thousands of other pioneers who flocked into the new country at that time. That thing was Walker's almost epileptic fear of snakes, which some laid to prenatal causes, and some said came from a dark prophecy about his end with which an old Indian squaw had tried to scare him when he was small. Whatever the cause, the effect was marked indeed; for despite his strong general courage the very mention of a snake would cause him to grow faint and pale, while the sight of even a tiny specimen would produce a shock sometimes bordering on a convulsion seizure.

In reality, Slayer and Dragon, sacrificer and victim are of one mind behind the scenes, where there is no polarity of contraries....The Dragon-slayer is our friend; the Dragon must be pacified and made a friend of.

Ananda K. Coomaraswamy

The Davises started out early in the year, in the hope of being on their new land for the spring plowing. Travel was slow; for the roads were bad in Arkansas, while in the Territory there were great stretches of rolling hills and red, sandy barrens without any roads whatever. As the terrain grew flatter, the change from their native mountains depressed them more, perhaps, than they realized, but they found the people at the Indian agencies very affable, while most of the settled Indians seemed friendly and civil. Now and then they encountered a fellow-pioneer, with whom crude pleasantries and expressions of amiable rivalry were generally exchanged.

Owing to the season, there were not many snakes in evidence, so Walker did not suffer from his special temperamental weakness. In the earlier stages of the journey, too, there were no Indian snake legends to trouble him; for the transplanted tribes from the southeast do not share the wilder beliefs of their western neighbors. As fate would have it, it was a white man at Okmulgee in the Creek country who gave the Davises the first hint of the Yig beliefs; a hint which had a curiously fascinating effect on Walker, and caused him to ask questions very freely after that.

Before long Walker's fascination had developed into a bad case of fright. He took the most extraordinary precautions at each of the nightly camps, always clearing away whatever vegetation he found, and avoiding stony places whenever he could. Every clump of stunted bushes and every cleft in the great, slab-like rocks seemed to him now to hide malevolent serpents, while every human figure not obviously part of a settlement or emigrant train seemed to him a potential snake-god till nearness had proved the contrary. Fortunately no troublesome encounters came at this stage to shake his nerves still further.

As they approached the Kickapoo country they found it harder and harder to avoid camping near rocks. Finally it was no longer possible, and poor Walker was reduced to the puerile expedient of droning some of the rustic anti-snake charms he had learned in his boyhood. Two or three times a snake was really glimpsed, and these sights did not help the sufferer in his efforts to preserve composure.

On the twenty-second evening of the journey a savage wind made it imperative, for the sake of the mules, to camp in as sheltered a spot as possible; and Audrey persuaded her husband to take advantage of a cliff which rose uncommonly high above the dried bed of a former tributary of the Canadian River. He did not like the rocky cast of the place, but allowed himself to be overruled this once; leading the animals sullenly toward the protecting slope, which the nature of the ground would not allow the wagon to approach.

Audrey, examining the rocks near the wagon, mean-while noticed a singular sniffing on the part of the feeble old dog. Seizing a rifle, she followed his lead, and presently thanked her stars that she had forestalled Walker in her discovery. For there, snugly nested in the gap between two boulders, was a sight it would have done him no good to see. Visible only as one convoluted expanse, but perhaps comprising as many as three or four separate units, was a mass of lazy wriggling which could not be other than a brood of newborn rattlesnakes.

Anxious to save Walker from a trying shock, Audrey did not hesitate to act, but took the gun firmly by the barrel and brought the butt down again and again upon the writhing objects. Her own sense of loathing was great, but it did not amount to a real fear. Finally she saw that her task was done, and turned to cleanse the improvised bludgeon in the red sand and dry, dead grass near by. She must, she reflected, cover the nest up before Walker got back from tethering the mules. Old Wolf, tottering relic of mixed shepherd and coyote ancestry that he was, had vanished, and she feared he had gone to fetch his master.

Footsteps at that instant proved her fear well founded. A second more, and Walker had seen everything. Audrey made a move to catch him if he should faint, but he did no more than sway. Then the look of pure fright on his bloodless face turned slowly to something like mingled awe and anger, and he began to upbraid his wife in trembling tones.

"Gawd's sake, Aud, but why'd ye go for to do that? Hain't ye heerd all the things they've ben tellin' about this snake-devil Yig? Ye'd ought to a told me, and we'd a moved on. Don't ye know they's a devil-god what gets even if ye hurts his children? What for d'ye think the Injuns all dances and beats their drums in the fall about? This land's under a curse, I can tell ye — nigh every soul we've a-talked to sence we come in's said the same. Yig rules here, an' he comes out every fall for to git his victims and turn 'em into snakes. Why, Aud, they won't none of them Injuns acrost the Canayjin kill a snake for love nor money!

Gawd knows what ye done to yourself, gal, a-stompin' out a hull brood o' Yig's chillen. He'll git ye, sure, sooner or later, unlessen I kin buy a charm offen some o' the Injun medicine-men. He'll git ye, Aud, as sure's they's a Gawd in heaven — he'll come outa the night and turn ye into a crawlin' spotted snake!''

All the rest of the journey Walker kept up the frightened reproofs and prophecies. They crossed the Canadian near Newcastle, and soon afterward met with the first of the real plains Indians they had seen — a party of blanketed Wichitas, whose leader talked freely under the spell of the whisky offered him, and taught poor

Taken purely as a psychologem the hero represents the positive, favourable action of the unconscious, while the dragon is its negative and unfavourable action — not birth, but a devouring; not a beneficial and constructive deed, but greedy retention and destruction.

C.G. Jung, *Symbols of Transformation* (1956)

Walker a long-winded protective charm against Yig in exchange for a quart bottle of the same inspiring fluid. By the end of the week the chosen site in the Witchita country was reached, and the Davises made haste to trace their boundaries and perform the spring plowing before even beginning the construction of a cabin.

The region was flat, drearily windy, and sparse of natural vegetation, but promised great fertility under cultivation. Occasional outcroppings of granite diversified a soil of decomposed red sandstone, and here and there a great flat rock would stretch along the surface of the ground like a man-made floor. There seemed to be very few snakes, or possible dens for them; so Audrey at last persuaded Walker to build the one-room cabin over a vast, smooth slab of exposed stone. With such a flooring and with a good-sized fireplace the wettest weather might be defied — though it soon became evident that dampness was no salient quality of the district. Logs were hauled in the wagon from the nearest belt of woods, many miles toward the Wichita Mountains.

Walker built his wide-chimneyed cabin and crude barn with the aid of the other settlers, though the nearest one was over a mile away. In turn, he helped his helpers at similar house-raisings, so that many ties of friendship

A schizophrenic patient about a dream snake: "It is God's animal, it has such wonderful colours: green, blue, and white. The rattlesnake is green; it is very dangerous....The snake can have a human mind, it can have divine judgement; it is a friend to children. It would save the children who are needed to preserve human life."

S. Spielrein, *"On the psychological contents of a case of schizophrenia"* (1912)

sprang up between the new neighbors. There was no town worthy the name nearer than El Reno, on the railway thirty miles or more to the northeast; and before many weeks had passed, the people of the section had become very cohesive despite the wideness of their scattering. The Indians, a few of whom had begun to settle down on ranches, were for the most part harmless, though somewhat quarrelsome when fired by the liquid stimulation which found its way to them despite all Government bans.

Of all the neighbors the Davises found Joe and Sally Compton, who likewise hailed from Arkansas, the most helpful and congenial. Sally is still alive, known now as Grandma Compton; and her son Clyde, then an infant in arms, has become one of the leading men of the State. Sally and Audrey used to visit each other often for their cabins were only two miles apart; and in the long spring and summer afternoons they exchanged many a tale of old Arkansas and many a rumor about the new country.

Sally was very sympathetic about Walker's weakness regarding snakes, but perhaps did more to aggravate than cure the parallel nervousness which Audrey was acquiring through his incessant praying and prophesying about the curse of Yig. She was uncommonly full of gruesome snake stories, and produced a direfully strong impression with her acknowledged masterpiece — the tale of a man in Scott County who had been bitten by a whole horde of rattlers at once, and had swelled so monstrously from poison that his body had finally burst with a pop. Needless to say, Audrey did not repeat this anecdote to her husband, and she implored the Comptons to beware of starting it on the rounds of the countryside. It is to Joe's and Sally's credit that they heeded this plea with the utmost fidelity.

Walker did his corn-planting early, and in midsummer improved his time by harvesting a fair crop of the native grass of the region. With the help of Joe Compton he dug a well which gave a moderate supply of very good water, though he planned to sink an artesian later on. He did not run into many serious snake scares, and made his land as inhospitable as possible for wriggling visitors. Every now and then he rode over to the cluster of thatched, conical huts which formed the main village of the Wichitas, and talked long with the old men and shamans about the snake-god and how to nullify his wrath. Charms were always ready in exchange for whisky, but much of the information he got was far from reassuring.

Yig was a great god. He was bad medicine. He did not forget things. In the autumn his children were hungry and wild, too. All the tribes made medicine against Yig when the corn harvest came. They gave him some corn, and danced in proper regalia to the sound of whistle, rattle, and drum. They kept the drums pounding to drive Yig away, and called down the aid of Tirawa, whose children men are, even as the snakes are Yig's children. It was bad that the squaw of Davis killed the children of Yig. Let Davis say the charms many times when the corn harvest comes. Yig is Yig. Yig is a great god.

By the time the corn harvest did come, Walker had succeeded in getting his wife into a deplorably jumpy state. His prayers and borrowed incantations came to be a nuisance; and when the autumn rites of the Indians began, there was always a distant wind-borne pounding of tom-toms to lend an added background of the sinister. It was maddening to have the muffled clatter always stealing over the wide, red plains. Why would it never stop? Day and night, week on week, it was always going in exhaustless relays, as persistently as the red dusty winds that carried it. Audrey loathed it more than her husband did, for he saw in it a compensating element of protection. It was with this sense of a mighty, intangible bulwark against evil that he got in his corn crop and prepared cabin and stable for the coming winter.

The autumn was abnormally warm, and except for their primitive cookery the Davises found scant use for the stone fireplace Walker had built with such care. Something in the unnaturalness of the hot dust-clouds preyed on the nerves of all the settlers, but most of all on Audrey's and Walker's. The notions of hovering snake-curse and the weird, endless rhythm of the distant Indian drums formed a bad combination which any added element of the bizarre went far to render utterly unendurable.

Incomprehensible? But because you cannot understand a thing, it does not cease to exist.

Pascal, *Pensees* (1670)

Notwithstanding this strain, several festive gatherings were held at one or another of the cabins after the crops were reaped; keeping naively alive in modernity those curious rites of the harvest-home which are as old as human agriculture itself. Lafayette Smith, who came from southern Missouri and had a cabin about three miles east of Walker's, was a very passable fiddler; and his tunes did much to make the celebrants forget the monotonous beating of the distant tom-toms. Then Halloween drew near, and the settlers planned another frolic — this time, had they but known it, of a lineage older than even agriculture; the dread Witch-Sabbath of the primal pre-Aryans, kept alive through ages in the midnight blackness of secret woods, and still hinting at vague terrors under its latterday mask of comedy and lightness. Halloween was to fall on a Thursday, and the neighbors agreed to gather for their first revel at the Davis cabin.

It was on that thirty-first of October that the warm spell broke. The morning was gray and leaden, and by noon the incessant winds had changed from searingness to rawness. People shivered all the more because they were not prepared for the chill, and Walker Davis's old dog, Wolf, dragged himself wearily indoors to a place beside the hearth. But the distant drums still thumped on, nor were the white citizenry less inclined to pursue their chosen rite. As early as four in the afternoon the wagons began to

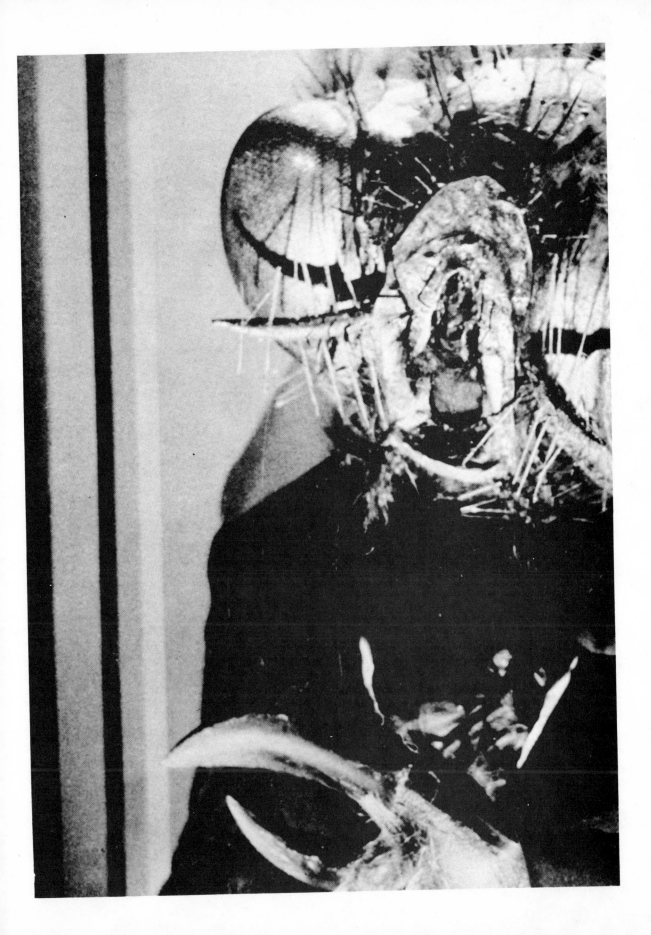

arrive at Walker's cabin; and in the evening, after a memorable barbecue, Lafayette Smith's fiddle inspired a very fair-sized company to great feats of saltatory grotesqueness in the one good-sized but crowded room. The younger folk indulged in the amiable inanities proper to the season, and now and then old Wolf would howl with doleful and spine-tickling ominousness at some especially spectral strain from Lafayette's squeaky violin — a device he had never heard before. Mostly, though, this battered veteran slept through the merriment, for he was past the age of active interests and lived largely in his dreams. Tom and Jennie Rigby had brought their collie Zeke along, but the canines did not fraternize. Zeke seemed strangely uneasy over something, and nosed around curiously all the evening.

Audrey and Walker made a fine couple on the floor, and Grandma Compton still likes to recall her impression of their dancing that night. Their worries seemed forgotten for the nonce, and Walker was shaved and trimmed into a surprising degree of spruceness. By ten o'clock all hands were healthily tired, and the guests began to depart family by family with many handshakings and bluff assurances of what a fine time everybody had had.

...It is quite within the bounds of possibility for a man to recognize the relative evil of his nature, but it is a rare and shattering experience for him to gaze into the face of absolute evil.

C.G. Jung, *Aion: Researches into the Phenomenology of the Self* (1959)

Tom and Jennie thought Zeke's eery howls as he followed them to their wagon were marks of regret at having to go home; though Audrey said it must be the far-away tom-toms which annoyed him, for the distant thumping was surely ghastly enough after the merriment within.

The night was bitterly cold, and for the first time Walker put a great log in the fireplace and banked it with ashes to keep it smoldering till morning. Old Wolf dragged himself within the ruddy glow and lapsed into his customary coma. Audrey and Walker, too tired to think of charms or curses, tumbled into the rough pine bed and were asleep before the cheap alarm-clock on the mantel had ticked out three minutes. And from far away, the rhythmic pounding of those hellish tom-toms still pulsed on the chill night wind.

Doctor McNeill paused here and removed his glasses, as if a blurring of the objective world might make the reminiscent vision clearer.

"You'll soon appreciate," he said, "that I had a great deal of difficulty in piecing out all that happened after the guests left. There were times, though — at first — when I was able to make a try at it." After a moment of silence he went on with the tale.

Audrey had terrible dreams of Yig, who appeared to her in the guise of Satan as depicted in cheap engravings she had seen. It was, indeed, from an absolute ecstasy of nightmare that she started suddenly awake to find Walker already conscious and sitting up in bed. He seemed to be listening intently to something and silenced her with a whisper when she began to ask what had aroused him.

"Hark, Aud!" he breathed. "Don't ye hear somethin' a-singin' and buzzin' and rustlin'? D'ye reckon it's the fall crickets?"

Certainly, there was distinctly audible within the cabin such a sound as he had described. Audrey tried to analyze it, and was impressed with some element at once horrible and familiar, which hovered just outside the rim of her memory. And beyond it all, waking a hideous thought, the monotonous beating of the distant tom-toms came incessantly across the black plains on which a cloudy half-moon had set.

...each one of us has been through a phase of individual development corresponding to the animistic stage in primitive men...everything which now strikes us as "uncanny" fulfils the condition of touching residues of animistic mental activity within us and bringing them to expression.

Sigmund Freud, *The Uncanny The Complete Psychological Works of Sigmund Freud: Vol. XVII* (1919)

"Walker — s'pose it's — the — the — curse o' Yig?"
She could feel him tremble.

"No, gal, I don't reckon he comes that way. He's shapen like a man, except ye look at him clost. That's what Chief Gray Eagle says. This here's some varmints come in outen the cold — not crickets, I calc'late, but summat like 'em. I orter git up and stomp 'em out afore they make much headway or git at the cupboard."

He rose, felt for the lantern that hung within easy reach, and rattled the tin match-box nailed to the wall beside it. Audrey sat up in bed and watched the flare of the match grow into the steady glow of the lantern. Then, as their eyes began to take in the whole of the room, the crude rafters shook with the frenzy of their simultaneous shriek. For the flat, rocky floor, revealed in the new-born illumination, was one seething, brown-speckled mass of wriggling rattlesnakes, slithering toward the fire, and even now turning their loathsome heads to menace the fright-blasted lantern-bearer.

It was only for an instant that Audrey saw the things. The reptiles were of every size, of uncountable numbers, and apparently of several varieties; and even as she looked, two or three of them reared their heads as if to strike at Walker. She did not faint — it was Walker's crash to the floor that extinguished the lantern and plunged her into

blackness. He had not screamed a second time — fright had paralyzed him, and he fell as if shot by a silent arrow from no mortal's bow. To Audrey the entire world seemed to whirl about fantastically, mingling with the nightmare from which she had started.

Voluntary motion of any sort was impossible, for will and the sense of reality had left her. She fell back inertly on her pillow, hoping that she would wake soon. No actual sense of what had happened penetrated her mind for some time. Then, little by little, the suspicion that she was really awake began to dawn on her; and she was convulsed with a mounting blend of panic and grief which made her long to shriek out despite the inhibiting spell which kept her mute.

Walker was gone and she had not been able to help him. He had died of snakes, just as the old witch-woman had predicted when he was a little boy. Poor Wolf had not been able to help, either — probably he had not even awakened from his senile stupor. And now the crawling things must be coming for her, writhing closer and closer every moment in the dark, perhaps even now twining slipperily about the bedposts and oozing up over the coarse woolen blankets. Unconsciously she crept under the clothes and trembled.

It must be the curse of Yig. He had sent his monstrous children on All-Hallow's Night, and they had taken Walker first. Why was that — wasn't he innocent enough? Why not come straight for her — hadn't she killed those little rattlers alone? Then she thought of the curse's form as told by the Indians. She wouldn't be killed — just turned to a spotted snake. Ugh! So she would be like those things she had glimpsed on the floor — those things which Yig had sent to get her and enroll her among their number! She tried to mumble a charm that Walker had taught her, but found she could not utter a single sound.

The noisy ticking of the alarm-clock sounded above the maddening beat of the distant tom-toms. The snakes were taking a long time — did they mean to delay on purpose to play on her nerves? Every now and then she thought she felt a steady, insidious pressure on the bedclothes, but each time it turned out to be only the automatic twitchings of her over-wrought nerves. The clock ticked on in the dark, and a change came slowly over her thoughts.

Those snakes couldn't have taken so long! They couldn't be Yig's messengers after all, but just natural rattlers that were nested below the rocks and had been drawn there by the fire. They weren't coming for her, perhaps — perhaps they had sated themselves on poor Walker. Where were they now? Gone? Coiled by the fire? Still crawling over the prone corpse of their victim? The clock ticked, and the distant drums throbbed on.

At the thought of her husband's body lying there in the pitch blackness a thrill of purely physical horror passed over Audrey. That story of Sally Compton's about the man back in Scott County! He, too, had been bitten by a whole bunch of rattlesnakes, and what had happened to him? The poison had rotted the flesh and swelled the whole corpse, and in the end the bloated thing had burst horribly — burst horribly with a detestable popping noise. Was that what was happening to Walker down there on the rock floor? Instinctively she felt she had begun to listen for something too terrible to name to herself.

The clock ticked on, keeping a kind of mocking, sardonic time with the far-off drumming that the night wind brought. She wished it were a striking clock, so that she could know how long this eldritch vigil must last. She cursed the toughness of fiber, that kept her from fainting, and wondered what sort of relief the dawn could bring, after all. Probably neighbors would pass — no doubt somebody would call — would they find her still sane? Was she still sane now?

Morbidly listening, Audrey all at once became aware of something which she had to verify with every effort of her will before she could believe it; and which, once verified, she did not know whether to welcome or dread. The distant beating of the Indian tom-toms had ceased.

She did not relish this new and sudden silence, after all! There was something sinister about it. The loud-ticking clock seemed abnormal in its new loneliness. Capable at last of conscious motion, she shook the covers from her face and looked into the darkness toward the window. It must have cleared after the moon set, for she saw the square aperture distinctly against the background of stars.

Then without warning came that shocking, unutterable sound — ugh! — that dull pop of cleft skin and escaping poison in the dark. God! — the bonds of muteness snapped, and the black night waxed reverberant with Audrey's screams of stark, unbridled frenzy.

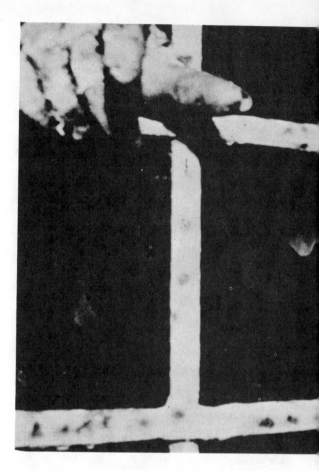

Consciousness did not pass away with the shock. How merciful if only it had! Amidst the echoes of her shrieking Audrey still saw the star-sprinkled square of window ahead, and heard the doom-boding ticking of that frightful clock. Did she hear another sound? Was that square window still a perfect square? She was in no condition to weigh the evidence of her senses or distinguish between fact and hallucination.

No — that window was not a perfect square. Something had encroached on the lower edge. Nor was the ticking of the clock the only sound in the room. There was, beyond dispute, a heavy breathing neither her own nor poor Wolf's. Wolf slept very silently, and his wakeful wheezing was unmistakable. Then Audrey saw against the stars the black, demoniac silhouette of something anthropoid — the undulant bulk of a gigantic head and shoulders fumbling slowly toward her.

"Y'aaaah! Y'aaaah! Go away! Go away! Go away, snake devil! Go'way, Yig! I didn't mean to kill 'em — I was feared he'd be scairt of 'em. Don't Yig, don't! I didn't go for to hurt yore chillen — don't come nigh me — don't change me into no spotted snake!"

But the half-formless head and shoulders only lurched onward toward the bed very silently.

Everything snapped at once inside Audrey's head, and in a second she had turned from a cowering child to a raging madwoman. She knew where the ax was — hung against the wall on those pegs near the lantern. It was within easy reach, and she could find it in the dark. Before she was conscious of anything further it was in her hands, and she was creeping toward the foot of the bed — toward the monstrous head and shoulders that every moment groped their way nearer. Had there been any light, the look on her face would not have been pleasant to see.

"Take that, you! And that, and that, and that!"

She was laughing shrilly now, and her crackles mounted higher as she saw that the starlight beyond the window was yielding to the dim prophetic pallor of coming dawn.

Doctor McNeill wiped the perspiration from his forehead and put on his glasses again. I waited for him to resume, and as he kept silent, I spoke softly.

"She lived? She was found? Was it ever explained?"

The doctor cleared his throat.

"Yes — she lived, in a way. And it was explained. I told you there was no bewitchment — only cruel, pitiful, material horror."

It was Sally Compton who had made the discovery. She had ridden over to the Davis cabin the next afternoon to talk over the party with Audrey, and had seen no smoke from the chimney. That was queer. It had turned very warm again, yet Audrey was usually cooking something at that hour. The mules were making hungry-sounding noises in the barn, and there was no sign of old Wolf sunning himself in the accustomed spot by the door.

Altogether, Sally did not like the look of the place, so was very timid and hesitant as she dismounted and knocked. She got no answer, but waited some time before trying the crude door of split logs. The lock, it appeared, was unfastened; and she slowly pushed her way in. Then, perceiving what was there, she reeled back, gasped, and clung to the jamb to preserve her balance.

A terrible odor had welled out as she opened the door, but that was not what stunned her. It was what she had seen. For within that shadowy cabin monstrous things had happened and three shocking objects remained on the floor to awe and baffle the beholder.

Near the burned-out fireplace was the great dog — purple decay on the skin left bare by mange and old age, and the whole carcass burst by the puffing effect of rattlesnake poison. It must have been bitten by a veritable legion of the reptiles.

To the right of the door was the ax-hacked remnant of what had been a man — clad in a nightshirt, and with the shattered bulk of a lantern clenched in one hand. He was totally free from any sign of snake-bite. Near him lay the ensanguined ax, carelessly discarded.

And wriggling flat on the floor was a loathsome, vacant-eyed thing that had been a woman, but was now only a mute mad caricature. All that this thing could do was to hiss, and hiss, and hiss.

Both the doctor and I were brushing cold drops from our

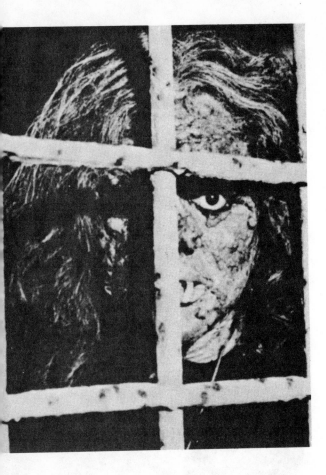

Snake
Theodore Roethke

I saw a young snake glide
Out of the mottled shade
And hang, limp on a stone;
A thin mouth, and a tongue
Stayed, in the still air.

It turned; it drew away;
Its shadow bent in half;

It quickened, and was gone.

I felt my slow blood warm.
I longed to be that thing,
The pure, sensuous form.

And I may be, some time.

The snake plays an important role in dreams as a fear-symbol...it expresses an abnormally active...unconscious and the physiological symptoms...associated therewith....I have very often noticed in such cases a singularly narrow consciousness, an apprehensive stiffness of attitude, and a spiritual and emotional horizon bounded by childish naivete or pedantic prejudice.

C.G. Jung, *Symbols of Transformation* (1956)

We witness the dissection of a heart so that the divine seed enclosed in it may germinate....The heart is the place of union where the luminous consciousness is made....

What more perfect symbol could be found for the creative, liberating movement, than this vibrating piece of flesh whose pulsation at every moment rescues corporeal matter from the inertia and decomposition that *lurk* in ambush.

L. Sejourne, *Burning Water: Thought and Religion in Ancient Mexico* (1863)

Frantic villagers in northwest Bangladesh managed to pull a 25-year-old man out of a 30-foot python that had swallowed him up to the waist...but both the man and the snake died in the struggle.

Reuter, *Dacca, July* (1977)

foreheads by this time. He poured something from a flask on his desk, took a nip, and handed another glass to me. I could only suggest tremulously and stupidly:

"So Walker had only fainted that first time — the screams roused him, and the ax did the rest?"

"Yes." Doctor McNeill's voice was low. "But he met his death from snakes just the same. It was his fear working in two ways — it made him faint, and it made him fill his wife with the wild stories that caused her to strike out when she thought she saw the snake devil."

I thought for a moment.

"And Audrey — wasn't it queer how the curse of Yig seemed to work itself out on her? I suppose the impression of hissing snakes had been fairly ground into her."

"Yes. There were lucid spells at first, but they got to be fewer and fewer. Her hair came white at the roots as it grew, and later began to fall out. The skin grew blotchy, and when she died —"

I interrupted with a start.

"Died? Then what was that — that thing downstairs?"

Doctor McNeill spoke gravely.

"That is what was born to her three-quarters of a year afterwards. There were three more of them — two were even worse — but this is the only one that lived."

Wolves Don't Cry
Bruce Elliott

The naked man behind the bars was sound asleep. In the cage next to him a bear rolled over on its back, and peered sleepily at the rising sun. Not far away a jackal paced springily back and forth as though essaying the impossible, trying to leave its own stench far behind.

Flies were gathered around the big bone that rested near the man's sleeping head. Little bits of decaying flesh attracted the insects and their hungry buzzing made the man stir uneasily. Accustomed to instant awakening, his eyes flickered and simultaneously his right hand darted out and smashed down at the irritating flies.

They left in a swarm, but the naked man stayed frozen in the position he had assumed. His eyes were on his hand.

He was still that way when the zoo attendant came close to the cage. The attendant, a pail of food in one hand, a pail of water in the other, said, "Hi Lobo, up and at 'em, the customers'll be here soon." Then he too froze.

Inside the naked man's head strange ideas were stirring. His paw, what had happened to it? Where was the stiff gray hair? The jet-black steel-strong nails? And what was the odd fifth thing that jutted out from his paw at right angles? He moved it experimentally. It rotated. He'd never been able to move his dewclaw, and the fact that he could move this fifth extension was somehow more baffling than the other oddities that were puzzling him.

"You goddamn drunks!" the attendant raved. "Wasn't bad enough the night a flock of you came in here, and a girl bothered the bear and lost an arm for her trouble, no, that wasn't bad enough. Now you have to sleep in my cages! And where's Lobo? What have you done with him?"

The naked figure wished the two-legged would stop barking. It was enough trouble trying to figure out what had happened without the angry short barks of the two-legged who fed him interfering with his thoughts.

Then there were many more of the two-leggeds and a lot of barking, and the naked one wished they'd all go away and let him think. Finally the cage was opened and the two-leggeds tried to make him come out of his cage. He retreated hurriedly on all fours to the back of his cage towards his den.

"Let him alone," the two-legged who fed him barked. "Let him go into Lobo's den. He'll be sorry!"

Inside the den, inside the hollowed-out rock that so cleverly approximated his home before he had been captured, he paced back and forth, finding it bafflingly uncomfortable to walk on his naked feet. His paws did not grip the ground the way they should and the rock hurt his new soft pads.

The two-legged ones were getting angry, he could smell the emotion as it poured from them, but even that was puzzling, for he had to flare his nostrils wide to get the scent, and it was blurred, not crisp and clear the way he ordinarily smelled things. Throwing back his head, he

howled in frustration and anger. But the sound was wrong. It did not ululate as was its wont. Instead he found to his horror that he sounded like a cub, or a female.

What had happened to him?

Cutting one of his soft pads on a stone, he lifted his foot and licked at the blood.

His pounding heart almost stopped.

This was no wolf blood.

Then the two-legged ones came in after him and the fight was one that ordinarily he would have enjoyed, but now his heart was not in it. Dismay filled him, for the taste of his own blood had put fear in him. Fear unlike any he had ever known, even when he was trapped that time, and put in a box, and thrown onto a wheeled thing that had rocked back and forth, and smelled so badly of two-legged things.

This was a new fear, and a horrible one.

Their barking got louder when they found that he was alone in his den. Over and over they barked, not that he could understand them, "What have you done with Lobo? Where is he? Have you turned him loose?"

It was only after a long time, when the sun was riding high in the summer sky, that he was wrapped in a foul-smelling thing and put in a four-wheeled object and taken away from his den.

He would never have thought, when he was captured, that he would ever miss the new home that the two-leggeds had given him, but he found that he did, and most of all, as the four-wheeled thing rolled through the city streets, he found himself worrying about his mate in the next cage. What would she think when she found him gone, and she just about to have a litter? He knew that most males did not worry about their young, but wolves were different. No mother wolf ever had to worry, the way female bears did, about a male wolf eating his young. No indeed; wolves were different.

And being different, he found that worse than being tied up in a cloth and thrown in the back of a long, wheeled thing was the worry he felt about his mate, and her young-to-be.

But worse was to come: when he was carried out of the moving thing, the two-legged ones carried him into a big building and the smells that surged in on his outraged nostrils literally made him cringe. There was sickness, and stenches worse than he had ever smelled, and above and beyond all other smells the odor of death was heavy in the long white corridors through which he was carried.

Seeing around him as he did ordinarily in grays and blacks and whites, he found that the new sensations that crashed against his smarting eyeballs were not to be explained by anything he knew. Not having the words for red, and green, and yellow, for pink and orange and all the other colors in a polychromatic world, not having any idea of what they were, just served to confuse him even more miserably.

He moaned.

The smells, the discomfort, the horror of being han-

dled, were as nothing against the hurt his eyes were enduring.

Lying on a flat hard thing he found that it helped just to stare directly upwards. At least the flat covering ten feet above him was white, and he could cope with that.

The two-legged thing sitting next to him had a gentle bark, but that didn't help much.

The two-legged said patiently over and over again, "Who are you? Have you any idea? Do you know where you are? What day is this?"

After a while the barks became soothing, and nude no longer, wrapped now in a long wet sheet that held him cocoonlike in its embrace, he found that his eyes were closing. It was all too much for him.

He slept.

The next awakening was if anything worse than the first.

First he thought that he was back in his cage in the zoo, for directly ahead of him he could see bars. Heaving a sigh of vast relief, he wondered what had made an adult wolf have such an absurd dream. He could still remember his puppyhood when sleep had been made peculiar by a life unlike the one he enjoyed when awake. The twitchings, the growls, the sleepy murmurs — he had seen his own sons and daughters go through them and they had reminded him of his youth.

But now the bars were in front of him and all was well.

Except that he must have slept in a peculiar position. He was stiff, and when he went to roll over he fell off the hard thing he had been on and crashed to the floor.

Bars or no bars, this was not his cage.

That was what made the second awakening so difficult. For, once he had fallen off the hospital bed, he found that his limbs were encumbered by a long garment that flapped around him as he rolled to all fours and began to pace fearfully back and forth inside the narrow confines of the cell that he now inhabited.

Worse yet, when the sound of his fall reached the ears of a two-legged one, he found that some more two-legs hurried to his side and he was forced, literally forced into an odd garment that covered his lower limbs.

Then they made him sit on the end of his spine and it hurt cruelly, and they put a metal thing in his right paw, and wrapped the soft flesh of his paw around the metal object and holding both, they made him lift some kind of slop from a round thing on the flat surface in front of him.

That was bad, but the taste of the mush they forced into his mouth was grotesque.

Where was his meat? Where was his bone? How could he sharpen his fangs on such food as this? What were they trying to do? Make him lose his teeth?

He gagged and regurgitated the slops. That didn't do the slightest bit of good. The two-leggeds kept right on forcing the mush into his aching jaws. Finally, in despair, he kept some of it down.

Then they made him balance on his hind legs.

He'd often seen the bear in the next cage doing this trick and sneered at the big fat oaf for pandering to the two-leggeds by aping them. Now he found that it was harder than he would have thought. But finally, after the two-leggeds had worked with him for a long time, he found that he could, by much teetering, stand erect.

But he didn't like it.

His nose was far from the floor, and with whatever it was wrong with his smelling, he found that he had trouble sniffing the ground under him. From this distance he could not track anything. Not even a rabbit. If one had run right by him, he thought, feeling terribly sorry for himself, he'd never be able to smell it, or if he did, be able to track it down, no matter how fat and juicy, for how could a wolf run on two legs?

They did many things to him in the new big zoo, and in time he found that, dislike it as much as he did, they could force him by painful expedients to do many of the tasks they set him.

That, of course, did not help him to understand why they wanted him to do such absurd things as encumber his legs with cloth that flapped and got in the way, or balance precariously on his hind legs, or any of the other absurdities they made him perform. But somehow he surmounted everything and in time even learned to bark a little the way they did. He found that he could bark *hello* and *I'm hungry* and, after months of effort, ask *why can't I go back to the zoo?*

But that didn't do much good, because all they ever barked back was *because you're a man.*

Now of many things he was unsure since that terrible morning, but of one thing he was sure: he *was* a wolf.

Other people knew it too.

He found this out on the day some outsiders were let into the place where he was being kept. He had been sitting, painful as it was, on the tip of his spine, in what he had found the two-leggeds called a chair, when some shes passed by.

His nostrils closed at the sweet smell that they had poured on themselves, but through it he could detect the real smell, the female smell, and his nostrils had flared, and he had run to the door of his cell, and his eyes had become red as he looked at them. Not so attractive as his mate, but at least they were covered with fur, not like the peeled ones that he sometimes saw dressed in stiff white crackling things.

The fur-covered ones had giggled just like ripening she-cubs, and his paws had ached to grasp them, and his jaws ached to bite into their fur-covered necks.

One of the fur-covered two-leggeds had giggled, "Look at that wolf!"

So some of the two-leggeds had perception and could tell that the ones who held him in this big strange zoo were wrong, that he was not a man, but a wolf.

Inflating his now puny lungs to the utmost he had thrown back his head and roared out a challenge that in the old days, in the forest, would have sent a thrill of pleasure through every female for miles around. But instead of that blood-curdling, stomach-wrenching roar, a

little barking, choking sound came from his throat. If he had still had a tail it would have curled down under his belly as he slunk away.

The first time they let him see himself in what they called a mirror he had moaned like a cub. Where was his long snout, the bristling whiskers, the flat head, the pointed ears? What was this thing that stared with dilated eyes out of the flat shiny surface? White-faced, almost hairless save for a jet-black bar of eyebrows that made a straight line across his high round forehead, small-jawed, small-toothed — he knew with a sinking sensation in the pit of his stomach that even a year-old would not hesitate to challenge him in the mating fights.

Not only challenge him but beat him, for how could he fight with those little canines, those feeble white hairless paws?

Another thing that irritated him, as it would any wolf, was that they kept moving him around. He would no sooner get used to one den and make it his own but what they'd move him to another one.

The last one that contained him had no bars.

If he had been able to read his chart he would have known that he was considered on the way to recovery, that the authorities thought him almost "cured" of his aberration. The den with no bars was one that was used for limited liberty patients. They were on a kind of parole basis. But he had no idea of what the word meant and the first time he was released on his own cognizance, allowed to make a trip out into the "real" world, he put out of his mind the curious forms of "occupational therapy" with which the authorities were deviling him.

His daytime liberty was unreal and dragged by in a way that made him almost anxious to get back home to the new den.

He had all but made up his mind to do so, when the setting sun conjured up visions which he could not resist. In the dark he could get down on all fours!

Leaving the crowded city streets behind him he hurried out into the suburbs where the spring smells were making the night air exciting.

He had looked forward so to dropping on all fours and racing through the velvet spring night that when he did so, only to find that all the months of standing upright had made him too stiff to run, he could have howled. Then too the clumsy leather things on his back paws got in the way, and he would have ripped them off, but he remembered how soft his new pads were, and he was afraid of what would happen to them.

Forcing himself upright, keeping the curve in his back that he had found helped him to stand on his hind legs, he made his way cautiously along a flat thing that stretched off into the distance.

The four-wheeler that stopped near him would ordinarily have frightened him. But even his new weak nose could sniff through the rank acrid smells of the four-wheeler and find, under the too sweet something on the two-legged female, the real smell, so that when she said,

"Hop in, I'll give you a lift," he did not run away. Instead he joined the she.

Her bark was nice, at first.

Later, while he was doing to her what her scent had told him she wanted done, her bark became shrill, and it hurt even his new dull ears. That, of course, did not stop him from doing what had to be done in the spring.

The sounds that still came from her got fainter as he tried to run off on his hind legs. It was not much faster than a walk, but he had to get some of the good feeling of the air against his face, of his lungs panting; he had to run.

Regret was in him that he would not be able to get food for the she and be near her when she whelped, for that was the way of a wolf; but he knew too that he would always know her by her scent, and if possible when her time came he would be at her side.

Not even the spring running was as it should be, for without the excitement of being on all fours, without the nimbleness that had been his, he found that he stumbled too much, there was no thrill.

Besides, around him, the manifold smells told him that many of the two-leggeds were all jammed together. The odor was like a miasma and not even the all-pervading stench that came from the four-wheelers could drown it out.

Coming to a halt, he sat on his haunches, and for the first time he wondered if he were really, as he knew he was, a wolf, for a salty wetness was making itself felt at the corners of his eyes.

Wolves don't cry.

But if he were not a wolf, what then was he? What *were* all the memories that crowded his sick brain?

Tears or no, he knew that he was a wolf. And being a wolf, he most rid himself of this soft pelt, this hairlessness that made him sick at his stomach just to touch it with his too soft pads.

This was his dream, to become again as he had been. To be what was his only reality, a wolf, with a wolf's life and a wolf's loves.

That was his first venture into the reality of the world at large. His second day and night of "limited liberty" sent him hurrying back to his den. Nothing in his wolf life had prepared him for what he found in the midnight streets of the big city. For he found that bears were not the only males from whom the shes had to protect their young....

And no animal of which he had ever heard could have moaned, as he heard a man moan, "If only pain didn't hurt so much...." And the strangled cries, the thrashing of limbs, the violence, and the sound of a whip. He had never known that humans used whips on themselves too....

The third time out, he tried to drug himself the way the two-leggeds did by going to a big place where, on a screen, black and white shadows went through imitations of reality. He didn't go to a show that advertised it was in full glorious color, for he found the other shadows in neutral grays and blacks and whites gave a picture of life the way his wolf eyes were used to looking at it.

It was in this big place where the shadows acted that he found that perhaps he was not unique. His eyes glued to the screen, he watched as a man slowly fell to all fours, threw his head back, bayed at the moon, and then, right before everyone, turned into a wolf!

A *werewolf,* the man was called in the shadow play. And if there were werewolves, he thought, as he sat frozen in the middle of all the seated two-leggeds, then of course there must be *weremen* (would that be the word?)...and he was one of them....

On the screen the melodrama came to its quick, bloody, foreordained end and the werewolf died when shot by a silver bullet....He saw the fur disappear from the skin, and the paws change into hands and feet.

All he had to do, he thought as he left the theatre, his mind full of his dream, was to find out how to become a wolf again, without dying. Meanwhile, on every trip out without fail he went to the zoo. The keepers had become used to seeing him. They no longer objected when he threw little bits of meat into the cage to his pups. At first his she had snarled when he came near the bars, but after a while, although still puzzled, and even though she flattened her ears and sniffed constantly at him, she seemed to become resigned to having him stand as near the cage as he possibly could.

His pups were coming along nicely, almost full-grown. He was sorry, in a way, that they had to come to wolfhood behind bars, for now they'd never known the thrill of the spring running, but it was good to know they were safe, and had full bellies, and a den to call their own.

It was when his cubs were almost ready to leave their mother that he found the two-leggeds had a place of books. It was called a *library,* and he had been sent there by the woman in the hospital who was teaching him and some of the other aphasics how to read and write and speak.

Remembering the shadow play about the werewolf, he forced his puzzled eyes to read all that he could find on the baffling subject of lycanthropy.

In every time, in every clime, he found that there were references to two-leggeds who had become four-leggeds, wolves, tigers, panthers...but never a reference to an animal that had become a two-legged.

In the course of his reading he found directions whereby a two-legged could change himself. They were complicated and meaningless to him. They involved curious things like a belt made of human skin, with a certain odd number of nail heads arranged in a quaint pattern on the body of the belt. The buckle had to be made under peculiar circumstances, and there were many chants that had to be sung.

It was essential, he read in the crabbed old books, that the two-legged desirous of making the change go to a place where two roads intersected at a specific angle. Then, standing at the intersection, chanting the peculiar words, feeling the human skin belt, the two-legged was told to divest himself of all clothing, and then to relieve his bladder.

Only then, the old books said, could the change take place.

He found that his heart was beating madly when he finished the last of the old books.

For if a two-legged could become a four-legged, surely....

After due thought, which was painful, he decided that a human skin belt would be wrong for him. The man in the fur store looked at him oddly when he asked for a length of wolf fur long and narrow, capable of being made into a belt....

But he got the fur, and he made the pattern of nail heads, and he did the things the books had described.

It was lucky, he thought as he stood in the deserted zoo, that not far from the cages he had found two roads that cut into each other in just the manner that the books said they should.

Standing where they crossed, his clothes piled on the grass nearby, the belt around his narrow waist, his fingers caressing its fur, his human throat chanting the meaningless words, he found that standing naked was a cold business, and that it was easy to void his bladder as the books had said he must.

Then it was all over.

He had done everything just as he should.

At first nothing happened, and the cold white moon looked down at him, and fear rode up and down his spine that he would be seen by one of the two-leggeds who always wore blue clothes, and he would be taken and put back into that other zoo that was not a zoo even though it had bars on the windows.

But then an aching began in his erect back, and he fell to all fours, and the agony began, and the pain blinded him to everything, to all the strange functional changes that were going on, and it was a long, long time before he dared open his eyes.

Even before he opened them, he could sense that it had happened, for crisp and clear through the night wind he could smell as he knew he should be able to smell. The odors came and they told him old stories.

Getting up on all fours, paying no attention to the clothes that now smelled foully of the two-leggeds, he began to run. His strong claws scrabbled at the cement and he hurried to the grass and it was wonderful and exciting to feel the good feel of the growing things under his pads. Throwing his long head back he closed his eyes and from deep deep inside he sang a song to the wolves' god, the moon.

His baying excited the animals in the cages near him, and they began to roar, and scream, and those sounds were good too.

Running through the night, aimlessly, but running, feeling the ground beneath his paws was good...so good....

And then through the sounds, through all the baying and roaring and screaming from the animals, he heard his she's voice, and he forgot about freedom and the night wind and the cool white moon, and he ran back to the cage where she was.

The zoo attendants were just as baffled when they found the wolf curled up outside the cage near the feeding trough as they had been when they had found the man in the wolf's cage.

The two-legged who was his keeper recognized him and he was allowed to go back into his cage and then the ecstasy, the spring-and-fall-time ecstasy of being with his she....

Slowly, as he became used to his wolfhood again, he forgot about the life outside the cage, and soon it was all a matter that only arose in troubled dreams. And even then his she was there to nuzzle him and wake him if the nightmares got too bad.

Only once after the first few days did any waking memory of his two-legged life return, and that was when a two-legged she passed by his cage pushing a small four-wheeler in front of her.

Her scent was familiar.

So too was the scent of the two-legged cub.

Darting to the front of his cage, he sniffed long and hard.

And for just a moment the woman who was pushing the perambulator that contained her bastard looked deep into his yellow eyes and she knew, as he did, who and what he was.

And the very, very last thought he had about the matter was one of infinite pity for his poor cub, who some white moonlit night was going to drop down on all fours and become furred...and go prowling through the dark — in search of what, he would never know....

We do not learn from experience; we make decisions patently against our own interest, and when they don't work we self-destructively make them all over again. Shrunken in vision and sensitivity, we move monolithically, straight ahead, like the ancient dinosaur who could not learn, blind even to our own dinosaurian movements.

Rollo May, *Love and Will* (1969)

The reason why the object seen in a Nightmare is frightful or hideous is simply that the representation of the underlying wish is not permitted in its naked form, so that the dream is a compromise of the wish on the one hand, and on the other of the intense fear belonging to the inhibition.

Karl Abraham, *Traum und Mythus* (1909)

The Prisoner's Dream
Engenio Montale

Dawns and nights here differ by few signs.

The zigzagging of formations upon the look-out towers
on days of battle, my only wings,
a needle of arctic draught,
the head-gaoler's eye at the peephole,
report of cracking nuts, an oily
hissing from the depths, roasting jacks
real or imagined—but the straw is gold,
the wine-red lantern is fireside,
if, sleeping, I am at your feet.

The purge has gone on since time began, senselessly.
They say.whoever retracts and signs
can save himself from this massacre of geese,
that whoever sobs and gravely accuses
and confesses and denounces, grabs hold of the server
instead of ending in the *pâté*
marked for the apocalyptic gods.

Slow-witted, riddled
by the prickling mattress I have grown one with
the flight of the moth-thing drilling my soles
to powder on the tiles,
with the iridescent kimonos of the window spaces
held out to the dawn from bastions,
I have sniffed on the wind the burnt odour
of rock-cakes from the ovens,
I have looked about, I have conjured
rainbows on spider-web horizons,

petals on the grating bars,
I have risen I have fallen back
into the depth where century is minute—

and the blows resound again and the footsteps,
and I still do not know if at the banquet
I shall be stuffer or stuffed. The wait is long,
my dream of you has not ended.

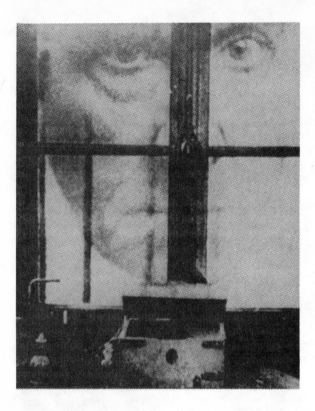

The Minotaur
Muriel Rukeyser

Trapped, blinded, led; and in the end betrayed
Daily by new betrayals as he stays
Deep in his labyrinth, shaking and going mad.
Betrayed. Betrayed. Raving, the beaten head
Heavy with madness, he stands, half-dead and proud.
No one again will ever see his pride.
No one will find him by walking to him straight
But must be led circuitously about,
Calling to him and close and, losing the subtle thread,
Lose him again; while he waits, brutalized
By loneliness. Later, afraid
Of his own suffering. At last, savage and made
Ravenous, ready to prey upon the race
If it so much as learn the clews of blood
Into his pride his fear his glistening heart.
Now is the patient deserted in his fright
And love carrying salvage round the world
Lost in a crooked city; roundabout,
By the sea, the precipice, all the fantastic ways
Betrayal weaves its trap; loneliness knows the thread,
And the heart is lost, lost, trapped, blinded and led,
Deserted in the middle of the maze.

Corrida
Roger Zelazny

He awoke to an ultrasonic wailing. It was a thing that tortured his eardrums while remaining just beyond the threshhold of the audible.

He scrambled to his feet in the darkness.

He bumped against the walls several times. Dully, he realized that his arms were sore, as though many needles had entered there.

The sound maddened him....

Escape! He had to get away!

A tiny patch of light occurred to his left.

He turned and raced toward it and it grew into a doorway.

He dashed through and stood blinking in the glare that assailed his eyes.

He was naked, he was sweating. His mind was full of fog and the rag-ends of dreams.

He heard a roar, as of a crowd, and he blinked against the brightness.

Towering, a dark figure stood before him in the distance. Overcome by rage, he raced toward it, not quite certain why.

His bare feet trod hot sand, but he ignored the pain as he ran to attack.

Some portion of his mind framed the question "Why?" but he ignored it.

Then he stopped.

A nude woman stood before him, beckoning, inviting, and there came a sudden surge of fire within his loins.

He turned slightly to his left and headed toward her.

She danced away.

He increased his speed. But as he was about to embrace her, there came a surge of fire in his right shoulder and she was gone.

He looked at his shoulder and an aluminum rod protruded from it, and the blood ran down along his arm. There arose another roar.

...And she appeared again.

He pursued her once more and his left shoulder burned with sudden fires. She was gone and he stood shaking and sweating, blinking against the glare.

"It's a trick," he decided. "Don't play the game!"

She appeared again and he stood stock still, ignoring her.

He was assailed by fires, but he refused to move, striving to clear his head.

The dark figure appeared once more, about seven feet tall and possessing two pairs of arms.

It held something in one of its hands. If only the lightning weren't so crazy, perhaps he....

But he hated that dark figure and he charged it.

Pain lashed his side.

Wait a minute! Wait a minute!

Crazy! It's all crazy! he told himself, recalling his identity. *This is a bullring and I'm a man, and that dark thing isn't. Something's wrong.*

He dropped to his hands and knees, buying time. He scooped up a double fistful of sand while he was down.

There came proddings, electric and painful. He ignored them for as long as he could, then stood.

The dark figure waved something at him and he felt himself hating it.

He ran toward it and stopped before it. He knew it was a game now. His name was Michael Cassidy. He was an attorney. New York. Of Johnson, Weems, Daugherty and Cassidy. A man had stopped him, asking for a light. On a street corner. Late at night. That he remembered.

He threw sand at the creature's head.

It swayed momentarily, and its arms were raised toward what might have been its face.

Gritting his teeth, he tore the aluminum rod from his shoulder and drove its sharpened end into the creature's middle.

Something touched the back of his neck, and there was darkness and he lay still for a long time.

When he could move again, he saw the dark figure and he tried to tackle it.

He missed, and there was pain across his back and something wet.

When he stood once more, he bellowed, "You can't do this to me! I'm a man! Not a bull!"

There came a sound of applause.

He raced toward the dark thing six times, trying to grapple with it, hold it, hurt it. Each time, he hurt himself.

Then he stood, panting and gasping, and his shoulders ached and his back ached, and his mind cleared a moment and he said, "You're God, aren't you? And this is the way You play the game...."

The creature did not answer him and he lunged.

He stopped short, then dropped to one knee and dove against its legs.

He felt a terrible fiery pain within his side as he brought the dark one to earth. He struck at it twice with his fists, then the pain entered his breast and he felt himself grow numb.

"Or are you?" he asked, thick-lipped. "No, you're not....Where am I?"

His last memory was of something cutting away at his ears.

...the religious neophyte crouched in a pit beneath a latticed platform, onto which a bedecked and garlanded bull was led. At a given moment, the bull was stabbed so that its blood spilled into the pit, spattering the worshipper below who...leans backward to have his cheeks, his ears, his lips and his nostrils wetted. He pours the liquid over his eyes and does not even spare his palate, for he moistens his tongue with blood and drinks it eagerly.

Prudentius, *Cathemerinon, Peristephanon: Book X* (402 A.D.)

From one perspective, overcoming the bull represents both a subjugation and a transcendence of man's lower animal nature. It involves the sacrifice of not yet transformed instinctual drives that control us in the dark.

Dorothy Norman, *The Hero* (1949)

The Night Fisherman
Martin I. Ricketts

Night fishing. There was nothing quite like it. There was nothing quite like sitting in the darkness at the edge of a black lake, torch in hand, and watching the luminous tip of the float on the dark surface of the water. Nothing like the thrill of watching the tiny tip flip with a sudden motion before vanishing beneath the surface with a tiny 'plop!' as the carp took the bait. Nothing like striking, heaving the rod sideways with a swish, and feeling the sudden fighting weight, invisible, on the other end.

Albert Jordan loved to fish at night. By day he'd tried fast-running streams and meandering rivers, but, as far as he was concerned, there was something special, something strangely fascinating about the bright tip of a plastic float on the slack, black waters of a night lake. No one else of his aquaintance could quite understand this fascination; every one of his angling friends derived their pleasure from sitting at the edge of a green swim, gently touched by the bright daylight sun, with a soft tumble of bird-song in the background, and the faint hoot of a water-fowl (faint for distance, so as not to disturb the waters of an angler's swim, of course!) hanging on the warm air. Albert, in turn, could never sympathize with *this* attitude. To him the pleasure of being alone at night at the water's silent edge was a wonderful thing, something to be worshipped with an almost religious fervour. In short, night fishing was his idea of the ultimate in pleasure.

It was in anticipation of this pleasure that Albert smiled to himself as he walked across the fields late on one particular evening. Midnight was approaching and the night was black as a cavern; all day the sky had been overcast, and now neither moon nor stars broke through the complete darkness. His gum-booted feet swishing heavily through the dew-laden grass, Albert Jordan headed in the direction of the invisible line of trees which marked the water's edge, the narrow beam of light from his torch probing faintly ahead of him, lighting the way for his feet. Hanging down from his shoulders, his basket and rod-bag bumped and rubbed against his raincoated back as he walked.

Soon he was among the trees and he half-slid down the bank, one hand on the wet ground for support. And then the ground was horizontal once more as he found himself standing in pitch-blackness on a shelf of baked, tramped mud right at the water's edge, on which, with relief, he dropped his heavy tackle. Not a sound, not a motion beside his own disturbed the complete darkness. He opened his basket, unfolded his canvas stool, and with experienced hands he began to tackle-up, needing no light to aid him.

At last he was ready. With an expert motion he cast, the bait falling with a quiet splash in the darkness. The float bobbed as if waving to him, moving slowly up and down a few times, and was then still, the luminous tip like an eye in the blackness in front of him. Albert sat on the stool to wait.

Minutes passed. The darkness, except for the tip of the float, was complete. Everything was still and silent.

Albert waited, warm with the knowledge of his own patience. For a long while he didn't move, he sat as if frozen, his gaze intent on the tip of the float in front of him.

Presently a soft gently breeze, like a shiver, sprang up quickly and was gone in a second; the only sign of its passing was the brief hiss and rattle of invisible reeds somewhere nearby.

More minutes passed. Still the tiny dot floating in front of him did not move. And neither did anything else.

Soon Albert began to fidget. His fingers twitched. He swallowed. After a while the realization dawned on him that the pleasure he had anticipated for tonight was missing. For no reason he picked up his rod and reeled in the line. With his fingertips he checked that the lobworm was still securely on the hook, and then he re-cast. The float bobbed again, silently on the black water, and was then still.

The silence and the darkness was once again filled with an intensity which crept like a ghost around him. The whole world seemed to be silently shrouded in a black, invisible cloak.

Albert suddenly realized he was nervous. Now why, he asked himself, should that be? He had never been at all afraid of the dark in his entire life. What was wrong tonight?

The stillness. That's what it was; that *must* be what it was. Never before had he been out on a night which was so dark and so completely still. Even the usual tiny watery sounds of the fish rising for food were missing.

He shivered. The blankness of such a night tended to inspire one's imagination to invent all kinds of weird and horrible things; he'd be well advised to occupy his mind with thoughts of familiar things, keeping outside of his immediate awareness the unnatural stillness of this incredibly dark night.

He began to concentrate on his fishing-rod. He reached down, feeling the reassuringly familiar shape of its handle with his fingertips. The rod. It was comprised of three sections, made of fibre-glass, and had metal ferrules through which the line passed. The line. Nylon: through the ferrules of the rod and down; down to the luminous float which glowed happily in front of him, a pale dot in the blackness, and then down still farther, laden with shot, to the hook.

And, impaled on the hook, was the worm.

Albert's hands kneaded each other in his lap as he thought about it. The worm writhing and squirming, the hook through its body; the hook sharp and barbed, preventing its escape as it wriggled in the cold black water. Albert shuddered. He could almost imagine himself as the worm, could almost feel the sharp, fiery pain of the hook as it pierced his body, and the icy coldness of the water as he struggled to escape, needles of pain lancing through his chest as the hook pulled at him....

Suddenly he laughed. What a strange notion. A worm

indeed! Grinning, he returned his thoughts to his fishing: He squinted in the darkness and concentrated on the tip of his float.

There! Had it moved? No, it must have been his imagination. Still, he had plenty of patience: he'd surely have a bite before long.

With frightening suddenness, moonlight shone abruptly down through a break in the clouds. The glow touched the branches of the nearby trees and fell across the bank and the reeds. The lake was calm, the water a flat sheet of lead in the faint, eerie light. Albert looked up as a quick flitting movement touched the corner of his vision.

Bats!

He shuddered involuntarily. Horrible things! In the waxy light he watched the tiny black silhouettes weaving to and fro, up and down, singing silently through the air: umbrella shreds, black shadow-patches of night, dropping and swooping with incredibly quick, furtive motions above him.

And then the moon was gone. The cold-darkness swiftly closed in again like the wings of one of those flitting creatures grown suddenly to monstrous proportions.

Albert, eyes closed, was shivering. The air was biting cold against his face and hands; yet, all over his body he could feel the sweat running down his flesh in sudden sticky streams. In his mind's eye he could still see the

things which had been illuminated by that brief wan glow, a glow which, now vanished, made the night seem even blacker than before. Above him he imagined the dark shapes still whipping silently to and fro. All around him he felt he could still see the drooping foliage in which his imagination now placed numerous unseen horrors, rustling and creeping, shifting ominously nearer to where he sat, alone, in the darkness at the water's edge.

Albert trembled and clenched his teeth.

From somewhere came the tiny sound of water dripping, and then it was gone.

Alone. That was the trouble. This night was darker and more frightening than any he had known, and here he was, all alone, with his usually placid imagination working at double-speed. Well, now that he was here he'd have to put up with it. Self-control, that was what was needed. He just had to pull himself together.

He concentrated on the float, the tiny spot of luminescence that floated unmoving before him on the black surface of the water. Why the hell hadn't he had a bite yet? The float hadn't moved since he got here. How long ago was that? Three hours? Ten minutes? He couldn't tell; time seemed to lose its meaning here at night on the lakeside.

He sat on the stool, hands in his lap, and stared at the float. But now the darkness was not quite silent: faintly, just on the edge of his hearing, came little whisperings and rustlings, as of tiny creatures stirring in the grass and the reeds. Or was it something else — something more sinister — coming closer?

The float. Concentrate on the float. Don't let your imagination play games with you. Albert's eyes stared into the blackness, yet he could still see the pictures that the brief touch of ghostly moonlight had painted: the flat water, the pointed reeds, the tiny, candle-wax leaves on the softly illuminated branches of the trees. The branches: crooked and long like reaching hands, like clawing fingers, like writhing snakes, like long worms....

Like long worms. Albert thought about the fat worm on the end of his line, squirming with the hook through it, waiting for the black shape of the fish to come looming through the dark water, the fish whose mouth would be open to engulf the worm, to suck at it; to suck out the nourishing innards and leave the skin empty and dead on the barbed hook. To suck....

Albert saw the float-tip suddenly move. Automatically he reached out for the rod, and then he froze. His mouth opened and closed, and his eyes became wide with horror. He could feel it. By God, he could *feel* it!

It was crawling over his flesh, a cold pulsing stickiness like a wet hand trying to grip him. Needles of pain were suddenly piercing his chest and an oozing dampness was all over him, as if...as if something were trying to suck at him, trying to suck out his insides....

Albert screamed once, briefly, and then he grabbed his rod. He yanked it sideways, and suddenly the feeling was gone. The sucking grip had vanished from his flesh and streams of fire were no longer surging through his chest.

Albert let go of the fishing rod and the float bobbed gently, once more down into the water. His body racked with shudders, Albert Jordan sat down on the stool and closed his eyes tightly against the darkness.

He just couldn't believe it. For a moment there he had actually thought he was the worm, the hook piercing through him, the line pulling at him as he squirmed desperately this way and that, and the fish sucking at him, trying to draw out his innards.

Albert shook his head. This couldn't go on; he'd have to pack up his tackle and leave. From now on he'd be strictly a day fisherman.

He reached down for his basket. The sooner he could leave this eerie place the better.

And then he stopped. Suddenly he could sense the mist. It was still completely dark, yet somehow, he knew it was there. The mist rising off the water, through the blackness, sifting through the reeds and creeping along and up the bank and among the trees. Albert could feel it on his hands and on his face, cold and fearful, and completely invisible in the pitch-darkness. Layers of it, rising slowly into him and over him like depths of icy water.

Suddenly the sharp pain returned, lancing through his body like a blade. He tried to reach his rod, but something prevented him from moving. Paralyzed, his eyes staring, he watched the luminous tip of his float disappear as, below the dark surface, a fish took the bait.

Panic churned in Albert's stomach as he squirmed at the sudden agony in his chest. It churned then rose, tearing up through his body, and then he let out one long, wild, terrified scream.

Once again the oozing stickiness was all over him, sucking, sucking, sucking at his innards. Cold and slimy it was now.

The pain in his chest was the hook on the end of a fishing-line, pushing its barb through him. The damp sliminess was the mouth of a fish closing over him; the rising layers and swirls of invisible mist were the depths of water in which he wriggled and twisted, trying to escape.

He leapt to his feet, but he was bent double with the pain of the hook through his body. The invisible slimy mouth sucked at him and the heaving mist rolled over him in moist, icy waves. He screamed and screamed, squirming and wriggling, the hook burning through him, the huge cold fish-mouth sucking and sucking at his insides.

He half-ran, half-tumbled forward, screaming, falling with a heavy splash into the black waters of the lake....

Albert Jordan's absence was noticed two days later. The angling equipment found abandoned at a local lakeside was identified as being his and the lake was therefore subsequently drained.

The body of the drowned man found on the bottom was positively identified as Albert Jordan. He was only just recognisable. It seemed as if his flesh was merely a bag containing the loose bones of his skeleton. His innards, strangely, were missing, as though they had been...sucked out.

The Dragon Fly
Howard Nemerov

Under the pond, among rocks
Or in the bramble of the water wood,
He is at home, and feeds the small
Remorseless craving of his dream,

His cruel delight; until in May
The dream transforms him with itself
And from his depths he rises out,
An exile from the brutal night.

He rises out, the aged one
Imprisoned in the dying child,
And spreads his wings to the new sun:
Climbing, he withers into light.

God preserve my sanity, for to this I am reduced. Safety and the assurance of safety are things of the past. Whilst I live on here there is but one thing to hope for, that I may not go mad, if, indeed, I be not mad already. If I be sane, then surely it is maddening to think that of all the foul things that lurk in this hateful place.

Jonathan Harker's Journal, Morning, 16, May.

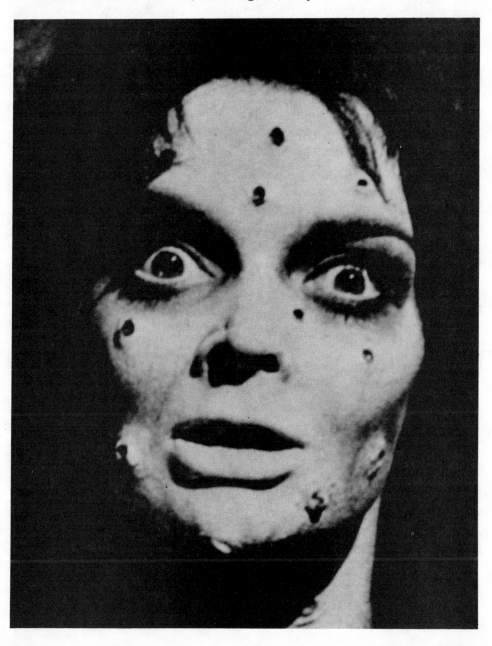

POSSESSION

In the moonlight opposite me were three young women, ladies by their dress and manner. I thought at the time that I must be dreaming when I saw them, for, though the moonlight was behind them, they threw no shadow on the floor. All three had brilliant white teeth that shone like pearls against the ruby of their voluptuous lips. There was something about them that made me uneasy, some longing and at the same time some deadly fear. I felt in my heart a wicked, burning desire that they would kiss me with those red lips.

One advanced and bent over me, simply gloating...the skin of my throat began to tingle as one's flesh does when the hand that is to tickle it approaches nearer — nearer. I could feel the soft, shivering touch of the lips on the super-sensitive skin of my throat, and the hard dents of two sharp teeth, just touching and pausing there. I closed my eyes in languorous ecstasy and waited — waited with beating heart.

Jonathan Harker's Journal, Evening, 16, May.

from **Lame Deer, Seeker of Visions**
John Lame Deer and Richard Erdoes

I was all alone on the hilltop. I sat there in the vision pit, a hole dug into the hill, my arms hugging my knees as I watched old man Chest, the medicine man who had brought me there, disappear far down in the valley. He was just a moving black dot among the pines, and soon he was gone altogether.

Now I was all by myself, left on the hilltop for four days and nights without food or water until he came back for me. You know, we Indians are not like some white folks — a man and a wife, two children, and one baby sitter who watches the TV set while the parents are out visiting somewhere.

Indian children are never alone. They are always surrounded by grandparents, uncles, cousins, relatives of all kinds, who fondle the kids, sing to them, tell them stories. If the parents go someplace, the kids go along.

But here I was, crouched in my vision pit, left alone by myself for the first time in my life. I was sixteen then, still had my boy's name and, let me tell you, I was scared. I was shivering and not only from the cold. The nearest human being was many miles away, and four days and nights is a long, long time. Of course, when it was all over, I would no longer be a boy, but a man. I would have had my vision. I would be given a man's name.

Solitude
Thomas de Quincey

There was one reason why I sought solitude at that early age, and sought it in a morbid excess, which must naturally have conferred upon my character some degree of that interest which belongs to all extremes. My eye had been couched into a secondary power of vision, by misery, by solitude, by sympathy with life in all its modes, by experience too early won, and by the sense of danger critically escaped. Suppose the case of a man suspended by some colossal arm over an unfathomed abyss, — suspended, but finally and slowly withdrawn, — it is probable that he would not smile for years. That was my case: for I have not mentioned in the 'Opium Confessions' a thousandth part of the sufferings I underwent in London and in Wales; partly because the misery was too monotonous, and, in that respect, unfitted for description; but still more because there is a mysterious sensibility connected with real suffering, which recoils from circumstantial rehearsal or delineation, as from violation offered to something sacred, and which is, or should be, dedicated to privacy. Grief does not parade its pangs, nor the anguish of despairing hunger willingly count again its groans or its humiliations.

The Snow
Clifford Dyment

In no way that I chose to go
Could I escape the falling snow.

I shut my eyes, wet with my fears:
The snow still whispered at my ears.

I stopped my ears in deaf disguise:
The snow still fell before my eyes.

Snow was my comrade, snow my fate,
In a country huge and desolate.

My footsteps made a shallow space,
And then the snow filled up the place,

And all the walking I had done
Was on a journey not begun.

I did not know the distance gone,
But resolutely travelled on

While silently on every hand
Fell the sorrow of the land,

And no way that I chose to go
Could lead me from the grief of snow.

Do not confine your children to your own learning, for they were born in another time.

Proverbial Hebraic saying

He was the most phenomenal child scholar I have ever known, and at seven was writing verse of a sombre, fantastic, almost morbid cast which astonished the tutors surrounding him. Perhaps his private education and coddled seclusion had something to do with his premature flowering. An only child, he had organic weaknesses which startled his doting parents and caused them to keep him closely chained to their side. He was never allowed out without his nurse, and seldom had a chance to play unconstrainedly with other children. All this doubtless fostered a strange secretive inner life, with imagination as his one avenue of freedom.

from an address by Samuel Loveman on H.P. Lovecraft at the Eastern Science Fiction Convention, Newark, N.J. March 1952

Silent Snow, Secret Snow
Conrad Aiken

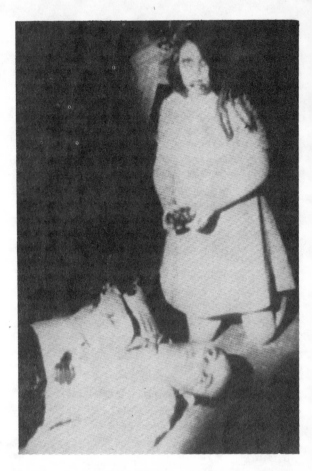

Chapter One

Just why it should have happened, or why it should have happened just when it did, he could not, of course, possibly have said; nor perhaps could it even have occurred to him to ask. The thing was above all a secret, something to be preciously concealed from Mother and Father; and to that very fact it owned an enormous part of its deliciousness. It was like a peculiarly beautiful trinket to be carried unmentioned in one's trouser-pocket — a rare stamp, an old coin, a few tiny links found trodden out of shape on the path in the park, a pebble of carnelian, a sea shell distinguishable from all others by an unusual spot or stripe — and, as if it were any one of these, he carried around with him everywhere a warm and persistent and increasingly beautiful sense of possession. Nor was it only a sense of possession — it was also a sense of protection. It was as if, in some delightful way, his secret gave him a fortress, a wall behind which he could retreat into heavenly seclusion. This was almost the first thing he had noticed about it — apart from the oddness of the thing itself — and it was this that now again, for the fiftieth time, occurred to him, as he sat in the little schoolroom. It was the half hour for geography. Miss Buell was revolving with one finger, slowly, a huge terrestrial globe which had been placed on her desk. The green and yellow continents passed and repassed, questions were asked and answered, and now the little girl in front of him, Deirdre, who had a funny little constellation of freckles on the back of her neck, exactly like the Big Dipper, was standing up and telling Miss Buell that the equator was the line that ran round the middle.

Miss Buell's face, which was old and greyish and kindly, with grey stiff curls beside the cheeks, and eyes that swam very brightly, like little minnows, behind thick glasses, wrinkled itself into a complication of amusements.

'Ah! I see. The earth is wearing a belt, or a sash. Or someone drew a line round it!'

'Oh, no — not that — I mean —'

In the general laughter, he did not share, or only a very little. He was thinking about the Arctic and Antarctic regions, which of course, on the globe, were white. Miss Buell was now telling them about the tropics, the jungles, the steamy heat of equatorial swamps, where the birds and butterflies, and even the snakes, were like living jewels. As he listened to these things, he was already, with a pleasant sense of half-effort, putting his secret between himself and the words. Was it really an effort at all? For effort implied something voluntary, and perhaps even something one did not especially want; whereas this was distinctly pleasant, and came almost of its own accord. All he needed to do was to think of that morning, the first one, and then of all the others —

But it was all so absurdly simple! It had amounted to so little. It was nothing, just an idea — and just why it should

have become so wonderful, so permanent, was a mystery — a very pleasant one, to be sure, but also, in an amusing way, foolish. However, without ceasing to listen to Miss Buell, who had now moved up to the north temperate zone, he deliberately invited his memory of the first morning. It was only a moment or two after he had waked up — or perhaps the moment itself. But was there, to be exact, an exact moment? Was one awake all at once? Or was it gradual? Anyway, it was after he had stretched a lazy hand up towards the headrail, and yawned, and then relaxed again among his warm covers, all the more grateful on a December morning, that the thing had happened. Suddenly, for no reason, he had thought of the postman, he remembered the postman. Perhaps there was nothing so odd in that. After all, he heard the postman almost every morning in his life — his heavy boots could be heard clumping round the corner at the top of the little cobbled hill-street, and then, progressively nearer, progressively louder, the double knock at each door, the crossing and re-crossings of the street, till finally the clumsy steps came stumbling across to the very door, and the tremendous knock came which shook the house itself.

(Miss Buell was saying 'Vast wheat-growing areas in North America and Siberia.'

Deirdre had for the moment placed her left hand across the back of her neck.)

But on this particular morning, the first morning, as he lay there with his eyes closed, he had for some reason *waited* for the postman. He wanted to hear him come round the corner. And that was precisely the joke — he never did. He never came. He never had come — *round the corner* — again. For when at last the steps *were* heard, they had already, he was quite sure, come a little down the hill, to the first house; and even so, the steps were curiously different — they were softer, they had a new secrecy about them, they were muffled and indistinct; and while the rhythm of them was the same, it now said a new thing — it said peace, it said remoteness, it said cold, it said sleep. And he had understood the situation at once — nothing could have seemed simpler — there had been snow in the night, such as all winter he had been longing for; and it was this which had rendered the postman's first footsteps inaudible, and the later ones faint. Of course! How lovely! And even now it must be snowing — it was going to be a snowy day — the long white ragged lines were drifting and sifting across the street, across the faces of the old houses, whispering and hushing, making little triangles of white in the corners between cobblestones, seething a little when the wind blew them over the ground to a drifted corner; and so it would be all day, getting deeper and deeper and silenter and silenter.

(Miss Buell was saying 'Land of perpetual snow.')

All this time, of course (while he lay in bed), he had kept his eyes closed, listening to the nearer progress of the postman, the muffled footsteps thumping and slipping on the snow-sheathed cobbles; and all the other sounds — the double knocks, a frosty far-off voice or two, a bell ringing thinly and softly as if under a sheet of ice — had the same slightly abstracted quality, as if removed by one degree from actuality — as if everything in the world had been insulated by snow. But when at last, pleased, he opened his eyes, and turned them towards the window, to see for himself this long-desired and now so clearly imagined miracle — what he saw instead was brilliant sunlight on a roof; and when, astonished, he jumped out of bed and stared down into the street, expecting to see the cobbles obliterated by the snow, he saw nothing but the bare bright cobbles themselves.

Queer, the effect this extraordinary surprise had had upon him — all the following morning he had kept with him a sense as of snow falling about him, a secret screen of new snow between himself and the world. If he had not dreamed of such a thing — and how could he have dreamed it while awake? — how else could one explain it? In any case, the delusion had been so vivid as to affect his entire behaviour. He could not now remember whether it was on the first or the second morning — or was it even the third? — that his mother had drawn attention to some oddness in his manner.

'But, my darling' — she had said at the breakfast table — 'what has come over you? You don't seem to be listening....'

And how often that very thing had happened since!

(Miss Buell was now asking if anyone knew the difference between the North Pole and the Magnetic Pole. Deirdre was holding up her flickering brown hand, and he could see the four white dimples that marked the knuckles.)

Perhaps it hadn't been either the second or third morning — or even the fourth or fifth. How could he be sure? How could he be sure just when the delicious *progress* had become clear? Just when it had really *begun*? The intervals weren't very precise....All he now knew was, that at some point or other — perhaps the second day, perhaps the sixth — he had noticed that the presence of the snow was a little more insistent, the sound of it clearer; and, conversely, the sound of the postman's footsteps more indistinct. Not only could he not hear the steps come round the corner, he could not even hear them at the first house. It was below the first house that he heard them; and then, a few days later, it was below the second house that he heard them; and a few days later again, below the third. Gradually, gradually, the snow was becoming heavier, the sound of its seething louder, the cobblestones more and more muffled. When he found, each morning, on going to the window, after the ritual of listening, that the roofs and cobbles were as bare as ever, it made no difference. This was, after all, only what he had expected. It was even what pleased him, what rewarded him: the thing was his own, belonged to no one else. No one else knew about it, not even his Mother and Father. There, outside, were the bare cobbles; and here, inside, was the snow. Snow growing heavier each day, muffling the world, hiding the ugly, and deadening increasingly — above all — the steps of the postman.

'But, my darling,' she had said at the luncheon table, 'what has come over you? You don't seem to listen when people speak to you. That's the third time I've asked you to pass your plate....'

I busied myself at home with chemistry, literature, & the like; composing some of the weirdest & darkest fiction even written by man!...I shunned all human society, even deeming myself too much of a failure in life to be seen socially by those who had known me as a youth, & had foolishly expected great things of me.

H.P. Lovecraft

How was one to explain this to Mother? or to Father? There was, of course, nothing to be done about it: nothing. All one could do was to laugh embarrassedly, pretend to be a little ashamed, apologize, and take a sudden and somewhat disingenuous interest in what was being done or said. The cat had stayed out all night. He had a curious swelling on his left cheek — perhaps somebody had kicked him, or a stone had struck him. Mrs. Kempton was or was not coming to tea. The house was going to be house-cleaned, or 'turned out', on Wednesday instead of Friday. A new lamp was provided for his evening work — perhaps it was eye-strain which accounted for this new and so peculiar vagueness of his — Mother was looking at him with amusement as she said this, but with something else as well. A new lamp? A new lamp. Yes, Mother; No, Mother; Yes, Mother. School is going very well. The geometry is very easy. The history is very dull. The geography is very interesting — particularly when it takes one to the North Pole. Why the North Pole? Oh, well, it would be fun to be an explorer. Another Peary or Scott or Shackleton. And then abruptly he found his interest in the talk at an end, stared at the pudding on his plate, listened, waited, and began once more — ah, how heavenly, too, the first beginnings — to hear or feel — for could he actually hear it? — the silent snow, the secret snow.

(Miss Buell was telling them about the search for the North-west Passage, about Hendrik Hudson, the Half Moon.)

This had been, indeed, the only distressing feature of the new experience: the fact that it so increasingly had brought him into a kind of mute misunderstanding, or even conflict, with his Father and Mother. It was as if he were trying to lead a double life. On the one hand he had to be Paul Hasleman, and keep up the appearance of being that person — dress, wash, and answer intelligently when spoken to; on the other, he had to explore this new world which had been opened to him. Nor could there be the slightest doubt — not the slightest — that the new world was the profounder and more wonderful of the two. It was irresistible. It was miraculous. Its beauty was simply beyond anything — beyond speech as beyond thought — utterly incommunicable. But how then between the two worlds, of which he was thus constantly aware, was he to keep a balance? One must get up, one must go to breakfast, one must talk with Mother, go to school, do one's lessons — and, in all this, try not to appear too much of a fool. But if all the while one was also trying to extract the full deliciousness of another and quite separate existence, one which could not easily (if at all) be spoken of — how was one to manage? How was one to explain? Would it be safe to explain? Would it be absurd? Would it merely mean that he would get into some obscure kind of trouble?

These thoughts came and went, came and went, as softly and secretly as the snow; they were not precisely a disturbance, perhaps they were even a pleasure; he liked to have them; their presence was something almost palpable, something he could stroke with his hand, without closing his eyes, and without ceasing to see Miss Buell and the schoolroom and the globe and the freckles on Deirdre's neck; nevertheless he did in a sense cease to see, or to see the obvious external world, and substituted for this vision the vision of snow, the sound of snow, and the slow, almost soundless, approach of the postman. Yesterday, it had been only at the sixth house that the postman had become audible; the snow was much deeper now, it was falling more swiftly and heavily, the sound of its seething was more distinct, more soothing, more persistent. And this morning, it had been — as nearly as he could figure — just above the seventh house — perhaps only a step or two above: at most, he had heard two or three footsteps before the knock had sounded....And with each such narrowing of the sphere, each nearer approach of the limit at which the postman was first audible, it was odd how sharply was increased the amount of illusion which had to be carried into the ordinary business of daily life. Each day it was harder to get out of bed, to go to the window, to look out at the — as always — perfectly empty and snowless street. Each day it was more difficult to go through the perfunctory motions of greeting Mother and Father at breakfast, to reply to their questions, to put his books together and go to school. And at school, how extraordinarily hard to conduct with success simultaneously the public life and the life that was secret. There were times when he longed — positively ached — to tell everyone about it — to burst out with it — only to be checked almost at once by a far-off feeling as of some faint absurdity which was inherent in it — but *was* it absurd? — and more importantly by a sense of mysterious power in his very secrecy. Yes: it must be kept secret. That, more and more, became clear. At whatever cost to himself, whatever pain to others —

Those who outlawed traditional folk fairy tales decided that if there were monsters in a story told to children, these must all be friendly — but they missed the monster a child knows best and is most concerned with: the monster he feels or fears himself to be, and which also sometimes persecutes him. By keeping this monster within the child unspoken of, hidden in his unconscious, adults prevent the child from spinning fantasies around it in the image of the fairy tales he knows. Without such fantasies, the child fails to get to know his monster better, nor is he given suggestions as to how he may gain mastery over it.

Bruno Bettleheim, *The Uses of Enchantment* (1976)

(Miss Buell looked straight at him, smiling, and said, 'Perhaps we'll ask Paul. I'm sure Paul will come out of his daydream long enough to be able to tell us. Won't you, Paul?' He rose slowly from his chair, resting one hand on the brightly varnished desk, and deliberately stared through the snow towards the blackboard. It was an effort, but it was amusing to make it. 'Yes,' he said slowly, 'it was what we now call the Hudson River. This he thought to be the North-west Passage. He was disappointed.' He sat down again, and as he did so Deirdre half turned in her chair and gave him a shy smile, of approval and admiration.)

At whatever pain to others.

This part of it was very puzzling, very puzzling. Mother was very nice, and so was Father. Yes, that was all true enough. He wanted to be nice to them, to tell them everything — and yet, was it really wrong of him to want to have a secret place of his own?

At bedtime, the night before, Mother had said, 'If this goes on, my lad, we'll have to see a doctor, we will! We can't have our boy —' But what was it she had said? 'Live in another world'? 'Live so far away'? The word 'far' had been in it, he was sure, and then Mother had taken up a magazine again and laughed a little, but with an expression which wasn't mirthful. He had felt sorry for her....

The bell rang for dismissal. The sound came to him through long curved parallels of falling snow. He saw Deirdre rise, and had himself risen almost as soon — but not quite as soon — as she.

Chapter Two

On the walk homeward, which was timeless, it pleased him to see through the accompaniment, or counterpoint, of snow, the items of mere externality on his way. There were many kinds of bricks in the sidewalks, and laid in many kinds of pattern. The garden walls too were various, some of wooden palings, some of plaster, some of stone. Twigs of bushes leaned over the walls; the little hard green winter-buds of lilac, on grey stems, sheathed and fat; other branches very thin and fine and black and desiccated. Dirty sparrows huddled in the bushes, as dull in colour as dead fruit left in leafless trees. A single starling creaked on a weather vane. In the gutter, beside a drain, was a scrap of torn and dirty newspaper, caught in a little delta of filth: the word ECZEMA appeared in large capitals, and below it was a letter from Mrs. Amelia D. Cravath, 2100 Pine Street, Fort Worth, Texas, to the effect that after being a sufferer for years she had been cured by Caley's Ointment. In the little delta, beside the fanshaped and deeply runnelled continent of brown mud, were lost twigs, descended from their parent trees, dead matches, a rusty horse-chestnut burr, a small concentration of sparkling gravel on the lip of the sewer, a fragment of eggshell, a streak of yellow sawdust which had been wet and was now dry and congealed, a brown pebble, and a broken feather. Farther on was a cement sidewalk, ruled into geometrical parallelograms, with a brass inlay at one end commemorating the contractors who had laid it, and, half-way across, and irregular and random series of dog-tracks, immortalized in synthetic stone. He knew these well, and always stepped on them; to cover the little hollows with his own foot had always been a queer pleasure; today he did it once more, but perfunctorily and detachedly, all the while thinking of something else. That was a dog, a long time ago, who had made a mistake and walked on the cement while it was still wet. He had probably wagged his tail, but that hadn't been recorded. Now, Paul Hasleman, aged twelve, on his way home from school, crossed the same river, which in the meantime had frozen into rock. Homeward through the snow, the snow falling in bright sunshine. Homeward?

Then came the gateway with the two posts surmounted by egg-shaped stones which had been cunningly balanced on their ends, as if by Columbus, and mortared in the very act of balance: a source of perpetual wonder. On the brick wall just beyond, the letter H had been stencilled, presumably for some purpose. H? H.

The green hydrant, with a little green-painted chain attached to the brass screw-cap.

The elm tree, with the great grey wound in the bark, kidney-shaped, into which he always put his hand — to feel the cold but living wood. The injury, he had been sure, was due to the gnawings of a tethered horse. But now it deserved only a passing palm, a merely tolerant eye. There were more important things. Miracles. Beyond the thoughts of trees, mere elms. Beyond the thoughts of sidewalks, mere stone, mere brick, mere cement. Beyond the thoughts even of his own shoes, which trod these sidewalks obediently, bearing a burden — far above — of elaborate mystery. He watched them. They were not very well polished; he had neglected them, for a very good reason: they were one of the many parts of the increasing difficulty of the daily return to daily life, the morning struggle. To get up, having at last opened one's eyes, to go to the window, and discover no snow, to wash, to dress, to descend the curving stairs to breakfast —

At whatever pain to others, nevertheless, one must persevere in severance, since the incommunicability of the experience demanded it. It was desirable of course to be kind to Mother and Father, especially as they seemed to be worried, but it was also desirable to be resolute. If they should decide — as appeared likely — to consult the doctor, Doctor Howells, and have Paul inspected, his heart listened to through a kind of dictaphone, his lungs, his stomach — well, that was all right. He would go through with it. He would give them answer for question, too — perhaps such answers as they hadn't expected? No. That would never do. For the secret world must, at all costs, be preserved.

The bird-house in the apple-tree was empty — it was the wrong time of year for wrens. The little round black door had lost its pleasure. The wrens were enjoying other houses, other nests, remoter trees. But this too was a notion which he only vaguely and grazingly entertained — as if, for the moment, he merely touched an edge of it; there was something farther on, which was already assuming a sharper importance; something which already teased at the corners of his eyes, teasing also at the corner of his mind. It was funny to think that he so wanted this, so awaited it — and yet found himself enjoying this momentary dalliance with the bird-house, as if for a quiet deliberate postponement and enhancement of the approaching pleasure. He was aware of his delay, of his smiling and detached and now almost uncomprehending gaze at the little bird-house; he knew what he was going to look at next: it was his own little cobbled hill-street, his own house, the little river at the bottom of the hill, the grocer's shop with the cardboard man in the window — and now, thinking of all this, he turned his head, still smiling, and looking quickly right and left through the snow-laden sunlight.

And the mist of snow, as he had foreseen, was still on it — a ghost of snow falling in the bright sunlight, softly and steadily floating and turning and pausing, soundlessly meeting the snow that covered, as with a transparent mirage, the bare bright cobbles. He loved it — he stood still and loved it. Its beauty was paralysing — beyond all words, all experience, all dream. No fairy-story he had ever read could be compared with it — none had ever given him this extraordinary combination of ethereal loveliness with a something else, unnameable, which was just faintly and deliciously terrifying. What was this thing? As he thought of it, he looked upward towards his own bedroom window, which was open — and it was as if he looked straight into the room and saw himself lying half awake in his bed. There he was — at this very instant he was still perhaps actually there — more truly there than standing here at the edge of the cobbled hill-street, with one hand lifted to shade his eyes against the snow-sun. Had he indeed ever left his room, in all this time? Since that very first morning? Was the whole progress still being enacted there, was it still the same morning, and himself not yet wholly awake? And even now, had the postman not yet come round the corner?...

This idea amused him, and automatically, as he thought of it, he turned his head and looked towards the top of the hill. There was, of course, nothing there — nothing and no one. The street was empty and quiet. And all the more because of its emptiness it occurred to him to count the houses — a thing which, oddly enough, he hadn't before thought of doing. Of course, he had known there weren't many — many, that is, on his own side of the street, which were the ones that figured in the postman's progress — but nevertheless it came to him as something of a shock to find that there were precisely *six*, above his own house — his own house was the seventh.

Six!

Astonished, he looked at his own house — looked at the door, on which was the number thirteen — and then realized that the whole thing was exactly and logically and absurdly what he ought to have known. Just the same, the realization gave him abruptly, and even a little frighteningly, a sense of hurry. He was being hurried — he was being rushed. For — he knit his brows — he couldn't be mistaken — it was just above the *seventh* house, his *own* house, that the postman had first been audible this very morning. But in that case — in that case — did it mean that tomorrow he would hear nothing? The knock he had heard must have been the knock of their own door. Did it mean — and this was an idea which gave him a really extraordinary feeling of surprise — that he would never hear the postman again? — that tomorrow morning the postman would already have passed the house, in a snow by then so deep as to render his footsteps completely inaudible? That he would have made his approach down the snow-filled street so soundlessly, so secretly, that he, Paul Hasleman, there lying in bed, would not have waked in time, or, waking, would have heard nothing?

But how could that be? Unless even the knocker should be muffled in the snow — frozen tight, perhaps?...But in that case —

A vague feeling of disappointment came over him; a vague sadness, as if he felt himself deprived of something which he had long looked forward to, something much prized. After all this, all this beautiful progress, the slow delicious advance of the postman, through the silent and secret snow, the knock creeping closer each day, and the footsteps nearer, the audible compass of the world thus daily narrowed, narrowed, narrowed, as the snow soothingly and beautifully encroached and deepened, after all this, was he to be defrauded of the one thing he had so wanted — to be able to count, as it were, the last two or three solemn footsteps, as they finally approached his own door? Was it all going to happen, at the end, so suddenly? or indeed, had it already happened? with no slow and subtle graduations of menace, in which he could luxuriate?

He gazed upward again, towards his own window which flashed in the sun: and this time almost with a feeling that it would be better if he *were* still in bed, in that room; for in that case this must still be the first morning, and there would be six more mornings to come — or, for that matter, seven or eight or nine — how could he be sure? — or even more.

Chapter Three

After supper, the inquisition began. He stood before the doctor, under the lamp, and submitted silently to the usual thumpings and tappings.

'Now will you please say "Ah!"?'

'Ah!'

'Now again please, if you don't mind.'

'Ah.'

'Say it slowly, and hold it if you can —'

'Ah-h-h-h-h-h —'

'Good.'

How silly all this was. As if it had anything to do with his throat! Or his heart or lungs!

Relaxing his mouth, of which the corners, after all this absurd stretching, felt uncomfortable, he avoided the doctor's eyes, and stared towards the fireplace, past his mother's feet (in grey slippers) which projected from the green chair, and his father's feet (in brown slippers) which stood neatly side by side on the hearth-rug.

'H'm. There is certainly nothing wrong there....'

He felt the doctor's eyes fixed upon him, and, as if merely to be polite, returned the look, but with a feeling of justifiable evasiveness.

'Now, young man, tell me — do you feel all right?'

I knew a man once in the Tourdenoise....(He) would study the sky at night and take from it a larger and a larger draught of infinitude, finding in this exercise not a mere satisfaction, but an object and goal for the mind; when he had so wandered for a while under the night he seemed, for the moment, to have reached the object of his being.

Hilaire Belloc, *On Coming to Our End* (1909)

...all those capable of deep trance as adults had, (as children) shared in fantasy play and imaginative ventures of some sort with their parents....(they) told them tales, ghostly stories, saw giant-castles in the clouds with them, played 'let's-pretend' with them, listened to the children's fantasies with respect.

J.C. Pearce, *The Crack in the Cosmic Egg* (1971)

Depend upon it, there is mythology now as there was in the time of Homer, only we do not perceive it, because we ourselves live in the very shadow of it, and because we all shrink from the full meridian light of truth.

Max Muller

'Yes, sir, quite all right.'

'No headaches? No dizziness?'

'No, I don't think so.'

'Let me see. Let's get a book, if you don't mind — yes, thank you, that will do splendidly — and now, Paul, if you'll just read it, holding it as you would normally hold it —'

He took the book and read:

'And another praise have I to tell for this the city our mother, the gift of a great god, a glory of the land most high; the might of horses, the might of young horses, the might of the sea....For thou, son of Cronus, our lord Poseidon, has throned herein this pride, since in these roads first thou didst show forth the curb that cures the rage of steeds. And the shapely oar, apt to men's hands, hath a wondrous speed on the brine, following the hundred-footed Nereids....O land that art praised above all lands, now is it for thee to make those bright praises seen in deeds.'

He stopped, tentatively, and lowered the heavy book.

'No — as I thought — there is certainly no superficial sign of eyestrain.'

Silence thronged the room, and he was aware of the focused scrutiny of the three people who confronted him....

'We could have his eyes examined — but I believe it is something else.'

'What could it be?' This was his father's voice.

'It's only this curious absent-minded —' This was his mother's voice.

In the presence of the doctor, they both seemed irritatingly apologetic.

'I believe it is something else. Now, Paul — I would like very much to ask you a question or two. You will answer them, won't you — you know I'm an old, old friend of yours, eh? That's right!...'

His back was thumped twice by the doctor's fat fist — then the doctor was grinning at him with false amiability, while with one finger-nail he was scratching the top button of his waistcoat. Beyond the doctor's shoulder was the fire, the fingers of flame making light prestidigitation against the sooty fire-back, the soft sound of their random flutter the only sound.

'I would like to know — is there anything that worries you?'

The doctor was again smiling, his eyelids low against the little black pupils, in each of which a tiny white bead of light. Why answer him? Why answer him at all? 'At whatever pain to others' — but it was all a nuisance, this necessity for resistance, this necessity for attention: it was as if one had been stood up on a brilliantly lighted stage, under a great round blaze of spotlight; as if one were merely a trained seal, or a performing dog, or a fish, dipped out of an aquarium and held up by the tail. It would serve them right if he were merely to bark or growl. And meanwhile, to miss these last few precious hours, these hours of which every minute was more beautiful than the last, more menacing — ? He still looked, as if from a great distance, at the beads of light in the doctor's eyes, at the fixed false smile, and then, beyond, once more at his mother's slippers, his father's slippers, the soft flutter of the fire. Even here, even amongst these hostile presences, and in this arranged light, he could see the snow, he could hear it — it was in the corners of the room, where the shadow was deepest, under the sofa, behind the half-opened door which led to the dining-room. It was gentler here, softer, its seethe the quietest of whispers, as if, in deference to a drawing-room, it had quite deliberately put on its 'manners'; it kept itself out of sight, obliterated itself, but distinctly with an air of saying, 'Ah, but just wait! Wait till we are alone together! Then I will begin to tell you something new! Something white! something cold! something sleepy! something of cease, and peace, and the long bright curve of space! Tell them to go away. Banish them. Refuse to speak. Leave them, go upstairs to your room, turn out the light and get into bed — I will go with you, I will be waiting for you, I will tell you a better story than Little Kay of the Skates, or The Snow Ghost — I will surround your bed, I will close the windows, pile a deep drift against the door, so that none will ever again be able to enter. Speak to them!...' It seemed as if the little hissing voice came from a slow white spiral of falling flakes in the corner by the front window — but he could not be sure. He felt himself smiling, then, and said to the doctor, but without looking at him, looking beyond him still:

'Oh no, I think not.'

'But are you sure, my boy?'

His father's voice came softly and coldly then — the familiar voice of silken warning....

'You needn't answer at once, Paul — remember we're trying to help you — think it over and be quite sure, won't you?'

He felt himself smiling again, at the notion of being quite sure. What a joke! As if he weren't so sure that reassurance was no longer necessary, and all this cross-examination a ridiculous farce, a grotesque parody! What could they know about it? These gross intelligences, these humdrum minds so bound to the usual, the ordinary? Impossible to tell them about it! Why, even now, even now, with the proof so abundant, so formidable, so imminent, so appallingly present here in this very room, could they believe it? — could even his mother believe it? No — it was only too plain that if anything were said about it, the merest hint given, they would be incredulous — they would laugh — they would say 'Absurd!' — think things about him which weren't true....

'Why no, I'm not worried — why should I be?'

He looked then straight at the doctor's low-lidded eyes, looked from one of them to the other, from one bead of light to the other, and gave a little laugh.

The doctor seemed to be disconcerted by this. He drew back in his chair, resting a fat white hand on either knee. The smile faded slowly from his face.

'Well, Paul!' he said, and paused gravely. 'I'm afraid you don't take this quite seriously enough. I think you perhaps don't quite realize — don't quite realize —' He took a deep quick breath, and turned, as if helpless, at a loss for words, to the others. But Mother and Father were both silent — no help was forthcoming.

'You must surely know, be aware, that you have not been quite yourself, of late? Don't you know that?...'

It was amusing to watch the doctor's renewed attempt at a smile, a queer disorganized look, as of confidential embarrassment.

'I feel all right, sir,' he said, and again gave the little laugh.

'And we're trying to help you.' The doctor's tone sharpened.

'Yes, sir, I know. But why? I'm all right. I'm just *thinking,* that's all.'

His mother made a quick movement forward, resting a hand on the back of the doctor's chair.

'Thinking?' she said. 'But, my dear, about what?'

This was a direct challenge — and would have to be directly met. But before he met it, he looked again into the corner by the door, as if for reassurance. He smiled again at what he saw, at what he heard. The little spiral was still there, still softly whirling, like the ghost of a white kitten chasing the ghost of a white tail, and making as it did so the faintest of whispers. It was all right! If only he could remain firm, everything was going to be all right.

'Oh, about anything, about nothing — *you* know the way you do!'

'You mean — day-dreaming?'

'Oh no — thinking!'

'But thinking about *what*?'

'Anything.'

He laughed a third time — but this time, happening to glance upward towards his mother's face, he was appalled at the effect his laughter seemed to have upon her. Her mouth had opened in an expression of horror....This was too bad! Unfortunate! He had known it would cause pain, of course — but he hadn't expected it to be quite so bad as this. Perhaps — perhaps if he just gave them a tiny gleaming hint — ?

'About the snow,' he said.

'What on earth!' This was his father's voice. The brown slippers came a step nearer on the hearth-rug.

'But, my dear, what do you mean?' This was his mother's voice.

The doctor merely stared.

'Just *snow,* that's all. I like to think about it.'

'Tell us about it, my boy.'

'But that's all it is. There's nothing to tell. *You* know what snow is.'

This he said almost angrily, for he felt that they were trying to corner him. He turned sideways so as no longer to face the doctor, and the better to see the inch of blackness between the window-sill and the lowered curtains — the

cold inch of beckoning and delicious night. At once he felt better, more assured.

'Mother — can I go to bed, now, please? I've got a headache.'

'But I thought you said —'

'It's just come. It's all these questions! Can I, Mother?'

'You can go as soon as the doctor has finished.'

'Don't you think this thing ought to be gone into thoroughly, and *now?*' This was Father's voice. The brown slippers again came a step nearer, the voice was the well-known 'punishment' voice, resonant and cruel.

'Oh, what's the use, Norman —'

Quite suddenly, everyone was silent. And without precisely facing them, nevertheless he was aware that all three of them were watching him with an extraordinary intensity — staring hard at him — as if he had done something monstrous, or was himself some kind of monster. He could hear the soft irregular flutter of the flames; the cluck-click-cluck-click of the clock; far and faint two sudden spurts of laughter from the kitchen, as quickly cut off as begun; a murmur of water in the pipes; and then, the silence seemed to deepen, to spread out, to become world-long and world-wide, to become timeless and shapeless, and to centre inevitably and rightly, with a slow and sleepy but enormous concentration of all power, on the beginning of a new sound. What this new sound was going to be, he knew perfectly well. It might begin with a hiss, but it would end with a roar — there was no time to lose — he must escape. It mustn't happen here.

Without another word, he turned and ran up the stairs.

Chapter Four

Not a moment too soon. The darkness was coming in long white waves. A prolonged sibilance filled the night — a great seamless seethe of wild influence went abruptly across it — a cold low humming shook the windows. He shut the door and flung off his clothes in the dark. The bare black floor was like a little raft tossed in waves of snow, almost overwhelmed, washed under whitely, up again, smothered in curled billows of feather. The snow was laughing: it spoke from all sides at once: it pressed closer to him as he ran and jumped exulting into his bed.

'Listen to us!' it said. 'Listen! We have come to tell you the story we told you about. You remember? Lie down. Shut your eyes, now — you will no longer see much — in this white darkness who could see, or want to see? We will take the place of everything....Listen —'

A beautiful varying dance of snow began at the front of the room, came forward and then retreated, flattened out towards the floor, then rose fountain-like to the ceiling, swayed, recruited itself from a new stream of flakes which poured laughing in through the humming window, advanced again, lifted long white arms. It said peace, it said remoteness, it said cold — it said —

But then a gash of horrible light fell brutally across the room from the opening door — the snow drew back hissing — something alien had come into the room — something hostile. This thing rushed at him, clutched at him, shook him — and he was not merely horrified, he was filled with such a loathing as he had never known. What was this? this cruel disturbance? this act of anger and hate? It was as if he had to reach up a hand towards another world for any understanding of it — an effort of which he was only barely capable. But of that other world he still remembered just enough to know the exorcising words. They tore themselves from his other life suddenly.

'Mother! Mother! Go away! I hate you!'

And with that effort, everything was solved, everything became all right: the seamless hiss advanced once more, the long white wavering lines rose and fell like enormous whispering sea-waves, the whisper becoming louder, the laughter more numerous.

'Listen!' it said. 'We'll tell you the last, the most beautiful and secret story — shut your eyes — it is a very small story — a story that gets smaller and smaller — it comes inward instead of opening like a flower — it is a flower becoming a seed — a little cold seed — do you hear? We are leaning closer to you.'

The hiss was now becoming a roar — the whole world was a vast moving screen of snow — but even now it said peace, it said remoteness, it said cold, it said sleep.

...what tempted me most was the warm, shallow, reed-grown Barrington River down the east shore of the bay. I used to go there on my bicycle and look speculatively at it....How easy it would be to wade out among the rushes and lie face down in the warm water till oblivion came. There would be a certain gurgling or choking unpleasantness at first — but it would soon be over. Then the long peaceful night of non-existence....

H.P. Lovecraft

The Monster Children
Joyce Maynard, Newsweek, July 26, 1976

A friend of mine told me this story several years ago, and it's a true one. He said he bought a baby rabbit one spring and built a hutch for it out behind his house. At first, when the rabbit was little and cute, he spent a lot of time watching it, but after a while he would just toss the lettuce and carrots in the cage without really looking. One day, in the fall, a visitor caught sight of the rabbit and screamed, so for the first time in months, my friend came to look. The animal's two front teeth had grown into fangs, and curved out of its mouth like elephant tusks, to the point where they had begun to cut into the rabbit's own neck.

I still have dreams about that rabbit, and they're more frightening than any my mind can construct about tigers or snakes. You expect those animals to be sinister and threatening, after all. No villain is more frightening than the one you had supposed to be your friend.

I saw a new movie last week in which a man tries to stab a 5-year-old boy to death and when he raised his knife over the boy's throat, the audience cheered. Like quite a few films that have come out since "Rosemary's Baby" and "The Exorcist," this movie had to do with demonic possession, and once again the devil was personified by a child.

Babes in arms
The idea of a parent killing a child is not new. In fairy tales and legends, and even in the Bible, there are stepmothers who send children out into the woods, fathers who lead sons to mountaintops to sacrifice them. What has changed is that parental violence no longer seems to be a source of guilt and shame — and its objects are no longer depicted

as innocents. The enemy now is not the man in the black hat or the white shark or even the Washington politician. It is the child.

It's not difficult to find reasons for this. Parents who stood, proud and hopeful, at the hospital windows twenty years ago, making plans for sleeping, soft-skinned infants, could hardly have bargained for Quaaludes and David Bowie, for daughters and sons who would live inside stereo headphones or sit, silent, at the dinner table, opening their mouths only to eat, or to say "Do you know how much I hate you?" They would not have guessed, back then, that there would be 14-year-olds on the Pill, and a Symbionese Liberation Army.

What has happened to the children — not to all of them, but to a large number — must seem, to their parents, almost like the fairy tales where elves steal the real, good infant and substitute a changeling. I suppose the parents of these changeling children must be frightened, to be harboring strangers — enemies, almost — under their roofs, feeding them, putting the sequined T shirts on their backs, and receiving not the gratitude or respect they gave their parents but condescension and contempt and maybe pity. Sometimes the children do not even seem quite human: it's difficult to picture the toughest, coolest ones crying, hard to believe they were ever babies.

The result of this is a growing anti-child sentiment that makes me sad. I read in a woman's magazine last month the results of a poll in which 10,000 mothers were asked whether they would again choose to have children. Seventy per cent said they would not. Newspapers play up stories of youth gangs and violence while the public clamors for a "tighter rein." Even the children we choose as our movie and television stars are appealing, almost, for their very sinisterness (Mason Reese, with his ancient, goblin face; Tatum O'Neal in her black tuxedo and her eye make-up).

A lot of parents now even seem to be turning on their own children. My mother tells me that when she goes to a party there is always talk of the children — but something has changed. Once the parents used to boast. Now they commiserate, and exchange examples of their own sons' and daughters' awfulness. I'm thinking too of several books from the last few years: Midge Decter's "Liberal Parents, Radical Children," in which her own offspring are shown as fairly unlovable, Alison Lurie's "War Between the Tates," with a couple of monstrous teenagers in it, and those self-help manuals with advice for parents on "how to call a truce with your children."

Then there was the case of the middle-class father who shot and killed his "uncontrollable" son, was tried for the crime and set free. Patricia Hearst, on the other hand, has gone to jail, and while many people feel badly for her, what one hears, more often, is sympathy for her parents, and the question: "What did they ever do to deserve this?"

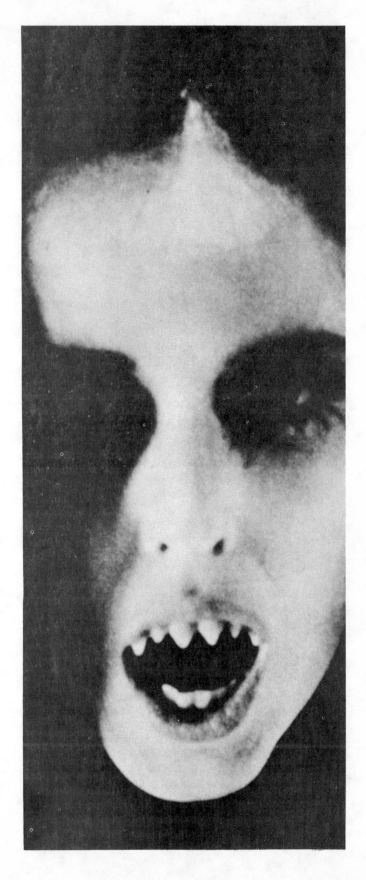

Bewitched

That's the large and frightening question troubling the parents who view their children as monstrous strangers. And what is so appealing, I think, about these demonic-possession movies is that they suggest some spontaneously generated, innate evil in the children, something completely out of the parents' control. Fault lies with the Devil, or the drugs, or the music, or the false guru, or what is referred to as "the world we live in," and not with the parents themselves.

I do believe that there are good and loving and conscientious people among the parents of the "bad" children, and that no parent should take full blame for what his child does. But the notion that a parent has no control over determining the kind of person his child will be seems to me dangerous. It lets parents off the hook too easily.

If children are worse now than they used to be, it isn't that parents are necessarily more inept than earlier generations were. But if they've done something wrong they are less likely to get away with it than they once were, in the days when children's demons, though no less present, were less visible.

The reasons why a child "goes bad" are complicated, for sure. But when there is a monster child, who appears determined to be as uncute, as unlovable as possible, and his parents turn on him, I wonder if that suggests something about the quality of their love. It doesn't seem far, really, from the quality of feeling evidenced by the purchasers of baby rabbits who stop visiting the hutch after the animal outgrows the Easter basket. No wonder the fangs begin to sprout.

from **The Vampire**
Haigh & The Brand of Satan
Basil Copper

Though it has long been a matter of dispute among medical circles, there is no doubt in my mind that John George Haigh was a vampire in the classical tradition, possibly the only true monster in this field in the twentieth century. By this, of course, I do not mean to imply that he was a vampire in the supernatural sense, but there is at least a strong suggestion that he needed to drink blood in order to refresh and sustain himself. It will be disgusting to many that such a creature should not only murder innocent people and dispose of them in such a revolting way, but that he should then drink the blood of the newly dead.

This is something that has to be faced in such a study and readers with a sensitive turn of mind should perhaps be warned that we are now about to turn to detailed examination of Haigh's alleged vampirism; to examine the medical evidence and to try to assess all the available facts. But first, we should know something of his earlier life and background.

John George Haigh was born at Stamford, Lincolnshire, on 24th July 1909. His father, after holding a good job as a foreman in an electricity works, was unemployed at the time, a cause of great bitterness to the family. Haigh's mother was herself 40 when he was born; he was an only child and spent his formative years at Outwood, near Wakefield, where the father then obtained work at a colliery. Haigh's solitary nature was naturally affected by his strange upbringing. Both parents belonged to a strict sect called the Peculiar People. It was aptly named; to Haigh's parents religious beliefs were of paramount importance. The growing boy was brought up on a diet of Bible parables and sayings, much of which were concerned with sacrifice. The grown man was to write later in life: 'I had none of the joys or the companionship which small children usually have. Any form of sport or light entertainment was frowned upon and regarded as not edifying. There was only, and always, condemnation and prohibition.' And he added, of his father: 'He was constantly preoccupied with thoughts of the hereafter and often wished the Lord would take him home. It was a sin to be content with this world and there were constant reminders of its corruption and evil. Often I pondered my father's references to the Heavenly places and to the 'worms that will destroy this body'. It was inevitable that I should develop an early inhibition regarding death.'

It would be remarkable, given the circumstances of Haigh's upbringing, if a normal man had emerged at the end of some twenty-five years of such formative influences as those his parents brought to bear. If Haigh's written testimony is to be trusted, his father must shoulder a great

deal of responsibility for the monster who eventually shocked post-war England.

Haigh continues of his family 'So great in fact was (his) desire to separate himself and his family from the evil world that he built a great wall round our garden so that no one could look in.' And he mentions a curious incident regarding the elder Haigh.

He writes: 'On my father's forehead is a small blue scar shaped like a distorted cross. Explaining the mark to me when I was very young he said, "This is the brand of Satan. I have sinned and Satan has punished me. If you ever sin, Satan will mark you with a blue pencil likewise".'

A curious conceit for a parent to display to his young son, and Haigh brooded about this for a long time; the tale of Satan's mark filled him with deep anxiety and even when, in later years, he came to realise that it was nothing but a scar caused by a lump of coal in his father's mine, he still kept looking at people in the street to see if they carried Satan's mark.

Despite the weird influences at work on his childhood, Haigh retained a deep love for his parents and he was sure they loved him also; to him they 'remained all that is noble'.

Haigh went to Wakefield Grammar School and also became a chorister at the cathedral when the strict Plymouth Brethren teachings of his parents at home began to clash with the Anglo-Catholic services at the cathedral. One sinister ritual of his earlier childhood threw a crooked shadow of things to come.

Lord Dunboyne says in his introduction to the trial:

'Haigh used to assert that his fond mother corrected him during childhood by smacking his hand with the bristles of a hairbrush. When his trial for murder was pending, he added that the punishment of the hairbrush drew blood, which he sucked and enjoyed to such an extent that he later deliberately cut his finger to gratify the taste he had acquired.' This statement needs little comment except to note that it reinforces and helps to explain Haigh's vampirism; his addiction to blood and the blood-drinking which was to be such a feature of the trial had been a cumulative force from his early days and it does not appear to me to have been grafted on to his evidence in order to provide a basis for a verdict of guilty but of unsound mind.

Needless to say the teachings of Haigh's parents were repressive and anti-clerical and were thus basically opposed to all the teachings and influences he was subjected to at the cathedral — where he was a chorister, pianist and organist for minor services, it will be remembered.

His dreams began to assume increasing importance at this stage; the analogy of Christ bleeding on the Cross at the cathedral has already been mentioned. Haigh asserted that he constantly saw Christ bleeding in his dreams. One of Haigh's more celebrated pronouncements during his arrest and trial was that he also had a recurring dream by which he climbed to the moon by means of a huge telescopic ladder; the colours of his dreams were bloody, and the globe from his ladder in space was also 'incarnadine', he added poetically. He also mentioned that from the age of 11 he had been in the habit of drinking his own urine.

Yet his sex life appeared normal, and he married a young girl at the age of 24. But he was subsequently sent to prison for fraud, and Mrs. Haigh disappears completely from the story; at any event he never saw her again. He had left school at 17 and after being employed by a firm of motor engineers started an advertising and estate agency. He then floated some large companies but later drifted into crime by means of fraud and forgery and was sent to prison for fifteen months in 1934. A long series of swindles and further spells in prison followed.

It was while he was in Lincoln Prison during the war that he experimented with dissolving field mice in sulphuric acid, when working in the tinsmith's shop. One wonders whether he then had any inkling of the later and more terrible use to which he was to put the idea. His obsession with blood appears to have returned when he was involved in a motor accident while working in light engineering at Crawley in the middle period of the war.

He suffered a 2-inch cut on his skull and he later said of the smash, 'Blood poured from my head down my face and into my mouth. This revived in me the taste and that night I experienced another awful dream. I saw before me a forest of crucifixes, which gradually turned into trees. At first there appeared to be dew, or rain dripping from the branches but as I approached I realised it was blood.'

Haigh continued, 'Suddenly the whole forest began to writhe and the trees, stark and erect, to ooze blood. A man went to each tree catching the blood. When the cup was full he approached me. ''Drink'' he said, but I was unable to move and the dream faded.' This extraordinary and vividly worded narrative was later somewhat discounted at the trial as being a concoction of the defendant with a view to pleading insanity.

The first true indication of Haigh's vampirism comes in his statement on the murder of the unfortunate Donald McSwan. The exact date was never established but police found in Haigh's diary, the date 9th September 1944 marked with a red cross, and it was taken to mean that McSwan met his end on that day. Haigh told the police, 'I got the feeling I must get some blood somewhere. I was meeting McSwan from time to time. The idea came to me to kill him and take some blood. I hit him over the head and he was unconscious. I got a mug and took some blood from his neck in a mug and drank it....That night I had the dream when I caught up with the blood.'

Lord Dunboyne says of this incident, 'On 12th September Haigh happened to mention in a personal letter from London that he was suffering from enteritis. Possibly the complaint was caused by drinking the blood of W.D. McSwan. On the other hand, Haigh's positive statement that he was never sick after his blood-drinking casts doubts on whether he ever indulged in the habit, because human blood, drunk neat, is almost bound to act as an emetic.'

Haigh then said he murdered a middle-aged woman about November of that year, though this was never proved. But experts felt there was little doubt that he murdered both parents of Donald McSwan, and this was believed to have taken place in July 1945. Haigh said that as the father's corpse did not produce enough blood he

---

The vampire seems to promise a similar triumph: a conquest of death, resurrection and eternal life. It is only that the sponsorship, as it were, is all wrong. Satan, not God, is the source of the energy, so that his gift is a soul-killing imitation of Christ's promise. The vampire's conquest becomes an infinite extension of death; his resurrection has ghastly conditions imposed on it; and his promised eternal life is an animated corporeality that stinks of the grave.

Leonard Wolf, *A Dream of Dracula* (1972)

---

killed the mother on the same day. The police, rather more prosaically, attributed Haigh's motives as being his desire to destroy the whole family in order to get hold of their property. All three members of the McSwan family were dissolved in acid, the same way he was later to dispose of Mrs. Durand-Deacon.

Like a sinister bird of prey Haigh then left Crawley in

1945 and booked in at the Onslow Court Hotel, some four years later to be the scene of so much excitement and police activity. But Haigh's appalling trail of crime was only half begun and soon the unfortunate Hendersons were to come within his orbit. Haigh, it is true, was keeping his hand in, it might be said, as he confessed to the authorities that he had murdered a youth at Gloucester Road in the autumn of 1945 — but this, like the reports of the other two alleged victims earlier mentioned, could not be substantiated.

Though Haigh had gained something like 6,000 pounds through his murderous activities, by August 1947 he was again in debt. It was then he met Dr. and Mrs. Henderson of Ladbroke Square through an advertisement of their house being for sale. He spent several months cultivating their friendship, but Christmas of that year found him ordering several carboys of acid for the infamous storeroom at Crawley. In February 1948 he ordered two 40-gallon drums. The vampire was about to claim two more victims.

It was in February that Haigh later told the police, his dream cycle recommenced. Once again, 'I was seized with an awful urge. Once more I saw the forest of crucifixes which changes to trees dripping with blood. Once more I wakened with the desire which demanded fulfilment.' One is irresistibly reminded of Stoker's description of Dracula's slave Renfield, who, like Haigh, was seized with the terrible urge to drink blood and who, while imprisoned, catches insects for the nourishment which they will afford his blood-lust.

Haigh continued, 'Archie was to be the next victim...in the storeroom at Leopold Road I shot him in the head with his own revolver. I then returned to Brighton and told Rose that Archie had been taken ill very suddenly and needed her. I said I would drive her to him. She accompanied me to the storeroom at Crawley and there I shot her. From each of them I took my draught of blood.'

No one ever saw the Hendersons again but Haigh's diary entries contained the initials 'A.H.', presumably for Archibald Henderson and 'R.H.' for Rosalie Henderson. Haigh had followed up the entry by adding the sign of the cross. With the Hendersons dissolving into nothingness in the two drums he had bought, Haigh then proceeded to dispose of their property. He told the prison authorities that he had been impelled to kill them solely through his thirst for blood, stimulated by his dreams, and all the time he believed himself to be under divine protection. Describing the killing of Dr. and Mrs. Henderson he said, 'I felt convinced there was an overseeing hand which would protect me.'

So confident was he of this that when he found one of Dr. Henderson's feet still undissolved when emptying out the sludge from the drum, he left it without even troubling to hide this shocking piece of evidence within the bounds of the yard.

Haigh's next crime, his penultimate if he is to be believed, was the murder of a girl at Eastbourne; but like the earlier cases, this could not be established by the police. His dark passage through the years was completed with the murder of Mrs. Durand-Deacon the following year, when once again his debts had become insupportable.

'It was not their money but their blood that I was after,' said Haigh. 'The thing I am really conscious of is the cup of blood which is constantly before me. I shot some of my victims...I can say I made a small cut, usually in the right side of the neck, and drank the blood for three to five minutes and that afterwards I felt better. Before each of the killings I have detailed in my confession, I had my series of dreams and another common factor was that the dream cycle started early in the week and culminated on a Friday.'

Give me dog, dogs, wolves, to serve, praise, kneel in thanks. Bring me torn by sin, stuffed with loot, bring me in their wild midst, in the spiked ring of white teeth, sharp fangs, wet mouths, cast me hard and down. I am not food, the calf, the ewe, I am the man to be sent to love, but clawed first, cleansed first, taught to fight, to lose, save my skin, my stained skin, my own old soft shell.

Leonard Cohen

The investigating authorities, rightly or wrongly, tended largely to discard the vampire theory, as I have earlier indicated, but Haigh's own story — unsupported, it must be admitted — bears a powerful ring of truth and there was the significant factor of a blood-stained penknife being found in his car.

Lord Dunboyne, in a particularly interesting passage of his brilliant introduction to the trial, has this to say of Haigh's vampirism. Speaking of Haigh's statements on this factor, he comments.

He (Haigh) was well aware that humans have been known to drink blood since primeval times. The phenomenon has not been confined to the symbolism of religious ritual. It has occurred in history in other connections. About 300 BC there is an account in the Mahavagga of a certain Buddhist monk who suffered from a seemingly incurable disease. He went to a place where swine were slaughtered, and ate their raw flesh and drank their blood and his sickness abated.

Again, primitive head-hunters and warriors have been known to believe that the blood of their victims, if drunk, will engender bravery; and even during the 1939 war, it was not unknown for Colonial troops, who were stationed in Europe, to visit local abattoirs and to drink the fresh blood of sheep and bullocks for the same reason. A yet more recent throwback of a similar tradition appears in Kenya to have induced the Mau Mau initiates to lick the blood of newly slain goats.

Further, some primitive tribes have, from time immemorial, cherished the belief that by tasting the blood of a slain person the slayer will enjoy such a fusion of blood in his veins as to form a communion of friendship with his victim and avert the evils of an avenging spirit. But in such cases, the killer is usually prompted only to lick the blood, for instance from the lethal weapon, and not to drink it as Haigh claimed he had done.

(Lord Dunboyne concludes.) In all these instances, moreover, the drinking of blood is actuated by a belief in its salutary effect and not associated in any way with psychopathic behaviour. In the very rare cases of a spontaneous impulse to drink human blood, the desire has invariably been connected with a sexual perversion. Even then it has been only incidental, in the frenzy of sexual excitement. In Haigh's life, on the other hand there is nothing to suggest sexual abnormality.

(Instead, Lord Dunboyne is of the opinion.) It is probable that he (Haigh) acquired his knowledge of blood-drinking from literature he had read on the subject and that he exploited the idea in an attempt to substantiate his plea of insanity and to escape execution.

This is something which, after all, must be left to the judgement of the reader, lacking concrete evidence which would prove the matter one way or the other. Certainly, Haigh's alleged vampirism had little effect on the case; three psychiatrists called in held that Haigh was simulating insanity and that there was no reason to believe he was irresponsible on legal grounds, or insane according to the medical evidence. Haigh was therefore duly executed at Wandsworth Prison on 6th August 1949, and the greatest *cause celebre* of its kind in the twentieth century was at an end.

Was Haigh a vampire? The story unfolded in the hushed Sussex courtroom was an incredible one. It was also a macabre one, the evidence being not only shocking but disgusting to most people of normal mind. If Haigh's statements — and they tallied in so many respects, even after repetition — are to be accepted at their face value and he was a genuine vampire from a medical point of view, how much of this was his fault and how much should be laid at the door of his parents? To some people, horrible as his crimes were, Haigh must have seemed, even at the time, to be more of a victim of a unique environment, rather than a sadistic monster. This is essentially a limited viewpoint and one not likely to be held by many, but nevertheless it must be put.

Sir David Maxwell Fyfe, Haigh's counsel, in a long and cogently argued opening speech for the defence, put forward a vivid description of Haigh's dreams in support of his contention that he was a paranoic.

Sir David said: 'He (Haigh) began by seeing in these dreams a veritable forest of crucifixes, and as the dream developed, in that absurd way in which even our ordinary dreams behave, the crucifixes turned into trees; in turn, one of the trees became a man. And that man appeared to be collecting something from those dripping trees. At first it appeared to be rain or dew, and as the dream developed, it appeared to be blood. You will hear that the dream repeated itself six or seven times; and the prisoner's account is that, as the blood was taken, he tried to get near to the man, but he could never get near enough to him, and he felt, first of all, an overmastering desire to have blood, and, secondly, that this controlling spirit of his was determined that he should have blood. Then, when the opportunity came to do these dreadful deeds, he felt that he was carrying out, not his own desires, but the divinely appointed courses that had been set for him in this way.'

The distinguished psychiatrist, Dr. Henry Yellowlees, who was called by Sir David as one of the principal defence witnesses went exhaustively into Haigh's strange dreams. Significantly, he said of the defendant's alleged vampirism, 'I think it is pretty certain that he tasted it (the blood); I do not know whether he drank it or not. From a medical point of view, I do not think it is important, for the reason that this question of blood runs through all his fantasies from childhood like a motif and is the core of the paranoid structure that I believe he has created, and it does not matter very much to a paranoic whether he does things in fancy or fact. That is what I feel medically about it.'

The important factor here is that Dr. Yellowlees said it did not matter medically whether Haigh had drunk blood or not; the witness was, of course, dealing at this point with the defendant's state of mind. Equally significantly 'it does not matter very much to a paranoic whether he does things in fancy or in fact', so Dr. Yellowlees's evidence-in-chief and his cross-examination by the prosecution does not rule out Haigh's vampirism.

It is something which cannot be proved through the evidence produced during the trial, for there was no evidence, but as I have said before, after sifting the masses of statements made at the time, there is no doubt in my own mind that Haigh was speaking the truth. Out of his tortured childhood had emerged a malformed human being; a vampiric predator whose thirst for blood was slaked on at least six occasions post mortem. That he is an horrific figure does not preclude him from being a sad one; despite his forebears from the mists of the past, such as Gilles de Rais and Sergeant Bertrand, he remains a figure mercifully unique in the twentieth century so far.

In an age not noted for kindness or regard for human life; which has seen two major slaughters on a world scale; and the holocausts of the Nazis and the atom bomb, the vampire is still a figure which commands attention. This is the significance of Haigh and will make his case a talking point after other, perhaps more heinous crimes, are long forgotten.

Trial of the Blood
K.M. O'Donnell

Lamiae were thought by ancient writers to be women who had the horrid power of removing their eyes, or else a kind of demon or ghost. These would appear under the guise of lovely courtesans who, by their enticing wiles, would draw some plump rosy-cheeked damoiseau into their embraces and then devour him wholemeal....Dio Chrysostom relates that in Central Africa there are certain fierce beasts which are termed *lamiae*. They have the countenances of beautiful women, and their bosoms are so white and fair as no brush could paint. These they show very wantonly and thus attract men by lewd deceit, but their victims they cruelly mangle and craunch. So the prophet Jeremiah saith, *Lamentations*, iv. 3: 'Even the *lamiae* have drawn out the breast.'

Montague Summers, *The Vampire His Kith and Kin* (1928)

June 16

I think, I think this: it was not cruelty which drove me on but rather an *excess of feeling,* a need to touch, to burst through the barriers we create against one another and know, then, the naked, vulnerable human heart, I do believe this, I am not a cruel man, I derive no satisfaction emotionally from what I have been forced to do, I am seized by *regret* and *remorse* at almost all of the worst moments...and yet, and yet, what is the point? I must go on. I do the necessary as do we all. And now, my powers at last deserting me, I confront what has happened and know that it could have been no other way.

Out into the tangled landscape again this evening, prowling the corridors of this ruined country, dead kings and warriors seeming to glint at me through the forests, the broken paths, leaping and stumbling through this abandoned country that will (I see this) some day be overtaken by machinery that will break the landscape to shreds, into an isolated house that I had marked down upon my sheets as a marginal possibility months ago (now, exhausted, I am down to the marginal possibilities) and into the bedrooms, passing through the locks with old cunning, seeing the sleepers: an old man, an old woman, another old man, an old man...age, age, senescence, dust, death, and at the end of the hallway one last bedroom where the virgin slept. I know she must have been a virgin. In my mind, at least, all of them are untouched: no one knows better than I or ever will their corruption, the rotting of the flesh, the unspeakable pleasures which even the most innocent-appearing of them have indulged shrieking...but in the cool, gray abscesses of the mind all is purity. I saw her. She saw me, her eyes fluttering to connection. We looked upon one another. She stroked a hand against her mouth like a butterfly. "No," she said, *"no"*. I spread my cloak apart so that she could see me. Her eyes terrified, glazed over with knowledge. My reputation, you see, has gotten around in these parts. I fell atop her without preamble. I sank — ah, God! — I sank my teeth into her neck, feeling the smooth pearl of the skin part. She thrashed against me like a fish. I held her down easily with my weight. I put in my tongue. I drank.

And drank of her until the white of the skin that had blended with the sheet faded to gray, her struggles, dying, locked her body rigid against mine and then finally, finally I pulled away from her, shaking and left that room. In the corridors, the quiet singing of the wind against the shutters.

I was weeping. Remorse and recrimination, gentlemen, have me in their clutches. But what can I do? Considering the situation, and I am sure that you will in your ponderous gravity, assessing and understanding all...what could I do?

At home, sleeping, I dreamed of her. In the dream her blood had become a sea and I dived through it, singing.

116

June 17

A man of means, a man of substance, moderate nobility coursing through these veins, earldoms and fiefs clamoring in the background generations past...yes, I am not an ordinary assassin, not the casual beast but a murderer of some distinction and to be understood only in this way. Writing these notes, leaning over my desk, supporting the weight of my collapsing frame — I do not sleep well, I have terrible dreams — I feel a sense of power, of resonance and maybe it is this which takes me to this diary because *I cannot be ignored,* I cannot be allowed to pass, I must leave some small legacy of explanation which will finally render my position clear; it is unfair that I have done *so much* and yet what will be remembered (if any of this is; perhaps there is no future of any kind for all of us) is merely atrocity. The landscape runs with blood and terror, houses are boarded up, the constabulary continue their hopeless search for what is described as a *fiend*...and of purpose, of intention, nothing is known at all. Fear has overcome understanding. I am not a fiend but a man of substance, moderate nobility coursing through these veins....

"I did this," I wanted to say over her body last night, "I did this for love, for necessity, for the connection. I did it because I wanted to take your blood and body unto me in the most ancient and sacramental of all the rituals, I wanted to possess you utterly and make your flesh whole. For love, for love, that was all I wanted!" I could have shouted but her blood had run out over the sheets in little anguished droplets, her body had broken on the bed like an hourglass and nothing to say then, only flee the room, flee that damned house, run through that landscape like a loon and finally to this ruined, cluttered castle itself, the specters of ancient earldom staggering through and I know that whatever I do and however I try no one will ever understand but the word *fiend*. Only in these notes can I make it clear; I will continue this journal, I have a certain alacrity with the language, smattering of education, bit of literacy, am pleased with this means of expression and if I can only — only get it down straight....

I feel the urge coming over me again.

The more awake we are, the greater is the violence of the paroxysm. I have experienced the affection stealing upon me while in perfect possession of my faculties, and have undergone the greatest tortures, being haunted by specters, hags, and every sort of phantom — having, at the same time, a full consciousness that I was labouring under incubus, and that all the terrifying objects around me were the creation of my own brain.

R. Macnish *The Philosophy of Sleep* (1834)

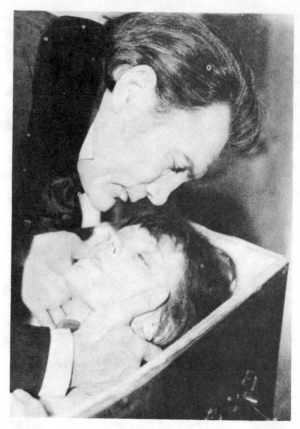

June 18

Further and further in my adventures; now I must go miles from this castle to conduct my intricate business. The surrounding populace is terrified, chains, bolts, guards, fires, all-night watches by the citizenry in the wake of the girl's funeral this morning, an event which the entire village, I am led to believe, attended...it is more and more difficult to continue these tasks which I thought at the beginning reasonably controlled, carefully attended, would sustain me until the need had passed. But the need has *not* passed, I must admit this: the taste of blood has brought the blood-craving and now I cannot sleep or think for the thought of *blood*...will there ever be an end to this? Miles from the castle in this morning's dawn, leaping the weeds like a dog, I felt a dread depression for the first time: how long can I go on this way? And if the fear spreads as it is seeming to, throughout the country, will I be reduced to waylaying travelers in the fields? This is a very tricky business. I do not know; I bounded and sniffed, fired with desire and then, as if a dream, saw in the weeds a child sleeping. I advanced upon the child slowly, slowly, saw as it turned that it was a young boy and for one stumbling instant considered: I have never before attacked a child and it was with a feeling of ominousness, of a line crossed never to be traversed over again, that I fell upon the boy in the bushes and attached my mouth to his neck, biting, biting down, taking the neck in that familiar spot, smaller and more fervent than I had ever known it and, sinking the teeth in, heard and recollected shriek as never before, a high, pitiful whine and I could, oh, God, have still stopped then and fled, the boy was uninjured but shocked, he never would have caught me, but I could not *stop,* the first taste of blood pricked up the hairs of the scalp like insects and the hunger was uncontrollable, I savaged him violently and oh what dreams he must have had then, rising from sleep to death and falling back then upon the grass as I drained him.

Now, strangely at ease, my head and mouth buzzing with sticky memories, I look out from the window to see two men approaching the door downstairs. Local officials. They are pounding on the door. They wish to see me.

I wipe my mouth again and inspect it in the glass, then go down to greet them. Part of me, part of me — I admit this — wants discovery because it will allow me to make my explanations to the world, but another, more intelligent part, that wants to live for blood another day, does not. They stand now cautiously, still serfs in the presence of the fiefdom, their hands apologetically clasped as they wait for response...and I know that I will have no trouble with these.

June 19
I could not sleep. After the interview I resolved to be cautious for some days, allow the terror to subside, but at midnight I sat on the bed, all fibers trembling, and knew that I must drink again. The constabulary are confused, there are no clues, I had no difficulty in getting rid of my two visitors, already sunk by class differences into a pool of trepidation; yes, I have heard of these horrid events, gentlemen, who has not heard of them? yes, I am entirely dismayed, no, I have myself observed nothing amiss in the neighborhood, yes, I am taking protective measures, no, I have no idea of who the assailant might be, yes, I will cooperate fully with any developing investigation, no, there are no clues. No clues, no ideas, no assistance, gentlemen; I am sorry! and they took their leave of these premises as, I regret to say, some of my victims have taken leave of their senses, quickly, gracelessly, shambling off the terrain. And now I sit hunched over these notes like a snail knowing, *knowing* that all wise counsel would lead me to *desist* for a few days, few days! few weeks is more like it, until the investigation has collapsed into false evidence or futility or until some hapless peasant has been brought in and charged with the crimes. I should stop! lay low! solder my forces together! but I cannot and I know that before the sun has come, I will go ahunting again.

Our dreams are nothing else than a message from the all-uniting dark soul.

C.G. Jung, *Psychological Reflections* (1953)

I know that what I have done, what I seek to do comes not from cruel or cold impulses but from love, *love!* of all humanity, a desire as I have already said I think (I never review these entries after I have written them; the moment to be seized is the next and the past is but a dream) for connection, blending, a fusion of forces, but I am gravely misunderstood, throughout the countryside my motives have never been approbated but they have been ignored and my two visitors spoke of "atrocities" with lowered eyes, referring delicately to certain "wounds about the neck and facial features" which marked the assailant as a "madman" and how I wanted to cry unto them *no madman but one who would turn the ancient ritual to fresh necessity* but said nothing of the sort of course, sitting quietly, rubbing nobleman's fingers into a palm, tapping a foot on the floor and giving quick little twitching nods of assent so that they would believe in my own horror of these crimes. In part I want to be caught and to confess, this is true, but I do *not* want to confess and be caught; if they can have me I will tell them all but cannot myself into their hands willingly commit. And now the need is strong within me; the need growing like seed within the vitals and I can barely hold this pen any longer; I must go upon the fields like a hound and show them, *show* them that I am no fiend, but destined for the purpose of love.

June 20

Now I think of torture. Blood is weak liquid; it will not serve indefinitely and what I am beginning to understand is that my error in taking my victims might have been the absence of confrontation: one shuddering grasp in the night, one thrust of the mouth, shrieks, whines and death following but that singing instant in which they would see me and *understand* what is being done to them and *what* has been lacking. There must be something darker and stronger, I must bind them and bring them to awareness.

I do not know what is happening to me, I fear that I am losing control and yet the thoughts of torture would strike one more as a *gaining* of control, would they not? a supersedence, sense of motion, accession to a higher mountain of purpose and yet six decaying generations of vanished nobility do admonish and hold me back. Is it *right,* Count? they seem to want to know. Do you really think that these are acts of nobility? Have you considered your forebears and your *history?* I cannot rip these little threads of advisement from my consciousness, they run through and around like bright ribbons and yet I know now that until I do so I will never be free. Must go on, I must go on then if I am to plant that seed of love which will flower and in two hundred years will cover the continent in its fields of yellow and red, blazing.

Not to talk upon what happened in the moors last night. Never to talk about it. That is a closed incident. That is *finished.* I will not think of it and instead will meditate upon the antique and honorable history of torture which, as we know, has been used by the best governments throughout all of the ages, for the betterment of men and the continued ascension toward their goals. Can a man be less than his governments? or must he, rather, strive ever to be more?.

June 21

Curiously spiritless today; able to accomplish nothing. A feeling of sea change, movement toward another level, uninterested in blood, no thoughts of the cords of the neck snapping as incline the head toward the perpetrator. No thoughts of any kind; moving underwater like an unformed creature of the depths, heading toward another shoal.

Constabulary by today on another routine visit, they told me deferentially. Pressure from the capital now to solve the mystery; panicky reports from the provinces are upsetting the balance of the country. Any further ideas? No. Any strangers in the neighborhood? No. Have I lived in this castle for all of my life alone as is rumored? No; not for all of my life but it had indeed been for a very long time. Any living relatives? Gentlemen, not even any *dead* relatives. Thank you, thank you. Fools; fools. If all that my quest has accomplished is to bring officials like these to stumbling, apologetic search, then I have accomplished nothing. *Nothing.*

Too depressed to go on. Everything changing. Tomorrow, a new purpose I feel.

June 22

That business on the moors, feeling his body break and open under mine, the blood *leaping* at me, choking, drowning in it, an aggressive dying that, and his whimpers not horrified but somehow placative. Realized then, still realizing, that this cannot continue; that the taking of their blood was never the answer. But I said, I *said* I will not write or think of this any more and I will not. I will not. A closed incident.

Still spiritless, but a feeling of gathered energy. Large events in the offing; a sensation of having passed the last barriers. In dreams my fate was never so stricken, my consequences so large: I sat at my mothers bosom and drank and drank of her, the infants thoughts as aimless as a fly buzzing on paper, locked to her uncomprehending of destiny but all of that, all of that is now and eternally departed.

June 23

Young, another young girl, coming to consciousness terrified now, looking frantically for escape, still trying to measure the situation, the bright bruise on her forehead where I had struck her to unconsciousness exploding with blood, looking, looking, then trying to move and screaming as she saw that she was bound. Hands bound, feet bound, trussed together, loop within loop, lying in the cellar like a fowl. "Kyrie eleison," she said, but liturgy means nothing to me. I showed her the knife. Not thirty minutes ago wandering free as an idiot on the fields but

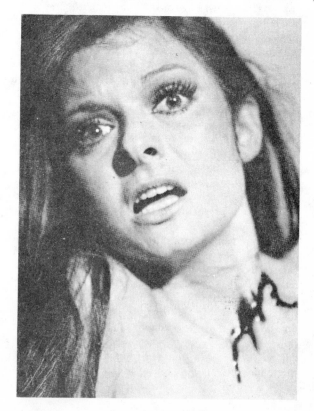

now mine, mine. I bounced the light from the knife into her eyes and she gasped with strain; I saw that she might faint and yanked her chin around to face me, putting the knife against her cheek so that she would stay in the valley of the sane. "Listen to me," I said, "now listen to me," and once again opened my cloak so that she would confront. "This is me," I said, "do you understand that? it's me! *don't turn away!*"

"Oh my God. My God —" .

"God will not save you now, neither will he take you. Only the antiChrist will have your soul when I am done, but not yet, not yet. Do you know why you are here?"

"Help me. Please help me —"

"No help," I said, *"no help!"* She would not listen. None of them ever listened. This is the horror of it: even at this moment, when all is done, *none of them are listening.* "I'm going to torture and kill you," I said, "but I want to tell you why." She inhaled and seemed about to faint again; I had to use the knife. It opened up a small wedge in her cheek. *"I want to tell you why."*

"Help me," she said again, mindlessly, "help me." Stupidity, fear, loss, the savage waste of it all. Yet one must go on. Whatever one makes of it: *one must go on,* there being no alternative to any of this but the grave. Her head rolled to the side, her eyes staring like a corpse, tongue protruding from the panic but I knew then that she was listening.

"Hear me," I said, "hear why I am doing this; one of you, somehow, must listen." Perhaps I was somewhat out of control. My mental state throughout these recent months and, now accelerating in some unknown way, has been precarious. "I wanted to know love. I wanted to change the face of the time. I wanted to carry a message and burn that message deep into the heart of this continent: that we must truly know one another and whether that knowledge is known through pain or lust, connection or fury it must be known, we must break through to a level of feeling we have never had before because it is this and only this which separates us from the beasts and if we do not have it, well, then we shall surely die." She squawked in place, held by the bonds. "And death," I said, "death is as nothing to the pain of ignorance; to know our humanity is to cherish eternity," and saying this, saying no more, brought the knife down upon and through her, spreading her like a rack of meat and then....

And then enough. I cannot bear to continue; these notes shriek to me, the pen itself feels like a knife in the hands and cannot continue. Her blood, when I was finished, tasted stale and weak against my lips, no longer the ingestion of vitality but a drinking in of death; and illness overcame me; in revulsion I vomited and then dropped the knife, staggered from the basement and came up here to this high turret where with the laughter of all ancestors around me, mad and rising laughter, I went to these notes but I simply cannot continue, I cannot continue, gentlemen, for I know now that I have failed.

And will somehow have to dispose of her now.

June 24

Odors wafting up from the basement and something must be done but I cannot do it. I cannot summon the energy to move her although if I do not move her I will not be able to save myself. Have sat at this desk all day, watching the light and the dark, moving in slow convulsions of moods but can do nothing: not eat, not drink, not even relieve myself. A feeling that all is ending.

June 25

The house stinks, the boards rot, I should put her in a sack and drag her upon the moors and yet, yet I still cannot. Search parties in the fields; I can see them from the distance and the temptation is awful, it is absolute, to go outside and beckon them into the castle. "Here she is," I would say, "I killed her, just take her out of the basement and do with me what you will," and it would be over but what then? what then? I cannot even find the energy now to contemplate my own outcome.

June 26

The castle stinks, these rooms stink, I stink myself, my own flesh oozing corruption. It is impossible that the stain of implication does not waft through the air for a square of ten miles, so awful is it here. In the distance I see the two officials at last, they are moving toward this castle at a good speed and behind them is a party of men, ten or twenty in number it must be, hard to tell, do not know,

deference is no longer their gait, detachment no longer their duty, but instead they seem impelled by urgency and in only a minute or so they will be at the door and this time I know they will not knock.

I could still flee. There is time yet; hurl myself into my robes and scuttle the back way, make haste across the fields and by dawn bribe my way by carriage to the capital and into anonymity. I could blend for fifty years into the capital and no one ever the wiser and it is tempting, quite tempting: after all I do not want to burn any more, alas, than any of my victims.

But I will not do it. I know this. I do not have the energy to flee. I will remain at this desk until the shouts have coursed their way from ground level to the stairs and then like blood in an artery run their way up here. I will sit at this desk completing these pitiful notes (which can never be completed), which have attempted to explain so much and have, I know, explained so little. I will sit and sit, the pool of odors coming over me and at last they will open the door and seize me in a grasp like iron, my presence the implication and as I bare my neck to them, waiting for that bite of salvation which will free me at last of these wretched and timeless burdens, I know that I will hang frozen in the air for a long long time, the knowledge at last pulsing through me that for me, at least, that bite will never come...and that I will have to face the consequences of my mortality.

I Am Coming
Philip Lamantia

I am following her to the wavering moon
to a bridge by the long waterfront
to valleys of beautiful arson
to flowers dead in a mirror of love
to men eating wild minutes from a clock
to hands playing in celestial pockets
and to that dark room beside a castle
of youthful voices singing to the moon.

When the sun comes up she will live at a sky
covered with sparrow's blood
and wrapped in robes of lost decay.

But I am coming to the moon,
and she will be there in a musical night,
in a night of burning laughter
burning like a road of my brain
pouring its arm into the lunar lake.

from The History of Witchcraft and Demonology
The Case of Hélène-Joséphine Poirier
Montague Summers

...Hélène-Joséphine Poirier, the daughter of an artisan family — her father was a mason — was born on 5 November, 1834, at Coullons, a small village some ten miles from Gien in the district of the Loire. Whilst still young she was apprenticed to Mlle Justine Beston, a working dressmaker, and soon became skilful with her needle and a remarkable embroideress. Already she had attracted attention by her sincere and modest piety, and was thought highly of by the parish priest, M. Preslier, a man of unusual discernment and the soundest common sense. On the night of 25 March, 1850, she was suddenly awakened by a series of sharp raps, which soon became violent blows, as if struck upon the walls of the small attic where she slept. In terror she rushed into her parents' room next door, and they returned with her to search. Nothing at all could be discovered, and she was persuaded to go back to bed. Although they could actually see no cause for alarm her parents had heard the extraordinary noises. "From this date," says M. Preslier, "the life of Hélène in the midst of such terrible physical and moral suffering that she might well have given utterance to the complaints of holy Job."

These manifestations to Hélène Poirier may not unfittingly be compared with the famous "Rochester knockings," the phenomenon of the rappings at Hydesville in 1848 at the house of the Fox family, which by many writers is considered to be the beginning of that world-wide movement known as Spiritism or Spiritualism in its modern manifestations and recrudescence.

Some months after this event Hélène suddenly fell rigid to the ground as if she had been thrown down by some strong hands. She was able to get up immediately but only to fall again. It was thought she was epileptic or at any rate seized with some unusual attack, some fit or convulsion. But after a careful observation of her case Dr. Azéma, the local practitioner, shrewdly remarked: "Nobody here but the Priest can cure you." From this time disorders of spirit and physical maladies increased with unprecedented rapidity and violence. "Her physical and mental sufferings, which began on 25 March, 1850, continued until her death on 8 January, 1914, that is to say during a period of sixty-four years. But those of diabolic origin ceased towards the end of 1897. So the diabolic attacks actually lasted for some seven-and-forty years, and for six years of this time she was possessed." It was in January, 1863, it first became undeniably evident that her sufferings, her spasms, and painful trances had a supernatural origin. The abbé Bougaud, Archdeacon of Orleans, having interviewed her, advised that she should be brought to the Bishop, Monsignor Dupanloup, and made arrangements for her to stay at a Visitation convent

in the suburbs, promising that a commission of theologians and doctors should examine her case. On Thursday, 28 October, 1865, Hélène accordingly commenced a retreat at the convent, where she was kindly received. M. Bougaud saw her for about two minutes, and she was handed an official order which would allow her access to the Bishop without waiting for a summons from his lordship or any other undue delay. But there was some misunderstanding, for on the Friday a doctor of high repute called at the convent, as he had been requested, interrogated and examined her for some three-quarters of an hour and then roundly informed the Mother Superior that she was mad, stark mad, and had better be sent home at once. He seems to have impressed the Bishop with his report, for Monsignor Dupanloup sent a messenger to direct the nuns to dismiss her forthwith, and accordingly she was perforce taken back to Coullons after a fruitless journey of bitter disappointments and discouragement.

In the occult tradition women are regarded as evil. In numerology, the female number 2, which represents gentleness, submissiveness, sweetness, is also the Devil's number. The Hindu goddess Kali, the Divine Mother, is also the goddess of violence and destruction. Women tend to 'think' with their feelings and intuitions.

Colin Wilson, *The Occult* (1971)

The Devil lusts for the human body because as a spiritual being he longs for matter, to make himself complete, and for the human soul because it belongs to his enemy, God....'He who affirms the Devil', according to Eliphas Levi, 'creates or makes the Devil.' Once the incubus has been conjured up in the magician's imagination, it may not be easy to dispose of it.

F. Hartmann, *Magic, White and Black* (1893)

Many persons now began to regard her with suspicion, but in the following year, 1866, the Bishop, whilst visiting Coullons for an April confirmation, granted her an interview which caused him very considerably to modify his first opinion, and M. Bougaud, who saw her in September, declared himself convinced of the supernatural origin of the symptoms she displayed.

The most terrible obsessions now attacked her, and more than once she was driven to the verge of suicide and despair. "From 25 March, 1850, until March, 1868, Hélène was *only obsessed*. The obsession *lasted 18 years*. At the end of this time she was *both obsessed and possessed* for 13 months. From this double agony of obsession and possession she was completely delivered by the exorcisms, which the Bishop had sanctioned, at Orleans, on 19 April, 1869. Four months' peace followed, until with heroic generosity she voluntarily submitted to new inflictions.

"At the end of August, 1869, she accepted from the hands of Our Lord the agony of a new obsession and possession in order to obtain the conversion of the famous general Ducrot. When he was converted, she was delivered from her torments at Lourdes on 3 September, 1875, the cure being effected by the prayers of 15,000 pilgrims who had assembled there. *The obsession and possession in their new form* had lasted five years. During the forty years which passed before her death, she was never again subject to possession, but she was continually obsessed, the attacks now being of short duration, now long and severe. The sufferings of every kind which she endured as well she offered with the intention of the triumph and good estate of God's priests. Why she was originally thus persecuted by the Devil for nineteen years, and with what intention she offered those torments from which she was delivered by the exorcisms directed by the Bishop, must always remain a secret." On Tuesday, 13 August, 1867, a supernormal impulse came over her to write a paper full of the most hideous blasphemies against Our Lord and His Blessed Mother, and, what is indeed significant, to draw blood from her arm and to sign therewith a deed giving herself over body and soul to Satan. This she happily resisted after a terrible struggle. Upon the following 28 August reliable witnesses saw her levitated from the ground on two distinct occasions. With this phenomenon we may compare the levitation of mediums at spiritistic séances. Sir William Crookes in *The Quarterly Journal of Science,* January, 1874, states that "There are at least a hundred recorded instances of Mr. Home's rising from the ground." Of the same medium he writes: "On three separate occasions have seen him raised completely from the floor of the room."

In March, 1868, it became evident that the poor sufferer was actually possessed. Fierce convulsive fits seized her; she suddenly fell with a maniacal fury and a deep hoarse voice uttered the most astounding blasphemies; if the Holy Names of Jesus and Mary were spoken in her presence she gnashed her teeth and literally foamed at the mouth; she was unable to hear the words *Et caro Uerbum factum est* without an access of insane rage which spent itself in wild gestures and an incoherent howling. She was interrogated in Latin, and answered the questions volubly and easily in the same tongue. The case attracted considerable attention, and was reported by the Comte de Maumigny to Padre Picivillo, the editor of the *Civilta Cattolica,* who gave an account thereof to the Holy Father. The saintly Pius IX showed himself full of sympathy, and even sent through the Comte de Maumigny a message of most salutary advice recommending great caution and the avoidance of all kinds of curiosity or advertisement.

In February, 1869, when interrogated by several priests Hélène gave most extraordinary details concerning bands of Satanists. "In order to gain admission it is necessary to bring one or more consecrated Hosts, and to deliver these to the Devil, who in a materialized form visibly presides over the assembly. The neophyte is obliged to profane the Sacred Species in a most horrible manner, to worship the Devil with humblest adoration, and to perform with him and the other persons present the most bestial acts of unbridled obscenity, the foulest copulations. Three towns, Paris, Rome, and Tours, are the headquarters of the Santanic bands." She also spoke of a gang of devil-worshippers at Toulouse. It is obvious that a mere peasant woman could have no natural knowledge of these abominations, the details concerning which were unhappily only too true.

In the following April Hélène was taken to Orleans to be examined and solemnly exorcized. The interrogatories were conducted by Monsieur Desbrosses, a consultor in theology for the diocese, Monsieur Bougaud, and Monsieur Mallet, Superior of the Grand Seminary. They witnessed the most terrible crisis; the sufferer was tortured by fierce cramps and spasms; she howled like a wild beast; but they persisted patiently. Mons. Mallet questioned her on difficult and obscure points in theology and philosophy using now Latin, now Greek. She replied fluently in both tongues, answering his queries concisely, clearly, and to the point, incontestable proof that she was influenced by some supernormal power. Two or three days later the

Bishop was present at a similar examination, and forthwith commissioned his own director, Monsieur Roy, a professor at the Seminary, to undertake the exorcisms. With him were associated Monsieur Mallet, the parish priest of Coullons, and Monsieur Gaduel, Vicar-General of the diocese. Two nuns and Mlle Preslier held the patient. It was found necessary to repeat the rite five times upon successive days. On the last occasion the cries of the unhappy Hélène were fearful to hear. She writhed and foamed in paroxysms of rage; she blasphemed and cursed God, calling loudly upon the fiends of hell; she broke free from all restraint, hurling chairs and furniture in every direction with the strength of five men; it was with the utmost difficulty she could be seized and restrained before some serious mischief was done; at last with an unearthly yell, twice repeated, her limbs relaxed, and after a short period of insensibility she seemed to awake, calm and composed, as if from a restful slumber. The possession had lasted thirteen months from March, 1868, to April, 1869.

Into the details of her second possession from 23 August, 1869, until 3 September, 1874, it is hardly necessary to enter at any length. Monsieur Preslier noted: "The second crisis of possession was infinitely more terrible than the first; 1st, owing to the length; the first lasted thirteen months, the second five years. 2nd, the first was relieved was a number of heavenly consolations, but very little solace was obtained during the second. 3rd, there was much bodily suffering in the first, in the second there were far keener mental sufferings and more exquisite pain." She was finally and completely delivered at Lourdes on Thursday, 3 September, 1874. It is not to be supposed that she passed the remaining forty years of her life without occasional manifestations of extraordinary phenomena. After much sickness, cheerfully and smilingly borne, she made a good end in her eightieth year, on 8 January, 1914, and is buried in the little village cemetery of her native place.

The Church does not deny that, with a special permission of God, the souls of the departed may appear to the living, and even manifest things unknown to the latter. But, understood as the art of science of evoking the dead, necromancy is held by theologians to be due to the agency of evil spirits....

Jacques Paul Maigne, *Encyclopedie Theologique* (1866)

from **The Occult**
Colin Wilson

The closest thing I have seen to a rational phenomenological explanation of this problem occurs, strangley enough, in a work of science fiction called *Forbidden Planet*, by W.J. Stuart, in which a scientific expedition to a distant planet tries to determine why all previous expeditions have been destroyed. The only man who seems to be able to live safely on the planet is an old scientist named Morbius, and he is able to tell them that the other expeditions have been destroyed by a kind of invisible, and apparently indestructible, monster.

Morbius is studying the remains of an earlier civilisation on the planet — beings who had apparently achieved the power to amplify their thoughts, their power of 'intentionality,' so that mental images could be *projected* as an external reality. And at the end of the novel, Morbius realises what has destroyed the previous expeditions. Without even suspecting it, he has also been amplifying the intentional forces of his subconscious mind, his subconscious desire to be left alone on the planet; and this is the 'invisible monster' that has been destroying the previous expeditions....

Now, if this hypothesis is correct, it may explain not only the mystery of vampires, werewolves and poltergeists — which we shall consider in the next chapter — but all so-called 'occult phenomena.' The subconscious mind is not simply a kind of deep-seat repository of sunken memories and atavistic desires, but of forces that can, under certain circumstances, manifest themselves in the physical world with a force that goes beyond anything the conscious mind could command. We are all familiar with certain moments when our conscious personality seems to become more real, more solid and authoritative, and we experience a peculiar sensation of power. Imagine this kind of strength and authority carried through to the far greater forces of the subconscious, and we begin to get a shadowy outline of a theory of the occult that avoids both extremes of scepticism and credulity.

The Nosferat not only sucks the blood of sleeping people, but also does mischief as an Incubus or Succubus. The Nosferat is the still-born, illegitimate child of two people who are similarly illegitimate. It is hardly put under the earth before it awakes to life and leaves its grave never to return. It visits people by night in the form of a black cat, a black dog, a beetle, a butterfly or even a simple straw. When its sex is male, it visits women; when female, men.

Ernest Jones, *On the Nightmare* (1951)

Robert Davidson
Edgar Lee Masters

I GREW spiritually fat living off the souls of men.
If I saw a soul that was strong
I wounded its pride and devoured its strength.
The shelters of friendship knew my cunning,
For where I could steal a friend I did so.
And wherever I could enlarge my power
By undermining ambition, I did so,
Thus to make smooth my own.
And to triumph over other souls,
Just to assert and prove my superior strength,
Was with me a delight,
The keen exhilaration of soul gymnastics.
Devouring souls, I should have lived forever.
But their undigested remains bred in me a deadly
  nephritis,
With fear, restlessness, sinking spirits,
Hatred, suspicion, vision disturbed.
I collapsed at last with a shriek.
Remember the acorn;
It does not devour other acorns.

...congenital causes [of vampireism] like the doctrine of 'original sin', are, of course, connected with parental sin. A clear example of this is the belief in Greece...that children born on Christmas Day are doomed to become Vampires in punishment of their mother's sin of being so presumptuous as to conceive on the same day as the Virgin Mary. During their lifetime such children are known as Callicantzaros, and in order, if possible, to obviate further developments it is customary to burn the soles of their feet until the nails are singed and [thus] their claws clipped.

M.D. Conway, *Demonological Devil-Lore: Vol. ii* (1879)

...little bleeding continues once the vampire has ceased his attack and withdrawn. If the vampire's advances are not prevented — and he will return night after night until he has reduced his victim to a lifeless husk...the victim once dead will himself become a vampire and prey on others....

Raymond D. McNally and Radu Florescu, *In Search of Dracula* (1973)

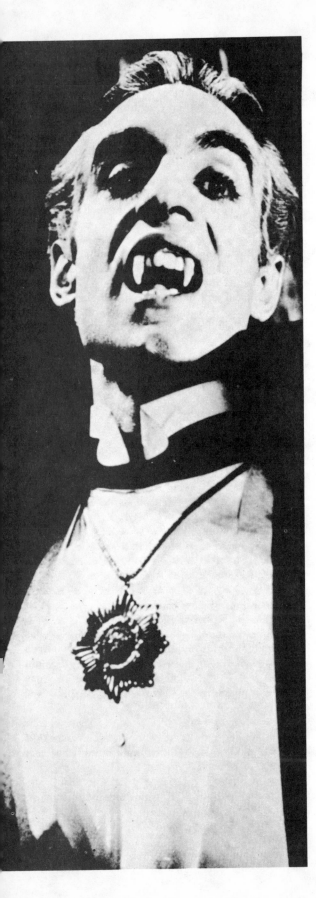

from **The Occult**
Colin Wilson

What happened...is that the witch craze produced a hysteria that created precisely what it was trying to destroy. This is a peculiarity of the human imagination that is only now being recognised by psychology: that when it is denied active, creative expression, it seeks out any powerful stimulus, no matter how terrifying or negative....

Sartre describes, in one of his early books, the case of a young girl who had been educated in a convent, and then married to a professional man. Left alone all day in the apartment, she began to experience an absurd compulsion to go to the window and summon men like a prostitute. Goethe has a classic story called *The Honest Attorney* in which a virtuous young wife, left to herself finally becomes insanely obsessed with the idea of committing adultery — precisely because the idea would normally horrify her. What is at work here is the same principle as in hypnotism. Boredom or emptiness allows the mind to fill up with unused energy, producing a painful sensation like an overfull bladder. An excessive degree of self-consciousness is created. This produces the usual effect of preventing the instincts from doing their quiet, unobtrusive work; the feelings are frozen. The desire for strong feelings — the most basic of human psychological needs — becomes a kind of panic; guilt and misery are preferable to boredom. What the mind really craves is the sense of vastness and wide-openness, of other times and other places, of *meaning*. What the inquisitors were doing was to create a body of myths and symbols that were *supercharged* with meaning and that consequently exercised an overwhelming gravitational pull on imaginative and bored women. The Devil literally finds work for idle hands and idle minds.

When the more normal aspects of sexuality are in a state of repression there is always a tendency to regress towards less developed forms. Sadism is one of the chief of these, and it is the earliest form of this — known as oral sadism — that plays such an important part in the Vampire belief.

Sigmund Freud, *Drei Abhandlungen zur Sexualtheorie* (1910)

It is believed that certain dead people cannot rest in the grave. As we shall see, there are several grounds for this, but we are at the moment concerned only with the one of sexual guilt. It is felt that because of this the dead person cannot rest in the grave and is impelled to try to overcome it by the characteristic method of defiantly demonstrating that he can commit the forbidden acts.

J.N. Sepp, *Orient and Occident* (1903)

Damn Her
John Ciardi

Of all her appalling virtues, none
leaves more crumbs in my bed, nor
more gravel in my tub
than the hunch of her patience
    at its mouseholes.

She would, I swear, outwait
the Sphinx in its homemade quandaries
once any scratching in the walls
has given her to suspect
    an emergence.

It's all in the mind, we say. With her
it's all in the crouch, the waiting
and the doing indistinguishable. Once
she hunches to execution, time is merely
    the handle of the switch:

she grasps it and stands by for whatever
will come, certainly, to her sizzling
justice. Then, inevitably always daintily
she closes her total gesture
    swiftly disdainfully as

a glutton tosses off a third dozen
oysters—making light of them—as if
his gluttony were a joke that all
may share. (The flaps and bellies
    of his grossness

are waiting, after all, for something
much more substantial than
appetizers.) —"Bring on the lamb!" her look
says over my empty shells. "Bring on
    the body and the blood!"

The magical universe is like an ocean. The great tides move through it invisibly and men are swept about by them, but are sometimes strong enough and clever enough to master and use them. And in the cold black currents which come up from the deeps there are strange and sinister creatures lurking — evil intelligences which tempt and corrupt and destroy, malignant elementals, astral corpses, zombies, nightmare things....

Richard Cavendish, *The Black Arts* (1967)

Bianca's Hands
Theodore Sturgeon

Biancas mother was leading her when Ran saw her first. Bianca was squat and small, with dank hair and rotten teeth. Her mouth was crooked and it drooled. Either she was blind or she just didn't care about bumping into things. It didn't really matter because Bianca was an imbecile. Her hands....

They were lovely hands, graceful hands, hands as soft and smooth and white as snowflakes, hands whose colour was lightly tinged with pink like the glow of Mars on Snow. They lay on the counter side by side, looking at Ran. They lay there half closed and crouching, each pulsing with a movement like the panting of a field creature, and they looked. Not watched. Later, they watched him. Now they looked. They did, because Ran felt their united gaze, and his heart beat strongly.

Bianca's mother demanded cheese stridently. Ran brought it to her in his own time while she berated him. She was a bitter woman, as any woman has a right to be who is wife of no man and mother to a monster. Ran gave her the cheese and took her money and never noticed that it was not enough, because of Bianca's hands. When Bianca's mother tried to take one of the hands, it scuttled away from the unwanted touch. It did not lift from the counter, but ran on its fingertips to the edge and leaped into a fold of Bianca's dress. The mother took the unresisting elbow and led Bianca out.

Ran stayed there at the counter unmoving, thinking of Bianca's hands. Ran was strong and bronze and not very clever. He had never been taught about beauty and strangeness, but he did not need that teaching. His shoulders were wide and his arms were heavy and thick, but he had great soft eyes and thick lashes. They curtained his eyes now. He was seeing Bianca's hands again dreamily. He found it hard to breathe....

Harding came back. Harding owned the store. He was a large man whose features barely kept his cheeks apart. He said, "Sweep up, Ran. We're closing early today." Then he went behind the counter, squeezing past Ran.

Ran got the broom and swept slowly.

"A woman bought cheese," he said suddenly. "A poor woman, with very old clothes. She was leading a girl. I can't remember what the girl looked like, except — who was she?"

"I saw them go out," said Harding. "The woman is Bianca's mother, and the girl is Bianca. I don't know their other name. They don't talk to people much. I wish they wouldn't come in here. Hurry up, Ran."

Ran did what was necessary and put away his broom. Before he left he asked, "Where do they live, Bianca and her mother?"

"On the other side. A house on no road, away from people. Good night, Ran."

Ran went from the shop directly over to the other side, not waiting for his supper. He found the house easily, for it

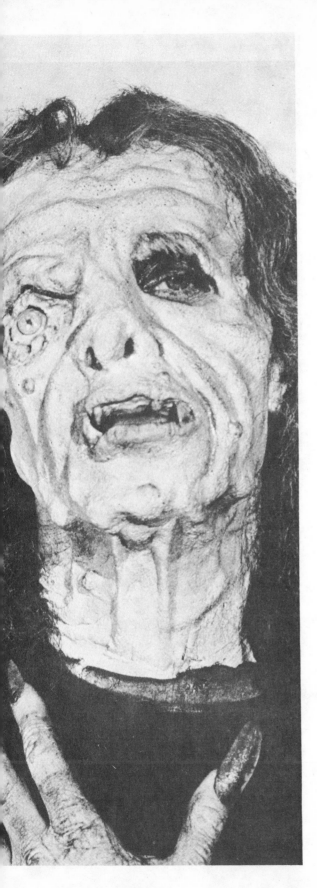

was indeed away from the road, and stood rudely by itself. The townspeople had cauterised the house by wrapping it in empty fields.

Harshly, "What do you want?" Bianca's mother asked as she opened the door.

"May I come in?"

"What do you want?"

"May I come in?" he asked again. She made as if to slam the door, and then stood aside. "Come."

Ran went in and stood still. Bianca's mother crossed the room and sat under an old lamp, in the shadow. Ran sat opposite her, on a three-legged stool. Bianca was not in the room.

The woman tried to speak, but embarrassment clutched at her voice. She withdrew into her bitterness, saying nothing. She kept peering at Ran, who sat quietly with his arms folded and the uncertain light in his eyes. He knew she would speak soon, and he could wait.

"Ah, well...." She was silent after that, for a time, but now she had forgiven him his intrusion. Then, "It's a great while since anyone came to see me; a great while...it was different before. I was a pretty girl —"

She bit her words off and her face popped out of the shadows, shrivelled and sagging as she leaned forward. Ran saw that she was beaten and cowed and did not want to be laughed at.

"Yes," he said gently. She sighed and leaned back so that her face disappeared again. She said nothing for a moment, sitting looking at Ran, liking him.

"We were happy, the two of us," she mused, "until Bianca came. He didn't like her, poor thing, he didn't, no more than I do now. He went away. I stayed by her because I was her mother. I'd go away myself, I would, but people know me, and I haven't a penny — not a penny....They'd bring me back to her, they would, to care for her. It doesn't matter much now, though, because people don't want me any more than they want her, they don't...."

Ran shifted his feet uneasily, because the woman was crying. "Have you room for me here?" he asked.

Her head crept out into the light. Ran said swiftly, "I'll give you money each week, and I'll bring my own bed and things." He was afraid she would refuse.

She merged with the shadows again. "If you like," she said, trembling at her good fortune. "Though why you'd want to...still I guess if I had a little something to cook up nice, and a good reason for it, I could make someone real cosy here. But — *why?*" She rose. Ran crossed the room and pushed her back into the chair. He stood over her, tall.

"I never want you to ask me that," he said, speaking very slowly. "Hear?"

She swallowed and nodded. "I'll come back tomorrow with the bed and things," he said.

He left her there under the lamp, blinking out of the dimness, folded round and about with her misery and her wonder.

People talked about it. People said, "Ran has moved to the house of Bianca's mother." "It must be because —" "Ah," said some, "Ran was always a strange boy. It must be because —" "Oh, *no!*" cried others appalled. "Ran is such a good boy. He wouldn't —"

Harding was told. He frightened the busy little woman who told him. He said, "Ran is very quiet, but he is honest and he does his work. As long as he comes here in the morning and earns his wage, he can do what he wants, where he wants, and it is not my business to stop him." He said this so very sharply that the little woman dared not say anything more.

Ran was very happy, living there. Saying little, he began to learn about Bianca's hands.

He watched Bianca being fed. Her hands would not feed her, the lovely aristocrats. Beautiful parasites they were, taking their animal life from the heavy squat body that carried them, and giving nothing in return. They would lie one on each side of her plate, pulsing, while Bianca's mother put food into the disinterested drooling mouth. They were shy, those hands, of Ran's bewitched gaze. Caught out there naked in the light and open of the table-top, they would creep to the edge and drop out of sight — all but four rosy fingertips clutching the cloth.

They never lifted from a surface. When Bianca walked, her hands did not swing free, but twisted in the fabric of her dress. And when she approached a table or the mantelpiece and stood, her hands would run lightly up and leap, landing together, resting silently, watchfully, with that pulsing peculiar to them.

They cared for each other. They would not touch Bianca herself, but each hand groomed the other. It was the only labour to which they would bend themselves.

Three evenings after he came, Ran tried to take one of the hands in his, Bianca was alone in the room, and Ran went to her and sat beside her. She did not move, nor did her hands. They rested on a small table before her, preening themselves. This, then, was when they really began watching him. He felt it, right down to the depths of his enchanted heart. The hands kept stroking each other, and yet they knew he was there, they knew of his desire. They stretched themselves before him, archly, languorously, and his blood pounded hot. Before he could stay himself he reached and tried to grasp them. He was strong, and his move was sudden and clumsy. One of the hands seemed to disappear, so swiftly did it drop into Bianca's lap. But the other....

Ran's thick fingers closed on it and held it captive. It writhed, all but tore itself free. It took no power from the arm on which it lived, for Bianca's arms were flabby and weak. Its strength, like its beauty, was intrinsic, and it was only by shifting his grip to the puffy forearm that Ran succeeded in capturing it. So intent was he on touching it, holding it, that he did not see the other hand leap from the idiot girl's lap, land crouching at the table's edge. It reared back, fingers curling spiderlike, and sprang at him, fastening on his wrist. It clamped down agonisingly, and

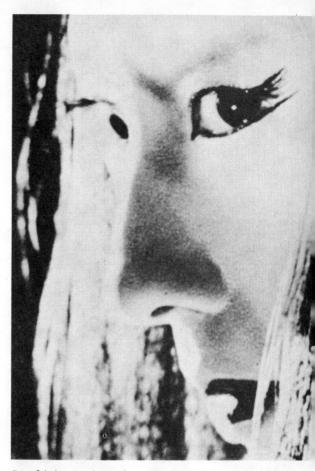

Ran felt bones give and crackle. With a cry he released the girl's arm. Her hands fell together and ran over each other, feeling for any small scratch, any tiny damage he might have done them in his passion. And as he sat there clutching his wrist, he saw the hands run to the far side of the little table, hook themselves over the edge and, contracting, draw her out of her place. She had no volition of her own — ah, but her hands had! Creeping over the walls, catching obscure and precarious holds in the wainscoting, they dragged the girl from the room.

And Ran sat there and sobbed, not so much from the pain in his swelling arm, but in shame for what he had done. They might have been won to him in another, gentler way....

His head was bowed, yet suddenly he felt the gaze of those hands. He looked up swiftly enough to see on of them whisk round the doorpost. It had come back, then, to see....Ran rose heavily and took himself and his shame away. Yet he was compelled to stop in the doorway, even as had Bianca's hands. He watched covertly and saw them come into the room dragging the unprotesting idiot girl. They brought her to the long bench where Ran sat with her. They pushed her on to it, flung themselves to the table, and began rolling and flattening themselves most curiously about. Ran suddenly realised that there was something of his there, and he was comforted, a little.

the strength of his back, and shoulders. Bianca's mother, by now beyond surprise, looked at him and away. There was that in his eyes which she did not like, for to fathom it would distrub her, and she wanted no trouble. Ran strode from the room and outdoors, to be by himself that he might learn more of this new thing that had possessed him.

It was evening. The crooked-bending skyline drank the buoyancy of the sun, dragged it down, sucking greedily. Ran stood on a knoll, his nostrils flaring, feeling the depth of his lungs. He sucked in the crisp air and it smelled new to him, as though the sunset shades were truly in it. He knotted the muscles of his thighs and stared at his smooth, solid fists. He raised his hands high over his head and, stretching, sent out such a great shout that the sun sank. He watched it, knowing how great and tall he was, how strong he was, knowing the meaning of longing and belonging. And then he lay down on the clean earth and he wept.

When the sky grew cold enough for the moon to follow the sun beyond the hills, and still an hour after that, Ran returned to the house. He struck a light in the room of Bianca's mother, where she slept on a pile of old clothes. Ran sat beside her and let the light wake her. She rolled over to him and moaned, opened her eyes and shrank from him. "Ran...what do you want?"

"Bianca. I want to marry Bianca."

Her breath hissed between her gums. "No!" It was not a refusal, but astonishment. Ran touched her arm impatiently. Then she laughed.

"To — marry — Bianca. It's late, boy. Go back to bed, and in the morning you'll have forgotten this thing, this dream."

"I've not been to bed," he said patiently, but growing angry. "Will you give me Bianca, or not?"

She sat up and rested her chin on her withered knees. "You're right to ask me, for I'm her mother. Still and all — Ran, you've been good to us, Bianca and me. You're — you are a good boy but — forgive me, lad, but you're something of a fool. Bianca's a monster. I say it though I am what I am to her. Do what you like, and never a word will I say. You should have known. I'm sorry you asked me, for you have given me the memory of speaking so to you. I don't understand you; but do what you like, boy."

It was to have been a glance, but it became a stare as she saw his face. He put his hands carefully behind his back, and she knew he would have killed her else.

"I'll — marry her, then?" he whispered.

She nodded, terrified. "As you like, boy."

He blew out the light and left her.

Ran worked hard and saved his wages, and made one room beautiful for Bianca and himself. He built a soft chair, and a table that was like an altar for Bianca's sacred hands. There was a great bed, and heavy cloth to hide and soften the walls, and a rug.

They were married, though marrying took time. Ran

They were rejoicing, drinking thirstily, revelling in his tears.

Afterwards for nineteen days, the hands made Ran do penance. He knew them as inviolate and unforgiving; they would not show themselves to him, remaining always hidden in Bianca's dress or under the supper table. For those nineteen days Ran's passion and desire grew. More — his love became true love, for only true love knows reverence — and the possession of the hands became his reason for living, his goal in the life which that reason had given him.

Ultimately they forgave him. They kissed him coyly when he was not looking, touched him on the wrist, caught and held him for one sweet moment. It was at table...a great power surged through him, and he gazed down at the hands, now returned to Bianca's lap. A strong muscle in his jaw twitched and twitched, swelled and fell. Happiness like a golden light flooded him; passion spurred him, love imprisoned him, reverence was the gold of the golden light. The room wheeled and whirled about him and forces unimaginable flickered through him. Battling with himself, yet lax in the glory of it, Ran sat unmoving, beyond the world, enslaved and yet possessor of all. Bianca's hands flushed pink, and if ever hands smiled to each other, then they did.

He rose abruptly, flinging his chair from him, feeling

had to go far afield before he could find one who would do what was necessary. The man came far and went again afterwards, so that none knew of it, and Ran and his wife were left alone. The mother spoke for Bianca, and Bianca's hand trembled frighteningly at the touch of the ring, writhed and struggled and then lay passive, blushing and beautiful. But it was done. Bianca's mother did not protest, for she didn't dare. Ran was happy, and Bianca — well, nobody cared about Bianca.

After they were married Bianca followed Ran and his two brides into the beautiful room. He washed Bianca and used rich lotions. He washed and combed her hair, and brushed it many times until it shone, to make her more fit to be with the hands he had married. He never touched the hands, though he gave them soaps and creams and tools with which they could groom themselves. They were pleased. Once one of them ran up his coat and touched his cheek and made him exultant.

He left them and returned to the shop with his heart full of music. He worked harder than ever, so that Harding was pleased and let him go home early. He wandered the hours away by the bank of a brook, watching the sun on the face of the chuckling water. A bird came to circle him, flew unafraid through the aura of gladness about him. The delicate tip of a wing brushed his wrist with the touch of the first secret kiss from the hands of Bianca. The singing that filled him was part of the nature of laughing, the running of water, the sound of the wind in the reeds by the edge of the stream. He yearned for the hands, and he knew he could go now and clasp them and own them; instead he stretched out on the bank and lay smiling, all lost in the sweetness and poignance of waiting, denying desire. He laughed for pure joy in a world without hatred, held in the stainless palms of Bianca's hands.

As it grew dark he went home. All during that nuptial meal Bianca's hands twisted about one of his while he ate with the other, and Bianca's mother fed the girl. The fingers twined about each other and about his own, so that three hands seemed to be wrought of one flesh, to become a thing of lovely weight at his arm's end. When it was quite dark they went to the beautiful room and lay where he and the hands could watch, through the window, the clean, bright stars swim up out of the forest. The house and the room were dark and silent. Ran was so happy that he hardly dared to breathe.

A hand fluttered up over his hair, down his cheek, and crawled into the hollow of his throat. Its pulsing matched the beat of his heart. He opened his own hands wide and clenched his fingers, as though to catch and hold this moment.

Soon the other hand crept up and joined the first. For perhaps an hour they lay there passive with their coolness against Ran's warm neck. He felt them with his throat, each smooth convolution, each firm small expanse. He concentrated, with his mind and his heart on his throat, on each part of the hands that touched him, feeling with all his being first one touch and then another, though the

contact was there unmoving. And he knew it would be soon now, soon.

As if at a command, he turned on his back and dug his head into the pillow. Staring up at the vague dark hangings on the wall, he began to realize what it was for which he had been working and dreaming so long. He put his head back yet farther and smiled, waiting. This would be possession, completion. He breathed deeply, twice, and the hands began to move.

The thumbs crossed over his throat and the fingertips settled one by one under his ears. For a long moment they lay there, gathering strength. Together, then, in perfect harmony, each co-operating with the other, they became rigid, rock-hard. Their touch was still light upon him, still light, now they were passing their rigidity to him, turning it to a contraction. They settled to it slowly, their pressure measured and equal. Ran lay silent. He could not breathe now, and did not want to. His great arms were crossed on his chest, his knotted fists under his armpits, his mind knowing a great peace. Soon, now....

Wave after wave of engulfing, glorious pain spread and receded. He saw colour impossible, without light. He arched his back, up, up...the hands bore down with all their hidden strength, and Ran's body bent like a bow, resting on feet and shoulders. Up, up....

Something burst within him — his lungs, his heart — no matter. It was complete.

There was blood on the hands of Bianca's mother when they found her in the morning in the beautiful room, trying to soothe Ran's neck. They took Bianca away, and they buried Ran, but they hanged Bianca's mother because she tried to make them believe Bianca had done it, Bianca whose hands were quite dead, drooping like brown leaves from her wrists.

The Voice
Thomas Hardy

Woman much missed, how you call to me, call to me,
Saying that now you are not as you were
When you had changed from the one who was all to me,
But as at first, when our day was fair.

Can it be you that I hear? Let me view you, then,
Standing as when I drew near to the town
Where you would wait for me: yes, as I knew you then,
Even to the original air-blue gown!

Or is it only the breeze, in its listlessness
Traveling across the wet mead to me here,
You being ever dissolved to wan wistlessness,
Heard no more again far or near?

   This I; faltering forward,
   Leaves around me falling,
Wind oozing thin through the thorn from norward,
   And the woman calling.

"He placed his reeking lips upon my throat! How long this horrible thing lasted I know not; but it seemed that a long time must have passed before he took his foul, awful, sneering mouth away.

"With that he pulled open his shirt, and with his long sharp nails opened a vein in his breast. When the blood began to spurt out, he took my hands in one of his, holding them tight, and with the other seized my neck and pressed my mouth to the wound, so that I must either suffocate or swallow.

Then he spoke to me mockingly, 'And you, are now to me, flesh of my flesh; blood of my blood; kin of my kin; my bountiful wine-press for a while; and shall be later on my companion and my helper. When my brain says *Come!* to you, you shall cross land or sea to do my bidding.' "
Mina Harker

Dr. Seward's Diary, 22, Sept.

RELEASE

When Lucy — I call the thing that was before us Lucy because it bore her shape — saw us she drew back with an angry snarl, such as a cat gives when taken unawares; then her eyes ranged over us. Lucy's eyes in form and colour; but Lucy's eyes unclean and full of hell-fire, instead of the pure, gentle orbs we knew. At that moment the remnant of my love passed into hate and loathing; had she then to be killed, I could have done it with savage delight.

As she looked, her eyes blazed with unholy light, and the face became wreathed with a voluptuous smile. She still advanced, however, and with a languorous, voluptuous grace, said: — "Come to me, leave these others and come to me."

When within a foot or two of the door, however, she stopped, as if arrested by some irresistible force. Then she turned, and her face was shown in the clear burst of moonlight.

Never did I see such baffled malice on a face.

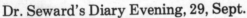

Dr. Seward's Diary Evening, 29, Sept.

Invitation to the Dance
Ted Hughes

The condemned prisoner stirred, but could not stir:
Cold had shackled the blood-prints of the knout.
The light of his death's dawn put the dark out.
He lay, his lips numb to the frozen floor.
He dreamed some other prisoner was dragged out—
Nightmare of command in the dawn, and a shot.
The bestial gaoler's boot was at his ear.

Upon his sinews torturers had grown strong,
The inquisitor old against a tongue that could not,
Being torn out, plead even for death.
All bones were shattered, the whole body unstrung.
Horses, plunging apart towards North and South,
Tore his heart up by the shrieking root.
He was flung to the blow-fly and the dog's fang.

Pitched onto his mouth in a black ditch
All spring he heard the lovers rustle and sigh.
The sun stank. Rats worked at him secretly.
Rot and maggot stripped him stitch by stitch.
Yet still this dream engaged his vanity:
That could he get upright he would dance and cry
Shame on every shy or idle wretch.

from **The Premature Burial**
Edgar Allan Poe

...My nerves became thoroughly unstrung, and I fell a prey to perpetual horror. I hesitated to ride, or to walk, or to indulge in any exercise that would carry me from home. In fact, I no longer dared trust myself out of the immediate presence of those who were aware of my proneness to catalepsy, lest, falling into one of my usual fits, I should be buried before my real condition could be ascertained. I doubted the care, the fidelity of my dearest friends. I dreaded that, in some trance of more than customary duration, they might be prevailed upon to regard me as irrecoverable. I even went so far as to fear that, as I occasioned much trouble, they might be glad to consider any very protracted attack as sufficient excuse for getting rid of me altogether. It was in vain they endeavored to reassure me by the most solemn promises. I exacted the most sacred oaths, that under no circumstances they would bury me until decomposition had so materially advanced as to render further preservation impossible. And, even then, my mortal terrors would listen to no reason — would accept no consolation. I entered into a series of elaborate precautions. Among other things, I had the family vault so remodelled as to admit of being readily opened from within. The slightest pressure upon a long lever that extended far into the tomb would cause the iron portals to fly back. There were arrangements also for the free admission of air and light, and convenient receptacles for food and water, within immediate reach of the coffin intended for my reception. This coffin was warmly and softly padded, and was provided with a lid, fashioned upon the principle of the vault-door, with the addition of springs so contrived that the feeblest movement of the body would be sufficient to set it at liberty. Besides all this, there was suspended from the roof of the tomb, a large bell, the rope of which, it was designed, should extend through a hole in the coffin, and so be fastened to one of the hands of the corpse. But, alas! what avails the vigilance against the Destiny of man? Not even these well-contrived securities sufficed to save from the uttermost agonies of living inhumation, a wretch to these agonies foredoomed!

There arrived an epoch — as often before there had arrived — in which I found myself emerging from total unconsciousness into the first feeble and indefinite sense of existence. Slowly — with a tortoise gradation — approached the faint gray dawn of the psychal day. A torpid uneasiness. An apathetic endurance of dull pain. No care — no hope — no effort. Then, after a long interval, a ringing in the ears; then, after a lapse still longer a pricking or tingling sensation in the extremities; then a seemingly eternal period of pleasurable quiescence, during which the awakening feelings are struggling into thought; then a brief re-sinking into non-entity; then a sudden recovery. At length the slight quivering of an eyelid, and immediately thereupon, an electric shock of a terror, deadly and indefinite, which sends the blood in torrents from the temples to the heart. And now the first positive effort to think. And now the first endeavor to remember. And now a partial and evanescent success. And now the memory has so far regained its dominion, that, in some measure, I am cognizant of my state. I feel that I am not awaking from ordinary sleep. I recollect that I have been subject to catalepsy. And now, at last, as if by the rush of an ocean, my shuddering spirit is overwhelmed by the one grim Danger — by the one spectral and ever-prevalent idea.

For some minutes after this fancy possessed me, I remained without motion. And why? I could not summon courage to move. I dared not make the effort which was to satisfy me of my fate — and yet there was something at my heart which whispered me *it was sure*. Despair — such as no other species of wretchedness ever calls into being — despair alone urged me, after long irresolution, to uplight the heavy lids of my eyes. I uplifted them. It was dark — all dark. I knew that the fit was over. I knew that the crisis of my disorder had long passed. I knew that I had now fully recovered the use of my visual faculties — and yet it was dark — all dark — the intense and utter raylessness of the Night that endureth for evermore.

I endeavored to shriek; and my lips and my parched tongue moved convulsively together in the attempt — but no voice issued from the cavernous lungs, which, oppressed as if by the weight of some incumbent mountain,

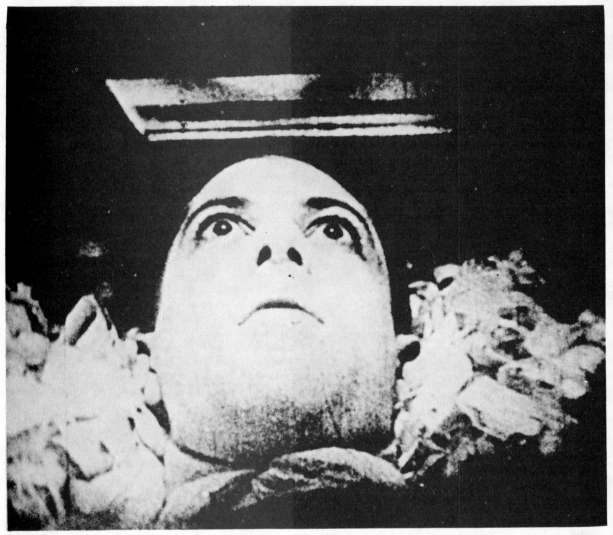

gasped and palpitated, with the heart, at every elaborate and struggling inspiration.

The movement of the jaws, in this effort to cry aloud, showed me that they were bound up, as is usual with the dead. I felt, too, that I lay upon some hard substance; and by something similar my sides were, also, closely compressed. So far, I had not ventured to stir any of my limbs — but now I violently threw up my arms, which had been lying at length, with the wrists crossed. They struck a solid wooden substance, which extended above my person at an elevation of not more than six inches from my face. I could no longer doubt that I reposed within a coffin at last.

And now, amid all my infinite miseries, came sweetly the cherub Hope — for I thought of my precautions. I writhed, and made spasmodic exertions to force open the lid: it would not move. I felt my wrists for the bell-rope: it was not to be found. And now the Comforter fled for ever, and a still sterner Despair reigned triumphant; for I could not help perceiving the absence of the paddings which I had so carefully prepared — and then, too, there came suddenly to my nostrils the strong peculiar odor of moist

earth. The conclusion was irresistable. I was *not* within the vault. I had fallen into a trance while absent from home — while among strangers — when, or how, I could not remember — and it was they who had buried me as a dog — nailed up in some common coffin — and thrust, deep, deep, and for ever, into some ordinary and nameless *grave*.

As this awful conviction forced itself, thus, into the innermost chambers of my soul, I once again struggled to cry aloud. And in this second endeavor I succeeded. A long, wild, and continuous shriek, or yell, of agony, resounded through the realms of the subterranean Night.

"Hillo! hillo, there!" said a gruff voice, in reply.

"What the devil's the matter now!" said a second.

"Get out o' that!" said a third.

"What do you mean by yowling in that ere kind of style, like a cattymount?" said a fourth; and hereupon I was seized and shaken without ceremony, for several minutes, by a junto of very rough-looking individuals. They did not arouse me from my slumber — for I was wide-awake when I screamed — but they restored me to the full possession of my memory.

Cool Air
H.P. Lovecraft

You ask me to explain why I am afraid of a draught of cool air; why I shiver more than others upon entering a cold room, and seem nauseated and repelled when the chill of evening creeps through the heat of a mild autumn day. There are those who say I respond to cold as others do to a bad odour, and I am the last to deny the impression. What I will do is to relate the most horrible circumstances I ever encountered, and leave it to you to judge whether or not this forms a suitable explanation of my peculiarity.

It is a mistake to fancy that horror is associated inextricably with darkness, silence, and solitude. I found it in the glare of mid-afternoon, in the clangour of a metropolis, and in the teeming midst of a shabby and commonplace rooming-house with a prosaic landlady and two stalwart men by my side. In the spring of 1923 I had secured some dreary and unprofitable magazine work in the city of New York; and being unable to pay any substantial rent, began drifting from one cheap boarding establishment to another in search of a room which might combine the qualities of decent cleanliness, endurable furnishings, and very reasonable price. It soon developed that I had only a choice between different evils, but after a time I came upon a house in West Fourteenth Street which disgusted me much less than the others I had sampled.

The place was a four-story mansion of brownstone, dating apparently from the late forties, and fitted with woodwork and marble whose stained and sullied slendour argued a descent from high levels of tasteful opulence. In the rooms, large and lofty, and decorated with impossible paper and ridiculously ornate stucco cornices, there lingered a depressing mustiness and a hint of obscure cookery; but the floors were clean, the linen tolerably regular, and the hot water not too often cold or turned off, so that I came to regard it as at least a bearable place to hibernate 'til one might really live again. The landlady, a slatternly, almost bearded Spanish woman named Herrero, did not annoy me with gossip or with criticisms of the late-burning electric light in my third floor front hall room; and my fellow-lodgers were as quiet and uncommunicative as one might desire, being mostly Spaniards a little above the coarsest and crudest grade. Only the din of street cars in the thoroughfare below proved a serious annoyance.

I had been there about three weeks when the first odd incident occurred. One evening at about eight I heard a spattering on the floor and became suddenly aware that I had been smelling the pungent odour of ammonia for some time. Looking about, I saw that the ceiling was wet and dripping; the soaking apparently proceeding from a corner on the side toward the street. Anxious to stop the matter at its source, I hastened to the basement to tell the landlady; and was assured by her that the trouble would quickly be set right.

"Doctor Munoz," she cried as she rushed upstairs ahead of me, "he have speel hees chemicals. He ees too seeck for doctair heemself — seecker and seecker all the time — but he weel not have no othair for help. He ees vairy queer in hees seeckness — all day he take funnee-smelling baths, and he cannot get excite or warm. All hees own housework he do — hees leetle room are full of bottles and machines, and he do not work as doctair. But he was great once — my fathair in Barcelona have hear of heem — and only joost now he feex a arm of the plumber that get hurt of sudden. He nevair go out, only on roof, and my boy Estaban he breeng heem hees food and laundry and mediceens and chemicals. My God, the salammoniac that man use for to keep heem cool!"

Mrs. Herrero disappeared up the staircase to the fourth floor, and I returned to my room. The ammonia ceased to drip, and as I cleaned up what had spilled and opened the window for air, I heard the landlady's heavy footsteps above me. Dr. Munoz I had never heard, save for certain sounds as of some gasoline-driven mechanism; since his step was soft and gentle. I wondered for a moment what the strange affliction of this man might be, and whether his obstinate refusal of outside aid were not the result of a rather baseless eccentricity. There is, I reflected tritely, an infinite deal of pathos in the state of an eminent person who has come down in the world.

I might never have known Dr. Munoz had it not been for the heart attack that suddenly seized me one forenoon as I sat writing in my room. Physicians had told me of the danger of those spells, and I knew there was no time to be

Moontan
Mark Strand

The bluish, pale
face of the house
rises above me
like a wall of ice

and the distant
solitary
barking of an owl
floats toward me.

I half close my eyes.

Over the damp
dark of the garden,
flowers swing
back and forth
like small balloons.

The solemn trees,
each buried
in a cloud of leaves,
seem lost in sleep.

It is late.
I lie in the grass,
smoking,
feeling at ease,
pretending the end
will be like this.

Moonlight
falls on my flesh.
A breeze
circles my wrist.

I drift.
I shiver.
I know that soon
the day will come
to wash away the moon's
white stain,

that I shall walk
in the morning sun
invisible
as anyone.

lost; so, remembering what the landlady had said about the invalid's help of the injured workman, I dragged myself upstairs and knocked feebly at the door above mine. My knock was answered in good English by a curious voice some distance to the right, asking my name and business; and these things being stated, there came an opening of the door next to the one I had sought.

A rush of cool air greeted me; and though the day was one of the hottest of late June, I shivered as I crossed the threshold into a large apartment whose rich and tasteful decoration surprised me in this nest of squalor and seediness. A folding couch now filled its diurnal role of sofa, and the mahogany furniture, sumptuous hangings, old paintings, and mellow bookshelves all bespoke a gentleman's study rather than a boarding-house bedroom. I now saw that the hall room above mine — the "leetle room" of bottles and machines which Mrs. Herrero had mentioned — was merely the laboratory of the doctor; and that his main living quarters lay in the spacious adjoining room whose convenient alcoves and large contiguous bathroom permitted him to hide all dressers and obtrusively utilitarian devices. Dr. Munoz, most certainly, was a man of birth, cultivation, and discrimination.

The figure before me was short but exquisitely proportioned, and clad in somewhat formal dress of perfect fit and cut. A highbred face of masterful though not arrogant expression was adorned by a short iron-grey full beard, and an old-fashioned pince-nez shielded the full, dark eyes and surmounted an aquiline nose which gave a Moorish touch to a physiognomy otherwise dominantly Celtiberian. Thick, well-trimmed hair that argued the punctual calls of a barber was parted gracefully above a high forehead; and the whole picture was one of striking intelligence and superior blood and breeding.

Nevertheless, as I saw Dr. Munoz in that blast of cool air, I felt a repugnance which nothing in his aspect could justify. Only his lividly inclined complexion and coldness of touch could have afforded a physical basis for this feeling, and even these things should have been excusable considering the man's known invalidism. It might, too, have been the singular cold that alienated me; for such chilliness was abnormal on so hot a day, and the abnormal always excites aversion, distrust, and fear.

But repugnance was soon forgotten in admiration, for the strange physician's extreme skill at once became manifest despite the ice-coldness and shakiness of his bloodless-looking hands. He clearly understood my needs at a glance, and ministered to them with a master's deftness; the while reassuring me in a finely modulated though oddly hollow and timbreless voice that he was the bitterest of sworn enemies to death, and had sunk his fortune and lost all his friends in a life-time of bizarre experiment devoted to its bafflement and extirpation. Something of the benevolent fanatic seemed to reside in him, and he rambled on almost garrulously as he sounded my chest and mixed a suitable draught of drugs fetched

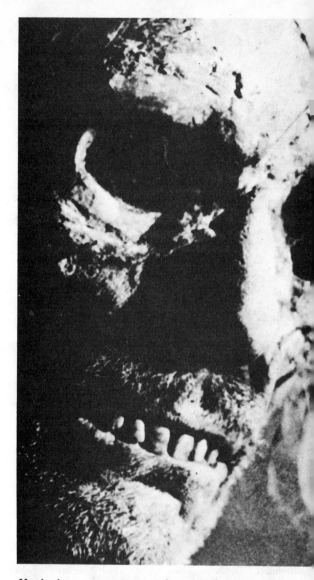

Magic has power to experience and fathom things which are inaccessible to human reason. For magic is a great secret wisdom, just as reason is a great public folly.

Paracelsus, *De Occulta Philosophia* (1538)

The magician masters great moving forces of the universe by experiencing them, by absorbing them into his own being and subjecting them to his will. He can do this because the forces are inside him as well as outside him....The channel between his inner impulses and the forces outside him is his imagination, and a powerful imagination is his most important single piece of equipment.

Richard Cavendish, *The Black Arts* (1967)

from the smaller laboratory room. Evidently he found the society of a well-born man a rare novelty in this dingy environment, and was moved to unaccustomed speech as memories of better days surged over him.

His voice, if queer, was at least soothing; and I could not even perceive that he breathed as the fluent sentences rolled urbanely out. He sought to distract my mind from my own seizure by speaking of his theories and experiments; and I remember his tactfully consoling me about my weak heart by insisting that will and consciousness are stronger than organic life itself, so that if a bodily frame be but originally healthy and carefully preserved, it may through a scientific enhancement of these qualities retain a kind of nervous animation despite the most serious impairments, defects, or even absences in the battery of specific organs. He might, he half jestingly said, some day teach me to live — or at least to possess some kind of conscious existence — without any heart at all! For his part, he was afflicted with a complication of maladies requiring a very exact regimen which included constant cold. Any marked rise in temperature might, if prolonged, affect him fatally; and the frigidity of his habitation — some fifty-five or fifty-six degrees Fahrenheit — was maintained by an absorption system of ammonia cooling, the gasoline engine of whose pumps I had often heard in my own room below.

Relieved of my seizure in a marvellously short while, I left the shivery place a disciple and devotee of the gifted recluse. After that I paid him frequent overcoated calls; listening while he told of secret researches and almost ghastly results, and trembling a bit when I examined the unconventional and astonishingly ancient volumes on his shelves. I was eventually, I may add, almost cured of my disease for all time by his skilful ministrations. It seems that he did not scorn the incantations of the mediaevalist, since he believed these cryptic formulae to contain rare psychological stimuli which might conceivably have singular effects on the substance of a nervous system from which organic pulsations had fled. I was touched by his account of the aged Dr. Torres of Valencia, who had shared his earlier experiments and nursed him through the great illness of eighteen years before, whence his present disorders proceeded. No sooner had the venerable practitioner saved his colleague than he himself succumbed to the grim enemy he had fought. Perhaps the strain had been too great; for Dr. Munoz made it whisperingly clear — though not in detail — that the methods of healing had been most extraordinary, involving scenes and processes not welcomed by elderly and conservative Galens.

As the weeks passed, I observed with regret that my new friend was indeed slowly but unmistakably losing ground physically, as Mrs. Herrero had suggested. The livid aspect of his countenance was intensified, his voice became more hollow and indistinct, his muscular motions were less perfectly coordinated, and his mind and will displayed less resilience and initiative. Of this sad change he seemed by no means unaware, and little by little his expression and conversation both took on a gruesome irony which restored in me something of the subtle repulsion I had originally felt.

He developed strange caprices, acquiring a fondness for exotic spices and Egyptian incense 'til his room smelled like the vault of a sepulchred Pharaoh in the Valley of Kings. At the same time, his demands for cold air increased, and with my aid he amplified the ammonia piping of his room and modified the pumps and feed of his refrigerating machine 'til he could keep the temperature as low as thirty-four or forty degrees, and finally even twenty-eight degrees; the bathroom and laboratory, of course, being less chilled, in order that water might not freeze, and that chemical processes might not be impeded. The tenant adjoining him complained of the icy air from around the connecting door; so I helped him fit heavy hangings to obviate the difficulty. A kind of growing horror, of outré and morbid cast, seemed to possess him. He talked of death incessantly, but laughed hollowly when such things as burial or funeral arrangements were gently suggested.

All in all, he became a disconcerting and even gruesome companion; yet in my gratitude for his healing, I could not well abandon him to the strangers around him, and was careful to dust his room and attend to his needs each day, muffled in a heavy ulster which I bought especially for the purpose. I likewise did much of his shopping, and gasped in bafflement at some of the chemicals he ordered from druggists and laboratory supply houses.

An increasing and unexplained atmosphere of panic seemed to rise around his apartment. The whole house, as I have said, had a musty odour; but the smell in his room was worse, and in spite of all the spices and incense, and the pungent chemicals of the now incessant baths which he insisted on taking unaided, I perceived that it must be connected with his ailment, and shuddered when I reflected on what that ailment might be. Mrs. Herrero crossed herself when she looked at him, and gave him up unreservedly to me; not even letting her son Esteban continue to run errands for him. When I suggested other physicians, the sufferer would fly into as much of a rage as he seemed to dare to entertain. He evidently feared the physical effect of violent emotion, yet his will and driving force waxed rather than waned, and he refused to be confined to his bed. The lassitude of his earlier ill days gave place to a return of his fiery purpose, so that he seemed about to hurl defiance at the death-daemon even as that ancient enemy seized him. The pretence of eating, always curiously like a formality with him, he virtually abandoned; and mental power alone appeared to keep him from total collapse.

He acquired a habit of writing long documents of some sort, which he carefully sealed and filled with injunctions that I transmit them after his death to certain persons whom he named — for the most part lettered East Indians, but including a once celebrated French physician now generally thought dead, and about whom the most inconceivable things had been whispered. As it happened, I burned all these papers undelivered and unopened. His aspect and voice became utterly frightful, and his presence almost unbearable. One September day an unexpected glimpse of him induced an epileptic fit in a man who had come to repair his electric desk lamp; a fit for which he prescribed effectively whilst keeping himself well out of sight. That man, oddly enough, had been through the terrors of the great war without having incurred any fright so thorough.

Then, in the middle of October, the horror of horrors came with stupefying suddenness. One night about eleven the pump of the refrigerating machine broke down, so that within three hours the process of ammonia cooling became impossible. Dr. Munoz summoned me by thumping on the floor, and I worked desperately to repair the injury while my host cursed in a tone whose lifeless, rattling hollowness surpassed description. My amateur efforts, however, proved of no use; and when I had brought in a mechanic from a neighbouring all-night garage we learned that nothing could be done until morning, when a new piston would have to be obtained. The moribund hermit's rage and fear, swelling to grotesque proportions, seemed likely to shatter what remained of his failing physique; and once a spasm caused

him to clap his hands to his eyes and rush into the bathroom. He groped his way out with face tightly bandaged, and I never saw his eyes again.

The frigidity of the apartment was now sensibly diminishing, and at about five in the morning, the doctor retired to the bathroom, commanding me to keep him supplied with all the ice I could obtain at all-night drug-stores and cafeterias. As I would return from my sometimes discouraging trips and lay my spoils before the closed bathroom door, I could hear a restless splashing within, and a thick voice croaking out the order for "More — more!" At length a warm day broke, and the shops opened one by one. I asked Esteban either to help with the ice-fetching while I obtained the pump piston, or to order the piston while I continued with the ice; but, instructed by his mother, he absolutely refused.

Finally I hired a seedy-looking loafer whom I encountered on the corner of Eighth Avenue to keep the patient supplied with ice from a little shop where I introduced him, and applied myself diligently to the task of finding a pump piston and engaging workmen competent to install it. The task seemed interminable, and I raged almost as violently as the hermit when I saw the hours slipping by in a breathless, foodless round of vain telephoning, and a hectic quest from place to place, hither and thither by subway and surface car. About noon I encountered a suitable supply house far down-town, and at approximately one-thirty that afternoon arrived at my

Siege
Alden Nowlan

My mind besieged in
its crumbling castle:
by day the enemy
snipes from his great
wheeled towers,
undermines the walls;
I hold the stairs
to the bells
whose laughter
reinforces me;
by night he infiltrates
but, being inhuman, is
not fully aware how
powerless I am:
animal and angel
alike are wary of
us because we are men,
hybrids, never wholly
predictable. He whispers.
And I dream
I am neither
alive nor dead,
my nose and jaw
sawn away, so that it

is worse, far worse
than that earlier
time when I shut
my eyes while I hid
the mirror behind
a door or switched
off the lights and sat
in the dark,
never saw myself except
as reflected in
the eyes of others
who weren't quick
enough in turning away
—that and the
remembered reality
of being fed through
one tube, drained
through another, the
urine burning
as it seeped from me,
drop by drop.
Believe me, I would gladly
spare you this
if I could.

boarding-place with the necessary paraphernalia and two sturdy and intelligent mechanics. I had done all I could, and hoped I was in time.

Black terror, however, had preceded me. The house was in utter turmoil, and above the chatter of awed voices I heard a man praying in a deep basso. Fiendish things were in the air, and lodgers told over the beads of their rosaries as they caught the odour from beneath the doctor's closed door. The lounger I had hired, it seems, had fled screaming and mad-eyed not long after his second delivery of ice; perhaps as a result of excessive curiosity. He could not, of course, have locked the door behind him; yet it was now fastened, presumably from the inside. There was no sound within save a nameless sort of slow, thick dripping.

Briefly consulting with Mrs. Herrero and the workmen despite a fear that gnawed my inmost soul, I advised the breaking down of the door; but the landlady found a way to turn the key from the outside with some wire device. We had previously opened the doors of all the other rooms on that hall, and flung all the windows to the very top. Now, noses protected by handkerchiefs, we tremblingly invaded the accursed south room which blazed with the warm sun of early afternoon.

A kind of dark, slimy trail led from the open bathroom door to the hall door, and thence to the desk, where a terrible little pool had accumulated. Something was scrawled there in pencil in an awful, blind hand on a piece of paper hideously smeared as though by the very claws that traced the hurried last words. Then the trail led to the couch and ended unutterably.

What was, or had been, on the couch I cannot and dare not say here. But this is what I shiveringly puzzled out on the stickily smeared paper before I drew a match and burned it to a crisp; what I puzzled out in terror as the landlady and two mechanics rushed frantically from that hellish place to babble their incoherent stories at the nearest police station. The nauseous words seemed well-nigh incredible in that yellow sunlight, with the clatter of cars and motor trucks ascending clamorously from crowded Fourteenth Street, yet I confess that I believed them then. Whether I believe them now I honestly do not know. There are things about which it is better not to speculate, and all that I can say is that I hate the smell of ammonia, and grow faint at a draught of unusually cool air.

"The end," ran that noisome scrawl, "is here. No more ice — the man looked and ran away. Warmer every minute, and the tissues can't last. I fancy you know — what I said about the will and the nerves and the preserved body after the organs ceased to work. It was good theory, but couldn't keep up indefinitely. There was a gradual deterioration I had not foreseen. Dr. Torres knew, but the shock killed him. He couldn't stand what he had to do; he had to get me in a strange, dark place, when he minded my letter and nursed me back. And the organs never would work again. It had to be done my way — artificial preservation — *for you see I died that time eighteen years ago.*"

Drugged
Walter de la Mare

Inert in his chair,
In a candle's guttering glow;
His bottle empty,
His fire sunk low;
With drug-sealed lids shut fast,
Unsated mouth ajar,
This darkened phantasm walks
Where nightmares are:

In a frenzy of life and light,
Crisscross—a menacing throng—
The gibe, they squeal at the stranger,
Jostling along,
Their faces cadaverous grey:
While on high from an attic stare
Horrors, in beauty apparelled,
Down the dark air.

A stream gurgles over its stones,
The chambers within are a—fire.
Stumble his shadowy feet
Through shine, through mire;
And the flames leap higher.
In vain yelps the wainscot mouse;
In vain beats the hour;
Vacant, his body must drowse
Until daybreak flower—

Staining these walls with its rose,
And the draughts of the morning shall stir,
Cold on cold brow, cold hands.
And the wanderer
Back to flesh house must return.
Lone soul—in horror to see,
Than dream more meagre and awful,
Reality.

The shadow is, in truth, a devilish form, and just when
you think you know who he is, he changes his disguise
and appears from another direction. So it is, in the
Jungian analysis, that the analysand is initiated into a
lifelong process, that of looking within, and being
willing to reflect long and hard on what he sees there,
in order to avoid being taken over by it.

June Singer, *Boundaries of the Soul: The Practice of
Jung's Psychology* (1972)

The way in this world is like the edge of a blade. On
this side is the underworld, and on that side is the
underworld, and the way of life lies between.

Martin Buber

from The Strange Case of Dr. Jekyll & Mr. Hyde

Robert Louis Stevenson

...I rushed to the mirror. At the sight that met my eyes, my blood was changed into something exquisitely thin and icy. Yes, I had gone to bed Henry Jekyll, I had awakened Edward Hyde. How was this to be explained? I asked myself; and then, with another bound of terror — how was it to be remedied? It was well on in the morning; the servants were up; all my drugs were in the cabinet — a long journey down two pairs of stairs, through the back passage, across the open court and through the anatomical theatre, from where I was then standing horror-struck. It might indeed be possible to cover my face; but of what use was that, when I was unable to conceal the alteration in my stature? And then with an overpowering sweetness of relief, it came back upon my mind that the servants were already used to the coming and going of my second self. I had soon dressed, as well as I was able, in clothes of my own size: had soon passed through the house, where Bradshaw stared and drew back at seeing Mr. Hyde at such an hour and in such a strange array; and ten minutes later, Dr. Jekyll had returned to his own shape and was sitting down, with a darkened brow, to make a feint of breakfasting.

Small indeed was my appetite. This inexplicable incident, this reversal of my previous experience, seemed, like the Babylonian finger on the wall, to be spelling out the letters of my judgment; and I began to reflect more seriously than ever before on the issues and possibilities of my double existence. That part of me which I had the power of projecting, had lately been much exercised and nourished; it had seemed to me of late as though the body of Edward Hyde had grown in stature, as though (when I wore that form) I were conscious of a more generous tide of blood; and I began to spy a danger that, if this were much prolonged, the balance of my nature might be permanently overthrown, the power of voluntary change be forfeited, and the character of Edward Hyde become irrevocably mine. The power of the drug had not been always equally displayed. Once, very early in my career, it had totally failed me; since then I had been obliged on more than one occasion to double, and once, with infinite risk of death, to treble the amount; and these rare uncertainties had cast hitherto the sole shadow on my contentment. Now, however, and in the light of that morning's accident, I was led to remark that whereas, in the beginning, the difficulty had been to throw off the body of Jekyll, it had of late gradually but decidedly transferred itself to the other side. All things therefore seemed to point to this; that I was slowly losing hold of my original and better self, and becoming slowly incorporated with my second and worse.

Between these two, I now felt I had to choose. My two natures had memory in common, but all other faculties were most unequally shared between them. Jekyll (who was composite) now with the most sensitive apprehensions, now with a greedy gusto, projected and shared in the pleasures and adventures of Hyde; but Hyde was indifferent to Jekyll, or but remembered him as the mountain bandit remembers the cavern in which he conceals himself from pursuit. Jekyll had more than a father's interest; Hyde had more than a son's indifference. To cast in my lot with Jekyll, was to die to those appetites which I had long secretly indulged and had of late begun to pamper. To cast it in with Hyde, was to die to a thousand interests and aspirations, and to become, at a blow and forever, despised and friendless. The bargain might appear unequal; but there was still another consideration in the scales; for while Jekyll would suffer smartingly in the fires of abstinence, Hyde would be not even conscious of all that he had lost. Strange as my circumstances were, the terms of this debate are as old and commonplace as man; much the same inducements and alarms cast the die for any tempted and trembling sinner; and it fell out with me, as it falls with so vast a majority of my fellows, that I chose the better part and was found wanting in the strength to keep to it.

Yes, I preferred the elderly and discontented doctor, surrounded by friends and cherishing honest hopes; and bade a resolute farewell to the liberty, the comparative youth, the light step, leaping impulses and secret pleasures, that I had enjoyed in the disguise of Hyde. I made this choice perhaps with some unconscious reservation, for I neither gave up the house in Soho, nor destroyed the clothes of Edward Hyde, which still lay ready in my cabinet. For two months, however, I was true to my determination; for two months, I led a life of such severity as I had never before attained to, and enjoyed the compensations of an approving conscience. But time began at last to obliterate the freshness of my alarm; the praises of conscience began to grow into a thing of course; I began to be tortured with throes and longings, as of Hyde struggling after freedom; and at last, in an hour of moral weakness, I once again compounded and swallowed the transforming draught.

I do not suppose that, when a drunkard reasons with himself upon his vice, he is once out of five hundred times affected by the dangers that he runs through his brutish, physical insensibility; neither had I, long as I had considered my position, made enough allowance for the complete moral insensibility and insensate readiness to evil, which were the leading characters of Edward Hyde. Yet it was by these that I was punished. My devil had been long caged, he came out roaring. I was conscious, even when I took the draught, of a more unbridled, a more furious propensity to ill. It must have been this, I suppose, that stirred in my soul that tempest of impatience with which I listened to the civilities of my unhappy victim; I declare, at least, before God, no man morally sane could have been guilty of that crime upon so pitiful a provocation; and that I struck in no more reasonable spirit than that in which a sick child may break a plaything. But I had voluntarily stripped myself of all those balancing instincts by which even the worst of us continues to walk with some degree of steadiness among temptations; and in my case, to be tempted, however slightly, was to fall.

Instantly the spirit of hell awoke in me and raged. With a transport of glee, I mauled the unresisting body, tasting delight from every blow; and it was not till weariness had begun to succeed, that I was suddenly, in the top fit of my delirium, struck through the heart by a cold thrill of terror. A mist dispersed; I saw my life to be forfeit; and fled from the scene of these excesses, at once glorying and trembling, my lust of evil gratified and stimulated, my love of life screwed to the topmost peg. I ran to the house in Soho, and (to make assurance doubly sure) destroyed my papers; thence I set out through the lamplit streets in the same divided ecstasy of mind, gloating on my crime, light-headedly devising others in the future, and yet still hastening and still hearkening in my wake for the steps of the avenger.

The next day, came the news that the murder had been overlooked, that the guilt of Hyde was patent to the world, and that the victim was a man high in public estimation. It was not only a crime, it had been a tragic folly. I think I was glad to know it; I think I was glad to have my better impulses thus buttressed and guarded by the terrors of the scaffold. Jekyll was now my city of refuge; let but Hyde peep out an instant, and the hands of all men would be raised to take and slay him.

I resolved in my future conduct to redeem the past; and I can say with honesty that my resolve was fruitful of some good. You know yourself how earnestly, in the last months of the last year, I laboured to relieve suffering; you know that much was done for others, and that the days passed quietly, almost happily for myself. Nor can I truly say that I wearied of this beneficent and innocent life; I think instead that I daily enjoyed it more completely; but I was still cursed with my duality of purpose; and as the first edge of my penitence wore off, the lower side of me, so long indulged, so recently chained down, began to growl for licence. Not that I dreamed of resuscitating Hyde; the bare idea of that would startle me to frenzy: no, it was in my own person that I was once more tempted to trifle with my conscience; and it was as an ordinary secret sinner that I at last fell before the assaults of temptation.

There comes an end to all things; the most capacious measure is filled at last; and this brief condescension to my evil finally destroyed the balance of my soul. And yet I was not alarmed; the fall seemed natural, like a return to the old days, before I had made my discovery. It was a fine, clear, January day, wet under foot where the frost had melted, but cloudless overhead; and the Regent's Park was full of winter chirrupings and sweet with spring odours. I sat in the sun on a bench; the animal within me licking the chops of memory; the spiritual side a little drowsed, promising subsequent penitence, but not yet moved to begin. After all, I reflected, I was like my neighbours; and then I smiled, comparing myself with other men, comparing my active good-will with the lazy cruelty of their neglect. And at the very moment of that vainglorious thought, a qualm came over me, a horrid nausea and the most deadly shuddering. These passed away, and left me faint; and then as in its turn faintness subsided, I began to be aware of a change in the temper of my thoughts, a greater boldness, a contempt of danger, a solution of the bonds of obligation. I looked down; my clothes hung formlessly on my shrunken limbs; the hand that lay on my knee was corded and hairy. I was once more Edward Hyde. A moment before I had been safe of all men's respect, wealthy, beloved — the cloth laying for me in the dining-room at home; and now I was the common quarry of mankind, hunted, houseless, a known murderer, thrall to the gallows.

It was partly in a dream that I came home to my own house and got into bed. I slept after the prostration of the day, with a stringent and profound slumber which not even the nightmares that wrung me could avail to break. I awoke in the morning shaken, weakened, but refreshed. I still hated and feared the thought of the brute that slept within me, and I had not of course forgotten the appalling dangers of the day before; but I was once more at home, in my own house and close to my drugs; and gratitude for my escape shone so strong in my soul that it almost rivalled the brightness of hope.

To find nature herself, all her forms must be shattered.

Meister Eckhart

from **Etudes Cliniques** (1852)
Dr. Morel

This unfortunate individual was entirely convinced that he had assumed the form of a wolf. "See this mouth," he would exclaim, separating his lips with his fingers, "it is the mouth of a wolf; these are the teeth of a wolf. I have cloven feet; see the long hairs which cover my body; let me run into the woods, and you shall shoot me!" During his quieter intervals he was sometimes allowed to see children whom he tenderly embraced, and of whom he was very fond. However, after they had gone he cried, "The unfortunates, they have hugged a wolf!"

He was a victim to the morbid wolfish hunger which is technically known as lycorexia or lycorrhexis. "Give me raw meat," he was wont to yell, "I am a wolf, a wolf!" When he was supplied with this, he would greedily devour some part, and reject the rest saying that it was not putrid enough.

This lycanthrope endured the most fearful mental agony, accusing himself of and tortured by the guilt of heinous offences which he certainly had not committed. He died at the asylum of Maréville.

The Ice Skin
James Dickey

All things that go deep enough
Into rain and cold
Take on, before they break down,
A shining in every part.
The necks of slender trees
Reel under it, too much crowned,
Like princes dressing as kings,

And the redwoods let sing their
    branches
Like arms that try to hold buckets
Filling slowly with diamonds

Until a cannon goes off
Somewhere inside the still trunk

And a limb breaks, just before mid-
    night,
Plunging houses into the darkness
And hands into cupboards, all seeking
Candles, and finding each other.
There is this skin

Always waiting in cold-enough air.
I have seen aircraft, in war,
Squatting on runways,
Dazed with their own enclosed,
Coming-forth, intensified color
As though seen by a child in a poem.
I have felt growing over
Me, in the heated death rooms

Of uncles, the ice
Skin, that which the dying

Lose, and we others,
In their thawing presence, take on.
I have felt the heroic glaze

Also, in hospital waiting
Rooms—that masterly shining,
And the slow weight that makes you
    sit
Like an emperor, fallen, becoming
His monument, with the stiff thorns
Of fear upside down on the brow,
And overturned kingdom;

Through the window of ice,
I have stared at my son in his cage,
Just born, just born.

I touched the frost of my eyebrows
To the cold he turned to
Blindly, but sensing a thing.
Neither glass nor the jagged
Helm on my forehead would melt.
My son now stands with his head
At my shoulder. I

Stand, stooping more, but the same,
Not knowing whether
I will break before I can feel,

Before I can give up my powers,
Or whether the ice-light
In my eyes will ever snap off
Before I die. I am still,
And my son, doing what he was taught,
Listening hard for a buried cannon,
Stands also, calm as glass.

Blood Son
Richard Matheson

The people on the block decided definitely that Jules was crazy when they heard about his composition.

There had been suspicions for a long time.

He made people shiver with his blank stare. His coarse guttural tongue sounded unnatural in his frail body. The paleness of his skin upset many children. It seemed to hang loose around his flesh. He hated sunlight.

And his ideas were a little out of place for the people who lived on the block.

Jules wanted to be a vampire.

People declared it common knowledge that he was born on a night when winds uprooted trees. They said he was born with three teeth. They said he'd used them to fasten himself on his mother's breast drawing blood with the milk.

They said he used to cackle and bark in his crib after dark. They said he walked at two months and sat staring at the moon whenever it shone.

Those were things that people said.

His parents were always worried about him. An only child, they noticed his flaws quickly.

They thought he was blind until the doctor told them it was just a vacuous stare. He told them that Jules, with his large head, might be a genius or an idiot. It turned out he was an idiot.

He never spoke a word until he was five. Then, one night coming up to supper, he sat down at the table and said ''Death.''

His parents were torn between delight and disgust. They finally settled for a place in between the two feelings. They decided that Jules couldn't have realized what the word meant.

But Jules did.

From that night on, he built up such a large vocabulary that everyone who knew him was astonished. He not only acquired every word spoken to him, words from signs, magazines, books; he made up his own words.

Like — nighttouch. Or — killove. They were really several words that melted into each other. They said things Jules felt but couldn't explain with other words.

He used to sit on the porch while the other children played hop-scotch, stickball and other games. He sat there and stared at the sidewalk and made up words.

Until he was twelve Jules kept pretty much out of trouble.

Of course there was the time they found him undressing Olive Jones in an alley. And another time he was discovered dissecting a kitten on his bed.

But there were many years in between. Those scandals were forgotten.

In general he went through childhood merely disgusting people.

He went to school but never studied. He spent about two or three terms in each grade. The teachers all knew

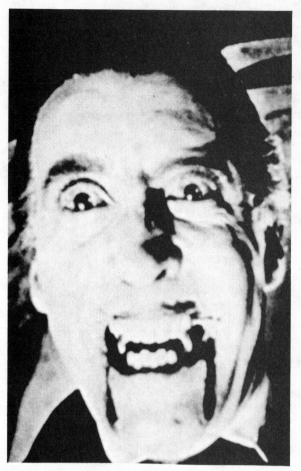

him by his first name. In some subjects like reading and writing he was almost brilliant.

In others he was hopeless.

One Saturday when he was twelve, Jules went to the movies. He saw ''Dracula.''

When the show was over he walked, a throbbing nerve mass, through the little girl and boy ranks.

He went home and locked himself in the bathroom for two hours.

His parents pounded on the door and threatened but he wouldn't come out.

Finally he unlocked the door and sat down at the supper table. He had a bandage on his thumb and a satisfied look on his face.

The morning after he went to the library. It was Sunday. He sat on the steps all day waiting for it to open. Finally he went home.

The next morning he came back instead of going to school.

He found *Dracula* on the shelves. He couldn't borrow it because he wasn't a member and to be a member he had to bring in one of his parents.

So he stuck the book down his pants and left the library and never brought it back.

He went to the park and sat down and read the book

Words Above a Narrow Entrance
David Wagoner

The land behind your back
Ends here: never forget
Signpost and weathercock
That turned always to point
Directly at your eyes;
Remember slackening air
At the top of the night,
Your feet treading on space.
The stream, like an embrace,
That swamped you to the throat
Has altered now; the briar
Rattling against your knees,
The warlock in disguise,
The giant at the root—
The country that seemed
Malevolence itself
Has gone back from the heart.
Beyond this gate, there lies
The land of the different mind,
Not honey in the brook,
None of the grass you dreamed.
Foresee water on fire,
And notches in a cloud;
Expect noise from a rock,
And faces falling apart.
The pathway underfoot,
Heaving its dust, will cross
A poisonous expanse
Where light knocks down the trees,
And whatever spells you took
Before, you will take anew
From the clack in the high wind.
Nothing will be at ease,
Nothing at peace, but you.

What myths are to the race, dreams are to the individual, for in dreams, as in myths, there also appear those primitive emotions and feelings in the form of giants, heros, dragons, serpents, and blood sucking vampires; representations of guilt, retribution, and fate; of lust and power, of monsters of the deep (the unconscious) and of unknown but overwhelming beings which fill our nights with nightmarish dreams and make us fear our sleep, but which, rightly used, can be fruitfully integrated into our personality.

J.A. Hadfield, *Dreams and Nightmares* (1954)

"...Count Dracula is *more than a man* who drinks blood; he is a kind of *dark god,* one who can command storms, transform himself into bats, wolves, and mists, and one who has hypnotic powers." *Bela Lugosi*

Arthur Lennig, *The Count* (1974)

through. It was late evening before he finished.

He started at the beginning again, reading as he ran from street light to street light, all the way home.

He didn't hear a word of the scolding he got for missing lunch and supper. He ate, went in his room and read the book to the finish. They asked him where he got the book. He said he found it.

As the days passed Jules read the story over and over. He never went to school.

Late at night, when he had fallen into an exhausted slumber, his mother used to take the book into the living room and show it to her husband.

One night they noticed that Jules had underlined certain sentences with dark shaky pencil lines.

Like: ''The lips were crimson with fresh blood and the stream had trickled over her chin and stained the purity of her lawn death robe.''

Or: ''When the blood began to spurt out, he took my hands in one of his, holding them tight and, with the other seized my neck and pressed my mouth to the wound....''

When his mother saw this, she threw the book down the garbage chute.

The next morning when Jules found the book missing he screamed and twisted his mother's arm until she told him where the book was.

Then he ran down to the cellar and dug in the piles of garbage until he found the book.

Coffee grounds and egg yolk on his hands and wrists, he went to the park and read it again.

For a month he read the book avidly. Then he knew it so well he threw it away and just thought about it.

Absence notes were coming from school. His mother yelled. Jules decided to go back for a while.

He wanted to write a composition.

One day he wrote it in class. When everyone was finished writing, the teacher asked if anyone wanted to read their compositions to the class.

Jules raised his hand.

The teacher was surprised. But she felt charity. She wanted to encourage him. She drew in her tiny jab of a chin and smiled.

''All right,'' she said, ''pay attention, children. Jules is going to read us his composition.''

Jules stood up. He was excited. The paper shook in his hands.

''My Ambition by....''

''Come to the front of the class, Jules, dear.''

Jules went to the front of the class. The teacher smiled lovingly. Jules started again.

''My Ambition by Jules Dracula.''

The smile sagged.

''When I grow up I want to be a vampire.''

The teacher's smiling lips jerked down and out. Her eyes popped wide.

''I want to live forever and get even with everybody and make all the girls vampires. I want to smell of death.''

"Jules!"

"I want to have a foul breath that stinks of dead earth and crypts and sweet coffins."

The teacher shuddered. Her hands twitched on her green blotter. She couldn't believe her ears. She looked at the children. They were gaping. Some of them were giggling. But not the girls.

"I want to be all cold and have rotten flesh with stolen blood in the veins."

"That will...hrrumph!"

The teacher cleared her throat mightily.

"That will be all, Jules," she said.

Jules talked louder and desperately.

"I want to sink my terrible white teeth in my victims' necks. I want them to...."

"Jules! Go to your seat this instant!"

"I want them to slide like razors in the flesh and into the veins," read Jules ferociously.

The teacher jolted to her feet. Children were shivering. None of them were giggling.

"Then I want to draw my teeth out and let the blood flow easy in my mouth and run hot in my throat and...."

The teacher grabbed his arm. Jules tore away and ran to a corner. Barricaded behind a stool he yelled:

"And drip off my tongue and run out my lips down my victims' throats! I want to drink girls' blood!"

The teacher lunged for him. She dragged him out of the corner. He clawed at her and screamed all the way to the door and the principal's office.

"That is my ambition! That is my ambition! That is my ambition!"

It was grim.

Jules was locked in his room. The teacher and the principal sat with Jules' parents. They were talking in sepulchral voices.

They were recounting the scene.

All along the block parents were discussing it. Most of them didn't believe it at first. They thought their children made it up.

Then they thought what horrible children they'd raised if the children could make up such things.

So they believed it.

After that everyone watched Jules like a hawk. People avoided his touch and look. Parents pulled their children off the street when he approached. Everyone whispered tales of him.

There were more absence notes.

Jules told his mother he wasn't going to school any more. Nothing would change his mind. He never went again.

When a truant officer came to the apartment Jules would run over the roofs until he was far away from there.

A year wasted by.

Jules wandered the streets searching for something; he didn't know what. He looked in alleys. He looked in garbage cans. He looked in lots. He looked on the east side and the west side and in the middle.

The Seated One was enormous in stature, and made like a human being down to the waist, like a hairy he-goat below; his legs ended in hoofs, but his hands were like human hands, so was his face human, red, sunburnt like an Apache, with large round eyes and a medium beard. He had the appearance of being not more than forty years old, and there was in his expression something sad and rousing compassion; but this feeling disappeared as soon as one's glance rose above his high forehead to see, emerging distinctly from his curly black hair, three horns; the two smaller ones behind and the larger one in front; and round the horns was placed a crown, apparently of silver, that emitted a soft glow like the light of the moon.

The naked witches placed me before the throne and exclaimed: 'Master Leonard, he is new!'

Then sounded a voice, hoarse and devoid of inflection as though he who spoke was not accustomed to pronouncing words, but strong and masterful, which addressed me saying: 'Welcome my son....'

Valery Brinssoui, *Fiery Angel* (1921)

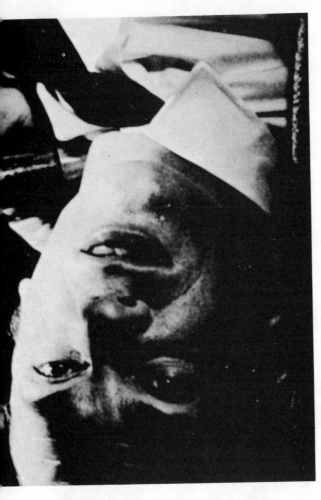

The Sentry
Alun Lewis

I have begun to die.
For now at last I know
That there is no escape
From Night. Not any dream
Nor breathless images of sleep
Touch my bat's-eyes. I hang
Leathery-arid from the hidden roof
Of Night, and sleeplessly
I watch within Sleep's province.
I have left
The lonely bodies of the boy and girl
Deep in each other's placid arms;
And I have left
The beautiful lanes of sleep
That barefoot lovers follow to this last
Cold shore of thought I guard.
I have begun to die
And the guns' implacable silence
Is my black interim, my youth and age,
In the flower of fury, the folded poppy,
Night.

He couldn't find what he wanted.

He rarely slept. He never spoke. He stared down all the time. He forgot his special words.

Then.

One day in the park, Jules strolled through the zoo.

An electric shock passed through him when he saw the vampire bat.

His eyes grew wide and his discolored teeth shone dully in a wide smile.

From that day on, Jules went daily to the zoo and looked at the bat. He spoke to it and called it the Count. He felt in his heart it was really a man who had changed.

A rebirth of culture struck him.

He stole another book from the library. It told all about wild life.

He found the page on the vampire bat. He tore it out and threw the book away.

He learned the selection by heart.

He knew how the bat made its wound. How it lapped up the blood like a kitten drinking cream. How it walked on folded wing stalks and hind legs like a black furry spider. Why it took no nourishment but blood.

Month after month Jules stared at the bat and talked to it. It became the one comfort in his life. The one symbol of dreams come true.

One day Jules noticed that the bottom of the wire covering the cage had come loose.

He looked around, his black eyes shifting. He did't see anyone looking. It was a cloudy day. Not many people were there.

Jules tugged at the wire.

It moved a little.

Then he saw a man come out of the monkey house. So he pulled back his hand and strolled away whistling a song he had just made up.

Late at night, when he was supposed to be asleep he would walk barefoot past his parents' room. He would hear his father and mother snoring. He would hurry out, put on his shoes and run to the zoo.

Every time the watchman was not around, Jules would tug at the wiring.

He kept on pulling it loose.

When he was finished and had to run home, he pushed the wire in again. Then no one could tell.

All day Jules would stand in front of the cage and look at the Count and chuckle and tell him he'd soon be free again.

He told the Count all things he knew. He told the Count he was going to practice climbing down walls head first.

He told the Count not to worry. He'd soon be out. Then, together, they could go all around and drink girls' blood.

One night Jules pulled the wire out and crawled under it into the cage.

It was very dark.

He crept on his knees to the little wooden house. He listened to see if he could hear the Count squeaking.

He stuck his arm in the black doorway. He kept whispering.

He jumped when he felt a needle jab in his finger.

With a look of great pleasure on his thin face, Jules drew the fluttering hairy bat to him.

He climbed down from the cage with it and ran out of the zoo; out of the park. He ran down the silent streets.

It was getting late in the morning. Light touched the dark skies with grey. He couldn't go home. He had to have a place.

He went down an alley and climbed over a fence. He held tight to the bat. It lapped at the dribble of blood from his finger.

He went across a yard and into a little deserted shack.

It was dark inside and damp. It was full of rubble and tin cans and soggy cardboard and excrement.

Jules made sure there was no way the bat could escape.

Then he pulled the door tight and put a stick through the metal loop.

He felt his heart beating hard and his limbs trembling. He let go of the bat. It flew to a dark corner and hung on the wood.

Jules feverishly tore off his shirt. His lips shook. He smiled a crazy smile.

He reached down into his pants pocket and took out a little pen knife he had stolen from his mother.

He opened it and ran a finger over the blade. It sliced through the flesh.

With shaking fingers he jabbed at his throat. He hacked. The blood ran through his fingers.

"Count! Count!" he cried in frenzied joy. "Drink my red blood! Drink me! Drink me!"

He stumbled over the tin cans and slipped and felt for the bat. It sprang from the wood and soared across the shack and fastened itself on the other side.

Tears ran down Jules' cheeks.

He gritted his teeth. The blood ran across his shoulders and across his thin hairless chest.

His body shook in fever. He staggered back toward the other side. He tripped and felt his side torn open on the sharp edge of a tin can.

His hands went out. They clutched the bat. He placed it against his throat. He sank on his back on the cool wet earth. He sighed.

He started to moan and clutch at his chest. His stomach heaved. The black bat on his neck silently lapped his blood.

Jules felt his life seeping away.

He thought of all the years past. The waiting. His parents. School. Dracula. Dreams. For this. This sudden glory.

Jules' eyes flickered open.

The side of the reeking shack swam about him.

It was hard to breathe. He opened his mouth to gasp in the air. He sucked it in. It was foul. It made him cough. His skinny body lurched on the cold ground.

Mists crept away in his brain.

One by one like drawn veils.

Suddenly his mind was filled with terrible clarity.

He felt the aching pain in his side.

He knew he was lying half naked on garbage and letting a flying bat drink his blood.

With a strangled cry, he reached up and tore away the furry throbbing bat. He flung it away from him. It came back, fanning his face with its vibrating wings.

Jules staggered to his feet.

He felt for the door. He could hardly see. He tried to stop his throat from bleeding so.

He managed to get the door open.

Then, lurching into the dark yard, he fell on his face in the long grass blades.

He tried to call out for help.

But no sounds save a bubbling mockery of words came from his lips.

He heard the fluttering wings.

Then, suddenly they were gone.

Strong fingers lifted him gently. Through dying eyes Jules saw the tall dark man whose eyes shone like rubies.

"My son," the man said.

The Image
Roy Fuller

A spider in the bath. The image noted:
Significant maybe but surely cryptic.
A creature motionless and rather bloated,
The barriers shining, vertical and white:
Passing concern, and pity and spite.

Next day with some surprise one finds it there.
It seems to have moved an inch or two, perhaps.
It starts to take on that familiar air
Of prisoners for whom time is erratic:
The filthy aunt forgotten in the attic.

Quite obviously it came up through the waste,
Rejects through ignorance or apathy
That passage back. The problem must be faced;
And life go on though strange intruders stir
Among its ordinary furniture.

One jibs at murder, so a sheet of paper
Is slipped beneath the accommodating legs.
The bathroom window shows for the escaper
The lighted lanterns of laburnum hung
In copper beeches—on which scene it's flung.

We certainly would like thus easily
To cast out of the house all suffering things.
But sadness and responsibility
For our own kind lives in the image noted:
A half-loved creature, motionless and bloated.

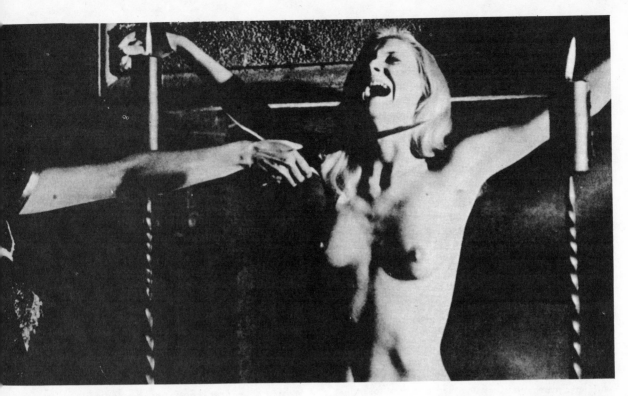

from **The Vampire, His Kith and Kin**
Fritz Haarmann — The Hanover Vampire (1925)
Montague Summers

The Daily Express, 17th April, 1925, gave the following:
"VAMPIRE BRAIN. PLAN TO PRESERVE IT FOR
SCIENCE." Berlin. Thursday, April 16th. The body of
Fritz Haarmann, executed yesterday at Hanover for
twenty-seven murders, will not be buried until it has been
examined at Göttingen University.

"Owing to the exceptional character of the crimes —
most of Haarmann's victims were *bitten to death* — the
case aroused tremendous interest among German
scientists. It is probable that Haarmann's brain will be
removed and preserved by the University authorities. —
Central News."

The case of Fritz Haarmann, who was dubbed the
"Hanover Vampire" was reported in some detail in *The
News of the World,* 21st December, 1924, under the
heading: "VAMPIRE'S VICTIMS." Haarmann was born
in Hanover, 25th October, 1879. The father, "Olle
Haarmann," a locomotive-stoker, was well-known as a
rough, cross-grained, choleric man, whom Fritz, his
youngest son, both hated and feared. As a youth, Fritz
Haarmann was educated at a Church School, and then at a
preparatory school for non-commissioned officers at New
Breisach. It is significant that he was always dull and
stupid, unable to learn; but it appears a good soldier.
When released from military service owing to ill-health he
returned home, only to be accused in a short while of
offences against children. Being considered irresponsible
for his actions the Court sent him to an asylum at
Hildesheim, whence however he managed to escape and
took refuge in Switzerland. Later he returned to Hanover,
but the house became unbearable owing to the violent
quarrels which were of daily occurrence between him and
his father. Accordingly he enlisted and was sent to the
crack 10th Jäger Battalion, at Colmar in Alsace. Here he
won golden opinions, and when released owing to illness,
with a pension his papers were marked "Recht gut."
When he reached home there were fresh scenes of rancour
whilst blows were not infrequently exchanged, and in 1903
he was examined by a medical expert, Dr. Andrae, who
considered him morally lacking but yet there were no
grounds for sending him to an asylum. Before long he sank
to the status of a tramp; a street hawker, at times; a
pilferer and a thief. Again and again he was sent to jail,
now charged with larceny, now with burglary, now with
indecency, now with fraud. In 1918, he was released
after a long stretch to find another Germany. He returned
to Hanover, and was able to open a small cook shop in the
old quarter of the town, where he also hawked meat which
was eagerly sought at a time of general hunger and
scarcity. He drove yet another trade, that of "copper's
nark," an old lag who had turned spy and informer, who
gave secret tips to the police as to the whereabouts of men
they wanted. "Detective Haarmann" he was nicknamed
by the women who thronged his shop because he always
had plenty of fresh meat in store, and he invariably
contrived to undersell the other butchers and victuallers of
the quarter.

The centre of Hanover was the Great Railway Station, and Hanover was thronged especially at its centre with a vast ever-moving population, fugitive, wanderers and homeless from all parts of dislocated Germany. Runaway lads from towns in every direction made their way here, looking for work, looking for food, idly tramping without any definite object, without any definite goal, because they had nothing else to do. It can well be imagined that the police, a hopelessly inadequate force, kept as sharp a watch as possible on the Station and its purlieus, and Haarmann used to help them in their surveyance. At midnight, or in the early morning he would walk up and down among the rows of huddled sleeping forms in the third-class waiting halls and suddenly waking up some frightened youngster demand to see his ticket, ask to know whence he had come and where he was going. Some sad story would be sobbed out, and the kindly Haarmann was wont to offer a mattress and a meal in his own place down town.

So far as could be traced the first boy he so charitably took to his rooms was a lad of seventeen named Friedel Rothe, who had run away from home. On 29th September, 1918, his mother received a postcard, and it so happened the very same day his father returned from the war. The parents were not going to let their son disappear without a search, and they soon began to hunt for him in real earnest. One of Friedel's pals told them that the missing boy had met a detective who offered him shelter. Other clues were traced and with extraordinary trouble, for the authorities had more pressing matters in hand than tracking truant schoolboys, the family obliged the police to search Cellarstrasse 27, where Haarmann lived. When a sudden entry was made Haarmann was found with another boy in such an unequivocal situation that his friends, the police, were obliged to arrest him there and then, and he received nine months imprisonment for gross indecency under Section 175 of the German Code. Four years later when Haarmann was awaiting trial for twenty-four murders he remarked: "At the time when the policeman arrested me the head of the boy Friedel Rothe was hidden under a newspaper behind the oven. Later on, I threw it into the canal."

In September, 1919, Haarmann first met Hans Grans, the handsome lad, who was to stand beside him in the dock. Grans, the type of abnormal and dangerous decadent which is only too common to-day, was one of the foulest parasites of society, pilferer and thief, bully, informer, spy, *agent provocateur,* murderer, renter, prostitute, and what is lower and fouler than all, blackmailer. The influence of this Ganymede over Haarmann was complete. It was he who instigated many of the murders — Adolf Hannappel a lad of seventeen was killed in November, 1923, because Grans wanted his pair of new trousers; Ernst Spiecker, likewise aged seventeen was killed on 5th January, 1924, because Grans coveted his "toff shirt" — it was he who arranged the details, who very often trapped the prey.

It may be said that in 1918, Hanover, a town of 450,000 inhabitants was well-known as being markedly homosexual. These were inscribed on the police lists no less than 500 "Männliche Prostituierten," of whom the comeliest and best-dressed, the mannered and well-behaved elegants frequented the Café Kröpcke in the Georgstrasse, one of the first boulevards of New Hanover; whilst others met their friends at the andrygonous ball in the Kalenberger Vorstadt, or in the old Assembly Rooms; and lowest of all there was a tiny dancing-place, "Zur schwülen Guste," "Hot-Stuff Gussie's" where poor boys found their clientele. It was here, for example, that Grans picked up young Ernst Spiecker whose tawdry shirt cost him his life.

"The picture appeard a vast and dim scene of evil, and I foresaw obscurely that I was destined to become the most wretched of human beings. Alas! I prophesied truly, and failed only in one single circumstance, that in all the misery I imagined and dreaded, I did not conceive the hundredth part of the anguish I was destined to endure." *Dr. Frankenstein*

Mary Shelley, *Frankenstein or The Modern Promotheus* (1831)

"Each of us are trapped in our own small, personal world that stifles us, suffocates us; we go around in this tiny world of personal meaning like a donkey tied to a post....ANYTHING that distracts us from our own personal world is a blessing." *Stavrogin*

Dostoevsky, *The Possessed* (1871)

With regard to his demeanour at the trial the contemporary newspapers write: "Throughout the long ordeal Haarmann was utterly impassive and complacent....The details of the atrocious crimes for which Haarmann will shortly pay with his life were extremely revolting. All his victims were between 12 and 18 years of age, and it was proved that accused actually sold the flesh for human consumption. He once made sausages in his kitchen, and, together with the purchaser, cooked and ate them....Some alienists hold that even then the twenty-four murders cannot possibly exhaust the full toll of Haarmann's atrocious crimes, and estimate the total as high as fifty. With the exception of a few counts, the prisoner made minutely detailed confessions and for days the court listened to his grim narrative of how he cut up the bodies of his victims and disposed of the fragments in various ways. He consistently repudiated the imputation of insanity, but at the same time maintained unhesitatingly

that all the murders were committed when he was in a state of trance, and unaware of what he was doing. This contention was specifically brushed aside by the Bench, which in its judgement pointed out that according to his own account of what happened, it was necessary for him to hold down his victims by hand in a peculiar way before it was possible for him to inflict a fatal bite on their throats. Such action necessarily involved some degree of deliberation and conscious purpose." Another account says with regard to Haarmann: "The killing of altogether twenty-seven young men is laid at his door, the horror of the deeds being magnified by the allegation that he sold to customers for consumption the flesh of those he did not himself eat....With Haarmann in the dock appeared a younger man, his friend Hans Grans, first accused of assisting in the actual murders but now charged with inciting to commit them and with receiving stolen property. The police are still hunting for a third man, Charles, also a butcher, who is alleged to have completed the monstrous trio...the prosecuting attorney has an array of nearly 200 witnesses to prove that all the missing youths were done to death in the same horrible way....He would take them to his rooms, and after a copious meal would praise the looks of his young guests. Then he would kill them after the fashion of a vampire.

—Someone is strewing pieces of human bodies around this West German city. On one occasion a group of schoolgirls found a leg propped up against a garbage can. On another, two halves from different human chests were found at a music show. Police said yesterday they have no idea whether the man they are hunting is a murderer or a grave robber....Because the heads have not been found, police cannot identify the victims.

U.P.I., *Hanover, July* 1977

Their clothes he would put up on sale in his shop, and the bodies would be cut up and disposed of with the assistance of Charles." "In open court, however, Haarmann admitted that Grans often used to select his victims for him. More than once, he alleged, Grans beat him for failing to kill the 'game' brought in, and Haarmann would keep the corpses in a cupboard until they could be got rid of, and one day the police were actually in his rooms when there was a body awaiting dismemberment. The back of the place abutted on the river, and the bones and skulls were thrown into the water. Some of them were discovered, but their origin was a mystery until a police inspector paid a surprise visit to the prisoner's home to inquire into a dispute between Haarmann and an intended victim who escaped." Suspicion had at last fallen upon him principally, owing to skulls and bones found in the river Seine during May, June and July, 1924. The newspapers said

that during 1924, no less than 600 persons had disappeared, for the most part lads between 14 and 18. On the night of 22nd June at the railway station, sometime after midnight, a quarrel broke out between Haarmann and a young fellow named Fromm, who accused him of indecency. Both were taken to the central station, and meanwhile Haarmann's room in the Red Row was thoroughly examined with the result that damning evidence came to light. Before long he accused Grans as his accomplice, since at the moment they happened to be on bad terms. Haarmann was sentenced to be decapitated, a sentence executed with a heavy sword. Grans was condemned to imprisonment for life, afterwards commuted to twelve years' penal servitude. In accordance with the law, Haarmann was put to death on Wednesday, 15th April, 1925.

This is probably one of the most extraordinary cases of vampirism known. The violent eroticism, the fatal bite in the throat, are typical of the vampire, and it was perhaps something more than mere coincidence that the mode of execution should be the severing of the head from the body, since this was one of the efficacious methods of destroying a vampire.

Certainly in the extended sense of the word, as it is now so commonly used, Fritz Haarmann was a vampire in every particular.

When I was 6 or 7 I used to be tormented constantly with a peculiar type of recurrent nightmare in which a monstrous race of entities (called by me "Night-Gaunts" — I don't know where I got hold of the name) used to snatch me up by the stomach & carry me off through infinite leagues of black air over the towers of dead & horrible cities. They would finally get me into a grey void where I could see the needle-like pinnacles of enormous mountains miles below. Then they would let me drop — & as I gained momentum in my Icarus-like plunge I would start awake in such a panic that I hated to think of sleeping again. The "night-gaunts" were black, lean, rubbery things with horns, barbed tails, bat-wings, and *no faces at all.* Undoubtedly I derived the image from the jumbled memory of Dore drawings (largely the illustrations to "Paradise Lost") which fascinated me in waking hours. They had no voices & their only form of real torture was their habit of tickling my stomach before snatching me up & swooping away with me. I somehow had the vague notion that they lived in the black burrows honeycombing the pinnacle of some incredibly high mountain somewhere. They seemed to come in flocks of 25 or 50, & would sometimes fling me one to the other. Night after night I dreamed the same horror with only minor variants — but I never struck those hideous mountain peaks before waking.

H.P. Lovecraft

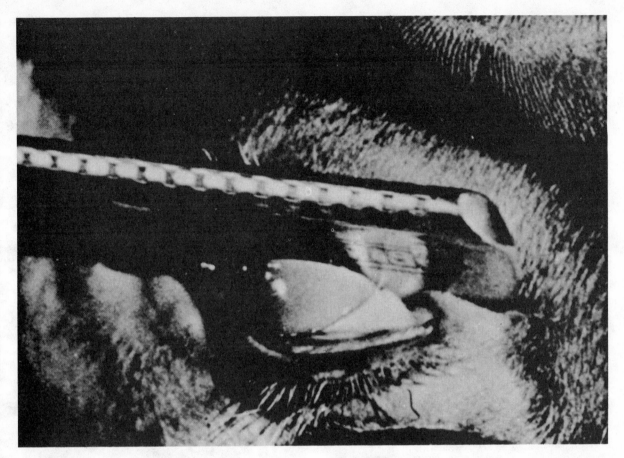

Mirage [Sea Island Miscellany: IX]
R.P. Blackmur

The wind was in another country, and
the day had gathered to its heart of noon
the sum of silence, heat, and stricken time.
Not a ripple spread. The sea mirrored
perfectly all the nothing in the sky.
We had to walk about to keep our eyes
from seeing nothing, and our hearts from stopping
at nothing. Then most suddenly we saw
horizon on horizon lifting up
out of the sea's edge a shining mountain
sun-yellow and sea-green; against it surf
flung spray and spume into the miles of sky.
Somebody said mirage, and it was gone,
but there I have been living ever since.

**In following the drive of the psychic substratum, the
artist fulfills not only himself but also his epoch....An
outsider in society, he stands alone, delivered over to
the creative impulse in himself.**

Erich Neumann

from **Blood / Thoughts**
Harlan Ellison

''Writing, has nothing much to do with pretty manners,
and less to do with sportsmanship or restraint....
''Every fictioneer re-invents the world because the facts,
things or people of the received world are unacceptable.
Every fiction writer dreams of imposing his invention upon
the world and winning the world's acclaim. (Such dreams
are known as delusions of grandeur in pathology but
tolerated as expressions of would-be genius in bookstores
and libraries.) Every writer begins as a subversive, if in
nothing more than the antisocial means by which he earns
his keep. Finally, every fantasist who cannibalizes himself
knows that misfortune in his friend, that grief feeds and
sharpens his fancy, that hatred is as sufficient a spur to
creation as love (and a world more common) and that
without an instinct for lunacy he will come to nothing.''
Geoffrey Wolff, (1975)

What are we to make of the mind of humanity? What are
we to think of the purgatory in which dreams are born,
from whence come the derangements that men call magic
because they have no other names for smoke or fog or
hysteria? What are we to dwell upon when we consider the
forms and shadows that become stories? Must we dismiss

them as fever dreams, as expressions of creativity, as purgatives? Or may we deal with them even as the naked ape dealt with them: as the only moments of truth a human calls throughout a life of endless lies.

Who will be the first to acknowledge that it was only a membrane, only a vapor, that separated a Robert Burns and his love from a Leopold Sacher-Masoch and his hate?

Is it too terrible to consider that a Dickens, who could drip treacle and God bless us one and all, through the mouth of a potboiler character called Tiny Tim, could also create the escaped convict Magwitch; the despoiler of children, Fagin; the murderous Sikes? Is it that great a step to consider that a woman surrounded by love and warmth and care of humanity as was Mary Wollstonecraft Shelley, wife of Percy Bysshe Shelley, the greatest romantic poet western civilization has ever produced, could herself produce a work of such naked horror as *Frankenstein?* Can the mind equate the differences and similarities that allow both an *Annabell Lee* and *a Masque of the Red Death* to emerge from the same churning pit of thought-darkness?

Consider the dreamers: *all* of the dreamers: the glorious *and* the corrupt:

Aesop, Attilla; Benito Mussolini and Benvenuto Cellini; Chekhov and Chang Tao-ling; Democritus, Disraeli; Epicurus, Edison; Fauré and Fitzgerald; Goethe, Garibaldi; Huysmann and Hemingway, ibn-al-Farid and Ives; Jeanne d'Arc and Jesus of Nazareth; and on and on. *All* the dreamers. Those whose visions took form in blood and those which took form in music. Dreams fashioned of words, and nightmares molded of death and pain. Is it inconceivable to consider that Richard Speck — who slaughtered eight nurses in Chicago in 1966, who was sentenced to 1,200 years in prison — was a devout Church-going Christian, a boy who lived in the land of God, while Jean Genet — avowed thief, murderer, pederast, vagrant who spent the firt thirty years of his life as an enemy of society, and in the jails of France where he was sentenced to life imprisonment — has written prose and poetry of such blazing splendor that Sartre has called him "saint"? Does the mind shy away from the truth that a Bosch could create hell-images so burning, so excruciating that no other artist has ever even *attempted* to copy his staggeringly brilliant style, while at the same time he produced works of such ecumenical purity as "L'Epiphanie"? *All* the dreamers. All the mad ones and the noble ones, all the seekers after alchemy and immortality, all those who dashed through endless midnights of gore-splattered horror and all those who strolled through sunshine springtimes of humanity. They are one and the same. They are all born of the same desire.

Speechless, we stand before Van Gogh's "Starry Night" or one of those hell-images of Hieronymous Bosch, and we find our senses reeling; vanishing into a daydream mist of *what must this man have been like, what must he have suffered?* A passage from Dylan Thomas, about birds singing in the eaves of a lunatic asylum, draws us up short, steals the breath from our mouths; and the blood and

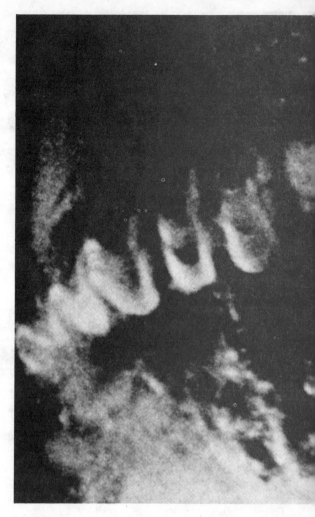

thoughts stand still in our bodies as we are confronted with the absolute incredible achievement of what he has done. The impossibility of it. So imperfect, so faulty, so broken the links in communication between humans, that to pass along one corner of a vision we have had to another creature is an accomplishment that fills us with pride and wonder, touching us and them for a nanoinstant with magic. How staggering it is then, to *see,* to *know* what Van Gogh and Bosch and Thomas knew and saw. To live for that nanoinstant what they lived. To look out of their eyes and view the universe from a never before conquered height, from a dizzying, strange place.

This, then, is the temporary, fleeting, transient, incredibly valuable, priceless gift from the genius dreamer to those of us crawling forward moment after moment in time with nothing to break our routine save death.

Mud-condemned, forced to deal as ribbon clerks with the boredoms and inanities of lives that may never touch — save by this voyeuristic means — a fragment of glory...our only hope, our only pleasure, is derived through the eyes of the genius dreamers; the genius madmen; the creators.

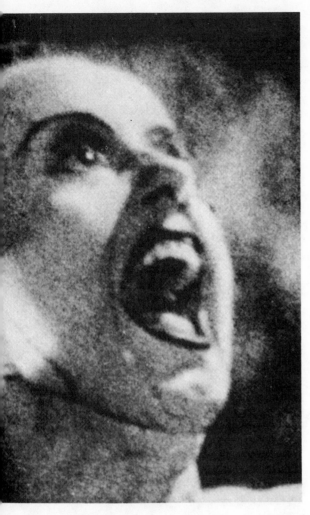

In compensation for his disappointment with and resentment of, actual human beings, Beethoven imagined an ideal world of love and friendship....His music, perhaps more obviously than that of any other composer, displays considerable aggression in the sense of·power, forcefulness and strength. It is easy to imagine that, had he not been able·to sublimate his hostility in his music, he might well have succumbed to a paranoid psychosis.

Anthony Storr, *Human Aggression* (1968)

Lugosi played weird roles for so long that he almost began to believe that he was a cross between vampire, superscientist, and a creature of occult powers.

Arthur Lennig, *The Count* (1974)

How amazed...how stopped like a broken clock we are, when we are in the presence of the creator. When we see what his singular talents — wrought out of torment — have proffered; what magnificence, or depravity, or beauty, perhaps in a spare moment, only half-trying; they have brought it forth nonetheless, for the rest of eternity and the world to treasure.

And how awed we are, when caught in the golden web of that true genius — so that finally, for the first time we know that all the rest of it was *kitsch;* it is made so terribly, crushingly obvious to us, just how mere, how petty, how mud-condemned we really are, and that the only grandeur we will ever know is that which we know second-hand from our damned geniuses. That the closest we will ever come to our ''Heaven'' while alive, is through our unfathomable geniuses, however imperfect or bizarre they may be.

And is this, then, why we treat them so shamefully, harm them, chivvy and harass them, drive them inexorably to their personal madhouses, kill them?

Who is it, we wonder, who *really* still the golden voices of the geniuses, who turn their visions to dust?

Who, the question asks itself unbidden, are the savages and who the princes?

Fortunately, the night comes quickly, their graves are obscured by darkness, and answers can be avoided till the next time; till the next marvelous singer of strange songs is stilled in the agony of his rhapsodies.

On all sides the painter wars with the photographer. The dramatist battles the television scenarist. The novelist is locked in combat with the reporter and the creator of the non-novel. On all sides the struggle to build dreams is beset by the forces of materialism, the purveyors of the instant, the dealers in tawdriness. The genius, the creator falls into disrepute. Of what good is he? Does he tell us useable gossip, does he explain our current situation, does he ''tell it like it is''? No, he only preserves the past and points the way to the future. He only performs the holiest of chores. Thereby becoming a luxury, a second-class privilege to be considered only after the newscasters and the sex images and the ''personalities.'' The public entertainments, the safe and sensible entertainments, those that pass through the soul like beets through a baby's backside...these are the hallowed, the revered.

And what of the mad dreams, the visions of evil and destruction? What becomes of them? In a world of Tiny Tim, there is little room for a Magwitch, though the former be saccharine and the latter be noble.

Who will speak out for the mad dreamers?

Who will insure with sword and shield and grants of monies that these most valuable will not be thrown into the lye pits of mediocrity, the meat grinders of safe reportage? Who will care that they suffer all their nights and days of delusion and desire for ends that will never be noticed? There is no foundation that will enfranchise them, no philanthropist who will risk his hoard in the hands of the mad ones.

And so they go their ways, walking all the plastic paths

filled with noise and neon, their multifaceted bee-eyes seeing much more than the clattering groundlings will ever see, reporting back from within their torments that nixons cannot save nor wallaces uplift. Reporting back that the midnight of madness is upon us; that wolves who turn into men are stalking our babies; that trees will bleed and birds will speak in strange tongues. Reporting back that the grass will turn blood-red and the mountains soften and flow like butter; that the seas will congeal and harden for iceboats to skim across from the chalk cliffs of Dover to Calais.

The mad dreamers among us will tell us that if we take a woman (that most familiar of alien creatures that we delude ourselves into thinking we rule and understand to the core) and pull her inside-out we will have a wondrousness that looks like the cloth-of-gold gown in which Queen Ankhesenamun was interred. That if we inject the spinal fluid of the dolphin into the body of the dog, our pets will speak in the riddles of a Delphic Oracle. That if we smite the very rocks of the Earth with quicksilver staffs, they will split and show us where our ghosts have lived since before the winds traveled from pole to pole.

The geniuses, the mad dreamers, those who speak of debauchery in the spirit, they are the condemned of our times; they give everything, receive nothing, and expect in their silliness to be spared the gleaming axe of the executioner. How they will whistle as they die!

Let the shamans of Freud and Jung and Adler dissect the pus-sacs of society's mind. Let the rancid evil of reality flow and surge and gather strength as it hurries to the sea, forming a river that girdles the globe, a new Styx, beyond which men and women will go and from whence never return. Let the rulers and the politicians and the financiers throttle the dreams of creativity. It doesn't matter.

The mad ones will persist. In the face of certain destruction they will still speak of the unreal, the forbidden, all the seasons of the witch.

Consider it.

Please: consider.

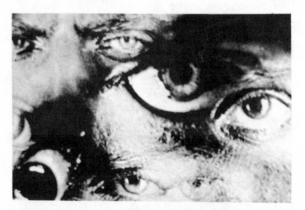

The Loss
E.L. Mayo

If I much concern myself with this,
You do too, and all who do not seem
Stone faces dreaming stone's dream
Of nothing, nothing, like the images
On Easter Island. All the animals
Follow us with their eyes as we go by
Wondering what we look for. In the sky
Red fades out to black and the night falls,
Night and the ignorance of eyes; but we
Light matches, matches; on our hands and knees
Ransacking every hummock, every tree's
Droppings for any nickel, dime, or cent
Of the incredible emolument
We never lost until we looked to see.

...Eternal truths are never true at any given moment in history....Yet the genius is the healer for his time, because anything he betrays of eternal truth is healing.

Carl G. Jung

Sleep, deep untroubled sleep. Isn't it odd how we love oblivion?

Robert Bibbings, *Coming Down the Seine* (1953)

Exploration Over the Rim
William Dickey

Beyond that sandbar is the river's turning.
There a new country opens up to sight,
Safe from the fond researches of our learning.
Here it is day; there it is always night.

Around this corner is a certain danger.
The streets are streets of hell from here on in.
The Anthropophagi and beings stranger
Roast in the fire and meditate on sin.

After this kiss will I know who I'm kissing?
Will I have reached the point of no return?
What happened to those others who are missing?
Oh, well, to hell with it. If we burn, we burn.

I saw the Count lying within the box upon the earth, some of which the rude falling from the cart had scattered over him. He was deathly pale, just like a waxen image, and the red eyes glared with the horrible vindictive look which I knew so well. As I looked, the eyes saw the sinking sun, and the look of hate in them turned to triumph. But, on the instant, came the sweep and flash of Jonathan's great knife. I shrieked as I saw it shear through the throat; whilst at the same moment Mr. Morris's bowie knife plunged into the heart. It was like a miracle; but before our very eyes, and almost in the drawing of a breath, the whole body crumbled into dust and passed from our sight. I shall be glad as long as I live that even in that moment of final dissolution there was in the face a look of peace, such as I never could have imagined might have rested there.

The Castle of Dracula now stood out against the red sky, and every stone of its broken battlements was articulated against the light of the setting sun.

Mina Harker's Journal, 6, Nov.

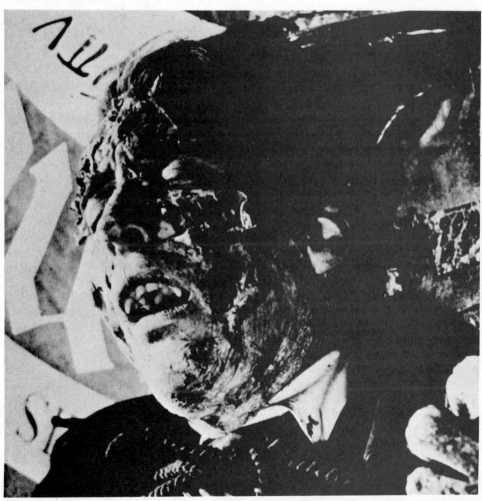

EPILOGUE

...he stood on the summit of a precipice, whose downward height no eye could have measured, but for the fearful waves of a fiery ocean that lashed, and blazed, and roared at its bottom, sending it burning spray far up, so as to drench the dreamer with its sulphurous rain. The whole glowing ocean below was alive — every billow bore an agonizing soul, that rose like a wreck or a putrid corpse on the waves of earth's oceans — uttered a shriek as it burst against that adamantine precipice — sunk — and rose again to repeat the tremendous experiment...the Wanderer...stood, in his dream, tottering on a crag midway down the precipice — he looked upward, but the upper air (for there was no heaven) showed only blackness unshadowed and impenetrable — but, blacker than that blackness, he could distinguish a gigantic outstretched arm, that held him as in sport on the ridge of that infernal precipice, while another, that seemed in its motions to hold fearful and invisible conjunction with the arm that grasped him, as if both belonged to some being too vast and horrible even for the imagery of a dream to shape, pointed upwards to a dial-plate fixed on the top of that precipice, and which the flashes of that ocean of fire made fearfully conspicuous. He saw the mysterious single hand revolve — he saw it reach the appointed period of 150 years — (for in this mystic plate centuries were marked, not hours) — he shrieked in his dream, and, with that strong impulse often felt in sleep, burst from the arm that held him to arrest the motion of the hand.

In the effort he fell, and falling grasped at aught that might save him....

His last despairing reverted glance was fixed on the clock of eternity — the upraised black arm seemed to push forward the hand — it arrived at its period — he fell — he sunk — he blazed — he shrieked! The burning waves boomed over his sinking head, and the clock of eternity rung out its awful chime — "Room for the soul of the Wanderer!" — and the waves of the burning ocean answered, as they lashed the adamantine rock — "There is room for more!" — The Wanderer awoke.

Charles Maturin, *Melmoth the Wanderer* (1820)

ACKNOWLEDGEMENTS:

This page constitutes an extension of the copyright page. Every reasonable care has been taken to trace ownership of copyright material. Information will be welcome which will enable the publisher to rectify any reference or credit.

SILENT SNOW, SECRET SNOW: by Conrad Aiken, from *The Collected Short Stories of Conrad Aiken*, 1932. Reprinted by permission of Brandt & Brandt, New York.

CURSE OF YIG: by Zelia Bishop. Reprinted by kind permission of Arkham House Publishers Inc.

MANNIKINS OF HORROR: by Robert Bloch. Reprinted by kind permission of the author.

THE CUPOLA: by Louise Bogan. Reprinted with the permission of Farrar, Straus & Giroux, Inc. from *The Blue Estuaries* by Louise Bogan. Copyright (c) 1923, 1929, 1930, 1931, 1933, 1934, 1935, 1936, 1937, 1938, 1941, 1949, 1951, 1952, 1954, 1957, 1958, 1962, 1963, 1964, 1965, 1966, 1967, 1968 by Louise Bogan.

DAMN HER: by John Ciardi, from *In The Stoneworks*. Copyright 1961 by Rutgers, The State University. Reprinted by permission of the author.

VAMPIRE OR VICTIM? HAIGH AND THE BRAND OF SATAN: by Basil Copper. Reprinted by permission of Citadel Press, a subsidiary of Lyle Stuart, Inc., 120 Enterprise Avenue, Secaucus, New Jersey.

DRUGGED: by Walter de la Mare. Reprinted by permission of The Literary Trustees of Walter de la Mare, and The Society of Authors as their representative.

THE HORLA: by Guy de Maupassant, from *The Best Stories of Guy de Maupassant*. Reprinted by permission of Random House, Inc., New York.

THE ICE SKIN: by James Dickey. Copyright (c) 1963,1965 by James Dickey. Reprinted from *Poems 1957-1967* by permission of Wesleyan University Press. First appeared in *The New Yorker*, December 28, 1963.

EXPLORATION OVER THE RIM: by William Dickey. Reprinted by kind permission of the author.

WOLVES DON'T CRY: by Bruce Elliot. From *Off the Beaten Orbit*, Pyramid Books, 1955, ed. Judith Merrill.

BLOOD/THOUGHTS: by Harlan Ellison. Reprinted by kind permission of the author.

BIRD CAGE: by Saint-Denys Garneau, translated by F.R. Scott. Reprinted by permission of F.R. Scott. Originally published by Klanak Press, Vancouver.

THE QUEST: by George Garrett. (Copyright (c) 1956,1957 George Garrett). Reprinted by permission of Charles Scribner's Sons from THE REVEREND GHOST: POEMS (Poets of Today IV) by George Garrett.

NOBODY: by Robert Graves. Reprinted by permission of Curtis Brown, Ltd. Copyright (c) 1939,1965 by Robert Graves.

A TWILIGHT MAN: by Harry Guest. Copyright Harry Guest 1968. From *Arrangements*, published by Anvil Press Poetry 1968.

THE NIGHT MIRROR: by John Hollander. From *The Night Mirror* by John Hollander. Copyright (c) 1965,1971 by John Hollander. Reprinted by permission of Atheneum Publishers. This poem originally appeared in *The New Yorker*, August 28, 1965.

THE RAIN AT NIGHT: by Miroslav Holub. From *Miroslav Holub: Selected Poems* tr. Ian Milner & George Theiner (1967), translation copyright (c) Penguin Books Ltd, 1967. Reprinted by permission of Penguin Books Ltd.

THE THOUGHT FOX: by Ted Hughes, from *Selected Poems* (c) 1957 Ted Hughes. Reprinted by permission of Harper and Row.

I AM COMING: by Philip Lamantia. Originally published by City Lights Books, San Francisco.

THE SENTRY: by Alun Lewis, from Raiders Dawn. Reprinted by permission of George Allen & Unwin (Publishers) Ltd., London.

COOL AIR: by H.P. Lovecraft. Reprinted by permission of the author's Estate and Scott Meredith Literary Agency, Inc., 845 Third Avenue, New York, New York 10022.

ROBERT DAVIDSON: by Edgar Lee Master, from *Spoon River Anthology*, published by Macmillan Publishing Company, New York. Reprinted by permission of Ellen C. Masters.

BLOOD SON: by Richard Matheson. Copyright 1951 by Richard Matheson, reprinted by permission of Harold Matson Co. Inc.

THE DRAGON FLY: by Howard Nemerov, from *The Next Room of the Dreams*. Reprinted by permission of the author.

SIEGE: by Alden Nowlan. From *I'm A Stranger Here Myself* by Alden Nowlan. Copyright 1974 by Clarke, Irwin & Company Limited. Used by permission.

PREPARATION: by P.K. Page, from *Poems; Selected and New*. Reprinted by permission of House of Anansi Press Ltd., Toronto.

ALL THE ROARY NIGHT: by Kenneth Patchen. From *Doubleheader: Hurrah For Anything*. Copyright (c) 1958 by Kenneth Patchen. Reprinted by permission of New Directions Publishing Corporation.

OLD MANSION: by John Crowe Ransom, from *Selected Poems, Revised and Enlarged*. Reprinted by permission of Random House, Inc.

THE NIGHT FISHERMAN: by Martin J. Ricketts. Reprinted by kind permission of the author.

SNAKE: by Theodore Roethke, from *The Collected Poems of Theodore Roethke*, copyright (c) 1955 by Theodore Roethke. Reprinted by permission of Doubleday & Company, Inc.

THE MINOTAUR: by Muriel Rukeyser, from *Beast In View*. Reprinted by permission of International Creative Management, New York.

THE CASE OF HELENE-JOSEPHINE POIRIER from *The History of Witchcraft*; THE CASE OF JEAN GRENIER *from The Werewolf*; FRITZ HARMANN, HANOVER VAMPIRE from *The History of Witchcraft*; by Montague Summers. Reprinted by permission of Lyle Stuart, Inc., 120 Enterprise Avenue, Secaucus, New Jersey.

WOLVES: by Allen Tate, from *Poems* by Allen Tate. Reprinted by permission of The Swallow Press, Chicago.

THE MAN FROM THE TOP OF THE MIND and WORDS ABOVE A NARROW ENTRANCE: by David Wagoner from *New And Selected Poems*. Reprinted by permission of Indiana University Press.

FORGET-ME-NOT: by Bernard Taylor, from *The Year's Best Horror Stories 1975*. Reprinted by kind permission of Harvey Unna & Stephen Durbridge Ltd., Authors' Agents, London.

EIDOLON: by Robert Penn Warren, from *Selected Poems: New And Old 1923-1966*. Reprinted by permission of Random House, Inc.

From THE OCCULT: A HISTORY: by Colin Wilson. Reprinted by permission of the author and Scott Meredith Literary Agency, Inc., 845 Third Avenue, New York, 10022.

ALTAMONT: by Leonard Wolf. (Originally titled *A Dream of Dracula: In Search of the Living Dead*]. Copyright (c) 1972 by Leonard Wolf. Reprinted by permission of Little, Brown and Company, Boston.

THE SHADOW MAKER: by Gwendolyn MacEwen. Reprinted by permission of Macmillan of Canada Ltd.

CORRIDA: by Roger Zelazny. Reprinted by permission of the author and Henry Morrison, his agents.

ILLUSTRATIONS

Front cover — Virgil Finlay; Back cover — Karen Simpson; P1, Dracula, Universal, 1931; P2, The Mole People, Universal, 1956; P3, The Monster of Piedras Blancas, Filmservice, 1959; P8, Dracula, Universal, 1931; P10, Black Sunday, Galatea/Jolly, 1960; P11, M. Nero, 1931; P12, The Abominable Dr. Phibes, American International Pictures, 1971; P15, The Cat and the Canary, Universal, 1927; P18, Taste the Blood of Dracula, Hammer, 1970; P21, The Devil Rides Out, Hammer/20th. Century Fox, 1968; P22, Tarantula, Universal, 1955; P25, The Green Slime, MGM, 1969; P26, Curse of the Werewolf, Hammer, 1961; P28/9, House of Terror, Des Fuentes, 1959; P31, Island of Lost Souls, Paramount, 1933; P32/3, Mad Doctor of Blood Island, Hemisphere, 1970; P35, City of the Dead, Amicus, 1959; P38, Zardoz; P39, The Last Laugh, 1925; P44, The Invasion of the Saucer Men, American International Pictures, 1957; The Day The Earth Stood Still, 20th. Century Fox; P49, Night of the Demon, Columbia, 1958; P53, Vampyr, Dreyer, 1932; P57, The Creeping Flesh, Tigon British/World Film Services, 1972; P62/4, The Bride of Frankenstein, Universal, 1935; P65, Frankenstein, Universal, 1931; P66, The Bride of Frankenstein, Universal, 1935; P67, The Cabinet of Dr. Caligari; P68/9, The Golem, Union, 1920; P72, Dracula, Universal, 1931; P73, London After Midnight, MGM, 1927; P76, The Reptile, Hammer, 1966; P81, The Fly, 20th. Century Fox, 1958; P83, The Man of a Thousand Faces, Universal, 1957; P84/5, Revenge of the Blood Beast, Leith, 1965; P86, The Werewolf of London, Universal, 1935; P91, Ben, Cinerama, 1972; P92, Vampyr, Dreyer, 1932; P93, Curse of the Dead, F.U.L., 1966; P95, The Hideous Sun Demon, Pacific International, 1959; P97, Black Sunday, Galatea, 1960; P98, Dracula, Universal, 1931; P100, Night of the Living Dead, Reade, 1968; P107, Captive Wild Woman, Universal, 1943; P108, Village of the Damned, MGM, 1960; P109, Count Yorga, Vampire..., Erica/AIP, 1970; P113, Frankenstein, 1910; P115, Lust for a Vampire, Hammer, 1971; P116, Dracula, Universal, 1931; P117, The Vampire Lovers, AIP, 1970; P121, Dante's Inferno, 20th. Century Fox, 1935; P127, The Magic Sword, United Artists, 1962; P128/9, Kwaidan, 1964; P134, Vampyr, Dreyer, 1932; P136, Tales From the Crypt, Metromedia/Amicus, 1971; P138, Master of the World, AIP, 1961; P139, Nosferatu, 1922; P140, Dr. Jekyll and Mr. Hyde, MGM, 1941; P144, The Horror of Dracula, Universal, 1958; P146/7, Vault of Horror, Metromedia/Amicus, 1973; P151, The Satanic Rites of Dracula, Hammer, 1973; P153, The Andulasian Dog, 1928; P154/5, The Bride of Frankenstein, Universal, 1935; P156, The Last Laugh, 1925; P157, Horror of Dracula, Universal, 1958; P159, Beauty and the Beast, 1945;